'I'll do anything it t

Acheron frowned, hi
narrowing. 'What's that

'What do you think? I'm desperate to keep Amber. If you have any suggestions on how I can be a better parent to her I'm willing to listen,' Tabby said.

'I thought you were offering me sex,' Acheron confided bluntly.

'Seriously?' Tabby gasped in shock at that misconception.

Acheron nodded cool confirmation.

Tabby was helplessly aware of the tension in the atmosphere. As she collided with his stunning dark-as-midnight gaze she saw a message even *she* couldn't ignore. He attracted her. This filthy rich Greek with his dazzling good-looks and hard-as-granite heart *attracted* her.

'There *is* a way you could keep Amber with you,' Ash drawled. 'But we would need to be married first,' he delivered smoothly.

He would not admit the truth that *he* would have a great deal riding on the arrangement as well. That acknowledgement would tip the power balance between them, and he refused to take that unnecessary risk. The less she knew, the better.

Lynne Graham was born in Northern Ireland and has been a keen Mills & Boon® reader since her teens. She is very happily married, with an understanding husband who has learned to cook since she started to write! Her five children keep her on her toes. She has a very large dog, which knocks everything over, a very small terrier, which barks a lot, and two cats. When time allows, Lynne is a keen gardener.

Recent titles by the same author:

CHALLENGING DANTE *(A Bride for a Billionaire)*
THE BILLIONAIRE'S TROPHY
  (A Bride for a Billionaire)
THE SHEIKH'S PRIZE *(A Bride for a Billionaire)*
A RICH MAN'S WHIM *(A Bride for a Billionaire)*

Did you know these are also available as eBooks?
Visit www.millsandboon.co.uk

THE DIMITRAKOS PROPOSITION

BY
LYNNE GRAHAM

MILLS & BOON

Published in Great Britain 2014
by Mills & Boon, an imprint of Harlequin (UK) Limited,
Eton House, 18-24 Paradise Road, Richmond, Surrey, TW9 1SR

© 2014 Lynne Graham

ISBN: 978 0 263 91106 0

Printed and bound in Spain
by Blackprint CPI, Barcelona

THE DIMITRAKOS
PROPOSITION

CHAPTER ONE

'BEARING IN MIND the history of the company's expansion and success, it *is* a most unjust will,' Stevos Vannou, Ash's lawyer, declared heavily in the simmering silence, a wary eye locked to the very tall, dark and powerfully built male across the office.

Acheron Dimitrakos, known as Ash to his inner circle, and Greek billionaire founder of the global giant DT Industries, said nothing. He did not trust himself to speak. Usually his control was absolute. But not today. He had trusted his father, Angelos, as far as he trusted anyone, which was to say *not* very much, but it had never once crossed his mind that the older man would even consider threatening the company that Ash had single-handedly built with the bombshell that his last will and testament had become. If Ash didn't marry within the year, he would lose half of the company to his stepmother and her children, who were already most amply provided for by the terms of his father's will. It was unthinkable; it was a brutally unfair demand, which ran contrary to every honourable scruple and the high standards that Ash had once believed the older man held dear to his heart. It just went to show—as if Ash had ever had any doubt—you couldn't trust anybody, and your nearest and dearest were the most likely to plunge a knife into your back when you were least expecting it.

'DT is *my* company,' Ash asserted between compressed lips.

'But regretfully not on paper,' Stevos countered gravely. 'On paper you never had your father transfer his interest to you. Even though it is indisputably the company that *you* built.'

Still, Ash said nothing. Cold dark eyes fringed with ridiculously long black lashes locked on the sweeping view of the City of London skyline that his penthouse office enjoyed, his lean, darkly handsome features set in hard, forbidding lines of restraint. 'A long court case disputing the will would seriously undermine the company's ability to trade,' he said eventually.

'Picking a wife would definitely be the lesser evil,' the lawyer suggested with a cynical chuckle. 'That's all you have to do to put everything back to normal.'

'My father knew I had no intention of ever marrying. That is exactly why he did this to me,' Ash ground out between clenched teeth, his temper momentarily escaping its leash as he thought of the utterly unhinged woman his misguided father had expected him to put in the role. 'I don't want a wife. I don't want children. I don't want *any* of that messing up my life!'

Stevos Vannou cleared his throat and treated his employer to a troubled appraisal. He had never seen Acheron Dimitrakos betray anger before or, indeed, any kind of emotion. The billionaire head of DT Industries was usually as cold as ice, possibly even colder, if his discarded lovers in the many tabloid stories were to be believed. His cool, logical approach, his reserve and lack of human sentiment were the stuff of legend. According to popular repute when one of his PAs had gone into labour at a board summit, he had told her to stay and finish the meeting.

'Forgive me if I'm being obtuse but I would suggest that any number of women would line up to marry you,' Ash's companion remarked cautiously, thinking of his own wife, who threatened to swoon if she even saw Acheron's face in print. 'Choosing would be more of a challenge than actually finding a wife.'

Ash clamped his mouth shut on an acid rejoinder, well aware the portly little Greek was out of his depth and only trying to be helpful even if stating the obvious was more than a little simplistic. He knew he could snap his fingers and get a wife as quickly and easily as he could get a woman into his bed. And he understood exactly why it was *so* easy: the money was the draw. He had a fleet of private jets and homes all over the world, not to mention servants who waited on him and his guests hand and foot. He paid well for good service. He was a generous lover too but every time he saw dollar signs in a woman's eyes it turned him off hard and fast. And more and more he noticed the dollar signs *before* he noticed the beautiful body and that was taking sex off the menu more often than he liked. He needed sex as he needed air to breathe, and couldn't really comprehend why he found the greed and manipulation that went with it so profoundly repellent. Evidently somewhere down inside him, buried so deep he couldn't root it out, there lurked an oversensitive streak he despised.

It was worse that Acheron knew exactly what lay behind the will and he could only marvel at his father's inability to appreciate that the woman he had tried to push Acheron towards was anathema to him. Six months before the older man's death there had been a big scene at his father's home, and Acheron had steered clear of visiting since then, which was simply one more nail in the coffin of the proposed bride-to-be. He had tried to talk to his stepmother about the problem but nobody had been willing to listen to common sense, least of all his father, who had been sufficiently impressed by the lady's acting ability to decide that the young woman he had raised from childhood would make his only son the perfect wife.

'Of course, perhaps it is possible that you could simply ignore the will and *buy* out your stepmother's interest in the company,' the lawyer suggested glibly.

Unimpressed, Ash shot the older man a sardonic glance. 'I will not pay for what is mine by right. Thank you for your time.'

Recognising the unmistakable note of dismissal, Stevos hastily stood up to leave while resolving to inform his colleagues of the situation immediately to sort out a plan of action. 'I'll put the best business minds in the firm on this challenge.'

Jaw line clenched as hard as a rock, Ash nodded even though he had little hope of a rescue plan. Experience told him that his father would have taken legal advice as well and would never have placed such a binding clause in his will without the assurance that it was virtually foolproof.

A wife, Ash reflected grimly. He had known since childhood that he would never take a wife and never father a child. That caring, loving gene had passed him by. He had no desire for anyone to grow up in his image or follow in his footsteps, nor did he wish to pass on the darkness he kept locked up inside himself. In fact, he didn't even like children, what little contact he had had with them simply bearing out his belief that children were noisy, difficult and annoying. Why would any sane adult want something that had to be looked after twenty-four hours a day and gave you sleepless nights into the bargain? In the same way why would any man want only one woman in his bed? The *same* woman, night after night, week after week. Ash shuddered at the very suggestion of such severe sexual confinement.

He recognised that he had a decision to make and he resolved to act fast before the news of that ridiculous will hit the marketplace and damaged the company he had built his life around.

'Nobody sees Mr Dimitrakos without an appointment *and* his prior agreement,' the svelte receptionist repeated frigidly. 'If you don't leave, Miss Glover, I will be forced to call Security to have you removed from the building.'

In answer, Tabby plonked her slight body back down on the plush seating in the reception area. Across from her sat an older man studying documents from a brief-case and talking urgently in a foreign language on his cell phone. Knowing she looked like hell did nothing for her confidence in such luxurious surroundings but she hadn't had a full night's sleep for some time, she no longer owned any decent clothes and she was desperate. Nothing *less* than desperation would have brought her to DT Industries seeking an interview with the absolute seven-letter-word of a man who had summarily refused to take any responsibility for the child whom Tabby loved with all her heart. Acheron Dimitrakos was a selfish, arrogant pig and what she had read about his womanising exploits in one of her clients' glossy scandal-sheet magazines had not improved her opinion. The man who had more money than Midas had turned his back on Amber without even expressing a desire to meet with Tabby as his co-guardian, or checking out the little girl's welfare.

The call to Security by Reception was duly made in clear crystalline tones undoubtedly intended to scare

Tabby off before the guards arrived. Her small face stiff, she stayed where she was, her slight body rigid with tension while she frantically tried to think up another plan of approach because gatecrashing Acheron's office wasn't going very well. But it wasn't as if she had had a choice, although she acknowledged that the situation was very serious indeed when such a callous personality became her last hope.

And then fate took a hand she wasn't expecting and she wasted a split second simply staring when she saw the tall dark man from the magazine pictures striding across Reception with a couple of suited men following in his wake. Tabby flew to her feet and raced after him. 'Mr Didmitrakos...Mr Dimitrakos!' she launched, stumbling over the syllables of his wretchedly complicated surname.

And at the exact same moment as her very tall and commanding quarry paused by the lift wearing an expression of sheer disbelief at her approach, the security guards came at a literal run, muttering fervent apologies to the man in front of her!

'I'm Amber's other guardian, Tabby Glover!' Tabby explained in feverish haste as both her arms were suddenly grabbed by the two men with him and she was yanked back a step from her proximity to him. 'I need to see you...I tried to get an appointment but I couldn't even though it's desperately important that we talk before the weekend!'

Security really was in need of sharpening up if they allowed him to be cornered on the top floor of his own building by a crazy woman, Ash reflected in exasperation. The young woman was wearing a worn jacket, track pants and trainers, her fair hair tied up in a high ponytail, pale shadowed face bare of make-up. She was small and plain, not at all the kind of woman who would have attracted his attention…although no sooner had he decided that than he noticed her remarkable blue eyes, which were an unusual violet in shade and dominated her pinched features.

'*Please!*' Tabby gasped. 'You can't be this selfish— nobody could be! Amber's father was a member of your family—'

'I have no family,' Ash informed her drily. 'Escort her out,' he told the security officers, who took over from his bodyguards in restraining Tabby even though she hadn't put up a struggle. 'And make sure this doesn't happen again.'

Taken aback that he wouldn't even give her five minutes of his time, that he betrayed no recognition even of Amber's name, Tabby was momentarily silenced. Then she swore at him like a fishwife, angrily employing language that had never left her lips before. In response, his brilliant dark eyes glittered with a raw angry hostility that momentarily shocked her because that cool front he wore evidently concealed much murkier depths.

'Mr Dimitrakos…?' Another voice interposed, and Tabby turned her head in surprise to see the older man who had been seated near her in the waiting area.

'The child—you'll recall your late cousin's guardianship request, which you turned down a couple of months ago?' Stevos Vannou hurtled forward to remind Acheron Dimitrakos in a quiet, respectful undertone.

An inconsequential memory pinged in the back of Ash's shrewd brain and drew his straight black brows together into a frown. 'What of it?'

'You selfish bastard!' Tabby raked at him, outraged by his lack of reaction and the consequences that his indifference to Amber's fate were about to visit on the child. 'I'll go to the press with this…you don't deserve anything better. All that wretched money and you can't do anything good with it!'

'*Siopi!* Keep quiet,' Acheron told her sternly in Greek and then English.

'And you and whose army is going to make me?' Tabby snapped back, unimpressed, the fighting spirit that had carried her through many years of loss and disappointment rising to the fore again to strengthen her backbone.

'What does she want?' Acheron asked his lawyer in English as if she weren't there.

'I suggest we take this back into your office,' Stevos remarked on a loaded hint.

Savage impatience gripped Ash. Only three days earlier he had returned from his father's funeral and, without even allowing for his grief at the older man's sudden death from a heart attack, it had turned into a very frustrating week. The very last thing he was in the mood for was a drama about some child he had never met and couldn't have cared less about. Troy Valtinos, oh, yes, he could remember now, a third cousin he had also *never* met, who had unexpectedly died and, in doing so, had attempted to commit his infant daughter to Ash's care. An act of sheer inexplicable insanity, Acheron reflected in exasperation, thinking back incredulously to that brief discussion with Stevos some months earlier. He was a childless single male without family back-up and he travelled constantly. What on earth could anyone have supposed he would do with an orphaned baby girl?

'I'm sorry I swore at you,' Tabby lied valiantly in an effort to build a bridge and win a hearing. 'I shouldn't have done that—'

'Your mouth belongs in the gutter,' Acheron breathed

icily and he addressed the security guards, 'Free her. You can take her out when I'm done with her.'

Tabby gritted her teeth together, straightened her jacket and ran uncertain hands down over her slender denim-clad thighs. Ash briefly studied her oval face, his attention lingering on her full pink mouth as a rare flight of sexual fantasy took him to the brink of picturing where else that mouth might be best employed other than in the gutter. The stirring at his groin put him in an even worse mood, reminding him of how long it had been since he had indulged his healthy libido. He knew he had to be in a very bad way if he could react to such an ignorant female.

'I'll give you five minutes of my valuable time,' Acheron breathed with chilling reluctance.

'Five minutes when a child's life and happiness hang in the balance? How very generous of you,' Tabby replied sarcastically.

Roaring rancour assailed Acheron because he wasn't accustomed to such rudeness, particularly not from women. 'You're insolent as well as vulgar.'

'It got me in the door, didn't it? Politeness got me nowhere,' Tabby traded, thinking of the many phone calls she had made in vain requests for an appointment. As for being called cheeky and vulgar, did she really care what some jumped-up, spoilt snob with loads of money thought about her? Yet her brain was already scolding her for her aggressive approach, telling her it was unwise. If she could get around the freeze front Acheron Dimitrakos wore to the world, he was in a position to help Amber while she was not. As far as Social Services were concerned, she could not be considered a suitable guardian for Amber because she was single, had no decent home and was virtually penniless.

'Start talking,' Ash urged, thrusting the door of his office shut.

'I need your help to keep Amber in my custody. I'm the only mother she's ever known and she's very attached to me. Social Services are planning to take her off me on Friday and place her in foster care with a view to having her adopted.'

'Isn't that the best plan in the circumstances?' Ash's lawyer, Stevos Vannou, interposed in a very reasonable voice as though it was an expected thing that she should be willing to surrender the child she loved. 'I seem to remember that you are single and living on benefits and that a child would be a considerable burden for you—'

Acheron had frozen the instant the phrase 'foster care' came his way but neither of his companions had noticed. It was a closely guarded secret that Ash, in spite of the fact his mother had been one of the richest Greek heiresses ever born, had once spent years of his life in foster care, shifted from home to home, family to family, enduring everything from genuine care to indifference to outright cruelty and abuse. And he had never, ever forgotten the experience.

'I haven't lived on benefits since Amber's mother, Sonia, passed away. I looked after Sonia until she died and that was why I couldn't work,' Tabby protested, and shot a glance brimming with offended pride at Acheron's still figure. 'Look, I'm not just some freeloader. A year ago Sonia and I owned our own business and it was thriving until Troy died and she fell ill. In the fallout, I lost everything as well. Amber is the most important thing in my world but, in spite of me being chosen as one of her guardians, there's no blood tie between Amber and me and that gives me very little real claim to her in law.'

'Why have you come to me?' Ash enquired drily.

Tabby rolled her eyes, helplessly inflamed by his attitude. 'Troy thought you were such a great guy—'

Ash tensed, telling himself that none of what she had told him was any of his business, yet the thought of an innocent baby going into foster care roused a riot of reactions inside him drawn from his own memories. 'But I never met Troy.'

'He did *try* to meet you because he said his mother, Olympia, used to work for your mother,' Tabby recounted.

Acheron suddenly frowned, straight black brows pleating as old memories stirred. Olympia Carolis, he recalled very well as having been one of his mother's carers. He had not appreciated when the guardianship issue had arisen that Troy was Olympia's son because he had only known her by her name before marriage, although if he stretched his memory to the limit he could vaguely recall that she had been expecting a child when she left his mother's employ. That child could only have been Troy.

'Troy was frantic to find a job here in London and you were his business idol,' Tabby told him curtly.

'His…*what*?' Ash repeated with derision.

'False flattery won't advance your cause,' Stevos Vannou declared, much more at home in the current meeting than he had been in the last, for the matter of the will would require considerable research of case law to handle.

'It wasn't false or flattery,' Tabby contradicted sharply, angry with the solicitor for taking that attitude and switching her attention back to Ash. 'It was the truth. Troy admired your business achievements very much. He even took the same business degree you did. That and the fact he saw you as head of his family explains why he put you down as a guardian in his will.'

'And there was I, innocent that I am, thinking it was

only because I was rich,' Acheron breathed with sardonic bite, his dark deep drawl vibrating down her spine.

'You really are a hateful, unfeeling creep!' Tabby slammed back at him tempestuously, fiery emotion ablaze in her violet eyes. 'Troy was a lovely man. Do you honestly think he realised that he was going to die at the age of twenty-four in a car accident? Or that his wife would suffer a stroke within hours of giving birth? Troy would never have taken a penny from anyone that he hadn't earned first.'

'Yet this lovely man left both his widow and child destitute,' Ash reminded her censoriously.

'He didn't have a job, and Sonia was earning enough money at the time through the business we owned. Neither of them could possibly have foreseen that both of them would be dead within a year of having that will drawn up.'

'But it was scarcely fair to name me as a guardian without prior discussion of the idea,' Acheron pointed out drily. 'The normal thing to do would have been to ask my permission first.'

Rigid with tension, Tabby made no comment. She recognised that he had a point but refused to acknowledge the direct hit.

'Perhaps you could tell us without further waste of time exactly what you imagine Mr Dimitrakos could do to help you?' Stevos Vannou sliced in, standing on the sidelines and thoroughly disconcerted by the sheer level of biting hostility erupting between his usually imperturbable employer and his visitor.

'I want to ask Mr Dimitrakos to support my wish to adopt Amber.'

'But is that a realistic goal, Miss Glover?' the lawyer countered immediately. 'You have no home, no money and no partner, and my own experience with Social Services and child-custody cases tells me that at the very least you need a stable lifestyle to be considered a suitable applicant to adopt.'

'What the heck does having or not having a partner have to do with it?' Tabby demanded defensively. 'This past year I've been far too busy to waste time looking for a man.'

'And with your approach it might have proved a considerable challenge,' Acheron interposed without hesitation.

Tabby opened and closed her lush mouth in angry disconcertion and took a seething step closer to the Greek billionaire. 'You accused me of having no manners? What about your own?' she snapped in outrage.

Studying the two adults before him squabbling and insulting each other much as his own teenaged children did, Stevos averted his attention from them both. 'Miss Glover? If you had had a partner it would certainly have made a big difference to your application. Raising a child today is a challenge and it is widely believed that *two* parents generally make that easier.'

'Well, unfortunately for me a partner isn't something I can dig up overnight!' Tabby exclaimed, wishing the wretched man would think of something other than picking holes in her suitability to adopt Amber. Didn't she have enough to worry about?

A germ of a wild idea leapt into Stevos's brain, and he skimmed his insightful gaze to Acheron and addressed him in Greek. 'You know, you could both help each other...'

Ash frowned. 'In what possible way?'

'She needs a stable home and partner to support her adoption application—you need a wife. With a little compromise on both sides and some serious legal negotiation, you could both achieve what you want and nobody would ever need to know the truth.'

Acheron was always quick on the uptake but for a split second he literally could not believe that Stevos had made that speech, could even have *dared* to suggest such an insane idea. He shot a disdainful glance at Tabby Glover and all her many obvious deficiencies and his black brows went skyward. 'You *have* to be out of your mind,' he told his lawyer with incredulity. 'She's a foul-mouthed girl from the back streets!'

'You've got the money to clean her up enough to pass in public,' the older man replied drily. 'I'm talking about a wife you *pay* to be your wife, not a normal wife. If you get married, *all* your problems with regard to ownership of the company go away—'

In brooding silence, Acheron focused on the one massive problem that would not go away in that scenario— Tabby Glover. *Not wife material* screeched every one of his sophisticated expectations, but he was also thinking about what he had learned about Troy Valtinos and his late mother, Olympia, and his conscience was bothering him on that score. 'I couldn't marry her. I don't like her—'

'Do you *need* to like her?' Stevos enquired quietly. 'I shouldn't have thought that was a basic requirement to meet the terms of a legal stipulation to protect your company. You own many properties. I'm sure you could put her in one of them and barely notice she was there.'

'Right at this moment the first thing on my agenda has to be the child,' Acheron startled his lawyer by asserting. 'I want to check up on her. I have been remiss in my responsibilities and too quick to dismiss them.'

'Look…' While Stevos was engaged in giving Ash an

alarmed look at that sudden uncharacteristic swerve of his into child-welfare territory, Tabby had folded her arms in frustration and she was glowering at the two men. 'If you two are going to keep on chatting in a foreign language and acting like I'm not here—'

'If only you were not,' Ash murmured silkily.

Tabby's hands balled into fists. 'I bet quite a few women have thumped you in your time!'

Shimmering eyes dark as sloes challenged her, his lean strong face slashing into a sudden smile of raw amusement. 'Not a one...'

Amber, Tabby reminded herself with painful impact, her heart clenching at the thought of the child she adored. She was here to ask for his help for Amber's sake, and Amber's needs were the most important consideration, not how objectionable she found the despicable man. His charismatic smile struck her like a deluge of icy water. He was incredibly, really quite breathtakingly, handsome and the fact that he found her amusing hurt. Of course, Tabby had never cherished many illusions about her desirability factor as a woman. Although she had always had a lot of male friends, she'd had very few boyfriends, and Sonia had once tactfully tried to hint that Tabby could be too sharp-tongued, too independent and too critical to appeal to the average male. Unfortunately, nobody had ever explained to Tabby how she could possibly have survived her challenging life without acquiring those seemingly unfeminine attributes.

'You want to meet the child?' Stevos stepped in quickly before war broke out again between his companions and wasted more time.

A sudden smile broke across Tabby's face like sunshine, and Acheron studied her intently, scanning her delicate features, realising that there could be an attractive female beneath the facade of bolshie belligerence. He liked women feminine, really, *really* feminine. She was crude and unkempt and the guardian of Olympia's granddaughter, he reminded himself doggedly, striving to concentrate on the most important element of the equation. And that was the child, *Amber*. He cursed the fact that he had not known of the connection sooner, cursed his own innate aversion to being tied down by anything other than business. He had no relatives, no loving relationships, no responsibility outside his company and that was how he liked his life. But not at the expense of basic decency. And his recollection of Olympia, who had frequently been kind and friendly to a boy everyone else had viewed as pure trouble, remained one of the few *good* memories Ash had of his childhood.

'Yes. I want to see the child as soon as possible,' Acheron confirmed.

Tabby tilted her head to one side, taken aback by his change of heart. 'What changed your mind?'

'I should have personally checked into her circumstances when I was informed of the guardianship,' Acheron breathed grimly, angry with himself for once at the elaborate and very protective support system around him that ensured that he was never troubled by too much detail about anything that might take his mind off business. 'But I will take care of that oversight now and be warned, Miss Glover, I will not support your application to adopt the little girl unless I reach the conclusion that you *are* a suitable carer. Thank you for your help, Stevos, but not for that last suggestion you made...' Sardonic dark eyes met the lawyer's frowning gaze. 'I'm afraid that idea belongs in fantasy land.'

CHAPTER TWO

'I COULD'VE DONE with some advance warning before you came to visit,' Tabby remarked thinly, after giving the uniformed chauffeur the address of the basement flat where she was currently staying, courtesy of her friend, Jack.

Jack, Sonia and Tabby had become fast friends and pseudo-siblings after passing their teenaged years in the same foster home.

Tabby eased slowly into the leather upholstered back seat of Acheron's unspeakably fancy limousine and studiously avoided staring starstruck at her surroundings but, dear heaven, it was a challenge not to stare at the built-in bar and entertainment centre. She had, however, enjoyed a mean moment of glorious one-upmanship when she sailed out of the front doors of the DT building with the doors held open by the same security guards who had, the hour before, manhandled her on the top floor.

'Obviously a warning would've been unwise. I need to see how you live without you putting on a special show for my benefit,' Acheron responded smoothly, flipping out a laptop onto the small table that emerged at the stab of a button from the division between front and back seats.

Tabby gritted her teeth at that frank admission. Any

kind of fake special show was not an option open to her in the tiny bedsit that she was currently sharing with Amber. It was purely thanks to Jack, who was a small-time builder and property developer, that she still had Amber with her and had not already been forced to move into a hostel for the homeless and give up Sonia's daughter. It hurt that her long-term friendship with Sonia counted for nothing next to the remote blood tie Acheron Dimitrakos had shared with Troy. What had they been? Troy's gran had been a cousin of Acheron's mother, so Acheron was what…a third cousin or something in relation to Amber? Yet Tabby had known and loved Sonia since she was ten years old. They had met in the children's institution where they were both terrorised by the older kids. Tabby, having grown up in a violent home, had been much more used to defending herself than the younger girl. Sonia, after all, had once been a loved child in a decent family and tragically orphaned by the accident in which her parents died. In comparison, Tabby had been forcibly removed by the authorities from an abusive home and no longer knew whether her parents were alive or dead. There had been a few supervised visits with them after she was first taken away, many attempts to rehabilitate her mother and father and cobble the family back together, but in reality her parents proved to be more attached to their irresponsible lifestyle than they had ever been to their child.

Acheron Dimitrakos worked steadily at his laptop, making no effort to start up a conversation. Tabby compressed her generous mouth and studied him. She knew he had already decided that she was a rubbish person from the very bottom of the social pile. She knew he had taken one look and made judgements based on her appearance…and, doubtless, her use of bad language, she conceded with a sneaking feeling of shame.

But then she doubted he knew what it felt like to be almost at the end of your tether. He was so…self-possessed, she decided resentfully, her violet gaze wandering over his bold bronzed profile, noting the slight curl in his thick black hair where it rested behind his ear and the extraordinary length of his dense inky-black eyelashes as he scrutinised the screen in front of him. Imagine a boyfriend with more impressive lashes than you have yourself, she ruminated, unimpressed, her soft mouth curling with disdain.

It annoyed her that he looked even more gorgeous in the flesh than he had in the magazine photographs. She had believed the photos must've been airbrushed to enhance his dark good looks but the evidence to the contrary was right before her. He had high aristocratic cheekbones, a perfectly straight nose and the wide, sensual mouth of a classic Greek statue. He was also extremely tall, broad-shouldered, narrow-hipped and long-legged—in fact, he was graced with every attractive male attribute possible.

Not a nice, caring person though, she reasoned staunchly, determined to concentrate on his flaws. Indeed, thinking of how he had outright refused to take any interest in Troy and Sonia's daughter, it was a challenge to understand why he should be suddenly bothering to come and see Amber now. She decided that she had made him feel guilty and that, after all, he *had* to have a conscience. Did that mean that he would support her application to adopt Amber? And even more importantly, would his opinion carry any weight with Social Services?

Acheron could not concentrate, which annoyed the hell out of him. Tabby Glover never sat still, and the constant movements of her slight small body on the seat beside him were an irritating distraction. He was too observant, he thought impatiently as he noted the bitten nails on her small hands, the shabbiness of her training shoes, the worn denim of jeans stretched taut over slender thighs, and he suppressed a sigh. He was out of his depth and although he had told Stevos to return to his office he was not enjoying the course he had set himself on. After all, what did he know about a young child's needs? Why did he feel guilty that he had already made up his mind to the hard fact that this young woman was not a fit sole guardian for a baby girl?

When the car came to a halt, Tabby slid out of the limo and bounced down the steps to stick her key in the front door of the basement flat. *Here goes,* she conceded nervously as she spread wide the door.

Ash froze one step inside, aghast at the indoor building site that comprised her accommodation. There was scaffolding, buckets and tools lying around, wires dangling everywhere, plasterboard walls. Tabby thrust open the first door to the left of the entrance.

Acheron followed her into a small room, packed with furniture and a table bearing a kettle and mini-oven and scattered with crumbs. Baby equipment littered almost every other surface. A teenage girl was seated on the bed with work files spread around her and when she saw Tabby she gathered up her files with a smile and stood up to leave. 'Amber's been great. She had a snack, enjoyed her bottle and she's been changed.'

'Thanks, Heather,' Tabby said quietly to the girl who lived in the apartment above. 'I appreciate your help.'

The child was sitting up in the cot wedged between the bed and the wall on one side. Acheron surveyed the child from a safe distance, noting the mop of black curls, the big brown eyes and the instant dazzling smile that rewarded Tabby's appearance.

'How's my darling girl?' Tabby asked, leaning over the cot to scoop up the little girl and hug her tight. Chubby arms wrapped round her throat while curious brown eyes inspected Acheron over Tabby's shoulder.

'What age is she?' Ash enquired.

'You should know,' Tabby said drily. 'She's over six months old.'

'Do the authorities know you're keeping her here?'

A flush of uneasy colour warmed Tabby's cheeks as she sat down on the bed because Amber was getting heavier by the day. 'No. I gave them Jack's address. He's a friend and he bought this apartment to renovate and sell on. He's allowing us to stay here out of the goodness of his heart. He hasn't the space for us at his own place.'

'How can you live in such a squalid dwelling with a young child and believe that you're doing the best you can for her?' Acheron condemned.

'Well, for a start, it's not squalid!' Tabby flared defensively and hurriedly rose to set Amber back into her cot. 'It's clean. We have heating and light and there's a fully functional bathroom through that door.' She pointed a hand to the opposite wall, and the gesture fell down in effectiveness because her arm shook and she hurriedly lowered it again. Tears were suddenly stinging the back of her eyes, and her head was starting to thump with the onset of a stress headache. 'For the moment I'm just doing the best I can but we're *managing*.'

'But you're not managing well enough,' Ash stated curtly. 'You shouldn't be keeping a young child in accommodation like this.'

Her brow pulsing with the band of tension tightening round it, Tabby lifted her hands to release the weight of her hair from the ponytail. Acheron watched a torrent of long blonde hair fall down to her waist and finally saw something he liked about her appearance: blonde hair that was natural unless he was very much mistaken, for that pale mass had no dark roots or streaky highlights.

'I'm doing the very best I can,' Tabby countered firmly, wondering why he was staring at her, her self-conscious streak on override, her pride still hurting from the 'squalid' comment.

'And how are you supporting yourself?' Acheron asked with a curled lip.

'I'm still cleaning. I didn't lose all my clients when I had to close my business down, and those I kept I'm still working for. I take Amber with me to the jobs. Most of my clients are out at work anyway so her coming with me doesn't bother them,' she admitted grudgingly. 'Take a look at her. She's clean and well fed and happy. We're rarely apart.'

Ash assimilated the information with a grim twist of his expressive mouth. 'I'm sorry, but your best isn't good enough. Nothing I've seen here will convince me otherwise. You don't have a proper home for the child. You're clearly living on the poverty line—'

'Money isn't everything!' Tabby protested. 'I love her and she loves me.'

Ash watched the slender blonde lean over the cot rail to gently stroke the little girl's head and saw the answering sunny smile that the gesture evoked. No such love or tenderness had featured in his childhood experience, and he fully recognised the fact, but he was also bone-deep practical and not given to changing his mind mid-course. 'Love isn't enough on its own. If you had a supportive family to back you and a proper home to raise her in I might feel differently, but you on your own with her in this dismal room and dragging her out with you to clean-ing jobs is *wrong*,' he pronounced with strong conviction. 'She could do better than this, she *should* have better than this and it is *her* needs and not your own that you should be weighing in the balance.'

'Are you saying that I'm selfish?' Tabby prompted in disbelief, because she had given up so much that was im-portant to her to take care first of Sonia, after she had suf-fered her first stroke, and ultimately her baby daughter.

Beneath the shocked onslaught of eyes the colour of rain-washed amethysts, Acheron's stubborn jaw line clenched hard and his mouth compressed. 'Yes. You have obviously done the best you can and given her continu-ity of care since her mother's death but now it's time for you to step back and put her best interests ahead of your own personal feelings.'

The tears glistening in Tabby's eyes overflowed, marking silvery trails on her cheeks, and for the first time in years Acheron felt like a real bastard and yet he had only told the truth as he saw it. *I love her and she loves me.* Yes, he could see the strength of the bond before him but it couldn't cover up the cracks in the long-term struggle for survival he saw for them both. Olympia's grandchild deserved more. Yet how did he put a price on the love and then dismiss it as if it were worthless?

'What age are you?' he pressed.

'Twenty-five.'

'I should've dealt with this situation when it first came up,' Acheron acknowledged grimly, thinking that she was surely far too young and immature to take on such a burden and that he should have taken immediate ac-tion to resolve the situation the instant the guardianship issue arose. It was his fault that Tabby Glover had been left to struggle on with the child while becoming more and more dangerously attached to her charge.

'Not if it meant parting Amber and me sooner,' Tabby argued. 'Can't you understand how much I care about her? Her mother and I became best friends when we were kids, and I'll be able to share my memories of her parents with her when she's old enough to want that information. Surely there's something you could do to help?'

But on a personal level, Acheron didn't want to be involved. He always avoided emotional situations and responsibilities that fell outside company business, and it had been that very detachment that had first roused his late father's concern that his only son should have set himself on such a solitary path.

Tabby searched Acheron's handsome features, marvelling at his masculine perfection even as she appraised the glitter of his dark-as-jet eyes and the hard tension round his wide, sensual mouth. 'I'll do anything it takes to keep her...'

Acheron frowned, his brow furrowing. 'What's that supposed to mean?'

'What do you think? I'm desperate to keep Amber. If you have any suggestions on how I can be a better parent to her, I'm willing to listen and take advice,' Tabby extended with the new-found humility of fear.

'I thought you were offering me sex,' Acheron confided bluntly.

'Seriously?' Tabby gasped in shock at that misconception. 'Does that happen to you a lot? I mean...women... just offering?'

Acheron nodded cool confirmation.

Her violet eyes widened in astonishment and she lifted her head, pale blonde hair cascading in a silken tangle round her shoulders with the movement. In the space of a split second she travelled from *possibly* pretty to decidedly beautiful in Acheron's estimation, and desire kindled; a desire he neither wanted nor intended to act on. His body was stubborn, though, and the pulse of heaviness at his groin was utterly disobedient to his brain, throwing up outrageous images of her lying on his bed, that lovely swathe of hair spread over his chest, that lush mouth gainfully employed in pleasuring him. He gritted his perfect white teeth, suppressing the outrageous fantasy, furiously conscious of the child's innocent presence and his unprecedented loss of self-discipline.

'Women just offer themselves? No wonder you're so full of yourself,' Tabby remarked helplessly, aware of the tension in the atmosphere, but unsure of its source as she stared back at him. She liked looking at him, didn't know why or exactly what it was about those lean sculpted features that fascinated her so much. But as she collided with his stunning dark-as-midnight gaze, liquid warmth surged between her legs and her nipples tightened, a message even she couldn't ignore or deny. He attracted her. The filthy rich Greek with his dazzling good looks and hard-as-granite heart *attracted* her. How foolish and deceptive physical chemistry could be, she reflected ruefully, embarrassment colouring her pale cheeks.

I'll do anything it takes to keep her... And suddenly Acheron, rigid with the force of his self-control, was reasoning with a new and unfamiliar sense of freedom to think outside the box and he was thinking, Why not? Why the hell not? Possibly Stevos's bright idea had not been as off the wall as it had first seemed. He and this strange girl both wanted something from each other, and he could certainly ensure that Amber benefitted from the deal in every way, thereby satisfying his uneasy conscience where the child was concerned.

'There *is* a way you could keep Amber with you.' Ash dangled the bait straight away, as always impatient to plunge to the heart of the matter.

Tabby leant forward where she sat, wide violet eyes intent on him. *'How?'*

'We could apply as a couple to adopt her—'

Thoroughly disconcerted by that unexpected suggestion, Tabby blinked. 'As a couple?'

'With my backing it could be achieved but we would need to be married first,' Ash delivered smoothly, deciding there and then that he would not admit the truth that he would have a great deal riding on the arrangement as well. That acknowledgement would tip the power balance between them and he refused to take that unnecessary risk and find himself being blackmailed. The less she knew, the less power she would have.

Astonishment was stamped on her small oval face. *'Married?'*

'For the sake of the adoption application. I should think that the most traditional approach would have the likeliest and quickest chance of success.'

'Let me get this straight…you're saying you would be willing to marry me to help me get permission to adopt Amber?' Tabby breathed in frank disbelief.

Acheron dealt her a sardonic look. 'Naturally I'm not suggesting a proper marriage. I'm suggesting the legal ceremony and a joint application to adopt her. We would then only have to give the appearance that we are living below the same roof for as long as it takes to complete the proceedings.'

So, not a real marriage, a *fake* one, she mused, but even so she was still transfixed by the concept and the idea that he might be willing to go to such lengths to help her. 'But why would you do that for us? A couple of months ago, you simply dismissed the idea that you could have any obligation towards Amber.'

'I wasn't aware then that she was Olympia Carolis's grandchild—'

'Olympia...who?' Tabby queried blankly.

'Troy's mother. I only knew her by the name she had before she married. I knew her when I was a child because she worked for my mother and lived with us,' Acheron volunteered with pronounced reluctance. 'I lost all contact with that side of the family after my mother died. But I liked Olympia. She was a good woman.'

'Yet you don't have the slightest true interest in Amber,' Tabby commented with a frown of incomprehension. 'You haven't even tried to hold her.'

'I'm not accustomed to babies and I don't want to frighten her,' Acheron excused himself glibly and watched her process his polite lie. 'I should've taken a greater interest in the child when I was first informed that I was one of her guardians. Your situation would not have reached crisis point had I accepted that commitment and taken my share of the responsibility.'

His admission of fault soothed Tabby, who had not been prepared for that amount of candour from him. He had made a mistake and was man enough to acknowledge it, an attitude that she respected. He had also moved a step closer to the cot and Amber, always a friendly baby, was beaming up at him in clear expectation of being lifted. But his lean brown hands clenched into taut stillness by his side, and she recognised that if anyone was frightened it was not Amber, it was *him*. Of course, he was an only child, and she assumed he had had little contact with young children because his rigid inhibited stance close to the baby spoke loudly for him.

'So, you've changed your mind and you think I should adopt her?'

'Not quite that,' Ash declared levelly. 'If we go ahead with this, I will be on the spot to oversee Amber's welfare and if I'm satisfied that you're a capable mother, I will release her fully into your care after we divorce. Naturally I will also ensure that when we part you have a proper home to raise her in.'

In other words, she would be on probation as a parent for the duration of the fake marriage, which was not good news on her terms. But Acheron Dimitrakos had to *really* care about what happened to Amber to be willing to get so involved and make such a sacrifice as marrying a stranger for the child's benefit alone, she thought ruefully, suddenly ashamed of her prejudices about him.

He would be killing two birds with one stone, Ash decided with satisfaction, solving all his problems in one decisive act. He would choose a discreet location for the ceremony but at the same time, if anyone was to be expected to believe that they were a couple and the marriage genuine, she would have to undergo a major makeover first.

'I'll take you home with me now,' Acheron pronounced. 'Bring the baby...leave everything else. My staff will pack your possessions.'

'Are you joking? Walk out the door with a strange man and move in with him?' Tabby breathed in stark disbelief. 'Do I look that naive and trusting?'

Acheron studied her levelly. 'You only get one chance with me and, I warn you, I'm not a patient man. I can't leave you and the child living here like this and, if we decide to go ahead with the marriage and adoption plan, there are things to be done, forms to be filled in without further waste of time.'

Tabby leapt up. As he shifted his feet in their highly polished leather shoes and elevated a sleek black brow in expectation he emanated impatience in invisible sparks, filling the atmosphere with tension. He thought he was doing her a favour and that she ought to jump to attention and follow his instructions and, because that was true, she wasn't going to argue with him. In fact, just for once, she was going to keep her ready tongue glued to the roof of her mouth and play nice to keep him happy and willing to help. Yes, she would trust him, but common sense suggested that a male as rich and gorgeous as he was had many more tempting sexual outlets than a woman as ordinary as she was.

'OK...' Tabby stuffed nappies and bottles and a tub of formula milk into the worn baby bag, and threaded Amber's chubby arms into a jacket that was slightly too small before strapping her into the car seat that she had had no use for since she had had to sell her car.

Acheron was already on his phone to his PA, telling her to engage an emergency nanny because he had no plans to trail the baby out shopping with them. The deal was done, only the details had to be dealt with now and he was in his element.

Ash stayed on the phone for the first ten minutes of their journey, rapping out instructions, making arrangements, telling Stevos to make a start on the paperwork. For the first time in a week he felt he was back in control of his life and it felt good. He stole a reluctant glance at Tabby, engaged in keeping Amber occupied by pointing out things through the windows. The awareness that Tabby Glover was going to prove very useful to him compressed his hard mouth because he was convinced that she would be difficult.

'Where are you taking us?' she asked, still in something of a daze after that discussion about adoption and marriage. She was scarcely able to credit that her and Amber's luck had turned a magical corner because Acheron Dimitrakos bore not the slightest resemblance to a fairy godmother.

'Back to my apartment where we will drop off… Amber,' Acheron advanced warily.

'And who are you planning to drop her off with? Your staff? *That's* not going to happen,' Tabby began forcefully.

'I have organised a nanny, who will be waiting for us. We will then go shopping to buy you some clothes.'

'Amber doesn't need a nanny and I don't need clothes.'

Acheron treated her to a scornful dark appraisal that burned colour into her cheeks. 'You're hardly dressed suitably. If we're to put on a convincing act, you need clothes,' he contradicted.

Anger flared in her violet eyes and her head turned sharply. 'I *don't* need—'

'Just say the word and I'll return you both to your clean and comfy basement,' Acheron told her in a lethally quiet tone of warning.

Tabby sucked in a sudden deep breath and held it, recognising that she was trapped, something she never ever allowed herself to be because being trapped meant being vulnerable. But if she said no, refused to toe the line, she would lose Amber for good. There would be no coming back from that development because once Amber was removed from her care, she would be gone for all time.

Had Acheron Dimitrakos been right to censure her selfishness in wanting to keep Sonia's daughter as her own? It was a painful thought. She hated to think that he could know better about anything but she knew that outsiders often saw more clearly than those directly involved. All she had to offer Amber was love, and he had said love wasn't enough. But Tabby valued love much more highly because she hadn't received it as a child and had often longed for the warm sense of acceptance, well-being and security that a loving parent could bestow. Only time would tell if Amber herself would agree that Tabby had made the wisest decision on her behalf.

Amber hugged Tabby in the lift on the way up to Acheron's apartment, the little girl clinging in reaction to Tabby's increasing tension. Acheron stood poised in the far corner of the mirrored compartment, a comfortable six feet three inches of solid masculine detachment. Tabby studied him in growing frustration, noting the aloof quality in his gaze, the forbidding cool of his lean, strong face. He was so unemotional about everything that he infuriated her. Here she was awash with conflicting emotions, terrified she was doing the wrong thing, putting her feelings rather than Amber's needs first…and whose fault was that? She had not doubted her ability to be a good mother until Acheron Dimitrakos crossed her path. Now she was facing the challenge of also surrendering her pride and her independence to meet his expectations.

'I don't think this is going to work,' she told him helplessly. 'We mix like oil and water.'

'A meeting of true minds is not required,' Ash imparted with sardonic bite. 'Stop arguing about every little thing. That irritates me.'

'A nanny is not a little thing. Who is she?'

'A highly trained professional from a reputable source. I would not put the child at risk.'

His intense dark eyes challenged her, and she looked away, her cheeks burning, her mouth dry, her grip on

Amber still a little tighter than it needed to be. For a split second she felt as though Amber were the only sure element left in the world that he was tearing apart and threatening to rebuild. He intimidated her, a truth that made her squirm. Yet he was willing to help her keep Amber, she reminded herself doggedly, and that should be her bottom line. Whatever it took she should bite the bullet and focus on the end game, not how bad it might feel getting there.

'Won't the sort of marriage you suggested be illegal?' she heard herself ask him abruptly. 'You know, a marriage that's just a fake?'

'Why would it be illegal?' he countered with icy cool. 'What goes on within any marriage is private.'

'But our marriage would be an act of deception.'

'You're splitting hairs. No one would be harmed by the deception. The marriage would simply present us as a conventional couple keen to adopt.'

'You're hopelessly out of date. Lots of couples don't get married these days,' Tabby pointed out.

'In my family we always get married when it comes to child-rearing,' Acheron told her smoothly.

That's right, remind me that I'm not from the same world! Tabby thought furiously, a flush of antagonism warming her face as embarrassment threatened to swallow her alive. Her parents had not been married and had probably never even thought of getting married to regularise her birth.

Her gaze strayed inexorably back to him until she connected with smoky dark deep-set eyes that made her tummy lurch and leap and heat rise in her pelvis. There was just something about him, she thought furiously, dragging her attention from him as the lift doors whirred open and she hastily stepped out into a hallway, some-

thing shockingly sexy and dangerous that broke through
her defences. She did not understand how he could act
like an unfeeling block of superior ice and still have that
effect on her.

CHAPTER THREE

THE NANNY, COMPLETE with a uniform that suggested she belonged to the very highest echelon of qualified nannies, awaited Acheron and Tabby in the spacious hall of Acheron's apartment and within minutes she had charmed Amber out of Tabby's arms and borne her off.

'Let's go,' Acheron urged impatiently. 'We have a lot to accomplish.'

'I don't like shopping,' Tabby breathed, literally cringing at the prospect of him paying for her clothes.

'Neither do I. In fact, usually the closest I get to shopping with a woman is giving her a credit card,' Acheron confided silkily. 'But I don't trust you to buy the right stuff.'

Mutinously silent as she slid back into the waiting limousine in the underground car park, Tabby shrugged a slight shoulder, determined not to battle with him when it was a battle she could not win. Even so, he could dress her up all he liked but it wouldn't change the person she truly was. No, she would be sensible and look on the clothing as a necessary prop for their masquerade, another move in what already felt more like a game than reality because in no realistic dimension did a girl like her marry a guy as rich and good-looking as him.

A personal shopper awaited them at Harrods where,

surprisingly enough, Acheron appeared to be in his element. Tabby did not attempt to impose her opinions and she hovered while Acheron pointed out what he liked and the correct size was lifted from the rail. She soon found herself in a changing cubicle with a heap of garments.

'Come out,' Ash instructed impatiently. 'I want to see you in the pink dress.'

Suppressing a groan, Tabby snaked into the classy little cocktail frock, reached down to flip off her socks and walked barefoot out of the cubicle.

Acheron frowned as she came to a halt and he strolled round her, staring at her slight figure in surprise. 'I didn't realise you were so tiny.'

Tabby gnawed at her lower lip, knowing she had skipped too many meals in recent months, painfully aware that she was too thin and that what delicate curves she had possessed had shrunk along with any excess body fat. 'I'm a lot stronger than I look,' she said defensively.

Acheron studied her doll-like dimensions with unabashed interest, his narrowed gaze running from her fragile shoulders down to her pale slender legs. He could've easily lifted her with one hand. He liked curves on a woman yet there was an aesthetically pleasing aspect to the pure delicacy of her build. Her breasts barely made an indent in the bodice of the dress and her hips made no imprint at all. Yet with that tousled mane of long blonde hair highlighting her pale oval face and bright violet eyes, she looked unusual and extraordinarily appealing. He wondered if he would crush her in bed and then squashed that crazy thought dead because sex would naturally not be featuring in their agreement. As she turned away, he froze, taken aback by the sight of the colourful rose tattoo marring the pale skin of her left forearm.

'That dress won't do,' Acheron told the assistant thinly. 'She needs a dress with sleeves to cover that.'

Gooseflesh crept over Tabby's exposed skin, and she clamped a hand over the skin marking she had forgotten about. Beneath her fingers she could feel the rougher skin of the scar tissue that the tattoo pretty much concealed from view, and her heart dropped to the pit of her stomach, remembered feelings of bitter pain and heartache gripping her in spite of the years that had passed since the wound was first inflicted. She had made the clear considered choice that she could live better with the tattoo than she could with that constant reminder of her wretched childhood catching her unawares every time she looked in the mirror. Of course, the skin ink wasn't perfect because the skin surface beneath it was far from perfect and the tattooist had warned her of the fact in advance. As it was, the rose, albeit a little blurred in its lines, had done the job it was designed to do, hiding the scar and providing a burial place for the bad memories. Only very rarely did Tabby think about it.

'How could you disfigure your body with that?' Acheron demanded in a driven undertone, his revulsion unhidden.

'It's of a good luck charm. I've had it for years,' Tabby told him unsteadily, her face pale and set.

The personal shopper was already approaching with a long-sleeved dress, and Tabby returned to the cubicle, her skin clammy now with the aftermath of shock—the shock of being forced back, however briefly, into her violent past. The rose was her lucky charm, which concealed the vivid reminder of what could happen when you loved someone unworthy of that trust. So, he didn't like tattoos; well, what was that to her? She put on the new dress, smoothed down the sleeves and, mustering her self-possession, she emerged again.

Acheron stared her up and down, his beautiful face curiously intent. Heat blossomed in her cheeks as he studied her with smouldering dark eyes, his tension palpable. Desire flickered low in her pelvis like kindling yearning for a spark, and she felt that craving shoot through every fibre of her body, from the dryness of her mouth to the swelling sensitivity of her nipples and the honeyed heat between her thighs. It made her feel light-headed and oddly intoxicated, and she blinked rapidly, severely disconcerted by the feelings.

'That will do,' he pronounced thickly.

She wanted to touch him so badly she had to clench her hands into fists to prevent herself from reaching out and making actual contact. She felt like a wasp being drawn to a honey trap and fiercely fought her reactions with every scrap of self-control left to her. Don't touch, *don't touch*, a little voice warned in the back of her head, but evidently he was listening to a different voice as he stalked closer and reached for her hands, pulling them into his, urging her closer, forcing her fingers to loosen within his grasp.

And Tabby looked up at him and froze, literally not daring to breathe. That close his eyes were no longer dark but a downright amazing and glorious swirl of honey, gold and caramel tones, enhanced by the spiky black lashes she envied. His fingers were feathering over hers with a gentleness she had not expected from so big and powerful a man and little tremors of response were filtering through her, undermining her self-control. She knew she wanted those expert hands on her body exploring much more secret places, and colour rose in her cheeks because she also knew she was out of her depth and drowning. In an abrupt movement, she wrenched her hands free and turned away, momentarily shutting her eyes in a gesture of angry self-loathing.

'Try on the rest of the clothes,' Acheron instructed coolly, not a flicker of lingering awareness in his dark deep voice.

Hot-faced, Tabby vanished back into the cubicle. Evidently he pressed all her buttons, and she had to stop letting him do that to her, had to stand firm. Of course he was sexy: he was a womaniser. He had insulted her with that crack about her tattoo and had then somehow switched that moment into something else by catching her hands in his and just looking at her. But she wasn't some impressionable little airhead vulnerable to the merest hint of interest from an attractive man, was she? Well, she *was* a virgin, she acknowledged grudgingly, as always stifling her unease about that glaring lack in her experience with men. After all she had not intentionally chosen to retain her virginity; it had just happened that way. No man had ever succeeded in making her want to get that close to him, and she had no plans to share a bed with someone simply to find out what it was like.

And then Acheron Dimitrakos had come along and turned everything she thought she knew on its head. For, although he attracted her, she didn't like him and didn't trust him either, so what did that say about her? That she had a reckless streak just like her long-lost and unlamented parents?

Tension seethed through Acheron. What the hell was the matter with him? He had been on the edge of crushing that soft, luscious mouth beneath his, close to wrecking the non-sexual relationship he envisaged between them. Impersonal would work the best and it shouldn't be that difficult, he reasoned impatiently, for they had nothing in common.

He watched her emerge again, clad in cropped wool trousers, high heels and a slinky little burgundy cashmere cardigan. She looked really good. She cleaned up incredibly well, he acknowledged grudgingly, gritting his teeth together as his gaze instinctively dropped to the sweet pouting swell of her small breasts beneath the clingy top.

He had done what he had to do, he reminded himself grimly. She was perfect for his purposes, for she had as much riding on the success of their arrangement as he had. Thankfully nothing in his life was going to change in the slightest: he had found the perfect wife, a non-wife...

He left Tabby alone with the shopper in the lingerie department and she chose the basics before heading for the children's department and choosing an entire new wardrobe for Amber, her heart singing at the prospect of seeing the little girl in new clothes that fitted her properly. The chauffeur saw to the stowing of her many bags in the capacious boot of the limousine, and she climbed in beside Acheron, who was talking on the phone in French. She recognised the language from lessons at school and raised her brows. So, that was at least *three* languages he spoke: Greek, English and now French. She refused to be impressed.

'We'll dine out tonight,' Acheron pronounced, putting the phone away.

'Why the heck would you want to do that?' Tabby demanded in dismay at the prospect.

'If we want to give the appearance of a normal couple, we need to be seen out together. Wear that dress.'

'Oh...' Tabby said nothing more while she wondered what social horrors dining out with him would entail.

She had never eaten out in a fancy restaurant, having always cravenly avoided such formal occasions, intimidated by the prospect of too much cutlery and superior serving staff, who would surely quickly spot that she was a takeaway girl at heart.

Two hours later, having showered and changed, Acheron opened the safe in his bedroom wall to remove a ring case he hadn't touched in years. The fabled emerald, which had reputedly once adorned a maharajah's crown, had belonged to his late mother and would do duty as an engagement ring. The very thought of putting the priceless jewel on Tabby's finger chilled Acheron's anti-commitment gene to the marrow, and he squared his broad shoulders, grateful that the engagement and the marriage that would follow would be one hundred per cent fake.

'Fine feathers make fine birds' had been one of her last foster mother's favourite sayings, Tabby recalled as she put on mascara, guiltily enjoying the fact that she had both the peace and the time to use cosmetics again. Make-up had been one of the first personal habits to fall by the wayside once she took on full-time care of Amber. But the nanny had been hired to work until eleven that night, leaving Amber free to dress up and go out like a lady of leisure. A *lady*? She grimaced at the word, doubting she could ever match that lofty description, and ran a brush through her freshly washed hair before grabbing the clutch that matched the shoes and leaving the room.

Acheron's apartment was vast, much bigger than she had expected. Tabby and Amber had been relegated to rooms at the very foot of the bedroom corridor, well away from the main reception areas as well as the principal bedroom suite, which seemed to be sited up a spiral staircase off the main hall. Acheron Dimitrakos lived like a king, she conceded with a shake of her head, wide-eyed at the opulence of the furnishings surrounding her and the fresh flowers blooming on every surface. They truly did come from different worlds. But the one trait they shared, she sensed, was an appreciation of hard slog and its rewards, so she hoped he would understand why she needed to continue to work.

'Put it on,' Acheron advised in the hall, planting an emerald ring unceremoniously into the palm of her hand.

Tabby frowned down at the gleaming jewel. 'What's it for?'

'Engagement ring…marriage?' Acheron groaned. 'Sometimes you're very slow on the uptake.'

Tabby rammed the beautiful ring down over her knuckle and squinted down at it, her colour high. 'I didn't know we were going for frills. I assumed you would choose more of a basic-package approach.'

'Since we'll be getting married pretty quickly and without a big splash our charade needs to look more convincing from the outset.'

'I'm already living with you and wearing clothes you bought for me,' she parried flatly. 'Isn't that enough of a show?'

'Many couples live together without marrying, many women have worn clothing I paid for,' Acheron derided. 'What we have has to look more serious.'

The restaurant was dimly lit and intimate and their table probably the best in the room. Certainly the attention that came their way from the staff was so constant that Tabby found it almost claustrophobic. Having studiously ignored her during the drive while talking on his phone, Acheron finally allowed himself the indulgence of looking at his bride-to-be. Her blonde mane tumbled round her shoulders framing a vivid and delicate little face dominated by violet eyes and a lush fuchsia-tinted mouth. He couldn't take his eyes off that mouth, a mouth modelled to make a man think of sin and sinning.

'How am I performing so far as your dress-up doll?' Tabby enquired mockingly to take her mind off the fact that she had still not established which knife and fork to use with the salad being brought to them.

'You answer back too much but you look amazing in the right clothes,' Acheron conceded, startling her with that compliment. 'So far I'm very satisfied with our bargain, and you can be assured that I will play my part.'

As he reached for one fork she reached for another and then changed course mid-movement, her gaze welded to his lean brown hands. *Just copy him*, her brain urged her.

'I've applied for a special licence. The legalities should be in place in time for the ceremony to be held on Thursday,' Acheron delivered. 'My lawyer is making all the arrangements and has contacted Social Services on our behalf with regard to our plans for Amber.'

'My word, he's a fast mover,' Tabby remarked breathlessly.

'You told me you didn't want the child to go into foster care,' he reminded her.

Her skin turned clammy at that daunting reminder of the unknown destination that would have awaited Amber had Tabby not gained his support. 'I don't but there are things we still haven't discussed. What am I supposed to do while we're pretending to be married?'

A winged ebony brow lifted. '*Do*? Nothing. You concentrate on being a mother and occasionally a wife. I will expect you to make a couple of appearances with me at public events. That is the sole commitment you have to make to me.'

'That's great because I want to start up my business again…in a small way,' Tabby admitted abruptly.

His handsome features clenched hard. 'No. That's out of the question. The child deserves a full-time mother.'

Tabby couldn't believe her ears. 'Most mothers work—'

'I will cover your financial requirements,' Acheron delivered with unquenchable cool. 'For the foreseeable future you will put the child's needs first and you will not work.'

Tabby gritted her teeth. 'I don't want to take your money.'

'Tough,' Acheron slotted in succinctly.

'You can't tell me what I can and can't do.'

'Can't I?'

Tabby's pulse had quickened until it felt as if it were beating in the foot of her throat, obstructing her ability to breathe and speak. Frustrated rage lay behind her choked silence as she stared across the table at him, her small face taut and pale. He was pulling strings as if she were a puppet. And wasn't she exactly that?

A chill settled over her rage, safely enclosing it. He was willing to help her to adopt Amber and she was stuck with his outdated idealistic attitude whether she liked it or not. Yes, she could walk away from him but if she did so she would also be walking away from the child she loved. And that, Tabby reflected hollowly, she could not do.

Amber had tugged at Tabby's heartstrings from the day she was born and Sonia was too weak, having suffered her first stroke within hours of the birth, even to hold her daughter. Consequently, for as long as Tabby needed Acheron's support she would have to conform to *his* expectations. Facing and accepting that ugly frightening truth had to be one of the most humbling experiences Tabby had ever known because it ran contrary to every tenet she had lived by since adulthood. The threat of no longer being in full charge of her life genuinely terrified Tabby.

'You seem to have lost your appetite,' Ash remarked, watching her move the food around her plate without lifting anything to her ripe pink mouth.

It was a steak cooked rare, not the way she liked it. But then she had coped with the menu being written in pretentious French simply by making the exact same menu choices as he had.

'You killed my appetite,' Tabby countered thinly.

A forbidding look flitted across his chiselled features. 'If restarting your business means that much to you, you should give up your desire to adopt a child, who will need much more of your time than you could give her as an independent businesswoman.'

Well, that certainly put his point of view across, Tabby conceded ruefully, sipping her water, ignoring the full wineglass beside it. She never touched alcohol, didn't trust the effect it might have on her, feared it might even awaken a craving she might find hard to control. She couldn't argue with Acheron Dimitrakos because setting up her business again *would* demand a great deal of her time. She compressed her lips, reasonably certain she could've coped without short-changing Amber but questioning for the first time whether or not that would have been fair to the child she loved. After all, she had personally never enjoyed the luxury of being a full-time mother and perhaps it would be more sensible to give that lifestyle a shot rather than dismissing it out of hand.

'Are we on the same page?' Acheron Dimitrakos asked impatiently over the cheese and crackers.

Mouth full at last of something she wanted to eat, Tabby nodded while trying not to imagine what it would feel like to be financially dependent on a man for the first time in her life.

As they emerged from the restaurant, Acheron banded an arm round her stiff spine, and she blinked in bewilderment at the daunting acknowledgement that they were literally surrounded by photographers. 'Smile,' he instructed her flatly.

And, hating it, she did as she was told.

'What was that all about?' she demanded once they were driving away.

'Public proof of our relationship,' Acheron supplied drily. 'There'll be an announcement of our engagement in *The Times* tomorrow.'

What relationship? Tabby thought with wry amusement. He said jump, she said how high? That was not a relationship, it was a dictatorship, but possibly he didn't know the difference.

The plaintive cry roused Acheron from a sound sleep. He listened for a while but the noise continued. After a moment, he rolled out of bed with a curse on his lips and reached the bedroom door, before groaning out loud and stalking back to rummage through a drawer and extract a pair of jeans. He hated having guests. He hated any interruption to his usual routine. But Tabby was a better option than a real wife, he reminded himself with satisfaction, and a good deal less likely to develop ambitious ideas about hanging on to her privileged position.

He pushed open the door of the nursery and saw the baby in the cot. It was kicking its arms and legs in furious activity, its little face screwed up as it loosed a wail that would have wakened the dead. Only, apparently, not her wannabe adoptive mother. Ash hovered by the cot, his wide, sensual mouth on a downward curve. The

baby sat up in a flash and looked expectant, even lifted
its arms as if she expected him to haul her to freedom. It
looked far too lively for a baby supposed to be sleeping.

'No more crying,' Ash decreed firmly. 'I don't like
crying.'

The baby's arms lowered, its rosebud mouth jutting
out in a pout while its bright brown eyes studied him
uncertainly.

'You see, crying gets you nowhere,' Ash explained
helpfully.

Another heartbroken sob emanated from the baby. She
looked incredibly sad and lonely, and Ash stifled a groan.

'Aren't you going to lift her? She needs comforting,'
Tabby murmured from the doorway, studying the little
tableau of inflexible male and needy baby. It was infuriating to register that she couldn't take her eyes off him
when he was wearing only a pair of jeans. He had a six-
pack that could have rivalled a top athlete's and his lean,
muscular bronzed chest was state-of-the-art perfection,
showcasing a male body that could have played a star-
ring role in any female fantasy.

'Why would I lift her?' Ash enquired with a raised
brow, flashing her a glance and noticing in that one
brief look that she was wearing a pale nightdress that
revealed more than it concealed of her tiny body while
she stood with her back turned to the light in the corridor. He glimpsed delicate little pink nipples and a pale
shadowy vee between her thighs, and his body reacted
with instantaneous arousal.

'Because if you expect our adoption application to im-
press the powers-that-be, you need to be confident that
you can handle Amber.'

'I will be perfectly confident if the situation demands
that of me, but at this hour of the day it would be very

unwise to remove her from the cot,' he declared. 'She's there for the whole night. It's two in the morning, in case you haven't noticed. Why raise her hopes by lifting her?'

Amber released another howl and, gripped by frustration, Tabby marched over to the cot, swept up the little girl and settled her without ceremony into Ash's arms. 'If she has a nightmare she needs comforting. She needs to know someone is there for her and a little cuddle usually soothes her.'

Amber was as shocked as Acheron to find herself in his arms. Wide brown eyes anxiously observed him. 'Cuddle?' Ash almost whispered the word in appalled disbelief. 'You actually expect me to cuddle her?'

CHAPTER FOUR

WITH A GASP of irritation, Tabby removed Amber from his awkward hold and pressed her close. 'Skin-to-skin contact is important,' she demonstrated, kissing Amber's hot brow.

'I'm not doing the kissing stuff either,' Acheron breathed witheringly.

'Then smooth her hair, rub her back, make her feel secure in other ways,' Tabby advised ruefully. 'Stop being so resistant to my suggestions.'

'And how do you suggest I do that? With a personality transplant?' Acheron derided. 'I'm no good with kids. I have no experience of that sort of affection.'

'It's never too late to learn,' Tabby told him with determination, settling Amber carefully back into his arms. 'Hold her closer, pet her. And please don't tell me you have no experience of petting women.'

'I don't pet them. I have sex with them. This is not an appropriate conversation to have around a child!' Acheron bit out in exasperation.

Picking up on his annoyance, Amber whimpered. He spread his fingers across her back in an uneasy rubbing motion.

'Bring her closer,' Tabby urged, approaching him to

tuck the baby into the curve of his shoulder. 'She's not going to bite.'

Acheron could never recall feeling quite so tense or uncomfortable. He knew what she wanted from him but he didn't want to do it. Then he thought of DT Industries, which would be one hundred per cent his only after the wedding, and he held the baby against him, deeming it a sacrifice worthy of such a result.

'And talk to her,' Tabby suggested.

'What about?' Acheron demanded with perfect seriousness, freezing as the baby nestled close of its own volition, disconcerted by the alien warmth and weight of her as she dug little hands into the flesh of his shoulder.

'Stocks and shares if you like. It doesn't matter at this age. It's the sound and tone of your voice that matters,' Tabby explained.

Acheron mumbled a Greek nursery rhyme.

'And if you walk around the room with her, it might make you feel more relaxed.'

Acheron gritted his teeth and started to tell the baby exactly what he thought of Tabby in Greek, careful to keep the antagonism out of his voice. Amber looked up at him with big trusting brown eyes, and he marvelled at her ability to award that amount of trust to a complete stranger. If the baby could try, he could as well even if it did stick in his throat to be listening to Tabby's instructions and following them. She maddened him, he acknowledged grimly, gently rubbing Amber's back as he talked. The baby slowly rested its head down on his shoulder.

'Give her to me,' Tabby murmured. 'She's going back to sleep.'

'And so ends lesson one,' Acheron mocked as she settled Amber back into the cot and covered her again.

Only it was not the child he was watching but Tabby. The pale grey silk glimmered in the dull light from the corridor, splaying across her thighs, outlining the plump little curves of her derriere as she bent over the cot rail, prominent nipples visible against the flimsy fabric as she straightened again.

Acheron was hard as a rock by the time he completed that far from fleeting appraisal. 'You might want to cover up more around me,' he commented. 'Or is this a come-on?'

Her violet eyes flew wide as she faltered at the door-way, and she flashed him an incredulous glance back over a narrow shoulder. 'Do you think you're irresist-ible or something?'

Acheron strode over to the doorway. 'You can't be that innocent. Men are fairly predictable when there is so much bare skin on display.'

'I am not on display,' Tabby countered furiously, cross-ing her arms defensively over her lightly clad length, sharply disconcerted by the idea that he could see her body beneath the nightie. 'When I came in I had no idea you would be in here.'

Acheron closed a hand around her wrist and tugged her into the corridor, shutting the door behind him. 'I like what I see,' he informed her softly.

Tabby stared up at him with fulminating force, noting the dark shadow of stubble outlining his stubborn jaw line and how that overnight growth enhanced his sheer masculinity. 'But I'm not offering myself.'

'No?' Acheron dipped his handsome head and nibbled at the corner of her inviting mouth, invading with his tongue as soon as she parted her succulent lips. Without further ado, he hauled her up against him, hands weav-ing across her slender back and then sliding up to glance over the taut peaks of her breasts in a caress that made her shiver.

That single kiss had unholy pulling power. Tabby bargained with herself to continue it. One second, just *one* second more to feel the hungry plunge of his tongue that raised a riot of damp heat low in her body and then his hands, dear heaven, his hands skimming, brushing the tender tips of her breasts before cupping her urgently sensitive flesh. 'No,' she told him shakily.

'No?' Wine-dark eyes glittered down at her, and her swollen mouth ran dry because she wanted another kiss, wanted the wildness she experienced beneath his skilled hands, wanted more with a ferocity that terrified her. Long fingers splayed to her spine, tipping her into revealing contact with the erection that his jeans could not conceal. 'We could have fun for an hour or two.'

'Do I strike you as that easy?' Tabby prompted tightly, outraged by the tone of his proposition. Did he think she was flattered by the idea of being his entertainment for a couple of hours? A quick and easy sexual convenience because there was no more appealing prospect available?

His stunning eyes narrowed. 'I don't make judgements like that about women. I'm not sexist. I enjoy sex. I'm sure you do as well.'

'You're wrong,' she began heatedly, thinking he was little different from the men who, having bought her a drink, had assumed that they were entitled to her body and could not comprehend her reluctance. Sex as a leisure-time pursuit was not her style.

'If you haven't enjoyed sex before then you've been with the wrong men,' Acheron assured her silkily, running a caressing finger along the ripe curve of her lower lip, and the breath feathered deliciously in her throat, a ripple of treacherous, unwelcome response quivering through her slender length.

'You're a class act in the persuasion stakes,' Tabby told him very drily, stepping back out of reach, fighting the unexpected chill of separation from the allure of his warm, vital body. 'But it's wasted on me—though I'm a virgin, I'm well aware that a man will tell you practically anything to get you into bed.'

'A...*virgin*?' Ash echoed in an astonished undertone, disbelief clenching his taut dark features. 'Seriously? Or is that a hook to pull me in deeper?'

Tabby slowly shook her head and then surrendered to laugh out loud. 'You are so suspicious of women it's not real. I don't want to pull you into anything. In fact, I think it would be a very bad idea for us to get that involved.'

'I wasn't thinking of involvement...I was thinking of sex,' Acheron traded smoothly. 'A simple exchange of pleasure.'

Tabby noted the way he even had to separate involvement from the act of sex and registered that he was positively phobic when it came to the concept of commitment. He did not want her to misunderstand what was on offer: a bodily exchange of pleasure, nothing more, no strings whatsoever. 'Goodnight,' she said gruffly, turning on her heel.

'A virgin...*seriously*?' Acheron breathed in her wake, the dark deep richness of his accented drawl vibrating through her in the stillness of the silent apartment.

Tabby turned her head slowly back to him. 'Seriously.'

Acheron frowned, dark brows drawing together, and stared at her, his eyes gleaming golden with curiosity and fascination in the overhead lights. 'But why?'

'I've never wanted to.' *Until now*, a little voice piped up in her brain, for that passionate kiss and the carnal caress of his well-shaped hands had roused more hunger in Tabby than she had ever felt in her life. A fierce physical hunger that she sensed could easily get out of hand.

'You wanted *me*, *hara mou*...' Acheron murmured with assurance as she walked away from him, blonde hair streaming down her back like a pale flowing river highlighting the curve of her bottom.

Tabby knew she should say nothing, but she couldn't resist the little devil inside herself that he provoked and she turned her head again, succumbing to temptation to murmur softly, 'But obviously...not enough.'

That crack might have affected some men like a challenge, Acheron mused broodingly as he strode back to his room for a cold shower, but he was not one of those men because logic had always ruled his libido. If he slept with her it would clearly get messy, and he hated messy relationships and didn't tolerate them for longer than it took to delete such women's numbers from his phone.

He reminded himself of the dire consequences of his last reckless encounter, and it was even worse that Tabby was still a virgin. He found that hard to credit but could not see any advantage in her telling such a lie. A woman who was still a virgin at twenty-five had to have *very* high expectations of her first lover for why else would she have waited so long? He would not be that man, would never fit that framework or meet the demands she would make. He had been warned and from now on he would keep his distance....

Tabby screened a yawn and settled Amber down on the rug at her feet. So far, it had been a very boring morning. Acheron's lawyer, Stevos, had arrived with a bundle of documents, which had been painstakingly filled in, and now he was engaged in explaining the pre-nuptial con-

tract to her clause by painful clause. Naturally Acheron
wanted to protect his wealth, and discussing the terms of
divorce before they even got as far as the wedding would
have been depressing had she been in love with him, but
she wasn't in love with him and couldn't have cared less
about his money.

'But I don't need anything like that amount of cash
to live on after the divorce,' Tabby protested worriedly.
'I know how to live well on a small budget and even a
quarter of that amount would be more than generous.'

'You're supposed to be out for all you can get,' Acheron chipped in helpfully from his restive stance by the
window. 'Sign the contract and forget about it. Once
you've lived in my world for a while, you'll find your
tastes have changed and that you want more.'

Tabby slung him a look of resentment. 'I only want
Amber out of this arrangement. I'm not going to turn
into a greedy, grasping manipulator overnight either!'

'Mr Dimitrakos simply wants you and the child to
enjoy a secure and comfortable future,' the lawyer interposed soothingly.

'No, Mr Dimitrakos wants to buy my loyalty and my
loyalty is not for sale!' Tabby replied with spirit. 'I very
much appreciate what he is doing to help me keep Amber
in my life and the very last thing I will do is take advantage of his generosity in any way. Please accept that.'

'*Sign,*' Acheron slotted with raw impatience. 'This
nonsense has taken up enough of my morning.'

'You mustn't forget to be present at the visit from
the social worker this afternoon,' Stevos reminded him
doggedly.

Stevos planted another document in front of Tabby
when she had signed the first. 'It's a standard confidentiality agreement, which will prevent you from talking

about the terms of your marriage to anyone outside this office.'

'That it's a big fat fake has to stay a secret,' Acheron interposed bluntly.

Suppressing a sigh, Tabby signed and then glanced up to watch Acheron as he talked to his lawyer in Greek. He was wearing a dark grey suit with a very subtle pinstripe and a purple shirt and he looked...absolutely amazing, as if he had stepped live out of a glossy magazine shoot. Sleek, sophisticated and breathtakingly handsome, he instantly commanded her gaze whenever he came within sight. There was no harm in looking at him and appreciating the view, she told herself ruefully. He was like a beautiful painting she could admire without needing to own, particularly as any woman with ideas of ownership where Acheron Dimitrakos was concerned was, in Tabby's opinion, in for a very rough ride.

They had shared the breakfast table in his dining room earlier that morning but the table was literally *all* they had shared. He had read his newspaper while she tended to Amber and munched toast, struggling to eat as quietly as a mouse in a cat's presence. It had proved neither sociable nor relaxed and she had already decided to eat her meals in the kitchen from now on.

'One of my assistants is going to take you shopping now for a wedding dress,' Acheron divulged as Tabby bent to lift Amber off the rug before she got her little hands on his shoelaces. 'And we will have to engage a nanny to take care of Amber when we're busy.'

Tabby straightened. 'I don't want a wedding dress... or a nanny.'

Scorching dark eyes assailed hers. 'Did I ask for your opinion?'

'No, but you're getting it, no extra charge.'

'A wedding dress is not negotiable.'

'Nothing's negotiable with you!'

Dark eyes flared sensual gold. 'If you were willing to try a little harder to please, you might be surprised,' he murmured huskily.

He was thinking about sex again: she *knew* it by the look in his eyes and the husky tone of his voice. Colour burned up hotly over her cheekbones as she dealt him a quelling glance.

'I'll be honest about this—I don't want to waste a wedding dress on a phony marriage. It just seems wrong,' Tabby admitted, lifting her chin. 'I want to save the white wedding dress for the day I do it for real.'

'Tough,' Acheron responded obstinately, moving closer. 'This may be a rush wedding but I want it to look as normal as possible and few women choose to get married without frills.'

Amber held out her arms to him and smiled.

'Cuddle her,' Tabby instructed, dumping the little girl into his startled arms. 'Practice makes perfect and, just as I have to look convincing at the wedding, you have to look convincing as an adoptive father-to-be this afternoon.'

Amber yanked at Acheron's silk tie with gusto and an appreciative grin suddenly slashed his mouth, shocking both his companions. 'Amber really doesn't give a damn about anything but attention and what amuses her in the moment.'

'A baby's needs are simple,' Tabby agreed wryly, striving not to react to that intensely charismatic smile of his, which made her want to smile back like a dream-struck idiot. Just looking at him, amusement falling from his features, she felt slightly light-headed and her tummy hollowed as if she were travelling downhill at breathtaking speed on a roller coaster. 'The nanny?'

'A necessity when you will have other calls on your time,' Acheron pronounced. 'Be practical.'

Tabby breathed in deep, reluctant to argue with him when the social services interview was to take place within a few hours. She took Amber back into her arms and strapped her into her buggy where the little girl screwed up her face and complained vehemently.

'She knows what she wants,' Acheron remarked. 'You will need to be firm as she gets older.'

'Obviously.'

'And you might find it a challenge to wear that wedding dress for real for some man when you already have a child in tow,' Acheron delivered with lethal cool. '*I* don't date single parents.'

'Tell me something that surprises me,' Tabby urged witheringly. 'You're too selfish, too concerned about protecting your own comfort level.'

'I just respect my limitations.'

'Nonsense. You can't stand the idea of having to consider someone else's needs before your own,' Tabby traded.

'So, what am I doing now in marrying you?' Acheron demanded curtly.

'You're righting the wrong you committed a couple of months ago when you refused to be Amber's guardian and no doubt that makes you feel so unselfish and perfect you think you're one hell of a guy!'

Listening to that exchange, Stevos was staring in shock at Tabby and her colour was high when she released the brake on the buggy and wheeled it out of the door.

Acheron's PA, Sharma, greeted her in the outer office and took her straight out to a limo for the shopping trip.

Tabby was surprised to be taken to an exclusive and very fashionable wedding boutique rather than a department store, but appreciated that with the time available it would be a challenge to come up with a sophisticated dress that fitted the bill. While Sharma played with Amber, Tabby tried on gowns, finally selecting the least fussy available and choosing the accessories suggested by the attentive proprietor. That achieved, she returned to Acheron's apartment and rang Jack to tell him that she was getting married and to invite him to the civil ceremony the following day.

'Is this a joke?' Jack asked.

'No. It is kind of sudden but I know exactly what I'm doing. Acheron wants to adopt Amber with me.'

'You've kept this very quiet. How long have you been seeing him for?' Jack enquired ruefully.

'A while. I didn't know it was going to turn serious or I'd have mentioned it sooner,' Tabby fibbed, wishing she could just have told the truth.

'It'll solve all your problems,' Jack pronounced with satisfaction. 'I've been really worried about you and Amber.'

Acheron turned up just in time for the interview with the social worker and swiftly proved a dab hand at twisting the truth, contriving to make it sound as if they had known each other far longer than they had. The older woman was so palpably impressed by Acheron and his incredible apartment that she asked few searching questions.

An hour later Tabby was feeding Amber and stealing bites from her own meal in the kitchen when Acheron appeared in the doorway, his expression thunderous. He swept up the highchair with Amber in it and turned on his heel.

'What on earth are you doing?' Tabby cried, racing after him.

Acheron set the chair down at one end of the dining table. 'We eat in here together. You do not eat in the kitchen like a member of my staff. That will not support the impression of a normal married couple.'

'I shouldn't think any of your staff could care less where we eat!' Tabby replied.

'But you need to be more cautious about appearances,' Acheron spelled out the warning grimly. 'Any one of my staff could sell a story to the tabloids and blow a massive hole in our pretence of being a couple.'

Tabby fell still. 'I never thought of that. Can't you trust your employees?'

'Most of them but there's always a rotten apple somewhere in the barrel,' Acheron answered with cynical cool.

Tabby nodded and returned to the kitchen to fetch her meal. He thought of every pitfall from every possible angle and it shook her that he had evidently already suffered that kind of betrayal from someone close to him. It was little wonder that he continually expected the worst from people, she reflected ruefully.

'Why were you eating in the kitchen?' he enquired as she settled at the table.

'I know you like your own space,' Tabby said quickly.

'You're not comfortable eating with me. I noticed that in the restaurant the first night,' Acheron commented, resting level dark eyes on her rising colour. 'You'll have to get over that.'

'Yes, but it was a strain that first night,' Tabby admitted, grudgingly opting for honesty. 'I couldn't read the menu because my French isn't up to it. I didn't even know which cutlery to use.'

A stab of remorse pierced Acheron. It had not even occurred to him that she might feel out of her depth at his favourite restaurant. 'Cutlery isn't important, *hara mou*—'

'Believe me, it *is* when you don't know which utensil to use.'

'In future, *ask*.' Acheron compressed his wide, sensual mouth, irritated that he had been so inconsiderate of the differences between them. 'I'm not…sensitive. I won't pick up on things like that unless you warn me. By the way, Sharma has engaged last night's nanny to work for us. I've also secured permission for us to take Amber abroad.'

'Abroad?' Tabby exclaimed. 'What are you talking about?'

'We're heading to Italy after the wedding. I have a house there. It will be easier to keep up the newly married act without an audience of friends and acquaintances looking on,' Acheron pointed out with irreproachable practicality.

Tabby woke early the next morning. Well, it was her wedding day even though it bore no resemblance to the very special event she had once dreamt the occasion would be. For a start, Sonia would not be there to play bridesmaid as the two women had always assumed she would, and momentarily Tabby's eyes stung with tears because sometimes the pain of losing her best friend felt like a wound that would never heal. She reminded herself that she still had Jack, but Jack was a man of few words and his girlfriend, Emma, was uneasy about his friendship with Tabby. As a result Tabby kept contact with Jack to the minimum. With a sigh, she rolled out of bed to go and tend to Amber and get dressed.

The nanny, Melinda, was in Amber's bedroom. Tabby had forgotten about the nanny, forgotten that she was no longer the only person available to care for the little girl, and Amber was already bathed, dressed and fed. A little pang of regret assailed Tabby because she had always enjoyed giving Amber her first peaceful feed of the day. But Sonia's daughter still greeted her with uninhibited love and affection, and Tabby buried her nose in the little girl's sweet-smelling hair and breathed deep, reminding herself why she was marrying Acheron and meeting his every demand. Amber was worth almost any sacrifice, she conceded feelingly.

The ceremony was to be held at an exclusive castle hotel, and Tabby was amazed at how much it had been possible to arrange at such speed. Then she reminded herself that Acheron's wealth would have ensured special attention and she scolded herself for being so naive.

Sharma had arranged for a hairstylist and a make-up artist to attend her at the apartment, and Tabby hoped that their professional skill would give her at least a hint of the glossy sophistication that Acheron's female companions usually exuded. As quick as she thought that, she wondered why his opinion should matter to her. Was it simply a matter of pride?

Sharma helped lace Tabby into her dress while the stylist adjusted the short flirty veil attached to the circlet of fresh flowers attached to Tabby's hair.

'With those flowers on your head you look like the Queen of Summer...' Sharma burbled enthusiastically. 'Mr Dimitrakos will be blown away.'

It dawned on Tabby for the first time that she was dealing with someone who thought she was about to attend a genuine wedding and she flushed with discomfiture, quite certain that the last thing Acheron would be was 'blown away'.

'And watching the boss go to so much trouble to get married in such a hurry is *so* romantic,' Sharma continued. 'I used to think he was so…er, cold, no offence intended…and then I saw him with the baby and realised how wrong I was. Of course fatherhood does change a man…'

And Tabby registered that Sharma had, not unnaturally, added two and two to make five in her assumption that Acheron was Amber's father. 'Actually, Amber is the daughter of my late best friend and Acheron's cousin,' she explained, deeming it wiser to put the other woman right on that score.

Grim-faced, Acheron paced while he awaited the arrival of the bridal car. He was very tense. It might be a fake wedding but with the arrival of his stepmother, Ianthe, and two of her adult children along with several good friends, it felt unnervingly real and he was already fed up with making polite conversation and pretending to be a happy bridegroom. Unhappily, a wedding without guests would not have been a very convincing affair, he reminded himself impatiently, and at least the woman whose attendance would have been least welcome had failed to show up. Stationed by the window of the function room adorned with flowers for the ceremony, he watched as a limousine embellished with white ribbons that fluttered in the breeze drew up at the hotel entrance.

Tabby stepped out in a sleek bell of rustling white fabric and petticoats, little shoulders bare, her veil and glorious streamers of golden-blonde hair blowing back from her oval face. Acheron's expressive mouth hardened even more, a nerve pulling taut at the corner of his lips. She looked as dainty and delicate as a doll and utterly ravishing, he noted in exasperation, cursing his all-too-male response to so feminine and alluring an image. Tabby didn't just clean up well, in Stevos's parlance; she cleaned up spectacular, Acheron conceded wryly, only absently registering the emergence of the new nanny clutching Amber, who was looking similarly festive in a candy-pink dress and matching hairband.

Tabby was guided straight into the ceremony where music was already playing. Her apprehensive glance took in the sea of faces and then lodged on Acheron and stayed there as if padlocked. *Whoosh!* She could feel all her defences being sucked away by the pure power of his compelling presence. He stared back at her, making no pretence of looking forward to the registrar, his stunning dark eyes golden and bright as sunlight in his lean face and so gorgeous he made something low in her body clench tight like a fist. Knees a tad wobbly, she walked down the short aisle between the seated guests and stilled by his side, the words of the brief ceremony washing over her while she frantically reminded herself that finding Acheron attractive was a one-way trip to disaster and not to be risked lest it should somehow threaten Amber's future as well.

He slid a ring onto her finger and she did the same for him. Afterwards, he retained his grip on her hand, ignoring her attempt to tug gently free, and suddenly there was a crowd of people round them murmuring congratulations, and introductions were being made.

His stepmother was a decorative blonde with a shrill voice and she had a son and a daughter by her side, both of whom seemed rather in awe of Acheron, which gave Tabby the impression that he had never been a true part of his father's family. Jack appeared with his girlfriend, Emma, and the other woman was friendlier than Tabby had ever seen her. Tabby chatted at length to Jack and turned only to find Acheron studying her, his handsome mouth compressed.

'Who was that?'

'Jack's an old friend and the only person I invited,' she proclaimed defensively.

'How much did you tell him?' Acheron enquired grimly.

'I told him nothing,' Tabby responded, wondering what his problem was. 'He thinks this is all for real.'

Drinks were being poured and toasts made by the time a tall, curvy brunette in a sapphire-blue suit swept into the room without warning.

Someone close to Tabby vented a groan. The brunette marched up to them like a woman on a mission and shot an outraged look at Acheron's stepmother, Ianthe. 'Mother, how could you take part in this insane charade when it goes against *my* interests?' she demanded loudly. 'I should have been the bride here today!'

'Let's not go there, Kasma,' her brother, Simeon, advised sheepishly. 'We're here to celebrate Ash's wedding, and I know you don't want to spoil the day by creating a scene.'

'Don't I?' Kasma struck an attitude, furious dark eyes glittering bright. She was a very beautiful woman with a great figure, a perfect face and a torrent of long dark hair, Tabby noted in a daze of agitation. 'Tell me, what has *she* got that I haven't, Acheron?' she demanded in a fierce tone of accusation.

Amber was starting to cry and Tabby took the opportunity to step out of the drama to join Melinda, the nanny, at the back of the room. After all, family squabbles and bitter ex-lovers were none of her business. Had Acheron had an affair with his stepsister? By the looks of it, it had been a rash move to utilise his charisma within the family circle, and she could understand why he had said on the first day that they met at his office that he had *no* family. His late father's family spoke to Acheron as politely as the strangers they so clearly were. Evidently he had never lived with them, which made her wonder who he *had* lived with when he was younger because Tabby was convinced she remembered his very famous mother's death being announced on television while she herself was still only a child.

Tabby took Amber into the baby-changing room, thinking that the histrionic Kasma would, with a little luck, be gone by the time she returned to sit down to a late and much-needed lunch.

But she was to have no such luck. No sooner had she finished undressing Amber than the door opened to frame Kasma's lush shape. 'Is that child Ash's?' she asked drily.

Tabby changed Amber, who was squirming like mad and craning her neck to look at the visitor. 'No.'

'I didn't think so,' Kasma said snidely. 'Ash has never been the daddy type.'

Exasperation kindling, Tabby straightened her shoulders and turned her head. 'Look, I don't know you and I'm busy here—'

'You know why Ash married you, don't you?' the brunette continued thinly. '*I* should have been Ash's bride. No one understands him as well as I do. Unfortunately for all three of us, he's too stubborn and proud to accept being forced to do what he should have done long ago.'

'I don't need to know what you're talking about,' Tabby told her uncomfortably. 'It's really none of my business.'

'How can you say that when by marrying Ash you're winning him a fortune?' Kasma demanded resentfully, her mother's vocal shrillness feeding into her sharp tone. 'According to the terms of his father's will if he stayed single until the end of the year he would lose half of *his* company to *my* family! And, of course, anyone who knows how Ash feels about his company would know that he would do virtually *anything* to protect it…even marry a totally unsuitable nobody from nowhere to maintain the status quo!'

CHAPTER FIVE

KASMA'S ACCUSATION RANG in Tabby's ears like a nasty echo during the flight to Italy. After the brunette's departure, lunch had proceeded quietly but Tabby had not had the advantage of a private moment in which to question Acheron. She had intended to raise the subject during the flight but Melinda was looking after Amber at the back of the cabin and she did not feel that she could speak freely.

Was it possible that Acheron had had a far more self-serving motive to marry than he had admitted? Tabby deemed it perfectly possible when she compared his refusal of all responsibility for Amber only months earlier with his sudden change of heart. Why on earth hadn't she been more suspicious of that rapid turnaround of his? He had to think she was as dumb as a rock, she thought painfully, feeling betrayed not only by his lack of honesty but also by her own gullibility. What terms had been included in his father's will? How could he possibly lose half of a company that belonged to him? And if Kasma's information was correct, why hadn't Acheron simply told Tabby the truth?

And the answer to that question could only be *power*, Tabby reflected with steadily mounting anger. As long as Tabby had believed that Acheron was doing her a favour for Amber's sake she had been willing to meet his every demand because she had been grateful to him, believing that he was making a big sacrifice even if theirs was only a fake marriage. But what if it wasn't like that at all? What if Acheron Dimitrakos had needed a conformable wife just as much as she needed the support and stability that would enable her to adopt Amber? That very much changed the picture and made them equals. But Acheron had never been prepared to treat Tabby as an equal. Acheron preferred to dictate and demand, not persuade and compromise. Well, those days were gone if Kasma had told her the truth…

'You're very quiet,' Acheron commented in the car driving them through the Tuscan countryside. She had changed out of her wedding gown before leaving London, and he had felt weirdly disappointed when he saw her wearing the violet dress he had personally chosen for her in London instead. The fabric and long sleeves were too heavy for a warmer climate and there was a flush of pink on her face in spite of the air conditioning. The colour, however, brought out the remarkable shade of her eyes and somehow accentuated the succulent fullness of her pink mouth.

Acheron breathed in slow and deep, dropped his gleaming gaze only for it to lodge on a slender knee and the soft pale skin beneath, which only made him wonder if her skin would feel as silky to the touch as it looked. He gritted his teeth, cursing his high-voltage libido. It had never once crossed his mind until now that, even with the options he had, a platonic relationship might still be a challenge, but evidently he was suffering from sexual frustration. Why else would he find her so appealing?

'I'm enjoying the views,' Tabby proclaimed stiltedly, so angry with him that she had to bite her lower lip before she started an argument while still trapped in the car with him. 'Where exactly are we going?'

'A villa in the hills. Like most of my properties it once belonged to my mother but I had it renovated last year.'

Despite her anger, curiosity stirred in Tabby. 'Your mother died when you were still quite young, didn't she?' she remarked.

His lean bronzed features clenched hard, dark golden eyes screening. 'Yes.'

The wall of reserve he used as a shield cast a forbidding shadow over his expressionless face. 'I lost my parents quite young too,' Tabby told him, rushing to fill the uneasy silence with an innate sensitivity towards his feelings that annoyed her. 'I went into foster care. That's where I met Jack and Amber's mum, Sonia.'

'I didn't realise you'd been in foster care,' Acheron breathed flatly, well aware she would not have had the escape route from that lifestyle that had eventually been granted by his inherited wealth.

'Well…' Tabby responded awkwardly, colliding with impenetrable midnight eyes heavily fringed by spiky black lashes and fighting a sensation of falling…and falling…and falling. 'They weren't the happiest years of my life but there were some good times. The last foster home I was in was the best and at least the three of us were together there.'

That appeared to be the end of that conversation as Acheron compressed his lips in grim silence while Tabby fought that light-headed sensation and struggled to focus on her anger. So, Acheron Dimitrakos was gorgeous and he kept on making her hormones sit up and take notice but he was also a skilled manipulator and deceiver and only a complete fool would forget the fact. In addition, it had not escaped her notice that he really wasn't interested in learning anything about her background and who she was as a person. But then had he ever seen her as a person in her own right? Or simply as someone he could easily use?

The car turned off the road and purred up a sloping driveway to the very large ochre-coloured stone building sprawling across the top of the hill. Tabby had to tense her lower lip to prevent her mouth from dropping open in comical awe because what he called a villa *she* would have called a palace. A fountain was playing a rainbow of sparkling water droplets down into a circular pool in the centre of a paved frontage already embellished with giant stone pots of glorious flowers. As she climbed out into the early evening sunshine, a flicker of movement from a shrubbery attracted her attention and a white peacock strutted out, unfurling his pristine feathers. The light caught his plumage as he unfurled it like a magnificent silver lace fan. The peacock posed, head high, one foot lifted, his confidence supreme in spite of his aloneness.

'You remind me of that bird,' Tabby muttered as the car carrying Amber and her nanny with the bodyguards drew up behind them.

Acheron raised an ebony brow enquiringly.

Embarrassed, Tabby shrugged. 'Never mind. Could we have a word in private?' she asked then.

'Of course,' he said without expression, but she didn't miss the frowning glance he shot in her direction as she moved to speak to Amber and her nanny. The little girl was fast asleep though, and a last feed and an early night were clearly what she most needed after a long and exhausting day.

The hall of the villa was breathtaking. Gleaming stretches of marble flooring ran below the arches that separated the reception areas. Tabby had never seen so many different shades of white utilised in a decor or anything so impractical for a household with a child in tow. Of course they would not be staying for long, she reminded herself, and Amber wasn't yet mobile so all the sharp-edged glass coffee tables and stylishly sited sculptural pieces on pedestals would scarcely endanger her.

'Very impressive,' she pronounced while Melinda followed the housekeeper up the wrought-iron and marble staircase.

'I have a few calls to make,' Acheron informed her and he was already swinging away, a tall, broad-shouldered male in a beautifully cut lightweight suit made of a fine fabric that gleamed in the light flooding through the windows.

'We have to talk...'

Over the years, far too many women had fired that same phrase at Acheron and had followed it with dramatic scenes and demands for more attention that he found abhorrent. His powerful frame tensed, his lean, strong face shuttering. 'Not now...later.'

'Yes...*now*,' Tabby emphasised without hesitation, violet eyes shimmering with anger, for she was not going to allow him to rudely brush her off as if she were the nobody from nowhere and of no account that Kasma had labelled her. If she toed his line and treated him like a superior being she would soon be thinking the same thing about herself.

'What is this about?' Acheron enquired coldly.

Tabby walked very deliberately out of the hall into the area furnished with incredibly opulent white sofas and slowly turned round, slim shoulders straight, chin lifted. 'Is it true that to retain ownership of your company your father's will required you to take a wife before the end of the year?'

His stubborn jaw line clenched. 'Where did you get that story from?' he asked grittily and then he released his breath with a measured hiss of comprehension. 'Kasma... *right*?'

'It's true, then,' Tabby gathered in furious disbelief. 'She told me the truth.'

'The terms of my father's will are nothing to do with you,' Acheron stated with chilling bite, his dark eyes deep and cold as the depths of the ocean.

But Tabby was in no mood to be intimidated. 'How dare you say that when getting married must've suited you every bit as much as it suited me? Didn't you think I deserved to know that?'

Acheron gritted his even white teeth together in a visible act of restraint. 'What difference can it possibly make to you?'

'I think it makes a *huge* difference!' Tabby slung back at him, violet eyes darkening with seething resentment. 'You made me feel as if you were doing me an enormous favour for Amber's benefit.'

'And wasn't I?' Acheron slotted in, utilising a tone that was not calculated to soothe wounded feelings.

'And you can stop being so rude right now!' Tabby launched at him, that derisive tone and superior appraisal of his lashing her like an offensive assault. 'Yes, Acheron, it *is* rude to interrupt and even more rude to look at me as if I'm some bug on the ground at your feet! I was completely honest with you but you, and no doubt your lawyer, deceived me.'

Eyes smouldering gold, Acheron was having trouble holding on to his temper. 'How you were deceived? I did exactly as I promised. I married you, I helped you to lodge an adoption application and I have ensured your future security. A lot of women would kill for one half of what I'm giving you!'

Her slender hands closed into irate fists. She wanted to pummel him as he stood there, the king of all he surveyed, cocooned from ordinary mortals and decent moral tenets by a level of wealth and success she could barely imagine. 'You are so arrogant, so hateful sometimes I want to hit you and I'm not a violent person!' Tabby hastened to declare in her own defence. 'Do you honestly not understand why I'm angry? I was frank with you. There were no lies, no pretences, no evasions. I believe I deserve the same respect from you.'

His wide, sensual mouth curled. 'This doesn't feel like respect.'

'Is this how you normally deal with an argument?'

'I don't have arguments with people,' Acheron responded levelly.

'Only because people probably spend all their time trying to please and flatter you, not because they always agree with you!' Tabby snapped back in vexation. 'For someone who appears very confrontational, you're actually avoiding the issue and refusing to respond to my natural annoyance.'

'I don't wish to prolong this argument, nor do I see anything natural about your annoyance,' Acheron admitted curtly. 'I don't make a habit of confiding in people. I'm a very private individual, and my father's will certainly falls into the confidential category.'

'I had the right to know that I didn't need to be grateful and submit to your every demand because you were getting even more out of this marriage than I was!' Tabby condemned, refusing to be sidetracked by a red herring like his reserve. 'You used my ignorance like a weapon against me!'

'The will was a matter of business and was of no conceivable interest to you,' Acheron stated in a raw undertone.

'Don't talk nonsense. Of course it was of interest to me that you had as much need to get married as I did!' she flashed back at him. 'It levels the playing field.'

'As far as I'm concerned, there *is* no playing field because this is not a game!' Acheron countered angrily. 'I married you and now that you're my wife, you're trying to take advantage of your position.'

Her violet eyes widened and she planted her tiny hands on her hips, just like a miniature fishwife getting ready to do battle, he decided, torn between grudging amusement and exasperation. 'Take advantage? How am I taking advantage? By standing up to you for once? By daring to state *my* side of the case?' she hissed back at him with simmering rancour.

Acheron strode forward, planted two hands over hers and hauled her up into the air before she could even guess his intention. He held her there, entrapped. 'You don't have a side of the case to argue, *moraki mou*—'

Enraged by his behaviour, Tabby glowered down at him. 'If you don't put me down, I'll kick you!' she launched at him furiously.

In response, Acheron banded her closely to his big powerful length, ensuring that her legs were as trapped as her hands. Dark golden eyes fringed by heavy black lashes held hers fast. 'There will be *no* kicking, *no* hitting, *no* bad language—'

'Says who?' Tabby bit out between gritted teeth.

'Your husband.' Acheron frowned as though that aspect had only just occurred to him and he was as much amused as irritated by the reality.

It was as if she were a firework and he had lit her

up inside. Rage blazed through Tabby. 'You are *not* my husband!'

Unholy amusement lit Acheron's eyes, whipping up the lighter tones she had noticed before and giving him an extraordinary appeal that made her mouth run dry and her tummy perform acrobatics. 'Then what am I?'

'A rat with a marriage certificate!' Tabby snapped at him informatively.

Acheron gave her a look of mock sympathy. '*Your* rat because you're stuck with me.'

'Put…me…down!' Tabby ground out fiercely. 'Or you'll regret it!'

'No, I much prefer this set-up to you shouting at me from across the room.'

'I was not shouting!'

'You were shouting,' Acheron repeated steadily. 'That is not how I conduct disputes.'

'I don't give a monkey's about how you like to conduct your disputes!' Tabby fired back.

It was those sparkling eyes, that incredibly succulent and inviting mouth of hers, Acheron mused abstractedly, conscious that she somehow hauled fiercely on every libidinous hormone he possessed and fired him up like a horny teenager. He didn't understand it, didn't care, didn't think he needed to, but without conscious volition he drew that tempting mouth up to his and crushed it under his, and the taste of her was as rich and fragrant and luscious as juicy strawberries on a summer day.

'No… No,' Tabby's dismayed objections, voiced as much to her wayward self as to him, were swallowed up by the hot, hungry pressure of his erotically charged mouth on hers.

Nobody had ever kissed Tabby as he did with all the passion of the volatile nature he kept under wraps, but which she sensed every time she was with him. He demanded and teased and the force of his sensual lips on hers followed by the invasive plunge of his tongue was unbelievably exciting and sexy.

He was very, *very* sexy, she acknowledged dimly, as if it was an excuse, and as he hoisted her higher to get a better grip on her slight body he let go of her hands and, instead of using them to get free of his hold, she balanced one on a broad shoulder and delved the fingers of the other into the springy, luxuriant depths of his black hair. With a guttural sound low in his throat he brought her down on something soft and yielding and then sealed her fast to the hard, driving length of his powerful frame.

And even as a faint current of alarm blipped somewhere in the back of Tabby's head she was aware of how much she loved feeling his strong, muscular body over and on hers. In fact, her every skin cell was leaping and bouncing with pent-up energy long before his fingers closed over the slight thrust of her achingly sensitive breast, and she strained up breathless and bound by a new tide of sensation. Indeed, desire had infiltrated her with such powerful effect that she scarcely knew what she was doing any more. Nothing had ever felt more necessary; nothing had ever felt more thrilling than the hot, hungry stimulation of his mouth and his hands. Spasms of excitement were quivering through her in a gathering storm. But then other sounds suddenly cancelled out those physical responses: a stifled gasp linked to the rattle of china and the sound of hastily receding footsteps.

'My goodness, what was that?' Tabby exclaimed, dragging her mouth from beneath his to find that she was lying on a sofa beneath him. *Beneath him*, her brain repeated, and her body went into panic mode when she collided with smouldering dark golden eyes and pushed at his shoulders, wriggling out from under his weight at frantic, feverish speed.

'Let's go to bed,' Acheron husked, closing long brown fingers over hers.

And it's just that simple and casual for him, she told herself angrily, furious that she had not contrived to resist him. She perched at the far end of the sofa, smoothing her tumbled blonde hair back from her brow, a slight tremor in her hands and her face so hot with mortification she could have boiled eggs on it. 'No, let's not…it would mess up things.'

'The bed would be more comfortable than the sofa,' Acheron declared single-mindedly.

'I'm not talking about *where*…I'm saying *no*, we're not going to do that!' Tabby slung back at him in frustration, wincing at the nagging bite of separation from his lean, hard body, fighting the ache of longing between her thighs with defiant determination. No way was she planning to be one more in a no doubt long line of easy women for Acheron, a mere female body to scratch an itch for a male unaccustomed to doing without sexual satisfaction.

Acheron sprawled back at the other end of the sofa, long powerful thighs spread so that she noticed, really couldn't help noticing, that that little tussle with her body had seriously aroused his. Her face burned even hotter and her tummy hollowed just looking at the prominent bulge at his pelvis, reactions to a physical craving she had never experienced before assailing her in an unwelcome wave.

All of a sudden and no thanks to Acheron for the lesson, she was realising why she was still a virgin. No other man had ever attracted her enough to make her drop her guard and yearn for sex. Sex, yes, that was all it would be, straightforward, unvarnished sex, not something a sensible woman would crave, and she was very sensible, wasn't she? *Wasn't she?* It really bothered her that even while thinking along those lines and carefully realigning her defences she was still fully engaged in appreciating the pure male beauty of Acheron's lean bronzed face and long, powerful body.

'You want me,' Acheron breathed a little raggedly. 'I want you.'

'Weird, isn't it…? I mean, we can't even be civil to each other,' Tabby pronounced shakily, still as out of breath as he was, recalling that wild entanglement and the fierce need he had sent powering through her and then suppressing the uncomfortable memory before standing up, smoothing down her dress with careful hands.

'Yet you burn me up, *hara mou*,' Acheron breathed huskily, springing upright with easy grace.

Tabby turned her head away. 'Let's not talk about that…you and me? It would be a very bad idea. We have as much in common as a cat and a dog. I'd like to see my room,' she completed, moving back with determination towards the hall.

'I'll show you. We've frightened off the staff,' Acheron volunteered with an unconcerned laugh. 'I think that noise was someone bringing us coffee and we were seen.'

'Yes, I can imagine what they saw,' Tabby cut in stiltedly, wishing he would drop the subject.

'Well, that's at least one person who will believe that we're genuine honeymooners,' Acheron replied nonchalantly, refusing to take the hint as he led the way up the marble staircase.

'But we're *not*,' she reminded him doggedly.

'You're not a very flexible personality, are you?'

'You'd roll me out like pastry if I was,' Tabby quipped. 'I'm still mad at you, Acheron. You took advantage of my ignorance.'

'I'm an alpha male, programmed at birth to take advantage,' Acheron pointed out with unapologetic cool. 'But you called me on it, which I wasn't expecting.'

He pushed open double doors at the end of the corridor and exposed a small hall containing two doors. 'That's my room.' He thrust open one door and then the second. 'And yours…'

Tabby worried at her full lower lip. 'Do we have to be so close?'

'I don't sleepwalk,' Acheron murmured silkily. 'But you're very welcome if you choose to visit.'

'I won't be doing that.' Tabby strolled in the big room, glancing into the en suite that led off and then into a dressing room to slide open a wardrobe, only to frown at the garments packed within. 'Didn't your last girlfriend take her clothes with her?'

'Those are yours. I ordered them,' Acheron explained. 'You'll need summer clothes here.'

Tabby spun back to study him with simmering violet eyes. 'I'm not a dress-up doll.'

'But you know that all I want to do is *undress* you, *moraki mou*.'

Tabby went pink again and compressed her lips.

'You blush like a bonfire,' Acheron remarked with sudden amusement as he strode off to make use of another door on the opposite side of the room that evidently led to his suite.

Tabby thought about turning the lock and then decided it would be petty, for surprisingly on that level she trusted him and had no fear that he might try to take what she was not prepared to offer. If she withstood his appeal, she was quite certain he would withstand hers and find some far more amusing and experienced quarry to pursue. Unfortunately, she didn't like the idea of him with another woman in the slightest and she told herself off for that because she knew she couldn't have it both ways. Either they were together or they were not; there was no halfway stage to explore.

Acheron stripped off for a cold shower. He was still ragingly erect and wondering when a woman had last turned him down. He couldn't remember, and the shock of Tabby's steely resolve still rankled. But it was a timely warning to steer clear, he reflected impatiently, his sensual mouth twisting as he stifled the urge to fantasise about having her tiny body wrapped round him while he satisfied them both. If she attached *that* much importance to sex, he definitely didn't want to get involved because sex meant no more to him than an appetite that required regular satisfaction.

Tabby rifled through the new wardrobe he had acquired for her without even mentioning his intent. She tugged out a long cotton dress that looked cool and, more importantly, covered up anything that she imagined a man might find tempting. If he kept his hands off her, she would keep her hands off him. She worried at her lower lip with her teeth. She had wanted to rip his clothes off him on that sofa, and the incredible strength of the hunger he had awakened still shocked her in retrospect. But nothing more was going to happen, *nothing*, she stressed inwardly with more force than cool. She could handle him, of course she could. He might be a very rich, very good-looking and very manipulative male but she had always had a good gut instinct about how best to look after herself.

Buoyed up by that knowledge, Tabby got changed, freshened up and went off to find out where the nursery had been set up.

CHAPTER SIX

'IT'S TIME YOU told me something about yourself,' Acheron declared, settling back into his seat and cradling his wineglass in one elegant hand.

Tabby was ill at ease. The grand dining room and the table festooned with flowers and fancy dishes for the first meal they were to share as a married couple made her feel like Cinderella arriving at the ball without a prince on hand to claim her. He had watched her watching him to see which cutlery to use, and the awareness had embarrassed her, making her wish that she had never confessed her ignorance. 'What sort of something?'

Acheron raised an ebony brow. 'Let's be basic—your background?'

He was so relaxed that he infuriated her, sheathed in tight faded denim jeans and a black shirt left undone at the throat. She had assumed he would dress up for dinner much as aristocrats seemed to do on television shows and, if she was honest, that was probably why she had picked the long dress. But instead of dressing up, Acheron had dressed *down* and, maddeningly, he still looked amazing, black hair curling a little from the shower, stubborn jaw line slightly rough with dark stubble, lustrous dark eyes pinned to her with uncompromising intensity and she couldn't read him, couldn't read him at all, hadn't a clue what he was thinking about.

'My background's not pretty,' she warned him.

He shrugged a shoulder in dismissal of that objection.

Tabby clenched her teeth and stiffened her backbone. 'I imagine my conception was an accident. My parents weren't married. My mother once told me they were going to give me up for adoption until they discovered that having a child meant they could get better housing and more benefits out of the welfare system. They were both druggies.'

Acheron no longer seemed quite so relaxed and he sat forward with a sudden frown. *Addicts?'*

'I warned you that it wasn't pretty. Their drug of choice was whatever was cheapest and most easily available. They weren't parents in the normal sense of the word, and I don't think they were even that keen on each other because they had terrible fights. I was simply the child who lived with them,' Tabby proffered tightly. 'And I got in the way…frequently because children have needs and they didn't meet them.'

Acheron forced his shoulders back into the chair, his astonishment at what she had told him concealed by his impassive expression. He almost told her then and there in a revelation that would have been unprecedented for him that they had much more in common than a cat and a dog.

'Have you heard enough?' Tabby enquired hopefully.

'I want to hear it *all*,' Acheron contradicted levelly, slowly comprehending the base level of painful isolation and insecurity from which that chippy, aggressive manner of hers had undoubtedly been forged. Tabby had been forced at an early age to learn to fight for her survival, and that he understood.

'I was the kid in the wrong clothes at school...when they got me there, which wasn't very often. Then my father started to take me with him as a lookout when he burgled houses,' she confided flatly, hating every word she was telling him but somehow needing him to know that she could handle her troubled, crime-infested childhood and indeed had moved far beyond it. 'Social Services got involved when he was caught in the act and eventually, because I was missing so much school and my parents were incapable of looking after me properly, I was put into care.'

'As was I,' Acheron admitted gruffly. 'I was ten years old. What age were you?'

Tabby stared back at him wide-eyed. '*You*...were in care? But your parents must have been *so* wealthy.'

'Which doesn't necessarily mean that they were any more responsible than yours,' Acheron pointed out drily. 'Believe me, my mother's money didn't protect me, although it did protect *her* until the day she died from an overdose. Her lawyers rushed her out of the country before she could be prosecuted for neglecting me.'

'What about your father?' Tabby prompted sickly, still shaken and appalled that he, who seemed so very assured and rich and protected, could ever have lived within the care system as she had. All at once she felt guilty about the assumptions she had made.

'His marriage to my mother only lasted about five minutes. When she got bored with him she told him that the child she was expecting—*me*—was the child of her previous lover...and he believed her,' Acheron explained flatly. 'He couldn't have afforded to fight her for custody in any case. I met him for the first time when I was in my twenties. He came to see me in London because a relative of his had noticed how very alike we looked in a newspaper photograph.'

'So what did your mother do with you?' Tabby asked, sipping at her glass of water.

'Very little. The trust who controlled her millions paid for a squad of carers to look after her and keep her worst excesses out of the newspapers. She was addicted to drugs too,' Acheron divulged tautly. 'But once I was no longer a baby none of her staff had a direct mandate to look after me, and my mother was, all too frequently, high as a kite. So I was left to my own devices, which eventually attracted the attention of the authorities. I had no other relatives to take responsibility for me.'

Painfully aware of the grim memories shadowing his eyes and the sad knowledge that his father could not have been waiting in the wings to take charge of him, Tabby stretched her hand across the table without even thinking about it and rested it down on his, where his long, elegant fingers were braced on the tablecloth. 'I'm sorry.'

His arrogant dark head came up at a combative angle even as he lifted his lynne to close it round hers, glancing down at their linked hands in virtual bewilderment as if he couldn't quite work out how that connection had happened. Dark colour crawled up to accentuate the high cheekbones that gave his face such strength and definition. 'Why would you be sorry? I imagine I got off lighter than you. I suspect you were physically mistreated...?'

Her oval face froze. 'Yes,' she almost whispered in confirmation.

'I only met with physical abuse *after* I entered the care system. I was an obnoxious little brat by then, semi-feral and may well have deserved what I got,' Acheron volunteered between gritted teeth.

'No child deserves pain,' Tabby argued.

'I endured two years of complete hell and innumerable different homes until my mother died and the trustees rescued me. I was sent off to boarding school for what remained of my childhood.'

Tabby's heart squeezed tight and her throat thickened at the awareness that just like her he had grown up knowing nothing of the love and security of a happy home and committed parents. She had been *so* wrong about him and it shamed her that she had been so biased purely because his late mother had been a famous Greek heiress. 'You never forget it…how powerless and lost you feel,' she framed unevenly.

Acheron looked across the table at her, his stunning dark golden eyes glittering. 'You leave it behind you, move on,' he told her squarely, suddenly releasing her hand.

'Yes, but it's always there somewhere in the back of your mind.' Starstruck even as she yanked her hand back, she collided with his eyes and the rare warmth of connection there and it made her feel not as if she was falling but instead flying high as a bird, breathless and thrilled.

'Not if you discipline yourself,' Acheron asserted smoothly.

'Tell me about your father's will,' Tabby urged, already dreading the return of the cold reserve that was beginning to clench his lean, darkly handsome features again.

'Some other time. We've raked over enough personal stuff for one evening…surely?' A sleek black emphatic brow lifted, the force of his will bearing down on her from the lambent glow of his beautiful lustrous dark eyes.

And Tabby, who was usually like a nail stuck to a magnet when in the grip of curiosity, quelled her desire to know more, conceding that, for a male as famously reticent as he was, he had been remarkably frank with her when he hadn't needed to be, for she knew of no stories referring to his dysfunctional upbringing that had ever appeared in the media. She swallowed back her questions and lifted a fork to attack the dessert that had been brought to the table.

'I'm crazy about meringue,' she confided. 'And this is perfectly cooked, crunchy on the outside, soft inside.'

A flashing smile crossed his wide, sensual mouth. 'A little like you, then? All fight on the surface and then all tender when it comes to another woman's child?'

In receipt of that rare smile, she felt her heart race. 'I only want Amber to have all the things I never had.'

'An admirable ambition. I've never had the desire to reproduce,' Acheron admitted, watching the tip of her tongue flick out to catch a tiny white crumb of meringue that could not possibly have tasted any sweeter than her lush mouth. Just like that he was hard as a rock again, imagining what else she might be able to do with her tongue, and the heavy pulse of mounting need at his groin was infuriating. It made him feel out of control and, because he despised that kind of weakness in any part of his life, he gritted his teeth and battled for restraint.

'I've never been the broody sort,' Tabby burbled, licking the fork before dipping it into the delicious dessert again, uncomfortably aware of the dark golden swoop of his gaze following her every move. 'But I was with Sonia when Amber was born and then I had to look after her the first few weeks until Sonia was strong enough after her stroke to leave hospital. I'm afraid that by that stage I was committed heart, soul and body to Amber…our attachment just happened and then Sonia had the second stroke and died immediately.' She paused, clashed with his caramel-shaded eyes and felt her mouth run dry. 'Please stop staring at me.'

'Then stop playing with the fork,' Acheron suggested huskily. 'Naturally I'm picturing you spread across the table as an infinitely more appealing main course than the one I've eaten.'

Surprised colour sprang into her face, and she dropped the fork with a clatter. 'Do you ever think of anything but sex?'

'And you're not thinking about it too?' Acheron derided thickly, studying her with burning intensity.

And the pink in her cheeks burned hotter than ever because he was perfectly correct. His raw masculine virility called to her on a visceral level. The table between them felt like a barrier she wanted to push out of the way. She wanted things she had never wanted before. She wanted to taste that intriguing little triangle of brown male skin visible below his throat, kiss a path along that stubborn jaw line, *touch*, explore. And even worse the mere thought of such experimentation made the blood race through her veins, her nipples tighten and push against her bodice while a liquid sensation of squirming warmth flowered between her thighs. *So, this is lust*, she told herself sharply. *Grow up and deal with it like a woman, not a frightened little girl*.

Acheron thrust back his chair and vaulted to his full commanding height of well over six feet. 'Come on…'

'No, sit down,' Tabby told him shakily, very much afraid that she knew exactly where he wanted her to go and even more afraid that she was ready to say yes, for never in her life had she ever felt anything as powerful as the primitive longing he awakened in her.

'Don't look at me like that and then try to tell me what to do, *hara mou*. It doesn't work,' Acheron advised, strolling round the table to move behind her and tug out the chair with her still seated in it.

'One of us has to try to be sensible,' Tabby protested in desperation.

Acheron bent down and scooped her out of the chair as if she were a child. *'Why?'* he queried thickly, his warm breath fanning her throat. 'We're not hurting anyone. We're both free agents. We can do as we like—'

'That's not how I live.'

'You've trapped yourself in a cage of irrational rules because that makes you feel safe,' Acheron countered, striding across the hall with her still cradled in his arms. 'But I can keep you safe too…'

Only he could still hurt her, just as easily as he could silence her arguments and sweep her literally off her feet, Tabby acknowledged feverishly even as her fingers reached up of their own accord to skate admiringly along the clean, hard line of his jaw. 'You don't make me feel safe.'

'But then you don't trust anyone,' Acheron countered with a swift downward glance at her anxious face. 'Neither do I. Even so, I *can* promise you that I won't lie to you.'

'Not much of a comfort when you could give tips to Machiavelli on how best to get your own way by nefarious means,' Tabby traded, provoking a surprised laugh from Acheron as he mounted the stairs. She knew decision time had come and gone and she wanted his mouth on hers so badly that it literally hurt even to think about it.

He lowered her to the carpet to open the first door, grabbed her hand as though he was afraid she would run off last minute and virtually dragged her into his bedroom. 'Now, I finally have you where I want you. Can you believe that this is our wedding night?'

'But it isn't…we're not really married.' Tabby leant back against his bedroom door, taut with tension because she was sincerely out of her comfort zone and could scarcely breathe for nerves. 'Let's not kid ourselves about that. Neither one of us ever had any plans to make this a proper marriage. I may be wearing a wedding ring but it's meaningless.'

Acheron didn't know a single woman of his acquaintance who would have reminded him of that fact at that precise moment, or who would have come to his bedroom without a carefully set agenda of ambitious and mercenary acquisition in mind. In the strangest possible way, Tabby was a breath of fresh air in his life, he reflected, uneasy with the thought.

'I know.' Like a hunter stalking a wary doe, Acheron approached and closed both of his hands over hers to pull her forward into his arms. 'But nothing that feels as exciting as this could possibly be meaningless,' he traded huskily.

'It's only hormones.'

'Says the woman who hasn't a clue what's going to be happening in that bed,' Acheron teased, feathering his mouth hungrily over the soft, silky contours of hers and making her shiver.

'Of course I know what happens…' But she still didn't quite know what she was doing there with him, breaking her rules of self-protection by letting him get that close, risking the vulnerability she always shunned. 'It's just sex,' she told him staunchly.

'It will be amazing sex,' Acheron predicted, skimming the straps down on her dress, pressing his hungry mouth to a slight-boned shoulder while pressing her close, letting her feel the hard-packed urgency in his lean body while reminding himself that he would have to go slow.

'I love your confidence,' Tabby whispered half under her breath.

'I thought it annoyed you.'

Tabby stretched up on tiptoe to link her arms round his neck and tug his handsome dark head down to her level. 'Shut up,' she told him helplessly, entrapped by dark eyes blazing like a banked golden fire across her face.

Acheron hoisted her off her feet and brought her down at the foot of the bed to flip off her shoes. 'I don't want to hurt you,' he admitted.

'If it hurts, it hurts,' Tabby said prosaically, determined not to surrender to apprehension because, with the single exception of her deep attachment to Amber, she had never felt as much as he made her feel either emotionally or physically. She supposed she was suffering from some kind of idiotic infatuation with him but assumed it would fade as time went on. 'Is this a one-time thing?' she asked him abruptly.

Engaged in slipping off her shoes, Acheron glanced back at her, amusement playing attractively about the wilful, passionate set of his mouth. 'You can't plan everything in advance, Tabby.'

'I do,' she told him tautly. 'I always need to know exactly where I am and what I'm doing.'

And his mouth claimed hers slow and deep and hungry and the tight knot of anxiety inside her unfurled because, in that moment, her senses locked to his, her body screaming with eagerness for more…more…more, and she couldn't stay focused the way she usually did. He unzipped the dress and extracted her from its folds with an ease and exactitude that briefly chilled her because she discovered she couldn't bear to think of him with the other lovers who must have honed his skills.

'What's wrong?' he prompted, more attuned to her than she had expected, instantly picking up on her renewed tension.

Perhaps she was, at heart, a terribly jealous, possessive person, she reasoned in mortification, troubled by her thoughts and wondering how she could possibly know what she was like when she had never enjoyed a deeper relationship with a man. There she perched, shivering a little in spite of the warmth of the room, suddenly conscious that she was clad only in bra and knickers and that her body was far from perfect.

'Nothing's wrong,' she breathed while he continued to study her troubled face with a frown. *'All right!'* she exclaimed as if he had repeated the question. 'I was just thinking that you're very smooth at stripping clothes off a woman!'

And Acheron burst out laughing, revelling in that honesty, appreciating that she would simply say whatever she thought without considering its impact and instead saying only what he might want to hear. That quality was another rarity in his world. 'Thank you…I think,' he teased.

'And you're still wearing too many clothes,' Tabby protested, all too aware of her own half-naked state as she struggled not to recall that she had really tiny breasts and was pretty skinny everywhere else where it was said to matter to a man. After all, regardless of her deficiencies, he wanted her. That was a certainty that buoyed her up as she watched dark golden eyes flare over her with unashamed desire and appreciation.

He laughed and shed his shirt, kicked off his shoes with the complete unselfconsciousness of a male who had never been inhibited in a woman's presence or constrained by the fear that a woman might not admire what he had to offer. Her throat ran dry as he unveiled the superb expanse of his bronzed torso, exposing the lean, ripped muscles of his six-pack. Poised there, black stubble darkening his handsome jaw, eyes glinting, hair tousled by her fingers with his jeans hanging low on his narrow hips as he unzipped them, he was as gorgeous as a tiger in his prime: glossy and strong and beautifully poised.

She tried and failed to swallow when she saw the tented effect of his boxers, the all too prominent evidence of his readiness outlined by the fine fabric. When his long, elegant hands began to sweep off that final garment she averted her attention and reached back awkwardly to unhook her bra, peeling it off before scrambling below the linen sheet to rip off her knickers in an effort to seem a little more in control than she was.

'I want you *so* much, *koukla mou*,' Acheron growled, yanking the sheet off her from the foot of the bed so that she sat up again, wide-eyed and thunderously aware of her nakedness. 'I also want to see you, *watch* you—'

'There's not a lot to see!' she gasped, her small body crowding back against the banked-up pillows.

Acheron locked a hand round one slender ankle and pulled her very gently down the bed. 'What I see is beautiful,' he breathed thickly, his hungry scrutiny skimming from the tangle of blonde curls at the apex of her thighs to the glorious hint of secret pink beneath and the mouth-watering swell of her breasts topped by prominent pale pink nipples. In one movement he was up on the bed by her side.

'I'm not.'

'Don't want to hear it!' he interrupted, long fingers fisting in the tumble of her golden hair to hold her still as he skated his mouth back and forth over her lips until they parted and his tongue speared inside, delving and exploring with a thoroughness that deprived her of breath and sanity. He could kiss, oh, yes, he could kiss, and then his fingers teased very gently at her straining nipples and he lowered his mouth there, catching a painfully sensitive peak between his lips and plucking it with a tugging intensity that made her nipple throb and arrowed heat straight down into her pelvis.

She trembled, and her spine arched as he pressed her flat on the mattress, dividing his attention now between the distended buds, suckling on her, flicking his tongue back and forth until the tingles of awareness rose like a tide to engulf her. She trembled, insanely aware of the gathering of heat and moisture between her thighs and the intolerable ache building there along with the desperate desire to be touched.

'You're very responsive,' Acheron purred, studying her with heavy-lidded eyes the colour of melted toffee set between the twin fringes of his black lashes. He skimmed a hand down her thigh, stroked her between her legs, and her hips shifted up in supplication. He possessed her swollen mouth again with carnal hunger before he sent a finger delving into her hot, damp heat.

A sound of helpless keening pleasure was wrenched from Tabby. All of a sudden everything she was feeling was centred in that one tormentingly sensitive area of her body. He settled his mouth to her throat and nuzzled a leisurely trail along the side of her neck, awakening nerve endings she had not known she possessed. What she could not understand was that in the space of minutes she had travelled from not being very sure of what she was doing to craving what he was offering with every straining sinew in her body.

'If at any stage you want me to stop, just say so, *koukla mou*,' Acheron husked.

'Wouldn't that be very difficult for you?' she whispered, her hand smoothing down over his muscled chest to discover the thrusting power of his erection.

'I'm not a teenager. I can control myself,' Acheron

growled, arching up into her hand as she traced the vel-
vet-smooth hardness of his shaft while marvelling at the
size of him. In that field, he had more than she had expected, more width, more length, and she didn't want
to think about how on earth he could make them fit as
nature had intended. With a slight but perceptible shud-
der of reaction he relocated her stroking fingers to his
muscled abdomen and added, 'As long as you don't do
too much of that.'

Satisfied that she could affect him as much as he affected her, Tabby lay back only to release a whimper of
startled sound as he circled her clitoris with expert fingers, unerringly striking the exact spot and the exact pace
that would drive her over the edge fastest. Her heart was
racing when he shifted down the bed, slid between her
thighs and employed his mouth there instead. She had
known about that, of course she had known, and had
never thought she could be that intimate with any man
but the insane pleasure he gave her drove all such logic
from her mind, and she gasped and writhed and cried
out. Enthralled by an exquisite torture of sensation that
built and built, her body leapt out of her control altogether and jerked spasmodically into an intense climax
that left her weak.

In the aftermath, Acheron rose up over her, lean, dark
features taut and flushed with hunger, and she could feel
the wide, blunt tip of him at the heart of her, pushing,
precisely stretching her inner sheath until a sudden sharp
pain made her cry out in surprise, and he froze in place.

'Do you want me to stop?' Acheron prompted raggedly.

'No point now.' Tabby could see he was in no condition to stop, could feel him hard and pulsing and alien inside her. In any case, the pain of his invasion had already

faded and the ache of hollow longing he had roused still lingered. She wrapped her arms round him, instinctively urging him on, fingers smoothing across the bronzed satin of his broad back.

'You're so tight,' he rasped, shifting with an athletic lift of his lean hips to surge into her again, deeper, further, harder in a technique that met every physical craving she hadn't known she had. 'I'm incredibly turned on.'

The flood of sensation returned as he withdrew and plunged back into her again, ensuring that she felt every inch of his penetration. The intensity of sensation shocked her and the powerful contracting bands in her pelvis turned her into a fizzing firework of wild excitement. He moved faster and she clung, riding out the electrifying storm of passion with a heart that seemed to be thumping in her eardrums. The explosion of raw pleasure that followed stunned her as the inner convulsions of her body clenched her every muscle tight as a fist. He vented a shuddering groan of completion while the waves of delight went on and on and on, coursing through her thoroughly fulfilled body.

In a dazed state of abstraction, Tabby lay in the tumbled bedding afterwards, watching Acheron stride across the room to retrieve something before vanishing into the bathroom, from which she soon heard the sound of running water. The instant their encounter had finished, the very moment he had attained release, he had rolled away from her and made no effort to touch her again. She was painfully aware of how much she would have liked him to hold her close in a caring, affectionate way that acknowledged their new intimacy and it disturbed her that she should feel so hurt by his withdrawal. After all, she wasn't looking for, or expecting, love or commitment, was she? No, she wasn't that naive.

She had slept with Acheron because for the very first time she had felt a fierce desire to experience that extra dimension with a man. But his swift departure from the bed had disappointed her, leaving her feeling ridiculously used and rejected. That was silly, she told herself firmly, because when it came to what they had just done he had not taken advantage of her in any way. Indeed, to some degree she was willing to acknowledge that *she* had taken advantage of *him* the moment she had estimated that he would undoubtedly possess the erotic skills that were most likely to ensure that she received pleasure from her first experience. That didn't, however, entitle him to forgiveness for disappointing her in the sensitive aftermath of sex.

Slithering out of bed, Tabby swiftly got dressed, finger-combing her tangled hair back off her damp brow before she approached the bathroom door.

A towel linked round his narrow bronzed hips, Acheron was in the act of stepping out of the shower cubicle.

'A-star for the sex, F for failure for the follow-up,' Tabby pronounced with scorn, mentally blocking out the lean, powerful vibrancy of his commanding presence. Yes, Acheron Dimitrakos was gorgeous but in her scheme of things that was unimportant in comparison to the way he treated her.

CHAPTER SEVEN

IN RECEIPT OF that attack, Acheron stiffened in astonishment and angled his arrogant dark head back, his black-as-jet eyes gleaming with angry incomprehension even as his attention lingered on how astonishingly lovely Tabby looked fresh from his bed with her long blonde hair in a waving, tousled mass round her shoulders, her small face warm with self-conscious colour and her ripe pink mouth still swollen from his kisses. Even as he fought to think clearly, his reaction to that view and those thoughts was instantaneous and very physical. 'What the hell are you talking about?'

'The instant you had your satisfaction you leapt out of bed and abandoned me as though I was suffering from some horrid contagious disease,' Tabby condemned. 'Not an experience I would be tempted to repeat—you made me feel like a whore!'

'That's melodramatic nonsense,' Acheron fielded with derision, willing back his increasing arousal with every fibre of his self-discipline.

'No, I don't think it is. You couldn't even bear to hold me close for thirty seconds,' Tabby reminded him doggedly. 'Well, I think it's sad that the only way you feel comfortable physically touching anyone is in a sexual way.'

Acheron cursed in Greek. 'You don't know me as well

as you think you do. But I warned you that I didn't do cuddling.'

'You think that excuses you?' Tabby asked with scornfully unimpressed eyes of violet blue dominating her flushed and furious face. 'It doesn't. It simply shows you up as selfish and inconsiderate, and I deserved better.'

'I don't fake affection for anyone just because it's the acceptable thing to do,' Acheron bit out between clenched teeth. 'And I have so little practice at it, I would feel foolish and uncomfortable!'

And that was the most strikingly truthful thing he had told her about himself to date, Tabby reckoned, stunned by the raw honesty of that irate reply. Indeed his admission of ignorance and discomfiture squeezed her heart like a clenched fist. Without even thinking about what she was doing, she closed the distance between them, deliberately invading his personal space to stretch her arms round his neck and look up at him.

'Practise on me,' she urged quietly. 'I practised on Amber. I wasn't a very touchy-feely person either before I got to hold her for the first time.'

Acheron swallowed hard, insanely aware that she was making a platonic approach and quite impervious to the reality that below the towel he was still ragingly erect. He didn't want to hug her as though she were his friend; he wanted to shag her senseless. But he knew that option wasn't in the ring at that moment and he closed his arms round her slowly and lifted her to the other side of the big bathroom. 'You shouldn't have got dressed again,' he scolded.

'I assumed we were done,' Tabby confided bluntly.

Acheron bent down and lifted the hem of her dress to take it off over her head. Totally disconcerted, Tabby froze there for a split second, her arms crossed defensively across her bare breasts. 'What are you doing?'

Acheron hooked a finger into her knickers and jerked them down, lifting her again into his arms to trail them off. 'I may have leapt out of bed but I *was* thinking about your comfort,' he breathed as he lowered her down into the warm embrace of the scented water filling the bath. 'Now lie back and relax.'

Thoroughly disconcerted, Tabby surveyed him in wonderment. 'You came in here and ran a bath for me?'

'I hurt you...I thought you'd be sore,' he breathed huskily as he lit the candles in the candelabra by the sink and doused the lights.

'It was just one of those things, not your fault.' But Tabby reddened and sank deeper into the soothingly warm water, resting her head weakly back on the cushioned padding on the rim. In truth she *was* sore, that part of her so tender she was now uncomfortably aware of her pelvic area. What a pair they were, she thought morosely. He couldn't do ordinary affection and she couldn't do sex.

There was a pop as Acheron released a cork from a champagne bottle and sent bubbling golden liquid down into a pair of goblets.

'Where did that come from? And the candles?' she pressed weakly.

'Honeymoon couple, wedding night? The staff had all the trimmings waiting in the bedroom... It would be a shame not to use them,' Acheron remarked, perching on the side of the bath to offer her a glass of champagne.

'No, thanks. I never drink,' she said stiltedly.

Acheron thrust the glass into her hand. 'Unless you have a drink problem, one glass isn't going to do any damage.'

Her small fingers tensed round the stem. 'No, I don't have a problem but my parents did.'

'That doesn't mean you have to avoid it altogether.'

'I always like to play it safe,' Tabby confided, taking a small sip of the champagne, tiny bubbles bursting below her nose and moistening her skin.

'I'm more of a risk-taker. I enjoy excitement,' Acheron traded wryly.

'I think I could've worked that out for myself.'

Acheron compressed his mouth, his eyes semi-concealed by his black lashes. 'I didn't stay in bed with you because I didn't want you to have unrealistic expectations of our relationship.'

She grasped what he meant immediately and wished she didn't, a tiny pang of hurt pinching somewhere down deep inside her. He didn't want her getting the idea that there was anything more complex between them than straightforward sex. 'I may be inexperienced but I'm not stupid,' Tabby told him with pride.

'And I'm not good with words if I gave you that impression,' Acheron acknowledged grimly. 'Tabby, I don't have conversations like this with women. I've never met a woman like you.'

'Are we *still* talking about me being a virgin?' Tabby asked in a small voice.

'I'm accustomed to women who know the score.'

'I know it too,' Tabby breathed, skimming a glance across his hard-edged profile, her chest tightening with a sense of constraint. 'I'm a very practical person.'

Acheron scanned her small, tight face, the set grip of her tiny hands over her raised knees as he read the valiant defensiveness she used as a screen and his stomach hollowed out at the prospect of hurting her. He had never felt that way around a woman before and he didn't like it at all. She might be fragile but she had made a choice, just as he had done, and they were both adults, he reminded himself impatiently as he straightened again.

At the same moment, Tabby sat up abruptly and set down the champagne flute, water sloshing noisily around her slight body. 'Oh, my goodness, what am I doing in here? I can't stay! The baby monitor is in my bedroom.'

'Melinda will take care of Amber's needs. Relax,' Acheron urged.

'Melinda can't be expected to work twenty-four hours a day. I told her I'd take care of Amber at night,' Tabby countered as she rolled onto her knees, concern for Amber overcoming her self-consciousness, and began to stand up. 'Pass me a towel—'

'No, you stay where you are,' Acheron instructed, his hand closing over her shoulder to press her back into the warm water again. 'I'll collect the monitor and check on Amber as well.'

Her violet eyes widened. '*You*...will?'

Acheron strode back into the bedroom to retrieve his jeans and wandered back to the doorway, dropping the towel with total unselfconsciousness to pull on the jeans. 'Why not? You've already shown me what to do with her if she's crying.'

'I wasn't expecting you to help,' Tabby commented. 'It's my job, not yours, after all.'

'Our arrangement isn't that clear cut. This is a joint venture when it comes to me requiring a wife and you requiring an adoptive father figure,' Acheron reminded her, turning on his heel.

Stiff with uncertainty, Tabby lay back in the warm water and sipped the champagne while still feeling thoroughly confused by Acheron's behaviour. She had got him wrong when she condemned him for abandoning her immediately after sex. But then, had the simple act of sex put him into a particularly good mood? Could a man be that basic? In consideration of her needs, he had run her a bath before he went for his shower. Now he was actually off to check on Amber for her as if the child was something more than the extra baggage she had assumed he deemed her to be. At the same time, however, he had also clearly felt the need to spell out the lowering message that the only thing between him and Tabby was sex. As if she didn't already know that!

Acheron was the ultimate womaniser, steering clear of involvement and commitment. And why shouldn't he? common sense asked. A young, handsome, wealthy male was in high demand in the world of women and had no need to settle on only one. In addition, Acheron had issues but then who didn't after such a childhood as they had both undergone? In remembrance, Tabby suppressed a shiver. He had probably learned just as she had that if you kept everyone at arm's length you didn't get hurt.

But Tabby had moved on from that self-protective stance when she first opened her heart to friendship with Sonia and then Amber and finally understood how much more warm and satisfying life could be with love and loyalty in it. She knew she had lost her business and her first home because she had chosen to personally care for Sonia and Amber but she had no regrets about the choices she had made.

Amber was now her sole responsibility, she recalled, while wondering what she was doing lying back in a luxury bathtub drinking champagne when the baby she loved might be in need of her. In an instant she had clambered dripping out of the bath and swathed herself in a big warm towel, hurriedly patting herself dry before reaching for her dress again. It was time to get back to the real world, she told herself urgently, and there was nothing 'real world' about lounging around lazily in Acheron's opulent bathroom.

Acheron groaned when he heard the baby crying through the monitor. The little plastic speaker was set on the dressing table and as he studied it he became aware that something had been written on the mirror.

'Go home, whore!' someone had printed with what looked like a red felt-tip pen.

Bemused, nerves still jumping at the sound of the baby crying, Acheron hesitated only a moment before striding into the bathroom to snatch up a towel, dampening it and walking back to wipe the mirror clean again before Tabby could see it. For a split second he paused, brooding over the disturbing awareness that only his household staff had access to the bedroom and that one of them clearly wasn't trustworthy. But why leave such a message for Tabby to find? he questioned furiously. She was his wife, his legal wife with every right to be in his house. Who would target Tabby? His handsome mouth down-curved: Kasma was the most likely suspect. Pure rage blazed in Acheron as he dug out his cell phone, called his head of security and brought him up to speed on the development. His temper uneven, he strode off to take care of the baby. She was only a baby, he told himself bracingly, of course he could handle one tiny baby without help.

Amber was sitting upright screaming at the top of her voice, her little face red as fire. Acheron hovered a few feet from the cot. 'Nothing's that bad,' he told Amber in what he hoped was a soothing tone.

Amber lifted up her arms expectantly.

'Do I need to come that close?' Acheron asked uneasily. 'I'm here. You're safe. I assure you that nothing bad is going to happen to you.'

Amber fixed bewildered brown eyes on him, tears

rolling down her crumpled face, and lifted her arms again in open demand.

Acheron released his breath on a slow measured hiss and moved closer. 'I'm no good at the cuddling stuff,' he warned her ruefully, reaching down to lift the child, who startled him by wrapping both arms tightly round his throat and hanging on as firmly to him as a monkey gripping a branch.

An exhausted sob sounded in his ear, and he splayed a big hand across the little girl's back and shifted his fingers in a vague circular motion aimed at soothing her fears. A vague shard of memory featuring a woman's face momentarily froze him where he stood. He didn't recall what age he had been but he had certainly been very small when the woman had come in the night to comfort him, rocking him in her arms and singing to him until he stopped crying. Had that woman been Olympia, Amber's late grandmother and his own mother's former carer? Who else could it have been? Only Olympia had ever shown him concern and treated him as if he was something other than a nuisance part of her well-paid job.

'I owe you,' he told Amber heavily and he rearranged her awkwardly in his arms and began to rock her, suppressing that rare memory of the past with the profound discomfort that such images always brought him. 'But even for you I can't sing.'

Amber startled him by smiling widely up at him, showing off her two front teeth, and he smiled back before he even knew what he was doing.

And that was how Tabby saw them when she came to a halt in the doorway: Acheron with a tousled black curl falling over his brow, his haunting dark eyes locked to Amber while the most glorious smile lifted his wide, sensual mouth. Barefoot and bare-chested, well-worn jeans hanging low on his lean hips, he looked both extravagantly handsome and unusually human at the same time. Her breath feathered in her throat and her mouth ran dry because that smile was pure sensual dynamite.

'Let me take her,' she proffered quietly. 'I'll put her back in bed.'

'We were managing fine,' Acheron announced, not without pride in the accomplishment as he settled Amber into Tabby's arms. 'Obviously she's not very choosy.'

'Well, you're wrong there. She can actually be quite choosy and can be difficult with some people,' Tabby admitted as she rested Amber down on the changing mat and deftly changed her before placing the child back into her cot, gently stroking her cheek when she grizzled. 'It's bedtime, sweetness. We don't play at bedtime.'

'I'll organise cover for the nights,' Acheron remarked as she joined him in the corridor.

'That's not necessary.'

'You can still go to her if you want but you can't be dragged out of bed *every* night,' he told her drily.

'I'm still the woman who wants to be her mother. It's my duty to be there for her,' Tabby reminded him gently. 'I don't want other people looking after her all the time.'

'Be reasonable.' Acheron paused outside the two doors that led into their separate bedrooms. 'Are you joining me for what remains of the night?'

The ease with which he asked the question disconcerted Tabby because she had assumed that once his lusty curiosity was satisfied she would no longer be of interest to him. His approach both pleased and annoyed her. 'I'm afraid if I did join you, there would have to be rules,' she murmured awkwardly, her hand closing on the handle of her own bedroom door.

'Rules?' Acheron repeated in wonderment. 'Is that your idea of a joke?'

'No, I rarely joke about serious stuff,' Tabby countered gently. 'If you want to hear the rules, ask me.'

'I don't do rules,' Acheron ground out between gritted teeth. 'Perhaps it has escaped your attention, but I'm not a misbehaving child!'

Tabby closed the door quietly in his face.

She had donned one of her slinky new nightdresses before the door opened again. She scrambled hastily below the top sheet and looked across the room enquiringly.

'What bloody rules?' Acheron slung at her, poised hands affixed to his lean hips, his hard-muscled abdomen prominent.

'One,' Tabby enumerated. 'Any relationship we have has to be exclusive and if you plan to stray you have to tell me and finish it decently. No secrets, no sneaking around on me.'

Acheron surveyed her with wild golden eyes of increasingly wrathful incredulity. 'I don't believe I'm hearing this!'

'*Two,*' Tabby continued unconcerned. 'You treat me with respect at all times. If I annoy you, we have it out but not around Amber.'

'You're absolutely out of your mind,' Acheron breathed with unsettling conviction while he studied her with seething, dark golden eyes. 'And I married you.'

'*Three,*' Tabby pronounced woodenly, although her colour was high and her hands clenched into fists by her side. 'I'm not a toy you can pick up and put down again whenever you feel like it. I'm not the entertainment when you're bored. If you treat me well, I will treat you equally well, but if you don't…well, all bets would be off then.'

'Na pas sto dialo!' Acheron murmured wrathfully. 'It means, go to hell, and take your precious rules with you!'

Tabby didn't breathe again until the door had snapped closed behind him and then she lay back in bed, her body feeling heavy as a stone dropped from a height, her tummy rolling like a boat on a storm-tossed sea. Well, that was one way of getting rid of Acheron without losing face, one way of ensuring he was forced to see her as an equal. What else could she have said? Sliding willy-nilly into a casual sexual affair with no boundaries was not her style and with a man as volatile as he was it would be a sure recipe for disaster. But now that the ultimate womanising, free-spirited man knew that she would make major demands, he would be careful to avoid her from now on.

And what sort of idiot was she to feel sad about that fact? She would get over her silly notions about him— of course she would, because there was really no other option open to her. He wanted one thing, she wanted another, so it was better to end it before it got messy and painful and humiliating. Better by far…

In the middle of the night, Acheron went for a cold shower. His erection wouldn't quit and he was still in an unholy rage. Rules, blasted rules. Was he suddenly back at school? Who did she think she was dealing with? Even more crucially, *what* did she think she was dealing with? Did she assume he had got into that bed and somehow signed up for the whole relationship charade? Trust a woman to take a concept as simple as sex and complicate it!

Even so, he was as furious with himself as he was with her. He had suspected that her naivety would lead to problems and he knew he should have listened to his misgivings. But just as the hot blood pulsing through his tense,

aching body wouldn't stop, his desire for her had proved
unrelenting. He'd had to know what she was like and he'd
found out and, even worse, she had been amazing and no
sooner had he stopped than he wanted to go again…and
again…and again. His even white teeth clenched hard.
That fast he was recalling the hot clenching of her tight
little body around him, an explicit memory that did nothing to cool his overheated libido.

'So, who's the cutest little baby in the world?' Tabby chattered the next morning while Amber waved her spoon in
the air, cheerfully responding to the warm, loving gush
of Tabby's appreciation.

Acheron suppressed a groan and slung himself down
into a chair by the dining table on the terrace. Baby talk
at breakfast time, one more thing she had brought into his
life that was not to his taste. First thing in the morning
he liked sex and silence and since he had had neither he
could not be expected to be in a good mood, he reasoned
impatiently. The sight of Tabby in a little red strappy top
and shorts that exposed far too much bare creamy skin for
his delectation didn't help. Even a glimpse of the tattoo
on her arm as she swivelled in her seat failed to switch
off the ever-ready pulse at his groin.

Tabby tried to scan Acheron without being obvious
about it, sending little flips of her eyes in his direction
with her lashes quickly dropping again. He was *so* beautiful; it was surely a sin for a male to be so beautiful
that she was challenged to stop staring at him. Even the
awareness of the lingering tenderness between her legs
couldn't dull her appreciation of that long, lean, powerful frame of his, gracefully draped in the chair like a
work of art to be admired. The sunlight glittered over his
black springy curls, and she wanted to run her fingers

through his hair, stroke that stubborn jaw line set like granite until she awakened that wonderful smile again. Disconcerted by her treacherous thoughts, Tabby twisted her head away, resisting temptation.

Amber extended both arms in Acheron's direction and beamed at him. 'Not right now, *koukla mou*,' he murmured. 'Have your breakfast first.'

That he had acknowledged Amber's presence but not hers aggravated Tabby. Last night she had only been a body but this morning she was evidently invisible into the bargain. 'Good morning, Acheron,' she said curtly.

'Kalimera, yineka mou,' Ash murmured silkily, noting the fiery brightness of her extraordinary violet eyes as she settled her gaze on him. 'Did you sleep well?'

'Like a log,' Tabby lied, wondering why he brought out a mean streak in her that she had never known she had.

A maid poured his coffee, and the rich aroma flared her nostrils, inexplicably reminding her that Sonia had become preternaturally sensitive to certain smells when she first fell pregnant with Amber and an edge of panic suddenly sliced through Tabby's surface calm. 'Last night…' she prompted abruptly, waiting with a rapidly beating heart and hot cheeks for the maid to retreat. 'You *did* use protection, didn't you?'

Magnificently nonchalant in the face of that intimate question, Acheron widened lustrous, dark golden eyes in mocking amusement. 'You think I would be stupid enough to neglect such a precaution?'

'I think in the heat of the moment if you wanted something enough you would take risks,' Tabby admitted tautly.

Acheron lifted a winged ebony brow and cocked his handsome head in Amber's direction. 'Not if it meant risking the acquisition of one of those,' he declared. 'Passion doesn't rule me.'

'Or me,' she echoed half under her breath. As she leant forward to help Amber clear her plate, her breasts stirred beneath her tee with the movement, pushing her unbearably sensitive nipples against the fabric, and made her think that a bra would have been a better idea than going without. Particularly in Acheron's radius.

The same view was not wasted on Acheron either, who recalled the precise pout of her delicate flesh and his almost overpowering desire to eat her alive. While the smouldering silence at the table stretched, the nanny entered and removed Amber from her chair to bear her off for a bath.

Acheron dragged in a deep, cooling breath of the sunshine laden air, knowing that, for the sake of peace and better understanding, he had to challenge Tabby's misconceptions. 'Your rules?' he mused with a dismissive shrug of one broad shoulder. '*My* rules? I never ever get involved with clingy, needy women.'

Coming at her out of nowhere, that statement crashed down on Tabby like a brick dropped on glass and her head flew up, violet eyes wide. 'Are you calling me clingy and needy?'

'What do you think?'

Tabby sprang out of her chair, the feet of it slamming back noisily across the tiles underfoot as she stabbed her hands down on the table for support. Anger had gripped her in a stormy surge. 'How dare you? I've never been clingy or needy in my life with a man!'

'Yet your first move is to try and hedge me round with rules. You want reassurance and promises about a future that is unknown to both of us,' Acheron reasoned with cold precision. 'I don't own a crystal ball.'

'I don't like the way you operate!' Tabby vented fiercely.

'Yet you know nothing about me. For years I've been exclusive in my affairs and I don't move on without saying so when I lose interest,' Acheron declared lazily, rising upright to study her, his brilliant, dark eyes hard and glittering. 'It is offensive that you should condemn me for lies and infidelity on the basis of your assumptions about my character.'

'You're so smooth…I wouldn't trust a word that came out of your mouth!' Tabby hurled at him accusingly, refusing to acknowledge that he had a point.

'Now who's guilty of prejudice?' Acheron riposted with soft sibilance. 'What do you find most offensive about me? My public-school education, my wealth or my lifestyle?'

Ferocious resentment held Tabby rigid where she stood, her small face taut and flushed with indignation, but it was the soft pink fullness of her lush mouth that welded Acheron's attention there. 'What I find most offensive is your certainty that you know best about *everything*!'

'I do know that we are poles apart and that this arrangement will work most efficiently if we stick to the original agreement we made.'

Tabby's tummy flipped as though she had gone down in a lift too fast, sheer strain locking her every muscle into tautness. 'You should've kept your blasted hands off me!' she slammed back.

Acheron flashed her a grim appraisal from his stunning golden eyes, and his mouth twisted sardonically. 'Sadly, I *couldn't*…'

And with that final admission, Acheron strode back into the air-conditioned cool of the villa and left her alone to contemplate the truly fabulous view. The rolling green

Tuscan hills stretched out before her marked out in a colourful patchwork of woodland, olive groves and vineyards. She snatched in a deeply shaken breath, the hot air scouring her lungs. He wanted them to return to the sensible terms of their platonic agreement, which was exactly what she had believed she wanted. Why, then, when she had achieved her goal, did she feel as though she had lost the battle? Indeed, instead of feeling relieved and reassured by his logical approach to their differences, she felt ridiculously hurt and abandoned…

CHAPTER EIGHT

TABBY ROLLED THE soft ball back to Amber where the child sat below the dappled shade of an ancient spreading oak tree. Amber rolled over and crawled to the edge of the rug, a look of glee in her bright eyes as she scanned the wide green expanse of freedom open before her.

Tabby marvelled at the speed with which the little girl had learned to embrace independent movement. One minute she had been rolling over and over again to explore further afield and the next she had perfected crawling. At just over seven months old she was a fairly early developer but she had always been a physically strong baby who met every developmental guideline in advance, and Tabby wasn't really surprised that Amber had discovered how to get around without adult assistance ahead of time. As she watched the little girl pulled a blade of grass and stuck it in her mouth.

'No…no,' she was saying while retrieving the grass when Melinda strolled up and offered to give her a break.

'Yes, and you're welcome,' Tabby confided ruefully. 'She's much more of a handful now, and I wouldn't mind a little break to sunbathe and read.'

'We can manage that. I'm going to put her in the buggy and take her for a walk,' the blonde nanny told her smoothly. 'I just love it here.'

Tabby glanced at the younger woman, wondering why she found it such a challenge to like her and feeling rather guilty about the fact. After all, Melinda was great with Amber, a diligent worker and friendly. Perhaps it was the hungry little glances she often saw Melinda aiming at Acheron that had prevented Tabby from bonding more with the other young woman. It was not that she was jealous, Tabby reasoned uneasily, simply that she wasn't comfortable with a woman prepared to show that much interest in the married man who employed her. In any case, and to be fair to all parties concerned, Acheron had shown not the smallest awareness of Melinda's curvaceous blonde allure.

'Any idea when we'll be leaving here yet?' Melinda asked as she gathered up Amber's toys and stuffed them in a bag.

'Not yet, sorry…my husband hasn't decided how long we'll be staying,' Tabby replied, wryly impressed by the way that possessive label slid off her tongue. But that, she had learned, was the easiest way to refer to Acheron in front of the staff.

Yet he was as much a husband as a caged tiger in a zoo would be, she conceded unhappily, lifting her book and her sunglasses and heading for the cool courtyard in which the pool was situated. For the past week she had barely seen Acheron, who confined himself to his office most of the day and often half the night to work. Even when he was around his phone was always ringing and his single-minded focus on business was exactly what she should have expected from a goal-orientated alpha male.

Occasionally he would join her for a cup of coffee at breakfast time and he generally put in a rather silent appearance at the dinner table, eating quickly and then politely excusing himself. He was a cool and distant companion at those meals and there was never so much as a hint of sexual awareness in either his looks or his conversation. It was as though that wild bout of passion on their wedding night was the product of her imagination alone, but Tabby still found it a distinct challenge to revert to treating him like a stranger and that embarrassed her, denting her pride and her belief in her own strength and independence because no woman of character should continue to crave the attention of a man set on treating her like the wallpaper.

Yet amazingly, infuriatingly, Acheron was playing an entirely different ball game with Amber. Melinda swore that Acheron never passed the nursery door without coming in to talk to and play with her charge and Amber had already learned to make a beeline for Acheron whenever he was in her vicinity. In fact, when it came to Acheron, Amber took her welcome for granted. Maybe Acheron's ego was flattered by the amount of attention Amber gave him. Maybe he was even belatedly discovering that he actually liked and enjoyed the company of children? How could she possibly know what motivated his interest? Tabby had not got through a week of virtually sleepless nights without acknowledging that she knew very little at all about Acheron Dimitrakos. Her husband was a mystery to her in almost every conceivable way.

Acheron stood at the window and groaned at the sight of Tabby arranging her slim pale body on a lounger like an exhibition banquet for the starving. A purple bikini cupped her rounded little breasts and slender hips and every shift of her slim thighs drew his considerable attention. He shifted uneasily, struggling to rein back the heavy pulse of arousal that was making his nights so long and frustrating.

Although he had kept watch, as he told himself a protective husband should do, he had yet to see Tabby go topless to eradicate the risk of tan marks. He frowned, not wanting her to show that amount of naked flesh when there were always staff roaming the grounds. It was very strange, he acknowledged in bewilderment, that in spite of the fact he thought it was a very old-fashioned attitude, which he would not have admitted even under torture, he didn't like the idea of anyone but him seeing any part of Tabby bare. He thought that there was a very weird possessive streak in him somewhere and blamed it on the surprising fact that he had become his wife's first lover.

His wife, a label he had never thought he would use, he conceded hard-mouthed, his dark eyes hooded and unusually reflective. Had Tabby genuinely been his wife, however, she would have been in his bed throughout the long hot hours of the afternoon abandoning herself to the demands of his passion and losing herself in the release he would have given her. As his body hardened afresh under the onslaught of that X-rated imagery he cursed bitterly under his breath.

Regretfully, Tabby had all the flexibility of a steel girder: he could do the rules or he could do cold showers. There would be no halfway measures, no get-out clause with her. It would be all or nothing and he knew he *couldn't* do it, couldn't walk that line and change himself to suit when he knew there was no future in it. It wouldn't be fair to her. Yet right at that precise moment Tabby's rules had more pulling power than a ten-ton truck.

That evening, Tabby selected a drop-dead gorgeous blue dress from the closet. Over the past week she had worn a different outfit every day, reasoning that the clothes were there and there was little point wasting them. In any case it would be downright silly to choose to overheat in the jeans and tops that were virtually all she had left of her own clothes since her life first began to unravel after she had lost her own home. Back then she had had to surrender an awful lot of her possessions, whittling her collection of clothing and objects down until she retained only what mattered most and what she could carry.

She tossed the dress on the bed, put on her make-up and brushed her hair, not that how she looked mattered when Acheron was treating her as though she were someone's maiden aunt. But then Acheron *wasn't* the reason why she took the trouble to dress up, she reminded herself staunchly. She did it for her own self-esteem and the knowledge that behaving, at least on the outside, like a rich honeymoon bride was part of her role. Clothed, she eased her feet into perilously high heels and surveyed herself critically in the mirror, mouth momentarily drooping while she wished she were taller, curvier and more striking in appearance…like Kasma? The Kasma whom Acheron never, ever mentioned? But then what business was Kasma of hers? The fiery fury, ignited only a week before by the discovery that Acheron would benefit as much as she did from their marriage, had drained away. After all, she had married Acheron for only one reason: to become Amber's adoptive mother, and all she needed to focus on now was getting through their little charade of a marriage as smoothly and painlessly as possible. Worrying about anything else, *wanting* anything else was unnecessarily stressful and stupid.

Acheron was crossing the hall when Tabby reached the head of the marble staircase. Obeying instinct, she threw her head back and straightened her spine even as she felt perspiration break out across her skin. There he was, sleek, outrageously good-looking and sophisticated even when clad in jeans and an open-necked shirt. Her heart went bumpety-bumpety-bump like a clock wound up too tight, and she gripped the bannister with an agitated hand to start down the stairs. Unfortunately for her, her leading foot went down, however, not onto a step but disorientatingly into mid-air and she tipped forward with a shocked cry of fright, her hand slipping its light hold on the stair rail, her whole body twisting as she tried to halt her fall so that her hip struck the edge of a hard marble step and her ankle was turned beneath her.

'I've got you!' Acheron bit out as the world steadied again.

Mercifully Tabby registered that she was no longer falling but that pain was biting all the way from her hip down her leg…no, not her leg, her ankle. She adjusted as Acheron swept her up into his arms with too much enthusiasm and her leg swung none too gently and she couldn't bite back the cry of pain that was wrenched from her throat. 'My ankle…'

'*Thee mou*…you could've been killed falling on these stairs!' Acheron breathed with a rawness that took her aback, striding back down into the hall with his arms tautly linked round her slight body. He called out in Greek until one of his security staff came running and then he rapped out instructions.

Against her cheek she could feel the still-accelerated pounding of his heart and she wasn't surprised that he was still high on adrenalin because he must have moved faster than the speed of light to intercept her fall. She felt quite queasy at the realisation that but for his timely intervention she might have fallen all the way down the marble staircase and broken her neck or at the very least a limb or two. Relief that she had only wrenched her ankle and bruised herself filtered slowly through her. 'I'm OK… Lucky you caught me in time.'

Acheron laid her down with exaggerated care on a sofa and squatted athletically down to her level. 'Did you feel anyone push you?' he asked, brilliant dark heavily fringed eyes locked to her face.

She was astounded at the tenor of that question; her violet eyes rounded. 'Why would anyone push me down the stairs?' she asked weakly. 'I lost my balance and tripped.'

Acheron frowned. 'Are you certain? I thought I saw someone pass by you on the landing just before you fell.'

'I didn't see or hear anyone.' Her brows pleated and her lashes screened her eyes, the heat of embarrassment washing away her pallor because she knew exactly *why* she had tripped but wild horses wouldn't have dragged the confession from her. 'Yes, of course I'm certain.'

If she hadn't been so busy admiring Acheron and trying to pose like a silly teenager to look her very best for his benefit, she would never have missed her step, Tabby was reflecting in deep, squirming chagrin.

'I'm afraid I have to move you again…I'll try not to hurt you,' Acheron told her, sliding his hands beneath her prone length. 'But I have to get you into a car to get you to a doctor.'

'For goodness' sake, I don't need a doctor!' Tabby exclaimed in growing embarrassment.

But over the next couple of hours while she was subjected to every possible medical examination at the nearest hospital, she might as well have been talking to a wall because Acheron refused to listen to a word she said. Furthermore, far from behaving like the cool, reserved male she was accustomed to dealing with, Acheron was clearly all wound up although why he was, she had no idea. He paced the floor outside her examination cubicle, talked to her through the curtain to check she was all right and not in too much discomfort, insisted on an X-ray being done while virtually ignoring the doctor who assured him that she was suffering from nothing more serious than some nasty bruising and a sprained ankle. Even more embarrassing, his security team spread out round them on full systems alert as if awaiting an imminent rocket attack on the casualty department.

'Ah…very much the adoring and anxious husband,' the middle-aged doctor chuckled in his ignorance.

If only the man knew how wrong he was, Tabby thought unhappily, feeling like a wretched nuisance and a malingerer taking up valuable medical attention when really there was nothing very much amiss with her.

If Tabby had died, it would have been *his* fault. Acheron brooded on that thought darkly, rage and guilt slivering through him in sickening waves and like nothing he had ever felt before. But then he had never been responsible for another life before and, though he would have liked to have thought otherwise, he believed that his wife was very much *his* responsibility. Naturally he was appalled by the suspicion that someone who worked for him might have attempted to hurt his wife. Having seen the rude message left on her bedroom mirror, he was unimpressed by her conviction that she had simply had an accident. In the split second it had taken for Tabby to lose her balance and topple she might not even have noticed that someone had lightly pushed her or tripped her up.

He was even more frustrated that his security staff had failed to come up with anything suspicious on any member of the villa staff. Acheron's mouth twisted. Unfortunately the Tuscan villa had rarely been used, hence the renovation the previous year and the hire of employees who were a new and unknown quantity and whose dependability would only be confirmed by the test of time. His lustrous eyes hardened and his stubborn mouth compressed into a tough line of determination. Tabby's safety was paramount and as he was very reluctant to frighten her with his suspicions. The wisest strategy would be to immediately vacate the villa and seek a more secure setting. That decision reached, Acheron gave the order, refusing to back down even when the chief of his security pointed out that such a move would entail rousing the baby from her bed as well. Regardless of the drawbacks of his plan, Acheron could hardly wait to get Tabby and the baby away from the Tuscan villa, which now, to his way of thinking, seemed a tainted place. He watched the doctor bandaging her swollen ankle, annoyance still gripping him that he had failed to prevent her from getting hurt.

'Sorry about all this.' Tabby sighed in the limo as they left the hospital.

'When you have an accident you don't need to apologise for it. How are you?' Acheron pressed.

'A bit battered and sore—nothing I won't quickly recover from,' Tabby responded with a smile. 'It'll certainly teach me to be more careful on stairs from now on.'

Acheron was quietly stunned. No woman of his acquaintance would have neglected to make a huge fuss over such an incident by exaggerating their injuries and demanding his sympathy and attention. Tabby, however, characteristically downplayed the episode and asked nothing of him, an acknowledgement that only increased his brooding discomfiture with the situation.

'Where on earth are we going?' Tabby enquired as he lifted her out of the limo and stowed her in the wheelchair already waiting for her use. 'Is this the airport?'

'Yes, we're flying to Sardinia,' Acheron said casually.

'Seriously? I mean, like *right now*?' Tabby stressed in disbelief. 'It's ten o'clock at night.'

'Amber and her nanny are already on board the helicopter, as is your luggage,' Acheron admitted.

There were many things Tabby could have said but she was fighting a dropped jaw and had already learned to think twice before she spoke her mind around Acheron. She clamped her lips firmly together and assumed that he was bored at the villa and that the evident appeal of a change of surroundings had persuaded him to act on impulse. Not only was he dragging Amber out of bed, but he was also forcing Tabby to travel when she was exhausted and in pain. Her lush mouth down-curved: he was being selfishly inconsiderate but she supposed that was normal behaviour for a male accustomed to thinking only of his own needs.

The helicopter was very noisy and Tabby, who hadn't eaten since lunchtime, was almost sick with hunger. She insisted on taking Amber from Melinda, though, and soothed the overtired baby herself. She was surprised when Acheron eased the drowsing child from her arms and settled her on his lap instead. Amber looked up at him, stuck her thumb back in her mouth and closed her eyes again, seemingly content with the exchange. Tabby must've dozed off at that point because she wakened confused by the bright light on her face and the jabs of pain from her ankle as Acheron carried her into a house.

'How do you feel?' he enquired again, stunning gaze sweeping her pale, taut face.

'I'll be fine—'

'Don't be a martyr—you look like death warmed over,' he countered impatiently. 'You're going straight to bed, *yineka mou*. I've organised food as well.'

A bed and a meal sounded very appealing to Tabby at that moment. He mounted a staircase and a faint breeze cooled her cheekbone. Her lashes swept up on a tall open window framed by pale fluttering draperies just as Acheron laid her down on a ginormous bed and began to carefully ease the bedding from beneath her. It struck her that for once he was being very kind and that set her teeth on edge.

'Why are you being so nice to me all of a sudden?' Tabby demanded abruptly.

That single question said so much that Acheron didn't want to hear just then that he almost groaned his frustration aloud. Leave it to Tabby, he thought ruefully. Leave it to Tabby to say what nobody else dared to say to Acheron Dimitrakos. He breathed in slowly. 'You're hurt.'

'You don't do rules and I don't do pity,' Tabby told him, tilting her chin in challenge.

'You're my wife.'

'Not really.'

'*Enough* my wife that I want to treat you like one,' Acheron contradicted almost harshly.

Tabby screened eyes blank with incomprehension and she was horribly tempted by an urge to slap him. He should have come with a dictionary or some sort of instruction manual that explained how he worked because once again she was all at sea as to what went on his complex and infuriating head.

'I want to make you feel better,' Acheron announced.

'No pity parties here, please.'

'I haven't behaved very well,' Acheron muttered in a harsh driven undertone. 'I am trying to make amends.'

'Pity's pity,' Tabby told him, unmoved by that argument.

Acheron came down on the bed beside her. There was

something wild about the glitter in his seething golden eyes as he gently knotted one hand in the fall of her golden hair and closed his mouth hungrily over hers. He sent a jolt of such savage hunger rocketing through her that she froze in sheer fright.

'Does that feel like pity?' he growled.

Tabby made no comment because she could barely breathe. She wanted him to do it again and for longer and was only just able to keep her hands off that lean, powerful body so very close to hers for the first time in a week. One little touch and he made her feel like a sex addict ready to run scarily out of control. In sudden retreat, she dropped her head and then mercifully they were interrupted by the entrance of a woman carrying a tray.

'You need to eat,' Acheron told her unnecessarily.

With his assistance, Tabby leant back against the pillows and lifted the knife and fork. She literally didn't *dare* look at him again, couldn't trust herself that far, knew that she couldn't risk reliving that burning, driving sensation of sexual need in his presence. Hungry though she undoubtedly was, she had to force herself to eat because the sheer level of tension holding her taut was suppressing her appetite. She ate in silence while Acheron paced restively round the big room, constantly drawing her eyes until she remembered that she couldn't afford to look, and in fact had to blank him out to stay in control. And what did that say about her? Was she really that weak that she couldn't withstand him? This guy who had virtually ignored her for the past week? The same one who had slept with her and then backed off at supersonic speed? Shame engulfed her, increasing the exhaustion she had been fighting to contain.

The tray was removed from her lap. Her lashes

drooped, eyes so heavy she literally couldn't hold them open any longer.

'Get some sleep,' Acheron urged, and for once she was in the mood to obey.

Tabby awoke with a piercing need to go to the bathroom, eyes flickering open on darkness and a strong feeling of disorientation. She struggled to sit up and gasped in dismay at the pain that shot through her ankle while she stretched out a wildly flailing hand in search of a bed-side light. Mercifully she found the switch attached to a hanging wire, and light illuminated the bedroom a scant second before the male lying on a sofa against the wall leapt upright.

'Ash?' she whispered in disbelief. 'What are you doing in here?'

Acheron was bare-chested and barefoot, low-slung denim jeans clinging to his lean hips. Her startled gaze clung to the muscled expanse of his magnificent bronzed torso and then flicked guiltily higher to take in the dark stubble masking his lower jaw and the unnerving intensity of eyes that glittered like black diamonds in the low light. 'I couldn't leave you in here alone.'

'Why not?' Tabby queried, her face hotter than fire as she forced herself to swivel her hips and shift her good leg off the edge of the bed. 'Why would you sleep on a sofa for my benefit?'

'What on earth are you trying to do?' Acheron de-manded, striding across the room.

'I need the bathroom,' she breathed between gritted teeth, mortification rolling over her like a tidal wave.

'You are so stubborn, *koukla mou*. Right now, you need help and I didn't want to put a stranger in here with you,' he admitted impatiently, pushing the walking stick resting against the bedside cabinet into her hand and then slowly pulling her upright to take advantage of its support. 'Now go slow or you'll hurt yourself.'

But Tabby had already worked out that there was no way of moving her leg without her ankle hurting her and she simply clenched her teeth and got on with it, tears stinging her eyes as she hobbled clumsily towards the connecting door he had already opened for her benefit.

Acheron groaned something in Greek and carefully scooped her up into his arms to carry her into the bathroom and gently settle her down on the stool by the vanity unit. 'Pain's always worse in the middle of the night. You'll feel better tomorrow,' he predicted. 'Shout when you're ready to go back to bed.'

Reckoning that there would be two blue moons in the sky before she willingly asked for his help, Tabby studied her tousled reflection in the mirror in cringing horror. She was still wearing the make-up she had put on for dinner the night before and she had panda eyes, sleep creases on her cheek and hideously messy hair. How come he looked gorgeous in the middle of the night but she looked like the Bride of Dracula?

She glanced down and fingered the skimpy nightdress she now wore and swallowed back a groan. Acheron must've undressed her. So what? He had already seen her naked, she reminded herself doggedly, so he had seen nothing new and it was very silly to be embarrassed about it. Levering herself upright, she took care of necessities and then made use of the facilities to clean herself up as best she could. Feeling considerably fresher but pale and stiff with the amount of pain her every movement had made her suffer, Tabby hobbled back out of the bathroom.

Acheron was waiting to scoop her up and deposit her back on the bed.

'I still don't understand what you're doing here with me,' she said weakly, perspiration breaking out on her brow.

'There're only three bedrooms in the main house. I knew you wouldn't want Amber staying away from you in the staff quarters and Melinda needed the third room,' Acheron explained drily.

'There's *only* three bedrooms?' Tabby remarked in amazement. 'You really didn't plan this move very well, did you?'

Acheron dealt her a fulminating appraisal in seething silence. 'It's three in the morning…let's talk about it tomorrow.'

Tabby watched him move back towards the sofa and released her breath on a reluctant sigh. 'Oh, for goodness' sake, share the bed… It's as big as a football pitch. I'm sure we can manage to avoid each other.'

Acheron swung round, his surprise unfeigned, but he said nothing. He switched out the light, and she lay very still in the darkness, listening to the sound of his jeans coming off and trying very hard not to picture what he looked like without them. The sheet moved, the mattress depressed and she forced herself to relax. She was safe as houses with him, she told herself wryly. Acheron was powered by reason, not emotion, not passion. He knew they were a match made in hell.

It was dawn by the time Tabby woke again. Soreness and stiffness assailed her with her first involuntary movement, and she screwed up her face in silent complaint. She turned her head only for her breath to hitch at the sight of Acheron lying asleep only inches away from her. His hair, rumpled into ebony curls, stood out in stark contrast to the white pillow case, his black lashes luxuriant fans that rimmed his strong cheekbones, his wilful passionate mouth full and relaxed. She couldn't stop staring at him. The sheet was wrapped round his hips, the corrugated musculature of his bronzed chest and abdomen exposed as well as a long, powerful, hair-roughened thigh. The pure haunting beauty of his perfectly sculpted body grabbed her by the throat and shook her inside out while heat pooled in her pelvis. She wanted to touch him; she wanted to touch him so badly it hurt to be denied.

His lashes swept up and he stretched slowly and languorously, long, taut muscles defined like ropes below his smooth brown skin. *'Kalimera, yineka mou.'*

Tabby arched a brow. 'Which *means…*?'

'Good morning, wife of mine,' Acheron translated with rich amusement lightening his dark eyes.

'I'm not yours,' Tabby hissed back faster than a striking rattler.

A lean brown hand lifted and wound slowly and carefully into the tumbled fall of her blonde hair, his glittering dark golden eyes hot as boiling honey on her skin. 'How else would you describe yourself? You married me and then you accepted my body into yours. Don't you appreciate that that means that we legally consummated our union?'

Seized by chagrin and confusion, Tabby stiffened. 'I…I…'

He covered her mouth with his, lingering to nibble teasingly at her full lower lip before moving on to taste her with explosive eroticism. A chemical reaction took place inside her, her body jerking in response while within seconds a giant mushroom of heated hunger and longing surged up inside her, blowing her best intentions to hell. Helpless in the grip of that sensual offensive, she kissed him back and his tongue drove deep between her lips with a raw sexual charge that roared through her like a rocket attack.

'Ash?' she mumbled when he freed her long enough to breathe again.

He stared down at her with lancing impatience, every line of him rigid with tension. 'To hell with your rules,' he growled in a tone of decision, his broad chest vibrating against her swollen breasts. 'I only play by my own.'

Those words were still ringing in her ears when he slid his hands underneath her and lifted her slowly onto her side. 'What are you doing?' she gasped.

'I'm making what we both need possible,' Acheron rasped in her ear, his warm breath fanning her neck as he buried his mouth in the sensitive slope between neck and shoulder while his hands slid up from her waist to cup her achingly tender breasts. 'As you're in no condition to run away, shout loud if you want to say no.'

In stark disconcertion her violet eyes opened to their fullest extent and locked onto the sofa he had occupied the night before. She had invited him into the bed in the first place. Had he assumed her body was included in the offer? Or was he just as entrapped as she was by the chemistry between them? Naturally that latter interpretation pleased her more but, in the midst of her pondering, long fingers plucked at the straining peaks of her breasts and actual thought became too much of a challenge.

Acheron tasted the soft white skin of her throat and the sweet scent of her enclosed him, heightening his arousal to an almost unbearable extent. In need of release he pressed his throbbing erection against her bottom, and she gasped and leant back into him while he lifted her nightdress to caress the swollen bounty of her small, taut breasts, paying special attention to her plump pink nipples. 'I love your breasts,' he told her thickly. 'They fit perfectly into my hands, *moli mou*.'

Every tiny muscle straining as she trembled, Tabby looked down at the fingers, so dark against her paler skin, expertly caressing her. Sharp biting arrows of need were spearing down between her legs where her indescribably sensitive flesh was tingling. She shifted and a faint sound of discomfort was wrenched from her as she accidentally moved her ankle.

'Lie still,' Acheron urged. 'You don't need to do anything. Let me do all the work.'

Her desire was already so strong that she wanted to scream, wanted to tell him what to do and to do it quickly. The shock of the thought and a vision of his reaction cooled her teeming thoughts. But she hadn't known, hadn't ever dreamt that a kiss and a little intimate touching could send her temperature shooting from zero to overload and she knew that she was finally understanding the very basic reason why he had become her first lover. He burned her up like a lightning strike, awakened a craving that overwhelmed her defences.

His hand shimmied down over her thigh, flirting, teasing more intimate areas without delivering on the promise. She ached, she actually ached deep down inside where she felt hollow and desperate, her entire being locked to the playful passage of that provocative hand. Fingertips traced her hidden core, stroking nerve endings that were impossibly delicate. She dragged in a sustaining breath while he nibbled an enervating path down the side of her extended throat. 'In a minute I'm going to kill you,' she swore shakily.

'No, you're going to ask me to do it again.'

'You really don't suffer from low self-esteem,' she noted even more unevenly, her breath catching in her convulsing throat as a fingertip brushed her clitoris, and flame leapt through her entire core.

'Not between the sheets…no,' Acheron agreed silkily. 'You've been told you're wonderful?'

'Many times. I'm filthy rich. Telling me I'm rubbish in bed—even if it's true—wouldn't be profitable,' he advanced with cynical cool.

Consternation seized Tabby. 'That's *awful*—'

'Awful,' he mimicked, stroking the most sensitive spot on her whole body so that she jackknifed back against him with a startled yelp.

'I don't want your money,' Tabby exclaimed helplessly. 'I just want your body!'

A stark little silence fell, and she squeezed her eyes tight shut in horror. *I didn't say that, I couldn't possibly have said that!*

'I've got no objections to that goal,' Acheron husked, biting at her ear lobe with erotic intent, ostensibly undeterred by her claim. 'It's earthy and honest…why not?'

He touched her again and her mortification drowned in a sea of shivering response. She lay back against him, tiny muscles twitching, soothed by the heat and strength of him even as that amplified physical contact heightened her awareness. With immense delicacy he stroked the seam of her femininity and then slid inside where she was warm and wet and, oh, so needy. She quivered, pitched straight to a high of longing that she couldn't quell or even control. He sank a finger inside her, and she jerked and gasped as he plunged slowly in and out, raising her temperature to boiling point, making her squirm and shift, forgetting even the twinges of pain in her ankle.

'Hot, tight, ready,' Acheron growled hungrily in her ear as she arched back into his lean, hard body, instinctively seeking the fulfilment that only he could give while he angled away from her to don a condom. 'I've been fantasising about this for days.'

'Days?' she parroted in surprise as he lifted her un-damaged leg to spread her open for him.

'Every night since that first night, every day I saw you in that teeny tiny bikini, *glyka mou*,' Acheron con-fided, tilting her forward, long fingers tightening their hold on her slender thigh as he entered her with a groan of intense masculine satisfaction.

A muffled scream of pleasure was torn from Tabby's throat as her body was forced to adjust to his size, her inner channel stretching to the brink of insane pleasure.

'All right?' Acheron murmured thickly.

'Well, I wouldn't want you to answer your phone right now!' Tabby admitted shakily, her heart thundering, her blood racing, her whole body thrumming with sensation as he eased back and then slammed into her again, jolt-ing her with wicked pleasure.

'No boundaries!' he ground out forcefully. 'No bound-aries between us!'

She couldn't think, couldn't speak for the intensity of what he was making her feel. He tugged her head back and took her mouth with passionate, driving need and the taste and heat of him scorched her all the while the slow, sure thrust of his engorged shaft stimulated her senses to an unbearable peak of excitement. Her hips writhed. The pace quickened. The heat built. She was crying out, sobbing she knew not what when her wayward body fi-nally clamped down convulsively on him and she soared over the edge in a frenzied crescendo of release that took her by storm.

Ecstasy was still rippling through her weak body in small blissful waves when he wrapped his arms round her and kept her close.

'You're amazing,' he husked.

'You too,' she whispered, exhaustion pinning her to the bed.

'And we're going to do this over and over again,' Acheron decreed with lethally sexy assurance. 'No more cold showers, no more separate beds, no more posing in teeny tiny bikinis I can't rip off.'

'Sleepy,' she framed apologetically.

'Sleep…you're going to need all your energy,' he said.

CHAPTER NINE

WHEN TABBY WOKE for the fourth time in twelve hours, she was totally disorientated and she blinked in the strong sunlight flooding through the French windows. A split second later, she sat up and checked her watch to discover that it was mid-afternoon.

My goodness, she had slept half the day away! In guilty dismay, she clambered awkwardly out of bed, learning that Acheron had got it right when he had suggested she would feel better in the morning. Her hip still ached like the very devil but the pain in her ankle had become more bearable. Curious to see her surroundings, having arrived in complete darkness the night before, she limped over to the French windows with the aid of her stick and went out onto the sunlit balcony to stand at the rail.

A craggy cove stretched out below her, the towering rocks encircling a stretch of pure white sand lapped by a turquoise sea so clear she could see the ocean bottom. The lush tree-filled gardens ran right to the edge of the beach. It was absolutely idyllic and very beautiful but Tabby's attention was drawn straight to the couple standing together in the rippling surf. Amber's pram was parked in the shadow of the rocks and Melinda, clad in a minuscule red bikini that exaggerated her bountiful curves, was talking with apparent urgency to Acheron, whose lean, powerful body was sheathed only in trunks.

It was an unexpectedly intimate and disturbing sight, and Tabby couldn't take her eyes off the couple, jealousy spearing through her with an immediacy that appalled her. She jerked in dismay and snatched in a startled breath when Melinda rested a hand down on Acheron's arm. To his credit the contact only lasted for a second because he took an immediate step back from the forward blonde and with a brief final word strode back across the sand towards the house. Tabby hobbled back hurriedly indoors to get dressed, her brain struggling to encompass what she had seen at the same time as she accepted that, yet again, the very foundations of her relationship with the man she had married had been demolished and everything had changed.

Sexual desire had stimulated that change, she conceded, shame slivering through her. *No boundaries*, Acheron had proclaimed with passion and he was certainly correct on that score: the rules she had tried to impose had been blown right out of the water along with her nonsensical belief that she could resist him. Even more pertinently, seeing Melinda touch Acheron had inflamed her with ferocious possessiveness and the sort of angry jealous feelings she had never before experienced. What did that say about her intelligence? What was she letting him do to her? Where were these violent conflicting emotions coming from? She was behaving like a lovesick idiot! Was that the problem? Had lust first sucked her in and then left her childishly infatuated with him?

Opening her as yet still packed cases, she extracted underwear and a long, loose sundress before stepping into the bathroom to freshen up. The whole process took her much longer than usual having to wash her hair in the sink, which was a challenge, and left the bathroom floor swimming by the time she had finished. When she finally emerged after mopping dry the floor, however, she felt more like herself with clean, tidy hair and a little make-up applied.

Acheron strolled into the bedroom and there Tabby was; captured in a patch of sunlight, long golden hair rippling down to softly frame her delicate features, her tiny body sylphlike in a pale blue dress that reflected her amazing eyes, which were currently pools of anxious troubled violet that evaded his. She was *so* open, *so* honest in her reactions, it literally shocked him. Nothing was concealed; nothing was hidden from him. His broad chest tightened as he expelled his breath and gritted his teeth. He could not begin to imagine how frighteningly vulnerable that lack of concealment and reserve made her. If he didn't act first, she was undoubtedly about to unleash a rash volley of accusations and questions about their renewed intimacy, which threatened to put them both right back where they had started after their car crash wedding night and her proclamation of her unnecessary rules.

'Tabby,' he murmured evenly, noting avidly that he could see the little points of her deliciously prominent nipples showing below the fine material of her dress as well as the slender outline of her shapely legs. An overpoweringly strong urge to claim her again assailed him.

'Ash,' she said breathlessly, studying his lean, darkly handsome features with a sinking heart because that fast she was out of breath and dizzy just looking at him. 'We need to talk.'

'No, we don't, *glyka mou*,' Acheron contradicted with stubborn assurance as he drew closer. 'Let's do this my way. We don't talk, we especially *don't* agonise over anything. It is what it is and we just enjoy it for as long as it lasts.'

He had snatched the confused words out of her mouth before she had even collected her thoughts enough to speak. She suspected that his solution was vintage Acheron in the field of relationships—say nothing, do nothing and the problem will go away. 'I wasn't about to agonise over anything,' she protested, swaying slightly because she found it hard to stand still for long and had to grip the walking stick in a tighter hold.

He closed hands round her forearms to steady her and slowly trailed his hands down to her waist. 'You can't help yourself.'

As she looked up at him, her lush full lips tingled and she was conscious of a sensation like prickling heat curling low in her pelvis. He angled his mouth down and kissed her with intoxicating urgency.

'Oh…' she said in breathless surprise at the development, her body humming into ready awareness with an enthusiasm that disconcerted her.

He lifted her dress slowly, brazen dark golden eyes locked to hers, daring her to object. Anticipation pierced her, sharp as a lance, liquid heat pooling between her thighs. His gaze not once leaving hers, he found her with his fingers, eased below her lace-edged panties and stroked and that fast she was hotter than the fires of hell, leaning up against him for support, making no objection when he gently lowered her back onto the bed. The stick fell forgotten on the floor.

'I only just got up,' she exclaimed, her surprise unconcealed.

'You should've waited here for me, *glyka mou,*' Acheron told her sibilantly.

'I can't believe you want me again already.' Tabby studied him with confused and wondering eyes.

'The instant I look at you I want you,' Acheron admitted in a slightly raw undertone because there was a lack of control and a weakness in such a truth that deeply disturbed him.

'Not the very first time you saw me,' she reminded him stubbornly.

'You swore at me…not your finest hour, *glyka mou*,' he mocked. 'Now that I know you, it wouldn't bother me at all or make me stop thinking that you're the hottest woman on the planet.'

Eyes wide with astonishment, Tabby was transfixed by that statement. 'You really mean that?'

'*You have to ask*? Here I am throwing you down on the bed to ravish and you have to ask how much I want you? I can't wait to get you horizontal and that's not OK,' Acheron groaned, yanking off her panties with scant ceremony and splaying her legs with a voracious hiss of all-male satisfaction, fully appreciating the pink glistening femininity he had exposed. 'No, don't spoil the view,' he censured when, hot-cheeked, she tried to scissor her thighs together again. 'I like to look and I *love* to appreciate.'

Tabby forced herself to remember that while he peeled off his trunks, revealing his long, thick erection. Heat rolled through her, moisture gathering at the heart of her along with a soul-deep yearning that should have terrified her. She realised that she was acting on instinct, not even pausing to think about what he had said, skipping the *agonising* as he had phrased it because what woman wished to be viewed in that light?

'*Thee mou*, hot, hot, hot,' Acheron rasped as he came down on top of her, punctuating every word with a passionate kiss and hands that traced every erogenous zone she possessed until her impatience steadily rose to match his.

Only then did he sink into her hard and fast, muttering something in Greek before he paused to press his lips to her brow. 'Am I hurting you?' he grated uneasily.

'Only if you stop,' she traded helplessly, her whole body clenching round him as possessively as her arms, hands smoothing over his satin-smooth back, clenching there, nails curving inward as he ground into her, and she cried out in helpless delight. Excitement rose in an unstoppable tide, and she lost the self she knew in it, living from one glorious moment of intense sensation to the next until the great gathering storm became too much to contain and the passion swept her off the heights down into the ecstatic rippling aftermath.

'Well, there wasn't much finesse about that,' Acheron remarked, cradling her up against him in a damp tangle of limbs. 'My apologies.'

'No need,' Tabby countered, pressing her mouth softly to his chest, revelling in the hot, musky smell of his skin and the closeness that he was embracing. 'It was another ten out of ten.'

'You're *grading* me now?' he demanded in obvious horror.

'If you drop down to a five or lower, I'll warn you,' Tabby teased, smiling because she felt amazingly light-hearted while she was studiously engaged in not agonising. The minute she forgot his maxim though the real world immediately flooded back and, assailed by those whirling doubts, insecurities and unanswered questions, she became tense again and marvelled that she had so easily suppressed what she had seen.

'I saw you with Melinda on the beach,' she told him

baldly, putting it right out there without holding back and judging her words and their effect.

Acheron's big powerful frame stiffened and he tilted her head back to study her troubled face. 'I'm bringing another nanny in to work with Melinda, who will eventually replace her. I've already made the arrangements. I don't want Amber upset by too sudden a change in staff,' he volunteered.

Tabby was wildly disconcerted by the announcement but relieved to know that Melinda would soon be moving on, while being impressed and touched that he had also been careful to consider Amber's need for consistent care. 'You're planning to sack Melinda?'

'She's on a temporary contract. We can let her go any time we like but I'd prefer to dispense with her services in the usual way. She knows a little too much about our marriage for my comfort.'

Frowning at that admission, Tabby prompted, 'What do you mean?'

'Melinda is clearly aware that we were using separate bedrooms at the villa. When we were on the beach she offered to share Amber's room so that I could take over hers,' Acheron explained grimly.

Wings of hot pink reddened Tabby's cheeks. Annoyance and embarrassment that their unconventional sleeping arrangements had evidently attracted the attention of the staff engulfed her. 'Perhaps she was planning to do a little wandering during the night once you were conveniently close. She *was* coming on to you, wasn't she?'

Lean, extravagantly handsome features impassive, stunning dark eyes screened, Acheron nodded. 'It happens.'

Tabby looked up at him, weak with relief that he had told her the truth without fanfare or fuss. 'Often?'

Acheron released a rueful chuckle at the innocence of that question. 'All the time. If I ignore it, it usually dies a natural death but Melinda doesn't take hints…possibly because she's already reached the conclusion that ours is not a normal marriage. She *could* take that information to the press, laying me open to a potential charge that I only married you to circumvent my father's will.'

Tabby grimaced. 'We'll have to work harder at being a more convincing couple. Share a room, spend time together, fake it up to behave more like a honeymoon couple is expected to behave.'

'But it doesn't have to be fake now,' Acheron pointed out with lazy assurance.

But in her heart she would know it *was* fake, Tabby reflected painfully. He gave her great sex but he wasn't offering to give her anything more. Maybe that was the only kind of giving he knew—short-term physical stuff with a built-in time limit, she conceded fairly, not wanting to judge him just because he was different. After all, was she any more evolved in the field of relationships? She wanted him *so* much, wanted his attention as much as Amber did, was willing to do whatever it took to hold that attention. But she was not willing to admit even to herself that he was also stirring up emotions that she was afraid she couldn't handle.

'Why did your father write a will that forced you to get married when you didn't want to?' Tabby asked quietly, knowing that that was the heart of the matter and the mystery that he had so far avoided explaining.

'In a nutshell? He wanted me to marry Kasma,' Acheron told her tersely, his beautiful mouth hardening. 'And I don't *ever* want to talk about that.'

With difficulty, Tabby swallowed an irritated comeback on that omission, knowing such a response would only reinforce his reserve and make him dig his stubborn heels in even harder. She could leave the thorny question of Kasma to one side for the moment and concentrate on other aspects. 'But surely your father knew how you felt? How close were the two of you?' Tabby persisted.

A tiny muscle pulled taut at the corner of his unsmiling jaw. 'I only met him in my late twenties,' he reminded her drily. 'I suppose it was more of a business relationship than most. His company was struggling. He asked me for advice. I went in to help and ended up taking over.'

'Didn't he resent that?'

'Not at all. He wasn't much of a businessman, more of a family man desperate to give his loved ones a secure future.'

'That was your stepmother and her children?'

Acheron compressed his lips. 'My father married her when her kids were very young and raised them as his own but I didn't meet them until about eighteen months before he died.'

'Why not?' Tabby asked in surprise.

'His family weren't relevant to me or to our relationship. They were strangers. There was no blood tie and I've never had a family, so I was very wary about getting involved in that side of his life. As things turned out, I was right to be wary and to have kept my distance for as long as I did,' he pronounced with dark finality.

A silence full of undertones enclosed them in the aftermath of that assurance, adding to Tabby's discomfiture. She was trying desperately to work out what his past relationship with his stepsister, Kasma, had entailed. Obviously there had been an affair that left the beautiful brunette with expectations that Acheron was not prepared to fulfil. Presumably the affair had ended badly with bitterness on both sides. Had some tragedy occurred? Had

Kasma fallen pregnant or some such thing? Mightn't that explain why his late father had got such a bee in his bonnet about Acheron marrying his stepdaughter? Certainly the other woman had believed very strongly that she was the only woman who should become Acheron's wife. Was Kasma in love with him? Or was she more fixated on his money and his status? But regardless of why Kasma wanted Acheron, what did it matter when *he* didn't want *her*? Tabby asked herself irritably, weary of suspicions that were winding up her tension for no good reason. If it was that simple though, why couldn't he just say so?

'I wish you didn't keep secrets. I wish you were more frank and straightforward about things,' she admitted before she could think better of it.

'You're so honest sometimes you terrify me, *glyka mou*,' Acheron confided ruefully. 'And if this honeymoon is going to work, we will each have to compromise our most cherished ideals.'

Acheron peered down at the red-rose tattoo adorning Tabby's slender arm with a frown and stroked a finger gently across it. 'The skin underneath feels rough and the design is already blurred. The tattooist must have damaged your skin.'

Tabby gritted her teeth, relaxation abandoned as she yanked her arm free of his light hold. 'Don't touch me there.'

Lustrous dark golden eyes scrutinised her from below inky-black lashes. 'Why not?'

'Are we about to have *another* one of those conversations in which you suggest that I go for laser treatment to have it removed?' Tabby condemned, her small face taut and pale as she decided it was time to tell him the truth, which would surely conclude his interest in the subject.

'If you must know, I won't have it removed because it's covering up an ugly scar. In fact, the scar was there first. The tattooist did a marvellous job but he couldn't have made the ink design perfect when my skin was far from perfect to begin with.'

His lean dark features were frowning now. 'What sort of a scar?'

'Take it from me…you really don't want to know,' Tabby told him warningly, pulling away from him to scramble to her feet in the shade of the pine trees that overhung the pinkish pale sand. After checking that Amber still lay splayed out on her blanket in sleeping abandonment, her olive-skinned chubby limbs protruding starfish fashion from her white *broderie anglaise* play-suit, her rosebud mouth soft and relaxed, Tabby stalked on down the beach, a slight figure clad in shorts and a bikini top.

Acheron, she thought, her hands knotting into fists, her teeth grinding together in angry frustration. There were times she wanted to throw him into the sea from a great height. She had thought *she* was the nosy one but he didn't quit once he was on a trail either. Even worse, he was a domineering perfectionist. Although he wasn't planning to spend the rest of his life with her and Amber, he still wanted to persuade her that she should have the tattoo removed and he was as relentless as a steam roller running down a hill. At breakfast he had asked her if she would be happy for Amber to get something similar done, and Tabby had been betrayed into looking in dismay at Amber's smooth soft forearm and Acheron, being Acheron, had noticed that revealing appraisal.

'So, you *do* regret getting it done,' he had exclaimed with satisfaction.

Yes, Acheron had some infuriating traits, she acknowledged, but over the past month in Sardinia he had also been a highly entertaining companion, a very sexy lover and a patient and caring father figure for Amber. At that moment, Tabby couldn't begin to work out how an entire four weeks had flashed past faster than the speed of light. The first week had been a challenge while she was still hobbling round with a stick and pretty much sentenced to passing her time at the beach house. But once her ankle had healed, they had begun to go out and about.

Snapshots of special moments they had shared filled her memory with more comforting images. They had climbed the massive staircase to the Bastione terrace to see the amazing panoramic view of the rooftops of Calgiari. While she was still wheezing from the climb and overheated from the sun, he had told her that there was actually a lift but that he had assumed that she would enjoy the full tourist experience more. It had taken several cocktails and the cooling effect of the lovely breeze on the terrace before she had forgiven him, and if she was truthful her resistance had only truly melted when he slid long brown fingers into hers in the lift on the way down again.

They had made an evening visit to Castelsardo, a beautiful village dominated by a magical citadel all lit up at night, to enjoy live music in the piazza. Amber had adored all the noise and bustle going on around her and Acheron had enjoyed the baby's bright-eyed fascination.

The following night, however, they had sought out more adult fun, dancing until dawn at the Billionaire club where Tabby had felt distinctly overshadowed by the number of gorgeous women, sleek and deadly as sharks, cruising for a wealthy hook-up. That Ash had acted as if he only had eyes for her and had kissed her passionately on the dance floor had done much to lift her self-esteem.

Memory after memory was now tumbling inside Tabby's head. For forty-eight hours they had sailed a yacht round the national park of La Maddalena, a group of protected and largely uninhabited islands teeming with flora and wildlife. The last night they had skinny dipped in a deserted cove and made love until the sun went down. Exhausted, she had wakened to find Acheron barbecuing their evening meal, stunning dark golden eyes smiling lazily at her and making her heart somersault like a trapeze artist.

Of course, they had done all the usual things as well, like strolling round the famous boutiques on the Costa Smeralda, an activity or a lack of activity that Acheron was astounded to discover bored his bride to tears.

'But you *must* want me to buy you something,' he had protested. 'You *must* have seen something you liked. You do realise that the only thing I've bought you since we arrived is that bed linen?'

Tabby had seen the exquisite bed linen in an upmarket handicrafts shop and her childhood memories of being clumsy with a needle and thread had given her a true appreciation of the amount of skill involved in producing such beautiful embroidery. That had been a purchase to treasure, a gift she truly loved, and only later had it occurred to her that she would never see that winter-weight linen spread across a bed that she shared with Acheron and that it would inevitably adorn a bed she slept in alone. Once the summer was over, their marriage would be history.

But then while she had known they would be faking their honeymoon and had dutifully posed with him for a persistent paparazzo, who had followed them round Porto Cervo, she had not appreciated the lengths Acheron might go to in making their relationship look genuine from the inside and the outside. So, if occasionally she got a little confused and thought about him as if he *were* her real husband, who could blame her for making that mistake?

Or for falling madly and irrevocably in love with him during the process, she reasoned wretchedly. After all, no man had ever treated her as well as he did, no man had ever made her so happy either, and only he had ever made love to her several times a day, *every* day, as if she were indeed the hottest, sexiest woman on the planet. Naturally her emotions had got involved and she suppressed them as best she could, knowing that the last thing Acheron required from her was angst and a broken heart, which would make him feel guilty and uncomfortable.

It wasn't his fault she had fallen for him either. It certainly wasn't as though he had misled her with promises about the future. In fact, right from the outset she had known that there was no future for them. He had never made any bones about that. Once they had succeeded to legally adopt Amber, their supposed marriage would be left to wither and die. Tabby would make a new life with the little girl she loved while she assumed Acheron would return to his workaholic, womanising existence. Would she ever see him again after the divorce? As she confronted that bleak prospect an agonising shard of pain slivered through Tabby and left a deep anguished ache in its wake. Would Acheron want to retain even the most distant relationship with Amber? Or would he decide on a clean break and act as if Amber didn't exist?

Acheron crossed the beach, noting how Tabby's figure had rounded out once she was eating decent food, recalling with quiet satisfaction that she no longer bit her nails—small changes that he valued.

'How did you get the scar concealed by the tattoo?' he demanded obstinately, interrupting Tabby's reverie and shooting her back to the present by wrapping both arms round her from behind, carefully preventing her from storming off again. 'Were you involved in an accident?'

'No…it wasn't an accident,' Tabby admitted, past recollections making her skin turn suddenly cold and clammy in spite of the heat of the sun.

He was being supportive, she reminded herself doggedly, guilt biting into her former annoyance with him. When Amber had cried half the night because she was teething and her gums were sore, Acheron had been right there beside her, helping to distract the little girl and calm her down enough to sleep again. She had not expected supportiveness from Acheron but his interest in Amber was anything but half-hearted. When it came to childcare, he took the rough with the smooth, serenely accepting that children weren't always sunny and smiling.

The new nanny currently working with Melinda was called Teresa, a warm, chattering Italian woman whose main source of interest was her charge. Within a week the English nanny would be leaving to take up a permanent position with a family in London.

'Tabby…I asked you a question,' Acheron reminded her with deeply unwelcome persistence. 'You said you didn't get the scar in an accident, so—'

Dredged from the teeming tumult of her frantic attempt to think about just about anything other than the past he was trying to dig up, Tabby lifted her head high and looked out to sea. 'My mother burned me with a hot iron because I knocked over a carton of milk,' she confessed without any expression at all.

'*Thee mou…*' Acheron growled in stricken disbelief, spinning her round to look at her pale set face and the yawning hurt still lingering in her violet eyes.

'I was never allowed to be with either of my parents

unsupervised again after that,' she explained woodenly. 'My mother went to prison for burning me and I never saw either of them again.'

Bewildered by the great surge of ferocious anger welling up inside him, Acheron crushed her slight body to his, both arms wrapping tightly round her. For some reason he registered that he was feeling sick and his hands weren't quite steady, and in that instant some inexplicable deep need that disturbed him was making it impossible for him not to touch her. 'That must've been a relief.'

'No, it wasn't. I loved them. They weren't very lovable people but they were all I had,' Tabby admitted thickly, her dry throat scratching over the words as if she was reluctant to voice them. She had learned as a young child that loving gestures would be rejected but now more than anything in the world she wanted to wrap her arms round Acheron and take full advantage of the comfort he was clumsily trying to offer her, only that pattern of early rejection and knowledge of how abandonment felt kept her body rigid and uninviting in the circle of his arms.

'I understand that,' Acheron breathed in a raw driven undertone. 'I rarely saw my mother but I still idolised her—'

'What a pair we are!' Tabby sniffed, her tension suddenly giving way as tears stung her eyes and overflowed, her overloaded reaction to having had to explain and indeed relive what she never, ever talked about to anyone.

Acheron stared down at her tear-stained visage, pale below his bronzed skin, his strong facial bones forbiddingly set. 'I can't bear to think of you being hurt like that, *yineka mou*—'

'Don't…don't talk about it!' Tabby urged feverishly. 'I try never to think about it but every time I saw the scar in the mirror as a teenager, I remembered it, and sometimes people asked what had happened to me. That's why I got the tattoo…to cover it up, hide it.'

'Then wear that tattoo with pride. It's a survival badge,' Acheron informed her with hard satisfaction. 'I wish you'd explained weeks ago but I understand now why you didn't.'

'Oh, for goodness' sake, let's talk about something more cheerful!' Tabby pleaded. 'Tell me something about you. I mean, you must have *some* happy childhood memories of your mother?'

Acheron closed an arm round her slight shoulders to press her back across the beach towards Amber. 'The night before my first day at school she presented me with a fantastically expensive pen engraved with my name. Of course, I was only allowed to use a pencil in class but naturally that didn't occur to her. She was very fond of flamboyant gestures, always telling me that only the very best was good enough for a Dimitrakos—'

'Maybe that was how she was brought up,' Tabby suggested quietly. 'But you still haven't explained why that pen made you happy.'

'Because generally she ignored me but that particular week she was fresh out of rehab and engaged in turning over a new leaf and it was the one and only time she made me feel that I genuinely mattered to her. She even gave me a whole speech about education being the most important thing in my life…that from a woman who dropped out of school as a teenager and couldn't read anything more challenging than a magazine,' he told her wryly.

'Do you still have the pen?'

'I think it was stolen.' He sent her a rueful charismatic smile that tilted her heart inside her chest and interfered with her breathing. 'But at least I have that one perfect moment to remember her by.'

* * *

Acheron could not relax until he had commissioned a special piece of jewellery for Tabby's upcoming birthday, which surprisingly fell in the same week as his own. That achieved, he worried about having taken that much trouble over a gift. What was wrong with him? What sort of man went to such lengths for a wife he was planning to divorce? *Keep it cool*, a little voice chimed in the back of his uneasy mind. But it had proved impossible to play it cool when confronted with the harsh reality of Tabby's childhood experiences, which had had the unexpected effect of showing Acheron that he had a good deal less to be bitter about with regard to his own. His mother had been a neglectful, selfish and inadequate parent but even at her worst he had never doubted that she loved him. And possibly, but for the malicious machinations of a third party, his father might have learned to love and appreciate him as well...

The constant flow of such unfamiliar thoughts assailing him kept him quiet over dinner. Aware of Tabby's anxious gaze, he was maddened by the knowledge that he wasn't feeling like himself any more and that, even in the midst of that disorientating experience, withdrawing his attention from her could make him feel guilty. Never a fan of great inner debates, or even in the habit of staging them, he was exasperated and bewildered by the emotions Tabby constantly churned up inside him. *She was too intense*, too rich for his blood. He needed to take a step back, he decided abruptly; he needed some distance, and the instant he made that decision he felt better and back in control again.

'I have to go away on business for a couple of days,' Acheron volunteered as he strode out of the bathroom, a towel negligently wrapped round his lean, muscular body. His black hair tousled and damp, his lean, devastatingly handsome face clean-shaven, he looked amazing and Tabby's mouth ran dry before she could even process what he had said.

Realising that he was leaving her, Tabby went rigid and then scolded herself because he had done very little work in recent weeks and could hardly be expected to maintain that lifestyle indefinitely. No, she had been spoilt by his constant company and had to learn fast how to adapt to his absence. Was that why he had been so quiet and distant over dinner? Had he worried about her reaction? Well, it was time to show him that she was strong and not the complaining type.

'I'll miss you, but we'll be fine,' she responded lightly.

Acheron ground his teeth together, having expected her to object or even offer to travel with him. This was definitely a moment when he had believed she would cling and make him feel suffocated. He watched her clamber into bed, slender as a willow wand, the modest nightdress concealing the hot, secret places he loved, and lust kicked in so fast he felt dizzy with it. Lustrous dark eyes veiling, he discarded the towel, doused the lights and joined her. *Not tonight*, he thought grimly, as though he was fighting a battle; tonight he could get by without her.

Eyes sparkling in the moonlight, Tabby rolled over to Acheron's side of the bed and ran delicate fingers hungrily across a hair-roughened thigh while her hair trailed over his pelvis.

Acheron closed his eyes in despair. He could always lie back and think of Greece. If he said no like a frightened virgin, he would probably upset her, and there was no point doing that, was there? Why risk upsetting her? She found his swelling shaft with her mouth, and his hips shifted upward in helpless encouragement. It crossed his mind that the divorce might upset her because she acted as if she was fond of him, looked at him as if he was special, dived on him in bed if he didn't dive on her first, never missed a chance to put her arms round him...although strangely *not* this afternoon on the beach when he had put his arms round her in an effort to offer sympathy for what his thoughtless questions had made her cruelly relive. A particularly strong wave of pleasure blanked out the subsequent thought about *why* she might not have responded, yet another thought he didn't want to have. All that sentimental stuff, he thought grimly—he never had been any good at that. He had probably been clumsy.

Afterwards, Acheron didn't hold her the way he usually did, and Tabby felt cold inside and abandoned. She curled up on her side, hating him, loving him, wanting him, fretting and reckoning that love was the worst torture in existence for a woman. There was no point always wanting what he wouldn't give her, didn't even *want* to give her, she reflected painfully. Their divorce was not only written in the stars but also written into a pre-nuptial contract from which there would be no escape.

And maybe he still had feelings for Kasma, whom he would not discuss although she had on several occasions worked the conversation helpfully round in that direction to give him an easy opening. But trying to get Acheron to talk about something he didn't want to talk about was like trying to get blood out of a stone. In her experience though, people only avoided topics that embarrassed or troubled them, so his failed relationship with Kasma must have gone deep indeed to leave behind such conspicuous and quite uncharacteristic sensitivity...

The following morning, Tabby drifted out of sleep to discover that Acheron had made an early departure and without leaving even a note. She spent a quiet day with Amber and it was the next day before the silence from Acheron began to niggle at her. He didn't have to stay in touch when he was only planning to be away forty-eight hours, she conceded ruefully, and she was not so needy that she required him to check in with her every day. But as she lay in the bed that felt empty without him the day stretched before Tabby like a blank slate, shorn of anticipation, excitement and happiness.

Thoroughly exasperated with her mood, she went for a shower and got dressed in the bathroom, emerging to catch a glimpse of her reflection in the tall cheval mirror across the bedroom and wonder why she couldn't see it properly. As she automatically moved closer to see what was amiss with the mirror she realised that someone had written something on it, and she frowned at it in bewilderment.

He's using you! Tabby was gobsmacked. Why would anyone write that on their mirror for her to see? Clearly it was meant to be personal, and presumably Acheron was the 'he' being referred to. What on earth did it mean? Whatever, it really spooked her that someone had come into their bedroom while she was in the bathroom and left a message presumably intended to shock and insult her. After all, only someone in the house could have had access to their room and that knowledge made gooseflesh blossom on her exposed skin.

Without hesitation she lifted the house phone and asked to speak to Ash's security chief, Dmitri. Almost before she had finished speaking, Dmitri joined her in the room to see the mirror for himself. If his forbidding expression was anything to go by, he took the matter very seriously. Dmitri, however, was a man of few words and she left him to it and went downstairs for breakfast.

CHAPTER TEN

'CAN I ASK you where you're planning to go?' Melinda asked with a sunny smile, joining her at the breakfast table, which she never dared to do when Acheron was around.

'Into Porto Cervo to shop,' Tabby admitted. 'I'm looking for a birthday present.'

'There's some great jewellery boutiques…try the Piazzetta delle Chiacchere,' Melinda advised helpfully.

Tabby nodded, feeling guilty about how much she disliked the curvaceous blonde who would, by the end of the week, mercifully be gone from the household to take up her new appointment. Since Teresa's arrival and increasing involvement with Amber, Melinda seemed to spend a lot of time hovering unnecessarily and watching their comings and goings. Once, Tabby had even suspected that the blonde was eavesdropping on her and Acheron. No doubt the nanny had now registered that their detached marriage had developed into something closer. Or was that only her own wishful thinking at work? Tabby wondered heavily.

Acheron had been gone only one day and she felt bereft. That was a pretty poor show for a strong, independent woman, she conceded shamefacedly. She missed him so much, and her outlook wasn't improved by her recollection of his unusual behaviour on that last night they had spent together. He had been silent and moody, extraordinarily uninvolved when she had made love to him, saying nothing, doing nothing, in fact, acting like a right—

'Miss Barnes?' Dmitri appeared in the doorway. 'Could I have a word with you?'

'*Right* now?' Melinda prompted with a sparkling smile that seemed wasted on the granite-faced older man.

'Now would be a good time,' Dmitri responded evenly.

Tabby left Teresa in charge of Amber, having decided that dragging the little girl out to trail round the shops during the hottest part of the day would be unwise. The message was still on the mirror when she walked past into the bathroom to renew her lipstick and it made her shiver. *He's using you.* Well, as far as their marriage was concerned they were using each other, she told herself doggedly. Although things had changed drastically once they began sharing a bed in reality. Was Acheron only sleeping with her because that intimacy added to the illusion of their having a normal marriage? After all, if he was seen out by the paparazzi with another woman while he was supposed to be a happily married new husband, it wouldn't look good. So, was she being used on that basis? But how could she call it using when she was in love with him and wanted him to make love to her? Did that make her a silly lovelorn fool? Or was *she* taking equal advantage of *him*?

From the instant Dmitri phoned him and broke the news, Acheron hadn't been able to stay still or think with his usual logic. Gripped by insane impatience and mounting concern, he just wanted to get back to Sardinia and stand watch over Tabby and Amber. Unfortunately for him, getting a last-minute slot for the jet to take off in

Athens and jumping the queue took longer than he had envisaged. He cursed the fact that he had left them behind in the first place, cursed his conviction that he should protect Tabby at all costs from what Kasma might do next.

Why had he chosen to leave Tabby when he actually wanted to be with her? What did that say about him? That he couldn't recognise his own emotions and was prone to running away from what he couldn't understand? Feelings had never been so intense for him before and he had been torn between a kind of intoxication at the fire of them and a kind of panic at knowing he was out of control. He had never allowed that to happen to him before but he'd had no choice. He had jumped on the panic as an excuse and now he was paying the price. Thee mou, *if anything was to happen to them*, he brooded darkly, his fists clenching aggressively just as his pilot signalled him from across the VIP lounge that they were good to go.

'I really do believe that your husband would prefer you to stay in today,' Dmitri informed Tabby quietly.

Unfortunately, Tabby was in no mood to be grounded like a child and marvelled that Acheron could even think he could give out orders that way through Dmitri, particularly when he had taken off himself at such short notice. What was it? Why was he trying to keep her on the home front? Some sort of control issue on his part? And poor Dmitri was embarrassed to have to say such a thing to her; she could see it in the older man.

'I'm sorry but it's really important that I go out today,' she said levelly. 'I have something I have to buy.'

'Then I'll accompany you and I'll drive, Mrs Dimitrakos,' Dmitri responded with determination.

For the sake of peace, Tabby nodded agreement but knew she was going to have to have a discussion with

Acheron with regard to the intense security presence he maintained in their lives. Was it really necessary that they be guarded and watched over every place they went? Was there a genuine risk of their being robbed or kidnapped? Was there some kind of specific threat out against Acheron?

'You'll be very bored,' she warned Dmitri as she settled into the passenger seat of the SUV and watched another car full of security men follow them out of the entrance to the beach house with wry acceptance.

'It's not a problem. I'm used to going shopping with my wife,' Dmitri told her calmly. 'She can stare at one shop window for ten minutes before she's satisfied she's seen everything.'

Tabby knew she would be even more of a drag because she didn't even know what she was planning to buy and was hoping to be inspired by something she saw. What did you buy for the man who had everything? The massive monthly allowance he had awarded her, however, had piled up in her bank account and thanks to his generosity she had got to spend very little of it, so she had plenty to spend.

Dmitri following behind her, Tabby prowled through the exclusive boutiques and jewellery outlets. Acheron wasn't the sort of guy who wore jewellery. He wore a wedding ring and occasionally cuff links and that was all. But short of copping out by buying him another silk tie when he already had a rail of them, what was she to give him for his thirty-first birthday? Mulling over that thorny issue, she saw the pen. Actually *the* pen was the only possible description for a pen that bore a world-famous designer label. It would cost a fortune, she reckoned. But equally fast she recalled the pen his mother had bought him and decided that the cost was less important than what it meant, although why she was so keen to buy a significant gift for a man who couldn't even be bothered to phone her, she couldn't explain. Maybe it was the desolate thought that the pen might survive with him a lot longer than their marriage and act as a reminder of what they had once shared. Depressing, much? She scolded herself impatiently for her downbeat thoughts.

She bought the pen and arranged for it to be inscribed with his name and the date. She had to make use of the platinum credit card he had given her to make the purchase and, while trying to act as if she spent such sums all the time, she was secretly horrified at spending so much money and worried that Acheron would think she had gone mad. Pale and shaken after that sobering experience, she told Dmitri that she wanted to go for a coffee. He led the way to an outdoor café and insisted on choosing a seat a couple of tables away from her.

She had just bought the most expensive pen in the history of the world, she reflected guiltily, and when he saw the bill he might well freak out and regret telling her that her card had no upper limit. She was sipping her latte slowly, savouring the caffeine, when a shadow fell across her table.

Kasma settled her long elegant body down smoothly into the seat opposite. 'You've been so unavailable you've forced me into all this cloak and dagger stuff,' she complained.

Totally taken aback by the other woman's appearance, Tabby stared at the beautiful brunette with wide, questioning eyes. 'What on earth are you doing here?'

'You're here, Ash is here…where else would I be?' Kasma asked, rolling big dark eyes in apparent disbelief at the question. 'I refuse to believe that you're so stupid that you can't accept that Ash belongs with me.'

'Miss Philippides…' Dmitri broke into the conversation, standing straight and tall beside Kasma's chair. 'Please leave—'

Kasma slung him a defiant glance. 'We're in a public place and I can go where I please on this island. We're not in Greece now.'

'May I suggest then that *we* leave, Mrs Dimitrakos?' Dmitri continued, regarding Tabby expectantly.

Tabby breathed in deep. 'When I've finished my coffee,' she murmured, determined to hear what Kasma had to say since she sure as heck wasn't going to receive any information from Acheron.

Grim-faced, Dmitri retreated to an even closer table.

'I believe in getting straight down to business,' Kasma informed her. 'How much money do you want to walk out on this absurd marriage?'

Dumbstruck, Tabby stared at the older woman. 'You can't be serious.'

'Oh, I'm always serious when it comes to Ash. We belong together and he would have married me, *not* you, had my stepfather not foolishly tried to force the issue in his will,' Kasma contended confidently. 'You must know how proud Ash is.'

'Staying here, entering into this dialogue is a very bad idea, Mrs Dimitrakos,' Dmitri leant closer to spell out.

Kasma shot a vicious burst of Greek at the older man and the look on her face was downright scary. With the sudden suspicion that Dmitri's advice to retreat from the scene might well be the most sensible move, Tabby lifted her bag, settled some money on the table for the bill and stood up. Before she walked away, however, she had something to say. 'No matter how much money you offered me I wouldn't walk out on Acheron,' she murmured tautly. 'I love him.'

'Not as much as I love him, you bitch!' Kasma launched at her in a seething shout of fury that shook Tabby rigid.

Cupping her elbow firmly in his hand, Dmitri walked her away from the café at a fast pace. 'Kasma Philippides is a dangerously unstable woman. Your husband has a restraining order out against her on Greek soil and she's not allowed to approach him or make a nuisance of herself there. You can't talk to her. You can't reason with her. We've learned that the hard way.'

'Ash should've warned me. If he'd warned me, I would've walked away immediately,' Tabby protested defensively. 'I could see that she was obsessed with him at the wedding but I didn't understand how much of a problem she was in his life.'

'He wasn't expecting her to follow you here. He had no idea she was on the island. By the way, he's flying back as we speak.'

Relief swept Tabby. He would finally have to tell her the whole story. But he had had to take out a legal restraining order to keep Kasma at a distance? What had driven him to take his father's stepdaughter to court? That must have taken some nerve, particularly while his father was still alive. Had Kasma been acting like some sort of psycho stalker?

They were driving along the coast road when she noticed that Dmitri kept on looking worriedly in the driving mirror. Tabby glanced over her shoulder to notice the bright red sports car behind them. The driver had long dark hair just like Kasma's.

'She's following us,' Dmitri told her flatly. 'Make sure your belt is safely fastened. I may have to take evasive manoeuvres but I've already alerted the police.'

'Evasive manoeuvres?' Tabby gasped when there was

a sudden jolt at the rear of the car. 'She's trying to ram us? Is she crazy in that tiny little car?'

Dmitri didn't answer. His concentration was on the road because he had speeded up. Tabby's heart was beating very, very fast as she watched in the mirror as the red car tried to catch up with them again. They were zooming round corners so fast that Tabby felt dizzy and she was still watching Kasma's car when it veered across the road into the path of another car travelling the other way.

'Oh, my word, she's crashed...hit someone else!'

Dmitri jammed on the brakes and rammed into Reverse to turn and drive back. He leapt out of the SUV. The team from the other security car were already attending to the victims of the crash, carrying the passenger to the verge, the driver, still conscious, stumbling after them. The red sports car had hit a wall and demolished part of it. Tabby slowly climbed out, her tummy heaving as she approached the scene of frantic activity. Dmitri was talking fast on his phone as he approached her. 'Stay in the car, Mrs Dimitrakos. You don't need to see this. Miss Philippides is dead.'

'*Dead?*' Tabby was stunned, barely able to credit that the woman who had been speaking to her only minutes earlier could have lost her life.

'She wasn't wearing a belt—she was thrown from the car.'

'And the people who were in the other car?' Tabby asked.

'Very lucky to be alive. The passenger has a head wound and the driver has a leg injury.'

Tabby nodded and got back slowly into the SUV, feeling oddly distanced from everything happening around her. That sensation, which she only vaguely recognised as shock, was still lingering when she gave a brief statement at the police station with a lawyer sitting in, volunteering information she couldn't understand in the local language. That completed, she was stowed in a waiting room with a cup of coffee until Acheron strode through the door. He stalked across the room, emanating stormy tension, and raised her out of her seat with two anxious hands.

'You are all right? Dmitri swore you were unhurt but I was afraid to believe him,' Acheron grated half under his breath, his lean, darkly handsome features taut and granite hard as he scanned her carefully from head to toe.

'Well, I was fine until you made me spill my coffee,' she responded unevenly, setting the mug down and rubbing ineffectually at the splashes now adorning her pale pink top. 'Are we free to leave?'

'Yes, I've made a statement. *Thee mou*,' Acheron murmured fiercely. 'Kasma had a knife in her bag!'

'A *knife*?' Tabby repeated in horror.

'But for Dmitri's presence she might have attacked you!' Acheron lifted a not quite steady hand and raked long brown fingers through his luxuriant black hair. 'I was so scared when I heard she'd come here, I felt sick,' he confided thickly.

'She's dead,' Tabby reminded him in an undertone.

Acheron released his pent-up breath and said heavily, 'Her brother, Simeon, is on his way to make the funeral arrangements. He's a decent man. I hope you don't mind but I've asked him to stay with us.'

'Of course, I don't mind. No matter what's happened, your father's family deserve your consideration and respect.'

'Melinda's flying back to London,' Acheron volunteered. 'She was responsible for the messages on the mirror.'

'Messages…there was *more* than one?' Tabby queried in consternation.

Acheron told her about the message he had seen at the villa in Tuscany and how Dmitri had instantly worked out that Melinda had to be the perpetrator when the nanny did it a second time. Confronted that same morning after breakfast by Dmitri, Melinda had confessed that Kasma had approached her in London and had offered her a lot of money to leave the messages and to spy on Acheron while keeping Kasma up to date with information on where they were staying. It was Melinda who had warned Dmitri that Kasma was actually on the island, news that had alarmed Acheron into making an immediate return.

The fountain of questions concerning Kasma that had disturbed Tabby earlier in the day was, by that stage, returning fast, but the haunted look in Acheron's lustrous dark eyes and the bleak set of his bronzed face silenced her. He escorted her out to a car, and she slid in, appreciating the air-conditioned cool on her overheated skin.

'I have a lot to explain,' Acheron acknowledged flatly and then he closed his hand over hers.

In a reflexive movement, Tabby rejected the contact and folded her hands together on her lap. 'After the way you behaved that last night and the fact that you haven't been in touch since, I think holding hands would be a bit of a joke,' she said bluntly. 'You don't need to pretend things you don't feel to pacify or comfort me. As you noted, I'm unhurt. It's been a horrible day but I'll get over it without leaning on you.'

'Maybe I want you to lean on me.'

Tabby raised a brow, unimpressed by that unlikely suggestion. 'I'd prefer to fall over and pick myself up. I've been doing it all my life and I've managed just fine.'

Acheron compressed his wide, sensual mouth. 'I

should have explained about her weeks ago but the subject of Kasma rouses a lot of bad memories…and reactions,' he admitted with curt reluctance.

'Kasma's the reason you thought someone might have
pushed me down the stairs at the villa,' Tabby grasped
finally.

'Maybe she made me a little paranoid but she did destroy my relationship with my father before he died.'

'And that's why he wrote that crazy will,' Tabby guessed.

'I told you that I only met my father's family about
eighteen months ago. I only agreed in the first place because it seemed to mean so much to him. What I didn't
mention before is that the week before that dinner engagement took place at his home, I met Kasma *without*
knowing I was meeting Kasma,' he told her grittily.

Tabby frowned. 'Without knowing it was her?' she
echoed. 'How? I mean, *why*?'

'I doubt if I could *ever* adequately explain why from
Kasma's point of view. She introduced herself to me as
Ariadne. She certainly knew who I was,' he delivered
with perceptible bitterness. 'I was in Paris on a stopover
between flights and she was staying in the same hotel.
I've never believed that was a coincidence. I believe I was
set up. I was alone. I was bored. She targeted me and I
fell for it…and you could not begin to understand how
deeply I regret taking the bait.'

Tabby was studying him with confused eyes. 'The bait?'

'I had a tacky one-night stand with her,' Acheron
ground out grudgingly, dark colour accentuating his
spectacular cheekbones, his jaw line clenching hard on
the admission. 'A couple of stolen hours from a busy
schedule of work and travel. I'm being honest here—it
meant nothing more to me. Although I treated her with

respect I never pretended at any stage that I wanted to see her again.'

Tabby averted her eyes, reflecting that respectful treatment would not have compensated Kasma for his ultimate rejection, when presumably she had persuaded herself that she could expect a much keener and less fleeting response.

'She picked me up in the hotel restaurant. Afterwards she started acting as though she knew me really well. To be frank, it was a freaky experience and I made my excuses and returned to my own room.'

Tabby was swallowing hard at a level of honesty she had not expected to receive from him. 'But if she already knew who you were, why did she lie about her own identity?'

Acheron shrugged a broad shoulder. 'Obviously because I would never have touched her had I known she was my father's precious little girl.'

'His precious little girl?' Tabby queried.

'Her mother was widowed when Kasma was only a baby. My father raised Kasma from the age of three. She was the apple of his eye, his favourite child, and he couldn't see any fault in her,' Acheron advanced tautly, his lips compressing. 'When I walked into the family dinner the week after the hotel encounter I was appalled to realise that Kasma was my father's stepchild and furious that she had lied to me and put me in that position, but that wasn't all I had to worry about. Before I could even decide how to behave, she stood up and announced that she had been saving a little surprise for everyone. And that surprise—according to her—was that she and I were *dating*.'

'Oh, my word…' Tabby was as stunned as he must've been by that development. 'And that one…er…episode at the hotel was really the extent of your relationship with her?'

'It was, but not according to Kasma. She had a very fertile imagination and over the months that followed she began acting like a stalker, flying round the world, turning up wherever I was,' he explained, lines of strain bracketing his mouth as he recalled that period. 'She tried to force her way into my life while telling my father a pack of lies about me. She told him I'd cheated on her, she told him I'd got her pregnant and then she told him she'd had a miscarriage. He fell for every one of her tales and nothing I could say would persuade him that my relationship with his stepdaughter was a fantasy she had made up. And having made that first mistake by getting involved with her that night at the hotel, I felt I had brought the whole nightmare down on my own head.'

'I don't think so—'

'It was casual sex but there was nothing casual about it,' Acheron opined grimly. 'I went to bed with a woman who was a stranger and maybe I deserved what I got.'

'Not when she set out to deliberately deceive you and then tried to trap you into a relationship,' Tabby declared stoutly. 'I don't agree with the way you behaved with her but she was obviously a disturbed personality.'

'She assaulted a woman I spent time with last year, which was why I was so concerned about your safety and Amber's.'

'What did she do?'

'She forced her way into my apartment and punched the woman while ranting about how I belonged to her.' He grimaced at the recollection. 'My father begged me to use my influence and prevent it from going to court but I was at the end of my rope. Kasma was dangerous and she needed treatment but as long as her family turned a blind eye and I swallowed what she was dishing out, she was free to do as she liked. The court accepted that she was lying and had never had a relationship with me and therefore had no excuse whatsoever for attacking the woman in my apartment and calling it a domestic dispute.'

'Didn't that convince your father that you were telling him the truth?'

'No, Kasma managed to convince him that I must've bribed someone and she had been stitched up by me to protect my own reputation,' he proffered with unconcealed regret. 'The sole saving grace was that after that court case I was able to take out a restraining order against her and at least that kept her out of my hair while I was on Greek soil.'

Tabby slowly shook her head, which was reeling with his revelations. 'Why didn't you tell me about her? Why wouldn't you explain?'

His bold bronzed profile clenched hard. 'I was ashamed of the whole business and I didn't want to frighten you either. My wealth didn't protect me from the fact that Kasma could still get to me almost everywhere I went. You have no idea how powerless I felt when she even managed to gatecrash the wedding because I didn't want to make a scene with my father's family present,' he confessed grittily. 'I didn't want to publicise my problems with her while my father was still alive either. She caused him enough grief with her wild stories about how badly I'd treated her.'

'So why on earth did he want you to marry her?' Tabby queried, struggling to understand that angle.

'He believed she loved me and he genuinely thought I owed her a wedding ring. He blamed me for her increasingly hysterical outbursts and strange behaviour.'

'That was probably easier for him than dealing with

the real problem, which was *her*. He would've had more faith in you if he had ever had the chance to get to know you properly,' Tabby opined, resting a soothing hand down on his. 'Kasma had the advantage and he trusted her and that gave her the power to put you through an awful ordeal.'

'It's over now,' Acheron reminded her flatly. 'Her brother, Simeon, believed me and tried to persuade her to see a therapist. Perhaps if she had listened she might not have died today.'

'It's not your fault though,' Tabby countered steadily. 'You weren't capable of fixing whatever was broken in her.'

Acheron groaned out loud. 'It's so *not* sexy that you feel sorry for me now.'

'I don't feel sorry for you. I just think you've been put through the mill a bit,' Tabby paraphrased awkwardly. 'No wonder you don't like clingy, needy women after that experience.'

'I wouldn't mind if you clung occasionally,' Acheron admitted.

Tabby rolled her eyes at him. 'Stop being such a smoothie…it's wasted on me.'

'What do you mean?' Acheron asked harshly as the limo drew up outside the beach house.

'It's not necessary to charm me. We both had good reasons to get married and that's the only fulfilment either of us require from our agreement. You got a wife and, hopefully, I will eventually be able to adopt Amber,' Tabby spelt out as she slid out of the car and walked into the house.

'That's not how I feel,' Acheron informed her stubbornly.

'We're not twin souls and nor are we required to be,'

Tabby flipped back, walking through to the lounge, which stood with doors wide open to the terrace and the view of the cove, draperies fluttering softly in the slight breeze that never seemed to leave the coast. 'I think we're overdue a little plain speaking here.'

Outside, she leant up against the rail bordering the terrace and folded her arms in a defensive position. She knew what she needed to say. She was more than half-way to getting her heart broken by the stupid, danger-ous pretence that she was on a *real* honeymoon with a *real* husband! How had she let that happen? How had she let herself fall in love with a male who was simply doing what he had to do to give the appearance of being a newly married man?

'Meaning?' Acheron prompted, stilling in the door-way, six feet plus inches of stunning male beauty and charisma.

Tabby looked him over with carefully blank eyes. He was gorgeous; he had always been gorgeous from the crown of his slightly curly black head to the soles of his equally perfect feet. He focused sizzling dark golden eyes on her with interrogative intensity.

'Tabby?' he prompted afresh.

'Unlike you I call a spade a spade. I don't wrap it up.'

'I appreciate that about you…that what you say you mean,' he countered steadily.

Tabby threw her slight shoulders back, violet eyes wide and appealing. 'Look, let's just bring the whole charade to an end here and now,' she urged. 'Melinda was spying on us and she's gone. We've done all the newly happily married stuff for weeks and now surely we can both go back to normal?'

'Normal?'

Tabby was wondering what the matter with him was,

for it was not like him to take a back seat in any argument. Furthermore, he looked strained, having lost colour while his spectacular strong bone structure had set rigid below his bronzed skin. 'We were strangers with a legal agreement, Ash,' she reminded him painfully. 'We've met the terms, put on the show and now surely we can return to being ourselves again behind closed doors at least?'

'Is that what you want?' he pressed curtly, lean brown hands closing into fists by his side. 'Don't you think this is a decision best shelved for a less traumatic day?'

Tabby lifted her chin, her heart squeezing tight inside her chest, pain like a sharp little arrow twisting inside her because, of course, it was not what she wanted. She wanted him; she was in love with him but she had to protect herself, had to force herself to accept that what they had shared was only a pretence. 'No.'

'You want to go back to where we started out?' Acheron demanded starkly.

Tabby dropped her shoulders, her eyes veiling. 'No, I just want us to be honest and not faking anything.'

Acheron breathed in very slow and deep, dark golden eyes glittering like fireworks below the shield of his luxuriant black lashes. 'I *haven't* been faking anything...'

Tabby's dazed mind ran over all the romancing, the sexing, the hand-holding, the fun, and she blinked in bemusement. 'But *of course* you were faking.'

'It may have started out that way, but it ended up real, *yineka mou.*' Acheron surveyed her steadily but she knew he was putting up a front because he was really, really tense.

'How...*real*?' Tabby questioned, her heart thumping like mad.

Acheron lifted his arms and spread his hands in an oddly defenceless gesture. 'I fell in love with you...'

Tabby almost fell over in shock, her brain refusing to accept that he could have said that he loved her. 'I don't believe you. You're just scared that I'm about to walk out on our marriage agreement and you'll lose your company—but you don't *need* to be scared of that happening because I wouldn't do that to you. I'm still as determined to adopt Amber as I ever was, so I couldn't do that even if I wanted to,' she pointed out honestly.

'When I try to say, "I love you" for the first time in my life to a woman, you could at least listen to what I'm saying and stop talking a lot of rubbish!' Acheron shot back at her with scorching effect.

Tabby was struck dumb by that little speech. He was serious? He wasn't joking, faking, trying to manipulate her in some nefarious way? She stared back at him fixedly.

'And it was bloody hard to say too!' Acheron added in angry complaint at her response.

'I'm in shock,' Tabby mumbled shakily. 'I didn't think you had any feelings for me.'

'I tried very hard not to. I fought it every step of the way,' Acheron admitted ruefully. 'But in the end you got to me and you got to me so hard I ran away from it.'

'Ran away?' Tabby almost whispered in growing disbelief.

'I was feeling strange and that's why I took off on business…to give myself a little breathing space,' Acheron qualified tautly. 'But the minute I got away I realised I only wanted to come back and be with you.'

Tabby blinked slowly, struggling to react to that explanation when all her crazy head was full of was a single statement: that he loved her. *He loves me.* She tasted the idea, savoured it, very nearly careened across the terrace and flattened him to the tiles in gratitude, but mercifully retained enough restraint to stay where she was. 'You got cold feet, didn't you?' she guessed.

Acheron nodded. 'It was a little overwhelming when I realised what was wrong with me.'

Tabby moved closer. 'No, it wasn't anything wrong with you. It was a good thing, a wonderful thing…you love me. I love you.'

'If you feel the same way I do, why the hell are you putting me through this torture?' Acheron demanded rawly.

Tabby almost laughed, a sense of intoxication gripping her as she searched his darkly handsome features and the masculine bewilderment etched there. 'Talking about love is torture?'

Acheron rested his arms down on her slim shoulders and breathed, 'I thought once I said it, that would be that, but I was scared you wouldn't feel the same way and that you wanted it all to be fake.'

Tabby closed her arms round him and snuggled close. 'No, real is much better than fake. So, does this mean we're really and truly married?'

'Absolutely,' Acheron confirmed, and bent to lift her up into his arms. 'It also means we're going to be adoptive parents together because I sort of developed a fondness for Amber as well. Seems this love business is contagious…'

'Wow…' Tabby framed as he carried her upstairs to their bedroom and Teresa, with the baby in her arms, retreated back into the nursery with a warm smile. 'But how did it happen?'

Acheron arranged her on the bed with the care of a man setting up an art installation and stared down at her for what felt like ages. 'I think it started when I realised I was with a woman who was willing to sacrifice her

home and her business to look after her sick best friend
and child. I respect that level of loyalty and unselfish-
ness. I respect what you were willing to do to retain
custody of Amber even though I was pretty rough and
crude about everything at the time. You stuck it out…
you stood up to me…'

'And out of that came love?' Tabby whispered in
shock.

'Out of those experiences came a woman I couldn't
live without,' traded Acheron with a tender look in his
lustrous dark eyes that she had never seen before. '*Thee
mou*…if you had still wanted the fake marriage and the
divorce I don't know what I would've done.'

'I don't want a divorce…I don't ever want to let go of
you,' Tabby confided against his shirtfront.

'That desire is just about to come in very handy,
agape mou,' Acheron murmured thickly, claiming her
ripe mouth with his own, sending a thrill of heat and anticipation travelling through her relaxed body.

About an hour later, Acheron leapt naked out of bed
to retrieve his trousers and dig into a pocket to produce
a jewellers' box, which he pressed into her hand. 'I know
it's not your birthday for another twenty-four hours but
this is burning a hole in my pocket,' he admitted ruefully.

Tabby opened the box to find an unusual ring in the
shape of a rose with a ruby at the centre.

'What do you think?' Acheron demanded anxiously.
'I wanted you to know that it was made in the image of
your tattoo because it will always remind me what made
you the special woman you are.'

'It's…gorgeous!' Tabby carolled as he removed his
late mother's engagement ring from her wedding finger
and replaced it with the new ring. The diamonds on the
rose petals caught the sunlight and cast a rainbow of lit-

tle sparkling reflections across the white bedding. 'But why on earth do you think I am so special when I'm so ordinary?'

'You're special because in spite of all the bad things that happened to you, you still have an open heart and a loving spirit. You love Amber, you love me—'

'So much,' Tabby emphasised feelingly as she smiled up at him. 'Although you might feel you love me a little less when you see what I spent on my credit card.'

'Never,' Acheron contradicted. 'You're the least extravagant person I know.'

'You might change your mind on that score,' she warned him, hoping he at least appreciated the gift of the pen on his birthday in three days' time.

'I love you,' he breathed softly, his attention locked on her smiling face.

He had fallen in love with her, he had genuinely fallen in love with her, Tabby savoured finally, and she allowed the happiness to well up inside her along with a sense of release from all anxiety. Somehow, by the most mysterious process of love known to mankind, two people who had loathed each other on sight because of their misconceptions had found love and formed a happy home and family and she was delirious with the joy of that miracle.

Tabby sucked in her tummy and studied the mirror. No, it was pointless: she was pregnant and there was no escaping that pregnant apple shape, no matter how well cut her maternity clothing was. With a wry smile at the foolishness of her vanity, Tabby went downstairs to check the last-minute arrangements for Amber's fourth birthday party.

The party was a catered affair, everything set up to entertain a whole posse of Amber's nursery-school friends.

There was a bouncy castle in the garden of their London town house, purchased after the birth of their first child, Andreus, who was already a rumbustious noisy toddler. Closely pursued by his nanny, Teresa, who had become as much a part of the family as the children, Andreus hurtled across the hall to throw his arms up to be lifted by his mother.

Tabby tried not to wince at the weight of her son, but, at eight months along in her second pregnancy, lifting a child who was already outstripping his peers in size was becoming quite a challenge. He hugged her tight, black curls like his father's silky against her throat, her own big blue eyes bright in his little smiling face. Sometimes, Tabby was still afraid that if she blinked her happy family life would disappear and she would discover she had been trapped in an inordinately convincing and wonderful daydream. And then she would look at Acheron and the children and she would be soothed by the closeness of their bonds.

Admittedly she would never have picked Acheron out as a keen father figure when she first met him, but exposure to Amber's charms had soon raised a desire in Acheron to have a child of his own. By the time the legalities of Amber's adoption had been settled and she had officially become their daughter, Tabby had been expecting Andreus. The little girl whom Tabby was currently carrying had been more of an accidental conception, thanks to a little spur-of-the-moment lovemaking on the beach in Sardinia where they had first found love, and which of all Acheron's properties they visited the most, although they had quickly extended the house to add on more bedroom capacity.

His father's widow, Ianthe, and her two surviving children had stayed with them there to attend Kasma's funeral. It had been a sad and sobering occasion but it had also done much to build a bridge between Ash and his father's former family. Ianthe had admitted to having been seriously worried about her daughter's mental health but Ash's late father, Angelos, had refused to face up to that reality. Kasma's brother, Simeon, and his family also had young children and the two couples had become close friends since that last sad encounter.

The front door opened and Andreus scrambled down from his mother's arms to hurl himself violently at Acheron, shouting, 'Dad!' at the top of his voice.

Tabby watched Acheron scoop his son up, and a warm smile curved her generous mouth because she never loved Acheron more than when she saw him with the children. He was kind, affectionate and patient, all the things that they had both so badly lacked when they were kids themselves. 'I thought you wouldn't make it back in time.'

'Where's the birthday girl?' Acheron enquired.

Amber came racing downstairs, a vivid little figure clad in a flouncy new party dress, and flung herself at her father with very little more circumspection than her toddler brother. 'You're here!' she carolled. 'You're here for my party.'

'Of course, I am,' Acheron said in the act of producing a present from behind his back, only to laugh as the housekeeper opened the door to let Amber's best friend and her mother enter and the two little girls went running off together. 'So much for being flavour of the month there!' he teased.

'But you're always my favourite flavour,' Tabby rushed to assure him in an undertone before she went to greet the arriving guests.

Acheron watched her acting hostess with quiet admiration. *His* Tabby, the best and luckiest find he had

ever made, always warm, sunny and bright and still the
most loving creature he had ever met. It didn't surprise
him in the slightest that he loved her more with every
passing year.

* * * * *

'It's good to know you don't have a problem with a woman being in charge.'

'This is a one time and one time only deal. My tolerance and acceptance will only stretch so far. Once I'm back on my feet again you'd be unwise to push any advantage you gained while I was laid up.'

Raising her brows, Kit responded smartly, 'When you're back on your feet again you'll no longer need my services, so such a possibility won't even arise. I'll be looking after another client… hopefully one a little less egotistical than you.'

Worryingly, any response he normally might have made to such an unflattering observation deserted Hal. The idea that Kit was already eagerly contemplating a new client—one 'a little less egotistical' than he was—seriously bothered him.

But he couldn't help but notice how her smooth alabaster cheeks had a faintly scarlet tint to them. *How interesting,* he thought. Perhaps it wasn't just his 'egotistical' nature that ruffled the coolly efficient redhead?

'You're blushing, Ms Blessington. Does it disturb you to get this close to your client? Because if it does I don't know how you're going to manage when you help me into my bath later,' he taunted.

The day **Maggie Cox** saw the film version of *Wuthering Heights*, with a beautiful Merle Oberon and a very handsome Laurence Olivier, was the day she became hooked on romance. From that day onwards she spent a lot of time dreaming up her own romances, secretly hoping that one day she might become published and get paid for doing what she loved most! Now that her dream is being realised, she wakes up every morning and counts her blessings. She is married to a gorgeous man, and is the mother of two wonderful sons. Her two other great passions in life—besides her family and reading/writing—are music and films.

Recent titles by the same author:

IN PETRAKIS'S POWER
WHAT HIS MONEY CAN'T HIDE
DISTRACTED BY HER VIRTUE
A DEVILISHLY DARK DEAL

Did you know these are also available as eBooks?
Visit www.millsandboon.co.uk

THE TYCOON'S DELICIOUS DISTRACTION

BY
MAGGIE COX

Published in Great Britain 2014
by Mills & Boon, an imprint of Harlequin (UK) Limited,
Eton House, 18-24 Paradise Road, Richmond, Surrey, TW9 1SR

© 2014 Maggie Cox

ISBN: 978 0 263 91106 0

Harlequin (UK) Limited's policy is to use papers that are natural, renewable and recyclable products and made from wood grown in sustainable forests. The logging and manufacturing processes conform to the legal environmental regulations of the country of origin.

Printed and bound in Spain
by Blackprint CPI, Barcelona

THE TYCOON'S DELICIOUS DISTRACTION

To the lovely Maddie
who is the bravest and wittiest girl I know!

CHAPTER ONE

In a fit of pique, Henry Treverne—Hal to his friends—wheeled himself along the parquet hallway up to the wall panel in the door and buzzed the concierge.

'If anyone else turns up for an interview today tell them I've come down with malaria, will you? I'm done with talking to fawning women who are convinced they can magic my problems away like Cinderella's fairy godmother, and I've also had my fill of the ones that gaze at me like I'm some kind of longed-for early Christmas present!'

'But, Mr Treverne, your next applicant is already here... Do you really think you've got malaria? If that's true, shouldn't you be in the hospital?'

The concierge of Hal's building—a down-to-earth young Londoner called Charlie—sounded understandably perturbed. Hefting a frustrated sigh, Hal tunnelled his fingers through the mane of coal-black hair that was in dire need of a proper cut and bit back a curse.

'Of course I haven't got malaria. I've just got back from Aspen, Colorado, not the damn Amazon!' He brought himself up short. 'What do you mean my next applicant is already here?'

Impatiently unfolding the scrunched-up piece of

paper lying on his lap, he couldn't help but succumb to a ripe curse, when he saw there was one more person the agency had scheduled him to see. A woman named Kit Blessington. God save him from one more insincere female desperate for the chance to be his 'carer' and in all probability make herself a nice little bonus by sell-ing a story about her experience to the press when he was back on his feet again.

'The lady arrived early and is waiting to see you, Mr Treverne.'

'Well, you can tell Ms Blessed, or whatever her name is, that I'm too tired to see anyone else today. Tell her she can come back tomorrow.'

'I'd rather see you now, if I could, Mr Treverne? After all, that was what was arranged. Plus, it's not convenient for me to come back tomorrow.'

Hal was taken aback by the assertively toned female voice that sounded in his ear. 'What do you mean, it's not convenient?' he growled. 'Are you in the market for a job or are you not?' His already bad mood plummeted even more. The woman clearly hadn't taken him seri-ously when he'd said he was too tired.

'I wouldn't be signed on with the agency if I wasn't interested in a job, Mr Treverne. And, by the way, my name is Blessington—not Blessed.'

'What's the reason you can't come back tomorrow?' Even as he ground out the question the back of Hal's neck prickled with intense dislike for this woman he hadn't even come face to face with yet.

'If you must know, I have another interview to attend in Edinburgh. I can't see you tomorrow if I'm travelling up to Scotland. That's why I'd like to keep my appoint-ment with you today.'

The frank confession rendered him momentarily dumbstruck. He wasn't best pleased that she'd arranged another interview when she hadn't even given him the courtesy of seeing *him* yet. What did she think she was playing at? Surely the agency must have told her who he was...that under the circumstances he had to be a priority?

'What the hell do you want to go to Scotland for?' he burst out, not caring that he sounded rude and unreasonable.

There was a brief pause, then in a level tone she replied, 'I go wherever the work takes me, Mr Treverne. We don't just work in the UK. The agency sends us all over Europe as well. Now, will you see me today or not?'

Feeling particularly belligerent, because inside the cast his leg was intolerably aching, and itching as well, Hal retorted, 'I'll give you ten minutes, Ms Blessington. Ten minutes should be ample time for me to glean whether you're suitable or not for the position, and whether it would indeed be better if you simply went ahead with your interview in Edinburgh. You'd better come up.'

'Thank you. I appreciate it. But just to reassure you, Mr Treverne, I too quite quickly make up my mind about whether I want to work for someone or not. So, yes...I'm sure it won't take long for either of us to reach a decision.'

She was playing verbal bat and ball with him, Hal realised, and it made him feel as if she was the one taking charge of the situation, not him. It certainly didn't bode well for her interview.

Damn his accident! It beggared belief that he'd surrendered to the crazy impulse to agree to a stupid contest on the ski slopes with his ex-business partner Simon. If his pride hadn't made him take the bait he wouldn't be in the intolerable position he was in now—recovering from a lengthy operation to help repair a badly damaged femur and unable to do all the things he had no doubt taken for granted and shouldn't have.

If he hadn't been in so much pain as the paramedics lifted him onto the stretcher, he would have checked to see if the concern Simon had so loudly expressed to the crowd that had gathered was sincere. *Hal very much doubted it.* He could just imagine the man who had always been his rival describing the scene to mutual colleagues and friends and commenting, *How the mighty are fallen...*

One thing was certain. Hal wasn't going to live down the ignominy of the painful incident any time soon.

Disgruntled and hurting, he punched the keypad to open the door and reversed the wheelchair a couple of feet back down the hall as he waited for the irritatingly forthright Ms Blessington to come in and be interviewed. In truth, he was absolutely prepared to dislike her on sight.

When he first glimpsed the gloriously red hair that rippled down over her slim shoulders as she came through the door he wasn't surprised. *It was said that redheads were feisty and opinionated.* And this particular redhead definitely had the look and stance of a public school head girl. He already knew that she was assertive—a woman who knew what she wanted and wasn't afraid to state it—and the unfussy green wool dress and almost military-style tartan jacket she wore with it suggested she selected her clothes more out of practicality than from any desire to make a fashion statement. The outfit might even have been bought at a charity shop. Yet the bright cerise stockings she'd teamed with sensible brown court shoes hinted at an intriguing rebellious streak that belied the illusion of 'needs must' and definitely gave Hal pause.

Lifting his head, he was momentarily taken aback to find his gaze captured by a pair of the prettiest corn-flower-blue eyes he'd ever seen. Even before she opened her mouth to speak he had concluded that the woman was a fascinating conundrum that under more condu-cive circumstances he might, just *might* be tempted to try and unravel. But when she next spoke any impulse to be more interested than he should be instantly vanished.

'I can see why you sounded so bad-tempered just now.' Frowning, she set a purple velvet shoulder bag down on the floor and purposefully stepped towards him, like an extremely efficient ward nurse intent on taking his temperature. 'If you don't mind my saying so, you do look rather uncomfortable. Your brow is beaded with sweat and I can see you're in pain. They told me at the agency that you'd broken your femur and that it was a bad break. Do you need a painkiller? If you tell me where they are I'll get them for you, if you'd like?'

'I've taken a couple—just a few minutes ago.'

For stupefying seconds the arresting floral scent his redoubtable interviewee wore transported Hal to a beau-tiful spring garden after a gentle rain had fallen, and it made it hard for him to think straight. It didn't help that she stood close enough for him to reach out and touch one of the fiery red coils of hair that cascaded over her shoulders, and the shockingly inappropriate impulse made his heart thunder inside his chest like a herd of galloping horses.

Taken aback by the surprising reaction, he coughed a little to clear his throat. 'The pills take a while to kick in. So, no, I don't need you to get me any more. The last thing I need is to feel comatose. I think we should just get on with the interview, don't you?'

'Of course.' The redhead's alabaster skin flushed a little, but quickly getting over any embarrassment she might have felt and levelling a searching glance at him, she asked, 'Instead of staying in that wheelchair, would you not prefer to conduct our interview lying on the sofa, with some cushions behind you for a while? I'm sure it would be a lot more comfortable. I can help you, if you'd like?'

'Ms Blessing?'

'Blessington.'

He should have known correction was inevitable, and Hal chewed down on his lip to stop himself from responding with something he might regret.

'Let's get one thing straight. I'm *not* looking to hire a facsimile of Florence Nightingale. I have round-the-clock access to a highly professional medical team if I want it. What I need—that is, the person I'm looking to hire—is someone who can be a temporary companion and help with all things practical while I recuperate. That's why I need a home help. I need someone not just to drive me wherever I want, to arrange for shopping to be delivered, make the odd cup of tea or coffee and rustle up a meal or a snack whenever I need it, but also someone with the ability to make intelligent conversation, who has an interest in music and film—two of the things that entertain me the most. I want this person to be on call twenty-four-seven in case I can't sleep and want some company."

The woman in front of him released the smallest sigh, but Hal didn't think it was because the criteria for the post that he'd outlined in any way daunted her. In fact the interested examination she'd submitted him to as he spoke had been unflinchingly direct.

'That's more or less what the agency told me you needed, Mr Treverne, and I want you to know that I have no problem with any of those things.'

'You've worked for clients with similar requirements before?'

'Yes. I recently worked for an actress recovering from a particularly bad bout of flu that had left her feeling extremely weak. I had to do many of the things you've mentioned for her too, until she could manage on her own again.'

The experience hadn't been a particularly good one for Kit, because the woman in question was spoilt and disagreeable. She had run her ragged for the six long weeks she'd worked for her, taking every opportunity to let her know how much she was admired and envied by her fellow thespians in the theatrical world for her beauty and acting prowess—her tone suggesting that Kit should feel privileged that she'd hired her.

But Kit hadn't felt resentful towards the woman, because she clearly hadn't been able to see how very unattractive her vanity and superior manner actually made her. During all the time Kit had been with her she hadn't had so much as one person call to see how she was doing. Kit had ended up feeling very sorry for her.

'And, seeing as I need you to be available round the clock, you're aware that this is a live-in position?'

Hal's arresting voice broke into her reverie.

'Most of the jobs with the agency *are*. Don't worry—all your requirements were explained to me in detail, Mr Treverne. Is there anything else you'd like to ask me?'

'Yes. How old are you?'

'I'm twenty-six.'

'And you don't have a "significant other" who might express reservations about you living-in? Especially when the person you'll be working for is male?' If Hal had hoped to rattle her with his slightly mocking inflection, he'd failed. His outspoken interviewee gave no visible sign whatsoever that the question had perturbed her in any way. Instead, she remained unshakably composed.

'I'm unattached, so there's no one in my life to express any reservations. In any case I wouldn't tolerate being in a relationship with someone who dictated what I could or couldn't do, or minded that I lived in if it was part of my job…which it clearly is.'

The blunt confession piqued Hal's curiosity even more. He found himself wondering what her story was. His sister Sam, who invariably liked to try and get to the root of someone's make-up, would no doubt presume the woman's outspoken and direct attitude had manifested itself as a result of her being bullied—either during her childhood or even in the recent past. Because of it, she'd probably made a mental decision not to let herself be intimidated by anyone ever again. He could almost hear Sam saying it. In Sam's psychology practice she'd seen plenty of clients with similar stories. Except it wasn't hard to guess that Ms Kit Blessington was no push-over… In Hal's view, only a fool would presume otherwise.

The notion didn't disturb him one jot. He'd rather have someone capable and strong-minded working for him than some shy wallflower who wouldn't say boo to a goose. It took him aback to realise that in the space of a few short minutes he'd become inexplicably fascinated by the woman. Fascinated or not, he reminded himself, it was hardly a good idea for him to be interested in a prospective employee…albeit a temporary one. At any rate, it wasn't a fascination that meant he was remotely attracted to her, he assured himself sternly. She might be unquestionably pretty, but she was no knock-out that he'd have trouble resisting should he hire her.

As if to remind him of the reason for them having this discussion at all, his leg started to throb like the blazes, and once again a wave of perspiration beaded his forehead. *Should he or shouldn't he give her a few days' trial to see if she was suitable?* God knew none of the other applicants he'd seen had been remotely suitable. Damn it, he needed someone capable and reliable to help him out as soon as possible or he'd be fit to be tied! His situation had already begun making him feel unbearably imprisoned, and for a man who was used to being so active—living life at 'breakneck speed', as his sister so often observed with concern—the experience was bordering on *torture*…

Giving the redhead a long, assessing glance, he said, 'Follow me into the living room and we can talk about this some more.' Hal's tone rang with the innate command that came only too easily to him. Would his potential home help be able to handle an often belligerent and exacting male who made no apology for it?

'You mean you want the interview to continue?'

'Well, I'm not inviting you into my living room to

get your opinion on the decor, Ms Blessington.' Even as he uttered the droll reply Hal registered that it was the first time he'd seen so much as a flicker of doubt in the woman's bright blue eyes—as if she'd momentarily feared her forthright manner might have talked her out of the job. As he turned away to steer the wheelchair further down the hall towards the living room he couldn't help mentally storing the information in case he ever had occasion to draw upon it. In his profession he'd long ago learned the wisdom of knowing his advantages when it came to relationships—professional or otherwise. And neither was he above using them...

Following behind the wheelchair, Kit used the time to further examine the man tagged as 'Lucky Henry' in the music business. Apparently, according to people in the know, he had the enviable gift of discovering potentially lucrative talent and backing it financially, expanding that talent even more, and obviously making himself even richer and more successful in the process as the artists he sponsored made platinum sales on their records and became the 'next big thing' in the pop industry.

Even though she didn't have the slightest desire to experience how the other half lived in that shallow, materialistic world—a world that in her opinion could only breed disappointment and unhappiness when an artist's star began to wane and they were no longer 'flavour of the month'—Kit couldn't deny she had often been intrigued as to what happened to the budding stars who *didn't* make it.

And, more than that, she was indisputably interested as to the motivation behind Henry Treverne's decision to become an impresario in such a dog-eat-dog profession. Having been a temporary home help to many celebrity clients, she'd done her research and learned that 'Lucky Henry' came from landed gentry and had grown up with every possible material advantage. Was money and success the only thing that inspired him because he'd already experienced being raised with the proverbial silver spoon in his mouth? *Surely the man must be a more complex character than his public persona suggested?*

Not only had he enjoyed every material advantage growing up, he was also blessed with an extraordinary physique and arresting good looks to boot. As Kit's gaze settled on broad, athletic shoulders in a cream cashmere sweater and thick dark hair curling somewhat rebelliously over the neckline she couldn't help wondering that if he should offer her the job, and if she accepted it, perhaps this time she really would be biting off more than she could chew. She might have deliberately given Henry Treverne the impression that she wasn't particularly concerned about whether he gave her the job or not because she'd already lined up another interview in Edinburgh, but the truth was it *did* matter to Kit—because the agency was paying the highest possible rate for this position and, as well as looking good on her résumé, it would really help boost her savings—savings she was eager to add to so that she might at long last buy the little bolthole she'd always yearned for.

'What's Kit short for?'

The question was fired at her as they reached the living room. Not answering immediately, Kit glanced round to get her bearings. The first thing that hit her was the bold oil painting of a man scaling what looked to be the sheer face of a glacier. Something about the tilt of the head, along with the colour of his hair and the breadth of his shoulders, made Kit realise that the daredevil mountaineer was Henry. Transfixed, it was hard for her to look away.

'That's you, isn't it?' she said.

His tight-lipped expression told her the question unsettled him.

'It is.'

Ignoring the opportunity to comment further—unlike most men, who notoriously loved to brag about their daring exploits—he remained stubbornly uncommunicative, so she returned her attention to the living room. She'd guessed his taste would veer towards the contemporary and she was right. The high-quality monochrome furniture that predominated was ultra-chic, with smooth clean lines, and it was arranged almost like a display of elite sculptures at an exhibition. Even though it had probably cost and arm and a leg to furnish, it was hardly the most inviting living room Kit had ever been in… However, the three streamlined ebony leather couches that took centre stage were strewn with brightly coloured Moroccan-style silk cushions that made her think he must have surrendered to a rogue impulse to inject some warmth into the arrangement.

'Kit is short for Katherine, and Katherine is spelt with a K.' Breaking off her reverie, she returned to his question regarding her name.

Her answer was the one she usually gave when quizzed about it. Her mother had been very particular about the spelling…it was the one decision in her life she'd appeared to have made with ease. *It was a far from a normal occurrence.* When it came to making informed decisions for herself and her daughter Elizabeth Blessington reacted to the task like a billiard ball run amok—decisions were random and precarious. How could they not be when they were invariably emotionally driven rather than made using reason and common sense? That was why Kit had found herself taking charge from such a ridiculously young age. While her friends had been playing with dolls or games Kit had usually been sitting in her mother's kitchen, trying to help find some practical solution to her latest dramatic dilemma—or if not that then consoling her because some unsuitable man she'd become infatuated with had once again let her down.

Elizabeth Blessington's choice of men had been disastrous, and the self-destructive pattern had begun with Kit's father. Ralph Cottonwood had been a genuine Romany gypsy who had selfishly abandoned Elizabeth when she'd become pregnant. In her mother's wistful words, 'He couldn't be tied down to a conventional married life when the allure of the open road would always call to him.'

Although Kit had missed not having a steady male influence in her life, she'd long ago decided that her itinerant father had probably done her and her mother a favour by not sticking around. One totally impractical parent with her head in the clouds had been quite enough to cope with…

'Why don't you sit down?'

Moving his wheelchair into the centre of the room, Henry vaguely waved his hand towards the couches.

'Okay.' As she settled herself Kit rested her hands together in her lap and patiently waited for him to continue. *A sudden realisation struck her.* She'd thought his eyes were green, but in the beam of gold sunlight that streamed through the windows she saw that they were a chameleon-like hazel, and fringed with enviably lustrous long black lashes. She'd have to be made of stone not to admire such a compelling visage…

'So tell me, Katherine with a K, what impulse led you into doing this kind of work?'

'I decided to do it because I like helping people.'

'And what qualifications do you have?'

The question didn't faze her, even though she'd often regretted her lack of opportunity to study for a profession. But with a mother who was often in financial trouble because she didn't have a clue how to manage money Kit had had no choice but to start work at sixteen so that she could contribute to the household income and help pay the rent.

'Do you mean professional qualifications?'

He nodded.

Pursing her lips for a moment, Kit quickly gathered her thoughts. 'I've done some fairly intensive first-aid training courses and completed a carer's certificate. But what I lack in professional qualifications I make up for by having plenty of "hands-on" experience in helping to take care of people. If you speak to Barbara—the manager at the agency—she'll clarify what I've said. I've been with her for the past five years and my record is exemplary. The agency standards are extremely high, and she wouldn't keep me on if I didn't help her live up to that.'

Her heart was thudding a little as she finished speaking, because Henry's expression had at first been perturbed and then somewhat amused. *Was he perhaps thinking she must be crazy if she thought he'd seriously consider taking on someone with minimal qualifications to work for him?* Kit hoped he would at least give her a chance to demonstrate her competence. Inexplicably, the thought of travelling up to Scotland tomorrow had strangely lost its appeal.

'It's lucky for you that I'm a risk-taker. Other people might call it reckless, but fortunately I don't much care what other people think. Okay, Ms Blessington, when can you start?'

He was going to give her a chance? Secretly elated, but careful not to show it, Kit strove for her usual composure. 'Are you saying that you'd like to offer me the job, Mr Treverne?'

He immediately combed his fingers through his unruly dark hair and scowled. 'Isn't that why you're here… because you want to work for me?'

'Yes, I am. But—'

'Firstly, don't call me Mr Treverne. It's far too formal. You can call me Hal. I'm sure you can guess that's not an invitation I extend to many, but for the purpose of ease of communication I'm extending it to you, Kit. And, yes…I'm offering you the job and I'd like you to start tomorrow. My sister assures me that the agency you work for does indeed have a good reputation for employing reliable and competent people—people who know how to employ discretion and respect confidentiality. That's especially important for businessmen in the public eye like me, as I'm sure you're aware? And, by the way, there's a confidentiality clause in the contract that I'll need to get you to sign. I trust you're okay with that?'

'Of course.'

Emitting a relieved sigh, Hal nodded. 'Then you can arrive tomorrow, just after breakfast. Depending on what kind of night I've had, I usually endeavour to have toast and coffee at around eight. There's one more thing…I have an appointment at the hospital at ten. You'll have to drive me.' Looking thoughtful, he paused, narrowing his chameleon-like gaze. 'I presume you'd like to accept the position?'

'Yes…yes, I would.' Rising to her feet, Kit walked towards him, her smile perhaps a little more cautious than usual. Henry Treverne was a commandingly attractive man and she wouldn't be truthful if she didn't privately admit that it worried her. It had never happened before but she'd often feared that if she fell for a man she worked for it would be the ruination of all her dreams and plans. Add to that the fact that he was still very much an unknown quantity with regard to what he would be like as an employer, she sensed, going by his brusque manner, that she would have her work cut out in proving to him he'd chosen the right person for the job.

'Thank you…thank you so much. I promise I won't let you down.'

'I sincerely hope you won't. The thought of having to interview prospective employees again fills me with horror after the parade of too-earnest applicants I've seen today.' Hal's lips shaped an ironic smile. 'Barring yourself, of course. If you're at all too earnest about having this job you hide it well. Would you like to see your room now?'

'Yes, I would.'

'Then follow me. In light of my accident, I thank God I chose an apartment that doesn't have stairs. For convenience, the room I've allocated you is next door to mine.' His hands resting lightly on the tyres of the wheelchair, Hal paused as another thought struck him.

'I won't give you a key because the revolving doors downstairs are never closed, and Charlie is usually there on the front desk if there's a problem. Plus, if you're out then that means I'm in, and all you need to do is get Charlie to buzz me to let me know you've returned. Okay?'

'But what if you've fallen asleep and don't hear the buzzer?'

'Unless I've been clubbed over the head by a particularly vindictive burglar you don't need to be concerned about that. I don't easily fall asleep—at least certainly not during the day. But, just to reassure you, Charlie has a spare key for emergencies.'

'That's good to know.'

'Then let's go and look at your room, shall we?'

CHAPTER TWO

IT HAD BEEN a hell of a day, Hal reflected, positioning his wheelchair in front of the bathroom mirror in order to brush his teeth. Although it was practically unheard of for him to turn in before midnight, since returning home from the hospital he'd cultivated the habit of retiring early in the hope of getting some longed-for rest. The irony was, no matter how early he went to bed, his sleep was unfailingly broken. First by episodes of agonising pain in his leg that meant he had to rise in order to take some pain relief and then by the inevitable visits to the bathroom—which was no easy feat when he had to hoist himself into his wheelchair to get there.

The one light on the horizon was he'd been advised that from tomorrow he could start using crutches. But he knew it would still be a fiasco, endeavouring to do all the commonplace things that he'd been used to taking for granted. Rubbing a hand round his dark stubbled jaw, then peering closer to examine the shocking bruised shadows beneath his eyes, he felt frustration and fury bite into him with all the force of a serrated steel clamp. *Was it usual to feel this fatigued after an accident? And was it normal that his emotions should be so tightly wound that he could scarcely contain them?*

His highly esteemed surgeon had assured him that it was…except the confirmation didn't help him to accept the fact. Thank God Sam had persuaded him to hire some practical help and companionship, with the aim of alleviating some of the frustration he felt round his compromised mobility and also to counter the boredom of being forced to spend so much time on his own.

If Sam hadn't been the manager of a busy psychology practice she would have willingly been there for Hal night and day if necessary. But she also had a husband with a demanding job, and Greg was surely entitled to spend his precious free time with his wife. As for Hal's so-called 'friends'…they were busy with their own demanding careers and pleasurable pursuits—and anyway none of them were the type to give up their time willingly for an invalid.

Appalled that he had begun to think of himself in such a scornful way, he quickly brushed his teeth, turned off the light, then returned to his bedroom grimly to face another disagreeable and painful night with nothing but his steadily worsening thoughts to keep him company.

As he lifted his hard-muscled frame out of the wheelchair and manoeuvred himself onto the bed he found himself fervently hoping that the feisty Kit Blessington's presence would at least be *bearable*. Perish the thought that she might be the type of woman who chattered incessantly about inconsequential things and would very quickly get on his nerves, making him bitterly regret hiring her—even if her practical skills *should* prove to be as competent as she'd indicated.

Hal was having an early-morning cup of coffee with his sister when, true to her word, Kit Blessington arrived at the agreed time. Sam had dropped in on her way to work, determined to meet Hal's new hired help as soon as possible, so she'd told him, her cat-like green eyes formidably serious. He knew it mattered to her a great deal that the woman passed muster because she adored her 'little' brother. He might resent her acting like his mother from time to time, but he didn't deny it felt good to have her unstinting regard and concern. Especially when the only communication he'd had from his father since the accident was a curt e-mail that had included the line, 'Didn't I always tell you that pride comes before a fall?'

Kick me while I'm down, why don't you? Hal had thought bitterly.

Tall and slender, with a gamine short hairstyle, his sister Sam looked as chic and sophisticated as always that morning in an elegant trouser suit. When Kit arrived the younger woman's bohemian, far more relaxed mode of dress couldn't have been more of a contrast. When he opened the door to let her in he saw that today her glorious red hair was precariously arranged up in a loose topknot that suggested it might easily topple at any moment, such must be the weight of the waving strands. Wearing a mint-green baggy knitted sweater beneath a man's battered tan flying jacket, along with a pair of slim-fitting caramel cords, she was transporting what looked to be a fairly hefty brown suitcase.

Hal immediately told her to put it down before she dislocated her shoulder, adding, 'What have you got in there? The kitchen sink?'

Flushing, she retorted, 'You *did* say that this was a live-in position? All I've brought with me are the strictest essentials, Mr Treverne.'

'Well, clearly they must indeed be essential if you're trying to lug *that* beast around,' he commented dryly.

Sam stepped up beside him and once Kit had sensibly lowered her suitcase down onto the parquet floor she leaned towards the younger woman to shake her hand.

'I'm very pleased to meet you, Ms Blessington. You've arrived just in the nick of time. Henry's got to get to grips with using his crutches today, so your presence will undoubtedly be appreciated. I'm Samantha Whyte, by the way—Henry's sister.'

'Hello. It's nice to meet you too, Ms Whyte. It's good to know that your brother has a close relative living nearby. It must be very reassuring for him in light of what he's coping with.'

'I don't live that near, but I'm close enough to call in whenever I can to check that he's okay. I have to warn you—Hal doesn't take to being confined very easily. Hal is what family and friends call him, by the way. He's apt to be like a bear with a sore head most days.'

'Do you two mind not talking about me as if I wasn't here?' Biting back an angry expletive, Hal violently reversed his wheelchair and headed back towards the kitchen.

'Don't mind him,' he heard Sam say soothingly behind him to Kit. 'As I said, he's a bit more irritable than usual since he broke his leg, but—'

'Don't you *dare* tell her that underneath my tetchy, disagreeable exterior I'm a veritable pussycat!' he yelled. 'Because I'm certainly *not!*'

His heart thumping hard inside his chest, Hal steered the wheelchair into the kitchen and straight away moved across to the oblong glass dining table to retrieve his rapidly cooling mug of coffee. He knew he was behaving like the worst bore in the world but he couldn't seem to help it. Tonight, before bed, he might just have to succumb to taking those sleeping pills his doctor had prescribed. Right now he'd probably take the strongest ones he could lay his hands on if they would help him get at least an hour of unbroken sleep. *'A bear with a sore head'* didn't come anywhere near to describing the infuriated way he felt.

'...and you'll need to consult with Hal's doctor today, when you take him to the hospital for his check-up, to get some advice on how best to help him.' Sam's voice carried clearly as she and Kit came down the hallway towards the kitchen. 'His knee joint and muscles were damaged when he broke his femur, and there's a certain process you have to know. Don't worry—it's not difficult. I think it's called the RICE technique, which stands for—'

'Rest, ice, compression and elevation,' Kit cut in quietly. 'I've been studying quite a comprehensive first-aid book since I was told that Mr Treverne had a broken femur. I've also spoken to one of my trainers at the centre where I took my first-aid courses.'

She'd been studying a first-aid book? Even though he was irritated at being discussed as though he were a recalcitrant schoolboy who'd complained about having to miss his school's sports day because he'd contracted chicken pox, Hal owned to feeling mildly surprised that his temporary employee would go to such lengths even before she knew if she had the job or not.

'I'm impressed.' Sam's voice contained the suggestion of a smile.

'Please don't be. My intention is simply to do a good job. It's no more than I would normally do when the person I've been hired to help is either recovering from an illness or an injury, Ms Whyte.'

'Please—call me Sam. At any rate, I've spoken to Hal's consultant about talking to you, so he's expecting you to ask.' They came into the kitchen. 'You can also check with the nurse who comes in once a week to visit him. Oh, and one more thing—there's also a cleaner who comes in twice a week to give the place a good going over. Mrs Baker is her name. So you won't have to spend too much time doing housework. My brother's welfare is your main priority. If he wants you to spend the entire day watching films or listening to music with him, then please don't hesitate.'

'Are you quite finished? Only I'm beginning to feel like some expendable extra in a hospital soap opera!' Scowling, Hal returned his mug of coffee to the table with a heavy slam, so that the now tepid beverage slopped over the lip and splashed onto his arm.

Without preamble, Kit moved across to the sink at lightning speed and grabbed the kitchen cloth that was folded over the tap. Then she hurried over to him, expertly dabbing the cloth on his exposed forearm and drying the spill. It was fortunate that he'd rolled up the sleeves of his cashmere sweater earlier, he thought wryly, because the blue was a favourite of his. But he guessed that, if required, his efficient new helper would no doubt have a handy solution for removing coffee stains from delicate fabrics too.

'Thanks,' he murmured when she had finished the clean-up.

'You're welcome.'

Her blue-eyed smile was fleeting, but with a jolt of surprise Hal straight away intuited that when she smiled properly—for instance when and if something pleased her—the gesture would light up her face and render her almost bewitching…

'Can I make you a fresh cup of coffee, Mr Treverne?' she asked.

Briefly catching his sister's amused glance over her shoulder, Hal shrugged. 'Yes—why not? I guess I'll be even more like a bear with a sore head if I don't have my usual quota of caffeine.'

'How do you take it?'

'Black with one sugar. You should make one for yourself too.'

'Thanks—I will. By the way, what time do you need to get to the hospital for your appointment?'

'Ten o'clock.'

'Of course. I remember that now.' The redhead gave him another fleeting smile. 'That gives us some time to have a general chat about things. For instance, you'll need to tell me what car I'm driving. Is it big enough to accommodate your wheelchair? Because if you're not used to using your crutches yet you're going to need it.'

Not wanting to contemplate the possibility of not being immediately expert at using crutches, Hal was terse. 'If it should transpire that I need the wheelchair—and I very much doubt it—then no doubt the hospital will supply one for my visit. The car you'll be driving me to my appointment in has plenty of leg room and is easy to drive…that is as long as you're a good driver?'

Again, if he'd thought to disconcert Kit then he was disappointed. With a confident toss of her head she moved over to the coffee machine and threw over her shoulder, 'I took my advanced driving test last year and passed with flying colours…so you can rest assured that I'm a good driver, Mr Treverne.'

'I thought we'd agreed you could call me Hal?'

'Do you mind if I call you Henry instead? Only using your friends' name for you sounds a little too over-familiar.'

Seeing the lightly mocking glint in his sister's eyes, Hal inwardly squirmed. No doubt his clever sister was thinking he'd met his match in the redoubtable Kit Blessington. But he would make it his mission to prove her wrong…see if he didn't!

'Well.' Sam leant down and dropped an affectionate peck on his cheek. 'I'll be off now. I'll leave you to the tender ministrations of Ms Blessington.' Her mouth curved into a satisfied and humorous grin.

'I'm not looking for her ministrations to be "tender",' he snapped. 'A decent level of competence will be enough.'

'A typical Hal response,' his sister remarked cheerily, winking at the other woman as she transported a mug of fresh coffee over to her brother. 'By the way, Kit, if you need me for anything…anything at all… you'll find my phone numbers on the noticeboard in Hal's study. You'll find that just to the side of a poster of the latest scantily clad supermodel. Look after him for me, won't you?'

'Of course.'

Unable to suppress a grin at his sister's amusing parting shot, Hal murmured, 'Bye, sis. Go easy with those wounded patients of yours, won't you?'

'What a lovely woman,' Kit remarked when Sam had departed.

'She is.' As he tunnelled his long fingers through hair

that hadn't seen a comb for more days than he cared to mention, Hal's smile was unrestrained. 'I agree. She's certainly one in a million.'

Momentarily dazzled by the twinkling hazel eyes and curved masculine mouth before her, Kit shrugged off her heavy jacket and arranged it on the back of one of the shaker-style dining chairs positioned around the table. Then she curled a stray strand of copper hair round her ear and in a brisk but friendly tone asked, 'Shall I help you get to grips with your walking aids now? We've got some spare time for you to practise before we leave for the hospital.'

Even though his smile had all but made her catch her breath she hadn't missed the fact that her employer's skin looked almost grey with tiredness, and her heart couldn't help but go out to him. More importantly, she reminded herself, she was there to do a job and help ease his burden and she was anxious to make a start.

'Wouldn't you like to take your luggage to your room first and unpack?'

Touched by his unexpected thoughtfulness, Kit shook her head.

'I can do that later. I'd rather help you first.'

Underneath what she guessed was a complexion that was far paler than usual, Hal flushed visibly.

'Crutches it is, then. You *do* realise you're going to have to let me lean on you a little while I get my balance?'

'That won't be a problem. I assure you that I'm much stronger than I look.'

'Why did I know you'd say that?'

For a second time Henry Treverne's devastating smile came very close to turning Kit's knees to water.

She fervently reminded herself to be on her guard round that killer smile. It would be extremely foolish to trust it. Once before she'd been beguiled by the smile of a handsome man and against her better judgement, had fallen into a brief affair with him. When the man in question had turned out to be married, Kit had been devastated. Not just because he had lied to her about being free, but because it had struck at the very core of her ability to trust herself. *There'd been no excuse.* After seeing what her mother had gone through with mendacious faithless men she ought to have known better. One thing was certain: she wouldn't make the same mistake twice...

Assuming the best 'head girl' tone she could muster, she said firmly to Hal, 'Well, I suppose we'd better get on with it, then.'

There was no disputing her new employer's indomitable spirit, Kit mused as, with her help, Henry carefully lowered himself onto a comfortable padded seat in the plush waiting room. But neither had it been hard to detect his frustration at not being able to master the use of his walking aids as smoothly and as effortlessly as he might have wished. Once again the sweat that had broken out on his brow had illustrated the effort it had taken him to get this far. They'd only walked the short distance from the car park, but it had clearly been a struggle for Hal. It made her even more determined to help him achieve the goal of being confident with the aids.

Leaning towards him, Kit freed his hands from holding the crutches and carefully leaned them against the wall behind him.

'You'd better go and tell the receptionist that I'm here.'

The sudden command sounded like a snarl of anger and resentment—a bit like a wounded animal. But she wasn't about to take Hal's surly mood personally. In her time working for the agency she'd encountered several 'tricky' customers and had soon learned how best to handle them. People were dealing with all kinds of challenges. Not just physical and mental ones, but also more commonplace dilemmas, like bereavement and loneliness and sometimes the heartache caused by a failed relationship.

Even though her mother had tested her patience to the nth degree, Kit was a naturally compassionate person, and it helped her more easily cope with the frayed tempers and impatience of some of the clients she cared for and not let their volatile reactions undermine her.

'Okay, I'll go and get you booked in. Do you have a patient card or a letter with your hospital number on?'

Hal sucked in a breath and blew it out again, as if even more exasperated. His eyes glinted, warning her that his temper was hanging by the slimmest of threads.

'Why? Do you think they don't know who I am?' he snapped.

Mentally taking a deep breath of her own, Kit said calmly, 'I'm sure the Queen herself has a patient number, and everybody knows who *she* is.'

'Never mind the backchat, Ms Blessington. Just go and tell them I'm here, will you?'

Had she imagined it or had that handsome carved mouth of his twitched ever so slightly with amusement? Acutely aware of the pretty young receptionist, who was gazing across the room at Hal as though he were some sublime visitation from heaven, Kit went to the desk.

'I'm here with Mr Henry Treverne. He has a ten o'clock appointment with his consultant Mr Shadik.'

Reluctantly withdrawing her gaze from Hal, the girl answered, 'I'll let him know that Mr Treverne is here right away.'

'Thank you.'

Returning to sit beside her brooding charge, Kit proffered what she hoped was a reassuring smile. 'Hopefully you won't have too long to wait.'

His dark eyebrows beetling together, Hal growled, 'However long the wait, it's far too long for my liking.'

'Don't you want help to get better?'

When he turned his head towards her she was treated to the full force of his powerful gaze.

'You may have noticed that asking for help and accepting it is not something that comes naturally to me.'

'Then perhaps when you're back to full strength again it might be something you could start to cultivate?'

'Yeah—and my father might train to climb Mount Everest!'

'I take it he's not a keen climber like you are, then?'

'The only thing he climbs are walls—especially when he hears of another "foolhardy escapade" of mine that he despairs of. That's why he didn't visit me in the hospital when I had this blasted accident. He's a man who's always erred on the side of safety. The only risks he ever takes are ones that he's sure will preserve the legacy of Falteringham House for the generations of the Treverne family to come.'

'Falteringham House? Is that the name of your family home?'

'Yes.'

'And your father really didn't visit you when you broke your leg?' *No wonder he was acting like some kind of wounded animal. It had clearly hurt him that his father had stayed away when he'd been injured.* She doubted that even her impractical, flighty mother would have behaved as callously.

Hal's expression was far away for a moment, and seconds later a tall, elegant man dressed in a tailored pinstriped suit that suggested he might just as easily be a wealthy lawyer as a surgeon presented himself in front of the man sitting beside her.

'Mr Treverne. It is good to see you again. Would you like to come into the examination room and I'll take a look at that leg, see how things are progressing?'

The comment was impatiently received with a disdainfully curled lip. 'The only thing that's progressed is the pain, Mr Shadik.'

'Then perhaps I need to prescribe some stronger medication for you. Let us go and discuss it, shall we?'

Glancing round at Kit, Hal nodded towards the crutches she'd leant against the wall.

'Give me a hand with those, would you? And you may as well come into the examination room with me and get the gist of what's happening.'

'I think that's a good idea.' Immediately pushing to her feet, Kit helped him safely secure the armrests before assisting him to stand. When he did, she observed that once again his indomitably handsome brow was beaded with sweat. The consultant had also noted it, and gravely shook his head.

'I am certain we can do much better as far as your pain relief is concerned, Henry, so please don't worry. Today is your first day on crutches, is it not?'

Hal briefly dipped his head in agreement.

'We'll get another X-ray and afterwards you can see the physio to make sure that you're using the aids properly... But I can see that you're already a natural.' The surgeon beamed.

Kit sensed that beneath his grim smile Henry was privately utilising every expletive he could lay his hands on, as well as inventing a few more choice ones of his own...

CHAPTER THREE

HAL HAD BEEN in dire need of a rest when they'd returned from the hospital. After the tedious rounds of X-rays and physiotherapy he'd endured, as well as a further consultation about the results with his surgeon, he'd been so exhausted that the only thing he'd longed for was at least a couple of hours of unbroken sleep.

In the living room he'd allowed Kit to assist him in getting comfortable on the couch, privately surprised at how used to her touch he was getting and how quickly he had started to trust it.

The biggest surprise of all had come when he'd learned what an amazingly confident driver she was. His top-of-the-range sporty four-by-four had been handled as expertly as if Hal was driving it himself. Any fears about her denting or damaging one of his favourite cars were happily unfounded.

But when Kit had been gently about to drape a cashmere throw over him as he lay back against the couch cushions he'd instantly reverted to type and snapped, 'For God's sake, woman! Stop fussing, will you?'

After that he'd despatched her to her room to unpack and acclimatise herself to her new surroundings, telling her to leave him in peace for a while. When she'd shut the door behind her, as he'd instructed, he'd closed his eyes only to find that the scent of her floral perfume lingered a little too disturbingly for his peace of mind. To compound the disturbance he'd also recalled just then how her precariously arranged topknot had finally collapsed during his consultation, spilling over her shoulders in a vivid autumnal riot of auburn silk. After that it had taken Hal quite a bit longer than he'd hoped to finally slip into the deep slumber he'd craved...

When he awoke it was to a darkened room, with thundering rain pouring outside. The downpour was so fierce that it lashed against the window panes as if trying to force an entry. It must be quite some storm for it to be so dark this early. Manoeuvring himself upright, he roughly scrubbed the backs of his knuckles across his eyelids and yawned. The sudden realisation that he was in dire need of the bathroom made him immediately seek out his walking aids. When he saw that they had been leant against an armchair a few feet away he muttered a ripe curse beneath his breath. How the *hell* was he supposed to reach them over there? The uncharacteristic sense of helplessness that swept over him made him feel even more irritated.

'Kit!' he yelled. 'Where the hell are you? I need you in here *now*!'

The door opened almost straight away and variously placed lamps flooded the room with softly diffused lighting. The first thing Hal noticed was that his new assistant had tamed her riot of auburn hair back into its precarious topknot. He didn't rightly know why that should be such a crime, but to his thinking it *was*.

'I need my crutches,' he said gruffly, carefully

swinging his legs to the floor. 'I'm pretty desperate to get to the bathroom.'

Without a word she immediately went across to the armchair to collect them, then returned to stand in front of him.

'It might be quicker if you lean on me and hop. It's just a few feet away, isn't it?'

'Sweetheart.' He glanced up into her pretty blue eyes and intoned, gravel-voiced, 'I'm six-foot-two and no lightweight. I have only your word that you're stronger than you look, and I'd rather not risk you getting a broken leg to match mine. Just help me with the crutches, will you?'

A little more *au fait* with the walking aids since his session with the physiotherapist, Hal was nonetheless pleased to see that Kit had waited for him when he emerged from the bathroom. Keeping a close eye on him, she silently accompanied him back down the hallway and into the living room.

'Would you like me to get on with dinner now?' she asked.

Dropping down onto the couch, he stared blankly out of the window, suddenly hypnotised by the still hammering rain. 'It looks pretty bleak out there, doesn't it?' he commented.

'Perhaps it's not so bad being forced to stay in this evening in light of the weather?'

There it was again...that surprisingly engaging smile. It completely transformed her otherwise serious demeanour and made Hal think she should smile more often. Not wanting to linger on the idea, he found himself nodding in agreement. For someone who prided himself on not letting even the most extreme weather conditions prevent him from doing what he wanted if he could help it, it was probably a first. Then it struck him what Kit had said just before that last remark.

His brows drawing together in puzzlement, he asked, 'Shouldn't we be having lunch first?'

'I'm afraid lunchtime has come and gone, Mr Treverne. You've been asleep since we got back from the hospital and that was nearly four hours ago. It's just after six in the evening.'

He was genuinely shocked. 'You're joking?'

The slender shoulders beneath the mint-green sweater lifted in a gently amused shrug. 'I promise you I'm not.'

'Did I take a sleeping pill before I napped? I don't remember...'

'No, you didn't. I think sheer exhaustion probably made you sleep so well. Anyway, you must be hungry. I saw that the fridge was well stocked and I took the liberty of making a beef bolognaise while you were sleeping. By the way, I checked with the agency that you weren't a vegetarian. I've just got to rustle up some pasta and I'll bring it in to you.'

'Sounds good. But I'll only eat it if you push me in my chair into the dining room and then come and join me. I really can't abide eating my meals off of a tray, and neither can I abide eating alone. I feel decrepit enough as it is in my sorry state, without acting like an invalid.'

Kit's expression was visibly perturbed. 'That sounds as though you believe you don't deserve any acknowledgement of your condition at all. Isn't that why you hired me in the first place, Mr Treverne? Because you needed some help?'

'How many times do I have to tell you to stop calling me Mr Treverne? And for pity's sake please don't keep referring to me as needing help. It's becoming the bane of my life.'

It wasn't her reference to his need that was bothering him, Kit guessed. It was the fact that for probably the first time ever this fit, active and no doubt fiercely independent businessman and sportsman *had* to be dependent on others...a state he undoubtedly despised. In truth, she entirely sympathised. She would hate it too.

'Well, I'll just go into the kitchen and cook the pasta, then I'll come back and take you into the dining room.'

Stretching out his hand for the mobile phone he'd left on the coffee table, Hal turned towards her.

'Take your time. I've got a couple of calls I want to make to my office first.'

'Okay. If you need me for anything, just call out.'

While Henry had been having his rest earlier Kit had made good use of the time to unpack, arrange her clothes in the walk-in wardrobe and arrange her toiletries in the bathroom. Despite there being an array of wonderfully scented products lined up on the shelves, she wouldn't be making use of them. After all, she was here to work, not as a guest. But she was more than appreciative of the beautiful room she'd been allocated. It had a lovely view of the large neatly mown communal gardens downstairs. The verdant green was bordered by a plethora of trees, plants and shrubs, and a person might almost fool herself that she was deep in the heart of the countryside instead of practically in the centre of London.

She'd also noticed the indisputably feminine touch that the room's decor suggested—such as the luxuri-

ous lilac curtains with matching swags that hung at the
windows and the array of colourful cushions that were
attractively arranged at the head of the Queen-sized
bed. The silk pillows were made up of various vintage
designs full of natural motifs like birds and flowers. *It
was definitely not a man's room.* In fact the decor was
the polar opposite of the very masculine chrome and
glass furnishings that the apartment's owner obviously
favoured. Was Hal's sister Sam's the female influence
that had helped design it?

Dropping strands of linguine into a pan of boiling water in the kitchen, Kit pushed back her hair and
frowned. *There'd been no mention of a girlfriend or
fiancée.* If Henry Treverne had either then surely she
would have been told of her existence in case the woman
dropped in or telephoned? In the newspaper reports
she'd read about the accident at the time there'd been no
mention of a girlfriend—which, considering his 'playboy' reputation, had surprised her. Telling herself he
must be between relationships, she dropped her shoulders and made herself relax. The job she did could be
testing enough without relatives or 'significant others'
keeping too close an eye on her. She always worked
best when her clients trusted her judgement enough to
know that she could be completely relied upon to take
good care of her charge.

In the dining room that also shared a view of the
communal gardens, Hal took four or five mouthfuls of
the fragrant pasta Kit had carefully prepared and across
the magnificent glass table gave her a rueful smile.

'This is really good,' he commented. 'But I can't say
the same is true of my appetite since the accident. I'm
afraid I'm going to have to leave it there. This must be

a first. Anyone who knows me well would tell you that it's unheard of for me to leave anything. Usually I can eat for England.'

'Trauma can affect people in many different ways,' Kit answered thoughtfully. 'As I'm sure your sister must have told you.'

'Trust me…she *has*. Sometimes I wish she wasn't quite so *all knowing*.'

Wanting to convey her reassurance, and sensing that underneath the dry wit he was probably feeling understandably low, she didn't hesitate to smile. 'You shouldn't worry about not having much of an appetite. I'm sure it will return in a few days, when you've started to feel more comfortable about getting round on your crutches and are getting more sleep. Rest is one of the greatest healers, but in our fast-paced culture it's too often overlooked.'

Hal's golden eyes narrowed interestedly. 'You sound as if you have some strong views on the subject?'

Laying her fork and spoon down on her plate, Kit took a few moments to mull over the remark. 'Moving so fast puts a lot of strain and pressure on the body as well as on the mind.' She sighed. 'Sometimes we need to remind ourselves that we aren't machines. We're flesh and blood and bone, and an overload of stress and pressure can tip us over the edge as well as cause accidents.'

'Then I take it you definitely wouldn't approve of someone who regularly pushes their body to the max in the pursuit of being the best he can in any sport or activity he participates in?'

'I presume you're talking about yourself?' Her gaze met his arresting hazel eyes and she saw his pupils flare teasingly.

'Yes, I am,' he confirmed, smiling. 'I put my heart and soul into everything I do…and I mean *everything.*'

Kit's body tightened at his emphasis and a distinct buzz of sensual heat sizzled through her. The strong re-action took her aback and caused her to feel unsettled for a moment. Willing back her composure—because in all likelihood it was second nature for a man like Hal to tease women and get them flustered—she reached for her fork with a matter-of-fact air and curled some linguine round it. The man was on a hiding to nothing if he thought to unhinge her with sexual innuendos to inflate his ego, she thought. *He'd soon come to learn that she was immune.*

'I'm sure that's commendable,' she commented, 'but it can also be dangerous when a desire to be competi-tive becomes the driving force in everything you do. Wasn't that how you came to have your accident in the first place?'

The teasing smile completely vanished from her companion's handsome face. 'I suppose you read that in the newspapers?' Plucking his linen napkin from where he'd laid it across his lap, Hal threw it down on the table in disgust and scowled. 'Newspaper reporters aren't exactly known for telling the truth, you know.'

'Was that a fabrication, then? That you were racing a business rival on a ski slope that's considered to be one of the most extreme terrains in the mountains?'

'You know what, Kit Blessington? If you ever think about a change of career you ought to consider becom-ing a public prosecutor. You certainly don't take any prisoners.'

Directly meeting his irritated glance, Kit shrugged. 'That's where you're wrong. I would hate to be responsible for condemning anyone…whether I was paid to do it or not. And although I don't think of what I do as a career, exactly, I'm quite happy earning my living at it and endeavouring to deliver a good service.'

Hearing the heavy sigh Hal emitted following her statement, she thought she'd better rein in her propensity to call a spade a spade before she talked herself out of a job. Antagonising a man who was already struggling to come to terms with an injury that severely restricted his usual activities was really not a good idea.

'I'm sorry if I've offended you with my opinions,' she said quickly. 'I have no desire to upset you. I suppose I just get a little passionate about the things that I believe are right.'

'Everyone is entitled to their views, and being passionate isn't a crime.'

There was the briefest suggestion of a smile on his beautifully carved lips and Kit was reassured.

'In my book being passionate just means that you care,' Henry continued, 'Which is why I take the risks I do in my work and in the sports that I love. And besides, it's in the male DNA to be competitive…survival of the fittest and all that.'

Unable to curb the impulse, she leaned towards him. 'I hear what you're saying, but don't you get tired of having to conform to that ethos all the time?'

Rolling his eyes, Hal grimaced. 'Right now I don't exactly have much choice, do I?'

'I tell you what…' Rising to her feet, Kit had a sudden brainwave. 'Why don't I make us a pot of coffee and I'll cut you a slice of home-made fruitcake to go with it? I know you didn't feel much like eating your dinner, but that could be dessert.'

'We've got home-made fruitcake?' His previously glum expression was transformed by the most beguiling boyish grin she had ever seen.

Crossing her arms over her mint-green sweater, she couldn't help smiling back. 'I brought it with me from home. I made it last night. When I rang the agency to confirm that I'd got the job the manager told me that it was one of your favourites.'

'Sam probably tipped her off. She knows I've a real weakness for cake…particularly fruitcake.'

'Well, then, why don't you just sit and relax and I'll go and get you some?'

'Don't forget the coffee.'

'I won't.'

As Hal lingered over his coffee Kit disappeared into the kitchen to stack the dishwasher. With a contented sigh he stretched out his long legs on the couch and winced as familiar intermittent pain shot down his calf. For once he didn't allow it to destroy his equilibrium. In truth, he regretted not making a better effort with the aromatic pasta Kit had cooked, but he'd immensely enjoyed the fruitcake she'd made. It was probably one of the best cakes he'd ever eaten. One thing was certain: if that was an example of her attention to detail on behalf of the people she worked for then she couldn't be faulted.

Utilising the remote device by his side, Hal turned up the volume on the soothing music he was listening to. If he could just learn to curtail the impatience and restlessness that had plagued him since the accident had immobilised him then perhaps he could start to enjoy the enforced rest that he was faced with? It had literally been *years* since he'd had some proper respite. Most days he lived his life as though he were in a race to get to the finish line first.

In a bid to divert the less than comfortable realisation, he returned his thoughts to Kit. There was something about the feisty redhead's presence that was undeniably reassuring. What had helped her become so capable and pragmatic? *He was curious to know.* Maybe over the next few days he would try to draw her out and get to know her a little? The women in his life had always bemoaned the fact that Hal didn't give them enough of his time and attention—be they the girlfriends he'd had or his sister Sam—because he was inevitably obsessed with work and also the high-octane sports activities he favoured. If he made it a bit of a project to find out more about Kit's background by conversing with her and really listening to what she had to say then it might help him learn how to improve his relationships with women in the future. *At any rate, it was worth a try.* Seeing as though all his usual distractions were denied him because of his injury, why not just embrace what was available instead?

Another knifing pain shot through his leg, but it was mostly concentrated on the muscles in his knee that had been damaged. Just as he reached down to massage it the door opened and Kit returned. As if intuiting he was in some discomfort, she came straight over to him with a concerned frown.

'I think I should get you some ice for that knee. But first let me put some pillows underneath you to elevate it. If we do that every day then it will help reduce the swelling.'

'You're the boss,' Hal quipped ruefully.

'It's good to know you don't have a problem with a woman being in charge.'

'This is a one time and one time only deal. My tolerance and acceptance will only stretch so far. Once I'm back on my feet again you'd be unwise to push any advantage you'd gained while I was laid up.'

Raising her brows, Kit responded smartly, 'When you're back on your feet again you'll no longer need my services, so such a possibility won't even arise. I'll be looking after another client…hopefully one a little less egotistical than you. Now, I'll just go and get a couple of pillows to elevate that knee.'

Any response he might normally have made to such an unflattering observation worryingly deserted Hal. The idea that Kit was already eagerly contemplating a new client—one 'a little less egotistical' than he was—seriously bothered him. And neither did he welcome the sense of vulnerability it left him with. Weakness of any kind didn't sit well with him.

As she exited the room to fetch the pillows he breathed out a disgruntled sigh. But when she returned carrying them, and leaned towards him to carry out the necessary manoeuvre, he immediately noted that her smooth alabaster cheeks had a faintly scarlet tint to them. *How interesting,* he thought. Perhaps it wasn't just his egotistical nature that ruffled this coolly efficient redhead?

'Lift up,' she instructed, her bright blue eyes skimming his features with the merest brief glance.

Raising himself in order that she could slide the pillows beneath him, Hal wasn't about to let the fact go unremarked…

'You're blushing, Ms Blessington. Does it disturb

you to get this close to your client? Because if it does I don't know how you're going to manage when you help me into my bath later,' he taunted.

Carefully assisting him to lower his legs down onto the pillows, Kit met his amused glance with a similarly mocking one.

'If you think it's going to make me squirm with embarrassment seeing an injured man in his birthday suit then I hate to disappoint you, *Mr Treverne*. Trust me— I've seen it all before!'

For the second time in a few short minutes Hal found himself worryingly bereft of an apt rejoinder and he didn't like it. He didn't like it *one* bit!

CHAPTER FOUR

THE LUXURIOUS BATHROOM adjacent to Hal's equally opulent bedroom had a vast sunken bath and shower and a gleaming marble floor with a striking snakeskin finish. If Kit hadn't known it to be true already, it screamed out that its owner was undoubtedly male, seriously charismatic and frighteningly rich. And so far her new employer was proving to be the most challenging one she'd ever worked for...

Dropping down onto a seriously comfy-looking chair, Hal handed over his crutches to her without preamble. It was nearly eleven o'clock at night and Kit knew that he was still tired, still hurting, and cranky because of it. Trying not to pay too much attention to the unhappy expression on his handsome face, she stood the crutches against the wall, leant down to the bath and turned on the taps.

As the water gushed out into the tub she glanced over her shoulder and asked, 'What kind of temperature do you like?'

'What?'

He was staring at her as though in a trance. Straightening, she crossed her arms over her chest, feeling as though she were suddenly being examined under the searching glare of an intense spotlight. It was hard to string a single coherent thought together when her heart felt as though she was careening downhill at breakneck speed because it beat so fast.

'I asked what kind of temperature you wanted?'

'Hot.'

Such a simple, commonplace word shouldn't sound so…so *provocative*. But it *did*. And it didn't help her case that she remembered telling Hal that she was hardly fazed by seeing a man's naked body and had 'seen it all before'. She didn't doubt he thought she must be referring to her intimate experiences. Perhaps he thought she'd had several? The truth was she'd had just one briefly intimate liaison and that had turned out to be an unmitigated *disaster*. She'd been stupidly bluffing when she'd made her comment, so that he wouldn't think he had the upper hand. And she'd called *him* egotistical!

'Okay,' she said.

'I'll need you to help me get in the water—also to put the waterproof cast protector on.'

'Of course.'

'Then I suppose I'd better get undressed.'

Swallowing hard at the very idea of seeing this man's toned, athletic body bared for her eyes only—albeit so that he could take a bath—Kit had to dig deep to retain her composure. 'Do you need any assistance with that?' she asked.

Hal's golden eyes glimmered almost painfully.

'Not to get undressed, no. But you might as well stay in here until I'm ready to get into the bath. Think you can do that?'

'No problem.' She sensed heat flare in her cheeks even before she answered.

'I'll put a towel round me to spare your blushes,' he declared, his tone indisputably provocative. 'Even though you've assured me that you've seen it all before.'

Kit might have known he wouldn't let her forget she'd said that. 'Do you want me to put in some bath salts or foam?' she enquired.

'Some of that blue stuff on the shelf will do,' he responded blithely, as if it scarcely mattered.

The 'blue stuff' he'd indicated was a seriously high-end exclusive product that probably cost the earth, she noted, a helpless little smile curving her lips. It certainly smelt nice. While Hal lifted off his sweater and T-shirt she kept herself occupied by watching over the bath-water and regularly testing the temperature. When he indicated that he was ready she turned off the taps and swivelled to see that he had wound a slim white bath-towel round the lower half of his torso, while he supported his injured leg on a handy footstool.

But that wasn't the only thing Kit noticed. Exposed in all their glory, the sheer tantalising breadth of his shoulders and his strongly defined biceps were even more magnificent than she'd guessed they would be. But she couldn't afford to let the fact distract her...not even for a second.

'The bath is ready, so I think we'd better get the cast protector on,' she said briskly.

'Then let's do it.'

With the waterproof protector fitted over his cast, Kit made sure to support him strongly as Hal gingerly lowered himself into the fragrant bubbles. Her heart raced in concern when she felt his muscles tensing and saw him bite his lip. 'Is the water too hot?' she breathed.

As she assisted him to position his injured leg on one of the marble bath sides he surprised her with an unrestrained grin. 'It's perfect. Just the way I like it.'

'Good…that's good.'

His even white teeth flashed another smile as he reached down beneath the bubbles to produce the now sopping wet towel that he'd wound round his hips to spare Kit's blushes. He handed it to her.

'You have no idea *how* good.'

Carrying the wet towel over to one of the pair of marble sinks to wring it out, she almost had to bite back a groan. She'd never known that just the sound of a man's voice could be such a turn-on. And it didn't help her to stay as safely immune as she wanted to when the man was as physically imposing and arresting as Hal Treverne.

She was appalled at herself for even daring to fantasise about someone like him when he had a reputation for dating some of the most beautiful women in the world. She didn't delude herself that she came anywhere *near* that elite category! She reminded herself of the cast-iron rules she always worked by—to be utterly professional and impartial at all times and definitely not to get personally involved. Particularly when the client was a stunningly attractive male who wasn't averse to teasing and provoking her. The last thing she wanted to do was find herself repeating the same soul-destroying pattern as her mother had…falling for a man who could only spell disaster. She'd already been burned by the brief, ill-judged liaison she'd had with a man who had turned out to be married…

'Kit?'

'Yes?' She finished wringing out the wet towel and turned her head to acknowledge him. The steam from the hot water had created a pall of fine damp mist over his sculpted cheekbones and had made his thick dark hair curl against his neck even more rebelliously. Aside from the fact that the mere sight of him challenged her on almost every level, Kit couldn't deny the pleasure she felt because he appeared so much more relaxed than she'd witnessed seeing him before.

'Will you wash my hair for me?'

It seemed she was going to have another challenge.

Helplessly, Kit swirled her tongue over her lips, because they'd suddenly dried. Leaving the damp towel coiled in the sink, she caught a glimpse of her own flushed face and startled blue eyes in the mirror. Her fiery copper hair was once again drifting free from its topknot and the bathroom steam had misted her porcelain skin to make her resemble a girl who had just got out of her lover's bed. Her insides executed a nervous cartwheel at the thought. *Particularly as the lover she'd automatically envisaged had been Hal...*

Smoothing her moist palms down over her jeans to dry them, Kit stepped slowly towards him. He was resting his head against the marble rim of the bath and she willed him not to notice how flushed she was. She desperately needed some time to restore her equilibrium. *For goodness' sake, he's injured,* she reminded herself. *I'm here to do a job and to help aid his recuperation by providing practical help...not to act like some silly infatuated schoolgirl around him!* She'd never been able to understand grown women who acted that way. And neither would she jeopardise her job or her peace of mind by mimicking them.

'Yes,' she replied. 'Of course I'll wash your hair. Do you have any preference as to what shampoo I should use?' It hadn't escaped her attention how laden with men's grooming products his bathroom shelves were, but once again he shrugged his shoulders as if the choice hardly signified.

'I don't have a preference. All I want is for you to wash my hair and help me feel halfway human again.'

'Okay. I'll just nip into the kitchen and get a jug so I can rinse the shampoo off. Won't be a minute.'

In the kitchen Kit found a suitable jug and gulped down a glass of cool water to help steady her nerves before returning to the steamy bathroom and the prospect of washing Hal Treverne's luxuriant dark hair...

Without a doubt Kit Blessington had a *sinful* touch, Hal reflected as her long graceful fingers massaged his scalp. It made him long for her to massage the rest of his battered and bruised body As well as giving him his broken femur and damaged knee, the accident hadn't spared him all the other aches and pains commensurate with a heavy fall.

Remembering the sight of her bending over the bath to run the water earlier, he noted that her fitted corduroy jeans couldn't help but emphasise her surprisingly lush curves. She had a derrière that resembled the most perfectly ripe peach. How could a healthy male specimen *not* fantasise about kissing it and perhaps taking a little nibble? It was only natural that his red-blooded imagination should start to linger irresistibly on the idea of making love to her. After all, he was only human, and having not had a woman in his bed for at least six months because of his killing work schedule and extra-curricular sporting pursuits he found his healthy libido was seriously starting to protest at the sexual drought he'd imposed on it. *Just because he had a broken leg it didn't mean that his need and desire for sex was broken too.*

Yet it didn't sit well with Hal that the sudden heated attraction he seemed to have developed towards Kit might compromise her in any way. Somehow he intuited that she wasn't a woman to take a sexual fling lightly...particularly not one with a man who had hired her to help him as he recuperated from an accident. So, no matter how tempting the alluring redhead was, he should leave well alone...for *both* their sakes, he decided.

Instead, he would carry out the intention he'd had earlier, to get to know her a little and engage her in conversation. He would encourage her to tell him a bit about *her* life rather than just talk about himself. God knew there was enough about his career and sporting exploits in the tabloids and magazines if she had a mind to read them... And it didn't stop there. There were plenty of unwelcome salacious reports about him too... Past associations with models and actresses, for instance, were embellished and exaggerated to the hilt. For some reason the thought of Kit reading about those made him wince...

'I'll rinse off the shampoo now,' she announced cheerfully. 'Then I'll get you some warm towels to dry yourself with. You can put your bathrobe on in the meantime.'

'Thanks, but just before you dash off there's something I have to do.' Spying a tiny bubble of foam on the tip of Kit's nose, where she had unthinkingly wiped the back of her hand across her face after washing his hair, Hal couldn't help staring.

'What's that?' she wanted to know. Her lips curved in an unknowingly sweet smile.

Unable to resist, he ordered huskily, 'Come here.'

'Why? What for?'

But even as she asked the question Kit was bending down towards him, to bring her face nearer to his, and the air between them thrummed with the kind of internal turbulence that was usually felt just before a lightning strike. Even though he might be dicing with danger, Hal couldn't ignore the irresistible impulse that had been building up inside him ever since she had helped him into the bath.

'You've got some foam on your nose,' he breathed, gently obliterating the tiny soap bubble with the pad of his thumb.

As soon as he'd seen to that he curved his hand round the back of her neck and brought her face down even closer to his. Her surprised breath fanned him softly just before he helplessly touched his mouth to hers for the briefest of seconds. He'd been longing to experience the taste of her, and it was a Herculean task not to surrender completely to the idea of kissing her more passionately, because everything about Kit Blessington had started to arouse him, Hal realised. Perhaps even more than it should, because in truth she should be strictly out of bounds to him.

Their association was nothing more than a professional one. She was the woman he'd hired as a home help. *But, oh, her cherry lips were sweet…*

Reluctantly he came to his senses and hastily withdrew. But he couldn't so easily escape the desire that burned in him as brightly and hotly as a flame that would not go out...

'You—we—we shouldn't have done that!' With her cheeks flushed and her eyes bright Kit self-consciously smoothed her hand down over her hip and reached for the jug of clean water she'd left on the bath side. 'I'd better rinse off your hair and then get those warm bath-towels for you.'

After rinsing the shampoo from his hair Kit grimly adhered to her task of helping Hal get out of the bath. She was careful not to meet his eyes so he wouldn't see that she was desperately struggling to maintain her composure. There was no hiding the fact that his naked physical form had deluged her with an uncomfortably primal awareness. That brief but inflammatory kiss he'd delivered had effectively turned her previously 'safe' little world upside down, and she didn't know how she was going to right it again.

Silently helping him into his bathrobe, Kit couldn't disguise her need to escape for a while. 'Will you be okay for a couple of minutes while I fetch those towels?'

'Of course. But don't be gone too long, will you? I might start to think you're trying to pretend that chaste little kiss we just shared didn't happen.'

Forcing herself to meet the undoubtedly mocking glance on Hal's face, she lifted her chin and delivered a deliberately droll reply of her own.

'I hate to dent your ego—I really do—but I've already forgotten about it. My focus is entirely on your welfare, just as it should be. When I return, I'll stay and help you dress, if you'd like? I'm aware you've already expended quite a bit of energy today, and you need to rest that leg.'

Hal predictably scowled. 'I don't need help dressing. Just bring me the towels. After that, rather than have you stay and help me, I'd prefer it if you just went and made me a hot drink.'

'Your wish is my command.'

'I wouldn't push your luck if I were you.'

'I wouldn't dare,' Kit murmured softly, and quickly exited the room...

She came back soon afterwards with the promised towels, then disappeared again to make his drink. Hal couldn't help feeling a little sombre. He'd told her that rather than staying to help him he'd prefer her to go and make him a hot drink, but it was a *lie*. He didn't prefer that she'd done that at all. His assertion that he didn't want her help because he hated being so reliant on her, and also because everything about her was arousing him...almost to the point of *pain*.

Hefting a heavy sigh, he glared down at his inanimate broken limb with a feeling that was very close to despair. Being left with too much time on his hands in which to berate himself for creating such a horrendous situation was hardly helpful. *He hated being left alone with his thoughts*. He'd rather go sky-diving or climb a glacial mountain without a guide rope any day. At least when he was doing that there wasn't any time for painful brooding—not when his attention had to be absolutely focused on the exhilarating and dangerous task in hand if he wanted to stay alive.

Breaking his leg and being forced to take time out from his usual activities had made Hal realise just how alone and fearful of the future he'd become lately. Having woken up to the fact that he'd deluded himself for too long that money, a successful career and the extreme sports he favoured were enough to keep his loneliness and sense of emptiness at bay, he was now faced with the realisation that in truth he'd been hiding from the one thing that might help counteract that…*having a genuinely intimate and meaningful relationship with a woman.* He'd avoided the possibility like the plague thus far, due to his dread fear of commitment. *In any case, he was hardly a good bet.* Aside from his restless nature, he was far too selfish and self-obsessed, and sooner or later the woman he chose would discover that and leave…*just as his mother had left his father when Hal and Sam were small…*

Uncomfortably ill at ease with that particular train of thought, he stood up abruptly on his good leg and reached out a hand for one of the crutches Kit had left standing against the wall close to his chair. Intent on positioning the padded rest under his arm, he lost his balance. Shockingly, he pitched forward onto the marble floor. Grunting out a furious expletive, because the force of the fall had momentarily robbed him of his breath, he stayed there for several humiliating seconds before coming to his senses and shouting for Kit.

He heard her run down the parquet corridor and for a moment couldn't help envying her ability to do just that—to run freely without hindrance…

'What on earth happened?'

Dropping to her haunches beside him in concern, she laid a hand gently on his back. Hal swore he could feel the warmth of her soft skin radiate through the thick towelling robe he wore.

Turning his head towards her, he grimaced. 'What

do you think happened? That I suddenly had a sudden perverse yen to lie face-down on the marble?'

Ignoring his mocking retort, Kit suddenly saw the walking aid lying on the floor beside him and realised what had happened.

'No, but I think you must have had a perverse yen to play Superman. No one is infallible, Henry...not even you. Why didn't you call me to come and help you stand up? That's what I'm here for. Are you hurt?'

'You mean apart from my pride? No. I don't think so. Help me get to my feet, then I can check.'

Upright again, and leaning on her with his hard-muscled arm draped round her shoulders, Kit guided him back to the bathroom chair. When he was comfortably settled she dropped down to her haunches again to check his knee and the protective cast for any new signs of damage. *Thankfully she couldn't find any.* She'd had the most awful fright when she saw that he'd fallen over, and she couldn't forgive herself for allowing him to persuade her to go and make a drink rather than stay with him as she should have done. She would never make the same mistake again, she vowed.

Glancing up, she witnessed a muscle visibly flinch in the side of his lean shadowed jaw. 'Everything looks okay but that doesn't mean you haven't damaged anything,' she said. 'Can you raise your injured leg off the floor a little for me, so that I can ascertain how much movement you've got?'

He did so with a rueful smile. Nothing appeared amiss, and Kit was temporarily able to relax. Rising to her feet, she resisted the sudden shocking impulse to comb his hair back from his forehead with her fingers. For goodness' sake! He wasn't a child! *But there'd been nothing remotely maternal about her urge to touch the dark silken locks.*

All the while she'd been helping him into the bath, washing his hair, then helping him out again, her senses had been taunted and aroused by his dangerously irresistible maleness and close proximity. The scent of his cologne along with the dizzying warmth of his body, seemed still to cling to her. Her very cells felt as though they'd been imbued with his essence. Not to mention the thrill of that brief kiss they'd shared...

In a bid to ground herself, she sucked in a steadying breath. 'I saw in the diary that the nurse is calling in tomorrow. That's good. I'll feel more reassured when she checks you over.'

'Worried about me, are you, Ms Blessington?'

The teasing glimmer in his compelling golden eyes reassured her that perhaps it *had* been only his pride that had been hurt. In any case, she wouldn't let herself rest on her laurels.

'Don't take it personally. I'd be worried about anyone in my care who had fallen over—especially someone who already has a broken leg. But you can be sure that next time I won't be so quick to believe you when you tell me you can manage on your own. That was an unforgivable mistake I made. If you want that hot drink I'll help you into the kitchen so that you can sit at the table with me. Then I think you should seriously consider going to bed.'

'That would sound like a much more attractive proposition if I didn't have to go there alone.'

Hal's huskily voiced statement—its meaning all too clear—nailed Kit's feet to the floor. The shock that eddied through her was so strong it made her feel dizzy.

Over a dry mouth, she answered, 'Is that so? Look, what you do in your private life is none of my business, but I'd urge you to give your body a chance to heal a bit more before you—before you—'

'Before I attend to needs of a more…shall we say… *personal* nature?'

After holding her stunned gaze for what seemed like a heart-pounding lifetime, with a wry twist of his lips he suddenly grimaced and shook his head.

'You're right, of course. But then it seems that you always *are*, Kit. I'd like to have a talk with you about how you came to be so eminently sensible. But right now I'm too tired, so our little chat will have to wait until tomorrow.'

Her acute discomfort at his previous incendiary comment thankfully easing, Kit collected Hal's walking aid and helped him get to his feet again. Once she was satisfied that he had his balance she walked by his side out into the corridor, then accompanied him into the kitchen…

CHAPTER FIVE

IT WAS IMPOSSIBLE to drift off into a relaxed sleep after the day's events—events that had upsettingly culminated in Hal's shocking fall. Kit thanked her lucky stars that he hadn't injured himself more, but she was still anxious to have the nurse check him over when she visited tomorrow. She prayed the woman wouldn't think she hadn't done her job properly because she'd left Hal unsupervised and in doing so proved herself incompetent. The last thing Kit wanted was to have her report back to Hal's sister with the suggestion that she hire someone else. It would be the first black mark on her unblemished record with the agency if she did.

Unable to banish the worry and doubt that plagued her, she thumped the luxurious feather pillow she'd been resting her head on and turned over onto her side. Her mind raced on. More than anything else she wanted Hal Treverne to see that she was the very best at what she did, and for him to realise that she was totally dedicated to helping aid his recovery.

Is that all you want him to see? That you're competent and good at what you do?

'Oh, for goodness' sake.'

Once more Kit sat up and drove her fingers restlessly

through her hair. The provoking question her mind had mocked her with was hardly conducive to her getting much sleep at all that night if she decided to explore it, she realised. *Yet she couldn't deny that the man disturbed her.* He made her more aware of her femininity than any other man had ever done before…especially when he kissed her!

The fact that he had a broken leg and was irritable and frustrated by his resultant immobility didn't make Kit any less aware of the man's undoubted charisma and sex appeal. But then, when she recalled that Hal had told her at the interview that he might need to call on her for company at night if he couldn't sleep, her heart skipped an anxious beat. People were apt to let their guard down more during the night-time hours. What would they talk about? Kit wouldn't dream of betraying any confidences he might share, but at the same time she hoped he wouldn't expect her to reveal any of her own. She'd never been at all easy talking about her past, and whenever it arose she'd developed a strategy of automatically glossing over the details and then acting as if it was hardly of any consequence.

'The past is in the past and that's where it should stay,' she'd comment, endeavouring for a blithe, cheery tone.

Would Hal Treverne break her cover and intuit that her guard was as strong as a portcullis slamming down to keep out the enemy if he should veer into that particular territory? And would he wonder why she was so reluctant to talk about it? Only tonight he'd vowed to talk to her about what had made her 'so eminently sensible' she recalled. His resolution had made her understandably anxious at the idea of even *briefly* having to revisit the circumstances and events that had shaped her. To discuss her past with him might threaten to open a can of worms that wouldn't easily be closed… It could also undo the self-confidence she'd built up over the past few years since working for the agency. *It might even destroy it completely.*

Making an abrupt decision to deal with whatever should transpire and not allow it to make her flustered, Kit resignedly combed her fingers through her freed mane of silken copper hair once again and lay back down. Deciding to draw upon the sheer determination and pragmatism she usually utilised to get her through life's challenges, she promised herself she would have a far less troubling day tomorrow, come what may. And on that reassuring note she finally allowed her eyes to drift closed…

The surprising realisation that hit Hal on opening his eyes the next morning was that for the first time since the accident he had astonishingly experienced an unbroken night's sleep. He'd slept through the night without waking even once. Barely able to believe it, he sat upright, bemusedly scrubbed his hand round his studded jaw and then pushed back the duvet. Yes, he'd taken two strong painkillers before retiring, but they had never worked as effectively before.

Had his redheaded guardian angel put some kind of spell on him? Glancing down at his injured leg, he saw that even the swelling on his damaged knee had diminished a little. That stupid fall of his last night hadn't hurt him at all. But it *had* acted as a warning to him not to refuse Kit's help when he needed it all because he was striving to be so damn independent! From now on he would endeavour to be more sensible. His swift recovery so that he could return to his busy life *depended* on it.

Although he had a bevy of reliable people working for him, he wouldn't be happy until he was back at the helm overseeing things and feeling satisfied that everything was being done properly and to the high standards he expected.

A short while after he had washed and dressed there was a knock on the door and his intention to be sensible was immediately put to the test as Kit came in, pushing his wheelchair. This morning she was wearing mouth-wateringly fitted blue jeans that hugged her slender hips and thighs as though paying devoted homage to her arresting contours and what looked to be a large-sized man's red and white check flannel shirt, encircled by a shiny red belt that showed off her ridiculously small waist. Once again her wavy auburn hair was threatening to tumble free from the topknot that never seemed quite able to secure it.

Hal stared. He couldn't help it. A bolt of white-hot heat shot through him at the thought of taking down that fiery hair, unbuttoning the ridiculous man's shirt she wore, freeing her breasts from her bra and kissing them until his lips and body were on fire from the sea of blissful pleasure that he would no doubt be drowning in...

'Good morning.' She smiled.

Feeling somewhat dazed by his heated reaction at seeing her again, Hal continued to make a personal inventory of her assets as though noticing them for the very first time. Her eyes were as blue as the brightest delphiniums that Mother Nature could devise, and her rosy cheeks and full red lips would surely tempt even the most devout monk to rethink his vows. Kissing them would be like tasting the sweetest ripe cherries he could imagine.

'Henry…are you all right?'

The most exquisite little frown he had ever seen puckered Kit's smooth alabaster brow. She *must* have put a spell on him. He had a creative mind, but never before in his entire romantic history to date had he thought of a woman's frown as being 'exquisite'. He sat on the edge of the vast king-sized bed, with his injured leg stretched out in front of him and resting on a footstool, and right then life felt surprisingly good. If this was what this incredible woman could do for him— make him feel happy to be alive in the midst of what he had previously deemed a *disaster*—then he'd be an absolute idiot to let her go.

At last he managed to convey his pleasure at seeing her to his lips. Shaping them into a pleased smile, he said, 'I'm absolutely fine. In fact I've never felt better.'

'I take it you're being sardonic?' Again Kit frowned, but this time the gesture was undoubtedly more perturbed.

'Not at all. I slept like a baby last night. Consequently I feel on top of the world.'

'Must have been those painkillers that you took.'

'Maybe.' With his smile still intact, Hal nonchalantly shrugged his big shoulders.

With a bemused sigh Kit manoeuvred the wheelchair a little closer towards him. 'Anyway…I thought I'd wheel you into the kitchen for breakfast this morning and save the wear and tear on your legs. Especially after that fall you had last night. You can use your crutches later, after you've seen the nurse and when you've rested up a bit.'

Even though her concerned declaration made Hal feel more like an eighty-year-old than a young, fit man at the height of his powers—or at least he *had been* until his accident—he was predisposed to forgive her, because the very welcome sleep he'd enjoyed last night, along with the growing realisation that she was somehow becoming important to him, made him feel much more amiable than he'd felt in a very long while. But he couldn't resist the opportunity to gently make fun of her. 'Save the wear and tear on my legs? Who was your last client, Kit? *Methuselah*?'

'Very funny. Why don't you get into the wheelchair and we'll go and get you some breakfast before the nurse arrives?'

At the table, Kit poured him a large mug of coffee and then sat opposite him to sip the cup of tea she'd made for herself.

'I'm so relieved to hear that you slept well last night,' she told him. 'I was worried that your fall might have given you a few extra aches and pains to keep you awake.'

'Well, it didn't. Like I said, I slept like a baby. By the way, what time is the nurse due?'

'I checked in the diary and she'll be here in about an hour. That gives me plenty of time to get you your breakfast. What can I get for you?'

'A couple of slices of wholemeal toast with marmalade will suffice. I rarely have much more than that.'

'Well...' Her rosy cheeks dimpled disarmingly. 'One of these mornings I'm hoping you'll let me cook you the full English. It's one of my specialties.'

Fielding another bolt of disturbing heat, because he'd realised how more and more attractive she was becoming to him, Hal leveled her a deliberately flirtatious smile. 'How could I refuse such an irresistible invitation? You certainly know how to tempt a man when he's down, Ms Blessington…especially when he's literally been knocked off his feet.'

His companion's even white teeth worried delicately at her fulsome lower lip.

'Are you saying that you're more susceptible to temptation when you're feeling low?'

Hal responded with a short, ironic laugh. 'I hardly need a reason to be more susceptible to temptation than I am already.' His voice had turned unwittingly husky and Kit's rosy cheeks turned even rosier, he noticed.

'Well…' Seizing the chance to free herself from his undoubtedly disconcerting examination, she got hurriedly to her feet. 'I'd better get on with making you that toast.'

'Don't forget to do some for yourself.'

'All I need in the morning is a cup of tea.'

His gaze swept pointedly up and down her figure. 'You'll fade away. You're not on some ridiculous diet, I hope?'

'No, I'm not.' Her expression was painfully affronted. 'Do you think I'd be on a diet at the expense of my health? I trust I have more common sense than that. In any case I'm a high-energy person and I don't easily put on weight. The more I do, the more I just burn it off.'

'Well, don't get too skinny.' Hal grinned, absent-mindedly stirring another teaspoon of sugar into his coffee. 'I like my women to have a decent amount of flesh on their bones.'

'Well…how fortunate that I'm not one of your women, then,' Kit returned smartly, delphinium-blue eyes flashing. 'In any case, according to the press, you certainly have plenty to choose from.'

So she *had* read those tiresome reports of his so-called salacious conduct in the newspapers. It seemed he wasn't going to get off lightly in her eyes…broken leg or no broken leg. She wouldn't be in a hurry to grant him any kind of dispensation. He silently balked at the idea that what she'd read about him might have already sullied her opinion.

'It may or may not interest you to know, but I haven't had a date in over six months now—and you really should be a bit more discerning about what you read in the tabloids, Kit. Maybe it's time you changed to a better class of newspaper?'

The flush on her face was akin to the shade of fresh beetroot, and Hal instantly regretted the biting comment. But it was too late to retract it.

'You're entitled to your opinion, of course. Would you like some more coffee with your toast, Mr Treverne?'

Moving over to the shiny stainless steel toaster on the counter, Kit had obviously decided not to get into a debate about the issue, and although he secretly craved her forgiveness for being so cutting Hal was undeniably relieved. *But he still wasn't able to let her have the last word…*

'So we're back to the more formal address now, are we? I told you I'd prefer it if you didn't call me that. Anyway…'

She turned just in time to see him raise a mocking eyebrow, his gaze unwavering and direct.

'...don't you think it's rather ridiculous when you've seen me buck naked in the bath?'

'You had a towel wrapped round you, as I recall.' Kit crossed her arms over her shirt and her glance was formidably fierce.

'A ridiculously *small* towel that left very little to the imagination, I'm sure.'

'Are you forgetting that I helped you into your robe afterwards?'

'No, I hadn't forgotten. I was merely being a gentleman and not mentioning it.'

With a bemused look, Kit sighed. 'At any rate, don't you think I have anything better to do than spend my time dwelling on what you look like naked?'

'No doubt you do. But don't bruise my already fragile ego by denying me the very healthy male fantasy of you lusting after my body in your spare time.'

'Oh, for goodness' sake...you're impossible!'

'I've been called worse things in my time.'

'I think we should just call a halt to this inane conversation right now and concentrate on having our breakfast, don't you?'

Once again Hal lifted a sardonic brow. 'You just told me that you don't eat breakfast.'

With a frustrated groan, Kit pushed back the tendril of auburn hair that had drifted onto her forehead and exasperatedly rolled her eyes. 'Well, I might just be driven to it to help me keep up my strength if you persist in trying to wind me up all day!'

It was perverse, but Hal privately admitted to a strange delight in knowing he could get to her—even if her reaction wasn't the usual smitten one he'd grown used to receiving from women.

Taking a couple of satisfying sips of his coffee, he gave her a disarming grin. 'I'll do my best not to aggravate you, sweetheart, really I will. But you surely can't deny a poor invalid these only too brief opportunities to brighten up his day? That is not unless you have a heart of stone?'

'So it's a "poor invalid" you are now, is it?'

'What else could I be when I'm stuck here in this wheelchair?' Suddenly, out of the blue, his mood turning on a sixpence, Hal's frustration at his immobility got the better of him. 'Trust me, angel. If I wasn't so incapacitated by this blasted broken leg I'd be chasing you round the room until I caught you and stole a long, satisfying kiss!' The very idea at being able to carry out such a threat instantly restored his good humour. 'Although I know *one* could never possibly be enough.'

'Don't you remember you already stole one yesterday?'

'You told me you'd forgotten about that. Maybe it left more of an impression than you admitted? Perhaps I should take a chance and steal another one to remind you how good it was?'

'I don't agree. Although I won't deny you your harmless little fantasy if it helps to keep your spirits up. Anything that aids your recovery is fine by me, because once you're up and about again, and you can get back to your busy life and the no doubt infinite number of women who find you so irresistible, you'll be a lot happier and my job here will be done.'

Just before she turned away to slot some bread into the toaster Hal saw her lips wrestle with the most mad-

dening grin and he couldn't help scowling because—
unbelievably—she had bettered him by finally getting
the last word...

Having pronounced him better than she'd hoped, the
cheerful nurse from the private hospital Hal attended
departed, promising to see him again in a week's time
and instructing him to call if he needed to see her
sooner. When she'd gone he told Kit that he intended
to work in his study until lunchtime and that she could
please herself what she did until then.

Cutting him down to size with the comments she'd
made in the kitchen before the nurse arrived had made
her regret being so outspoken, because since then he'd
fallen worryingly silent and there had been no more provocative banter between them. Even though her blood
had throbbed like honey heated over a slow-burning
flame when Hal had confessed he wished he could
chase her round the room and steal another kiss...

Kit knew she shouldn't encourage any more flirtatious comments because it would only make it harder
not to see him again when her job came to an end. Besides, she knew he couldn't possibly be serious about
wanting to kiss her for a second time. She was certain
that the brief but delicious kiss he'd delivered yesterday
had only come about because the circumstances had
been so helplessly intimate. After all, you couldn't get
much more intimate than helping a man into the bath
and washing his hair, Kit reflected, her blood heating
at the memory.

Besides, according to the press, he'd dated some of
the most beautiful women in the world. There was no
way on God's good green earth that Kit could ever hope

to match up to any of them…but then nor would she want to. *If* she ever fell in love with someone it would have to be with a man who wasn't so easily seduced by the temptations of the world, or one who felt he had to keep up some kind of glossy 'action man' image to be accepted by it.

No…none of that would be necessary, because the man she settled on would soon learn that he was with a woman who truly loved him for himself…*not* for what he could achieve or provide materially. Biting her lip, because she'd been drawn into mulling over a scenario that she rarely allowed herself to dwell on, Kit started in surprise when five minutes later Hal called her into his study.

After knocking and entering the room, Kit stared wide-eyed at the proudly displayed evidence of his achievement—awards he'd received from the music industry and stunning photographs of the various sporting challenges he'd participated in round the world. The only evidence of anything more personal was a lovely silver-framed portrait of his sister Sam.

Unable to help herself, Kit twitched her lips in amusement when her glance collided with the calendar above Hal's desk. The photograph depicting the current month *was* of a generously curved, famous blonde model wearing a white bikini… Scratch that… *Nearly* wearing a white bikini. She was still smiling when her gaze returned to Hal and saw that his chameleon-gold eyes were studying her intently, as if he was wondering what she made of all the awards and pictures on show… *never mind the audacious calendar.*

'You must be very proud of all your achievements,' she commented brightly. She didn't anticipate the downturned mouth and impatient shrug he gave her in response.

'There are other things I'd like to achieve more,' he answered intriguingly.

'Like what, exactly?'

The handsome features were instantly guarded. 'It's not something I feel inclined to discuss right now, if you don't mind.'

'I don't mind at all.'

Kit genuinely meant that, but she couldn't help but be curious as to what exactly Hal Treverne wanted to achieve that was even more commendable than what he'd attained already. Was there any goal or pursuit in the privileged world he inhabited that he *hadn't* accomplished or excelled at? *It didn't seem likely.*

Lightly folding her arms over her flannel shirt, she asked, 'What did you call me in for?'

Leaning back in his leather chair, he extracted a business card from his leather wallet and handed it to her.

'I'd like you to book a table for two at this restaurant for lunch today. Tell them that I'd like one of the more private tables, with some space around it so that I can stretch out my leg.'

Briefly examining the card and recognising the name of an elite Michelin-starred restaurant that the rich and famous were known to frequent, Kit quickly scanned her memory banks for easily accessible nearby parking in the area.

As if reading her mind, Hal said, 'You don't have to worry about parking. The concierge will have a member of staff do that for us when we arrive.'

'Okay. What time should I book the table for?'

'Half past one will be fine.'

'And are you meeting your guest at the restaurant?' Her heart thudded heavily at the thought that he was probably meeting some nubile blonde who was his latest lady-friend. Kit didn't quite buy his assertion that he hadn't dated in over six months. A man like Hal Treverne wouldn't be without a woman for very long—not if his colourful reputation was anything to go by.

'What guest?' He was looking distinctly perplexed. 'It's *you* I'm going to lunch with, Kit. Isn't that obvious?'

Now her heart thudded even harder. 'But you're booking a table at one of the most fashionable eateries in town. Do I have to dress up? If I do then I can't go. My wardrobe doesn't stretch to anything remotely suitable for a restaurant like that, and I don't want to embarrass you.'

'Embarrass me? You obviously don't get out a lot do you, sweetheart?' Tunnelling his fingers through his thick mane of dark curls, Hal shook his head bemusedly. 'You don't need fashionable clothing, or indeed any adornment other than that mane of glorious fiery hair and those beautiful blue eyes of yours, to make you fit to appear in any fancy restaurant in the world. Besides, I've frequented this particular establishment more times than I care to mention, and trust me...' the sculpted lips shaped themselves into an irrepressible grin '...the owner—who happens to be a personal friend of mine—would cut off his right arm rather than risk losing my custom.'

Silently reeling from the totally unexpected effusive compliment she'd just received, and the fact that yet again he had called her sweetheart, Kit struggled for a moment to reply.

'All right, then. I'll go ahead and make the reservation.'

'Good. Now, as much as I regret bringing our little tête-à-tête' to an end, I suppose I'd better get on with some work. By the way, Mrs Baker, my cleaning lady, is due in soon. Let her in and introduce yourself, will you?'

'Of course.'

'Good.'

As he turned his attention back to the paperwork strewn untidily across his desk Kit quietly let herself out, wondering what she could do to help make her more impervious to Hal Treverne's irresistible charm and charisma if she were to continue to stay working for him.

CHAPTER SIX

IN ADMIRATION, HAL had seen Kit turn what might have been a somewhat awkward entrance into the restaurant into a flawlessly smooth operation that he could never have managed on his own. Even though he was well-known, and it had no doubt not gone unnoticed by the other notable diners that he'd been injured in a foolish skiing accident, Hal hated the idea of inviting unnecessary attention when all he wanted to do was enjoy some of the finest cuisine in the country in peace with his chosen companion.

But even when he'd happened to catch someone's inquisitive gaze Kit's gracious smile and softly spoken reassuring words at his side had helped him to brush it off and they had proceeded to their table unhindered.

Pleased that his confidence in walking with the aids was definitely improving, Hal relaxed. His spirits rose even more when he saw that it was his beautiful Titian-haired companion who was drawing most of the attentive glances that came their way—he certainly wasn't above feeling some typically masculine pride at having an attractive companion.

The interest in Kit had started with the charming French *maître d'*, who had all but gone into Gallic ecstasy at the sight of her rippling burnished hair. She wore it loose at Hal's request, because he'd wanted to see it unbound again. And it hadn't been hard to detect the curious minds of the other diners avidly whirring at their entrance into the restaurant. They must be wondering about their relationship, putting two and two together and undoubtedly making five...

But whatever people were imagining about his association with Kit Hal couldn't deny that his idea of making their relationship more intimate had been growing stronger the more time they spent together, and he longed to make it a reality.

'Can I tempt you with some wine?' he asked as Kit's extraordinary blue eyes gravely studied her copy of the leather-bound menu.

'Wine?' She blinked up at him in astonishment. 'I'm driving. Did you forget?'

Unbelievably, he *had*. He was so lost in his contemplation of her captivating features that it seemed he had forgotten how to think straight. Embarrassed heat pulsed through his bloodstream and he knew it must have invaded his face. The atypical reaction made him feel like an inexperienced schoolboy instead of a thirty-two-year-old man who had always been supremely confident around women... *It was hardly a feeling he welcomed.*

'I confess I did. It's a shame. They have some incredible wine here.' Lifting his own copy of the menu, he attempted to peruse it.

Taking him by surprise, Kit leaned across and curled her elegantly slim hand round his.

'It doesn't mean that you shouldn't have a glass if

you want one. Although I'd advise you not to overdo it since you're taking medication at the moment.'

Hal hardly registered her words because the touch of her skin against his was like receiving an electric shock that left him reeling. Now he didn't just *like* her touch, he realised…he had begun avidly to *crave* it. But as his heartbeat slowly started to return to its normal rhythm he couldn't deny that she'd pricked his pride by reminding him of his current despised condition.

'I might have known my personal guardian angel would remind me of that fact. How fortunate that you always seem to be here when I need you, Kit.'

She instantly withdrew her hand. *He might have slapped her face.*

'That's what you're paying me for, isn't it…? To be a help to you while you recuperate?' She made a show of being interested in the menu again but her gaze returned almost immediately to examine him. 'If you don't like the way I'm doing my job perhaps you'd be happier with someone else?'

'Don't do this. Not here.' Lowering his voice, Hal glanced briefly across the packed restaurant. Then, leaning towards her with a frown, he said, 'It might be interpreted that we're having a personal relationship and it's not going very well. I don't want anyone getting the wrong impression and for a story to find its way into the tabloids so they can belittle me like they usually do.'

Her alabaster complexion flushed cerise and he realised he could have chosen his words a lot more carefully.

'What do you mean by the wrong impression? I'm nobody,' Kit demanded softly. 'It's not as if I'm your wife or girlfriend. Who cares what anyone else thinks?'

'*I* do.' He swallowed hard. It was impossible to tear his gaze away because he was mortified to think that he'd insulted her...*hurt* her, even. If he had, then he had a profound desire to make things right again. 'And I didn't mean to imply that it bothers me if people think our relationship is personal. Did you think it would? You sell yourself short if you do. You're a very beautiful woman, Kit, and it wouldn't be beyond anyone's understanding if I was attracted to you.'

'Now it's *my* turn to ask you not to do this. I'd prefer it if we both remembered why I'm here and didn't lose sight of that in some pointless, ridiculous fantasy.'

Self-consciously she'd lowered her voice, but the pink flush on her cheeks rendered her so irresistibly pretty that Hal didn't think twice about reaching out his hand to gently stroke his fingertips across her cheek.

Kit bit down on her lip as though pained. 'Don't. The waiter's coming towards us and we haven't even discussed what we're going to eat yet.'

'I heartily recommend the herb-crusted lamb. Trust me—what they do with it is close to *orgasmic*.' Grinning, Hal kissed his fingers with a deliberately theatrical flourish.

Kit had just about recovered her composure in time, he saw, as the waiter appeared to ask smilingly if they'd made their selection. Giving Hal the barest warning glance, she unhesitatingly went for the lamb. Despite the warning, he couldn't resist giving her a teasing wink of acknowledgment that she'd taken him at his word and succumbed to his enthusiastic recommendation without a murmur. He took it as a good sign that she trusted him.

'Well, well, well! I see the walking wounded has returned to the land of the living, looking as disgustingly handsome and fit as ever…despite the broken leg!'

Hal was seriously starting to relax and enjoy Kit's company, as well as his indisputably delicious meal, when a familiar male voice sent a disagreeable chill down his back. Looking up, he came face to face with the insincere smile of his ex-business partner Simon Rigden.

Simon was wearing his trademark designer suit, and his mid-brown hair was slicked back and as perfectly styled as always. But his over-familiar air and polished appearance weren't about to make Hal feel remotely friendly or predisposed to let bygones be bygones. The man was a wily snake and he'd be a fool to forget that for a second time. The pity was that he hadn't recognised it as being the case when they'd first met and he had stupidly made him his partner…

Ignoring the slightly pudgy hand held out before him in greeting, he took his time in touching his linen napkin to his lips, then emitted a weary sigh. 'If your aim was to ruin my day by appearing like this then you're wasting your time, Simon. That skiing accident on the Aspen slopes confirmed the realisation I already had about you…of what a conniving, merciless little weasel you are.'

Glancing across the restaurant, Hal saw a couple of similarly dressed businessmen he didn't know from Adam raise their glasses to him in a presumptuous gesture of acknowledgement. Clearly his one-time friend and business partner had company—and perhaps not so *savoury* company.

'Why don't you just slink back to what I'm sure are your equally disagreeable companions and endeavour to ruin their day instead? I have every confidence you'll more than succeed.'

Beneath the tan that he liked to keep topped up with frequent trips to the Caribbean and other fashionable hot spots round the world, Simon visibly flushed. But then exerting a little sweat and doing an honest day's work had never been one of his biggest priorities, Hal recalled. It was one of the reasons he had paid him off— in hindsight far too generously—and brought their partnership to an end. In another era Simon Rigden would have been known as being a reprehensible *louche,* he was certain.

'You're obviously feeling bitter because I won our little bet that I was a better skier than you and that I could beat you on what's known to be one of the most challenging slopes in the world,' Simon accused him mockingly. 'You feel humiliated that you crashed into that snowbank in front of several of your cronies. Everyone knows how much you hate to lose, but you weren't exactly "Lucky Henry" that day—were you, Hal?'

'You'd better leave before I signal the *maître d'* and have you thrown out for being a nuisance.'

'And risk having your reckless reputation highlighted once again in the tabloids? Although I'll concede this restaurant *does* make an admirable effort to keep out the riff-raff, one or two hacks always manage to sneak under the radar. See any faces you don't recognise?'

Hal bristled. 'Why don't you just get out of *my* face and leave me and my companion to enjoy our lunch in peace?'

The other man's gaze swung interestedly across the table to Kit.

'And who might *you* be, sweetheart? I must say I'm

surprised. I thought our friend's preference was for voluptuous blondes—not dainty little redheads who look like they come straight out of the Renaissance. But I suppose you must possess one or two sexy little tricks to keep him keen. You'll certainly need to invent a few more of those if you're going to keep him happy whilst he's immobile. I hear it was a particularly bad break, and my guess is his recuperation is going to be a long one. But if his interest starts to wane at any time, sweetheart, you should give me a call.'

His pudgy hand dived into his wallet to extract a business card. He threw it down in front of Kit in a gesture clearly meant to insult. 'I've had my surfeit of blondes lately, and I must admit, I could use a change.'

The look on Hal's face would have put the fear of God into a man with any modicum of sensitivity.

'Carry on in that vein, Rigden,' he warned, 'and I swear you'll live to regret it. Now, get out of my sight! You're not fit to even *look* at her. In fact you'd better get out of here quick—before I call the police.'

'It's all right, Henry. I can deal with this.' Calmly taking a sip of her orange juice, with both men staring at her in mute fascination, Kit followed up this remark with another confident assertion. 'I'd rather take my chances in a pool of piranhas than waste even a second of my time on an unsavoury character like you, Mr… er…?' Coolly she picked up the business card that had been so insultingly flung down in front of her and read the name on it out loud. *'Mr Simon Rigden.'* Pinning him with a direct and frosty glare, she finished, 'You can be sure I'll remember that, if I'm ever interviewed as a witness when Mr Treverne takes you to court on a charge of harassment. One thing's for sure—it won't enhance your reputation.'

'*Touché*,' Hal murmured beneath his breath.

'You little—' Flushing, the businessman abruptly turned on his heel and promptly left the restaurant, not even troubling to return to his companions and explain the reason he was leaving.

Given the looks of resignation on their faces, Hal deduced they weren't at all surprised by his sudden exit. Some people just had a knack for self-sabotage...

Immediately returning his gaze to the much more pleasing sight of his Titian-haired companion, he asked, 'What made you do that?'

'You mean cut him down to size and stand up for myself?'

'Yes.'

Kit's blue eyes flashed. 'Let's just say I've had plenty of experience in dealing with men like him. My mother brought men like Simon Rigden home with monotonous and painful regularity in her search for the man of her dreams. Needless to say it was a fruitless and soul-destroying exercise. Unfailingly, her dreams turned into a nightmare. She wasn't the best judge of men. And when each of those men took what they wanted and then abandoned her—which they did, without exception—I was the one left to pick up the pieces and try and convince her that what didn't kill her would make her stronger. Except that it never did...' Her gaze looked far away for a moment. 'Make her stronger, I mean...'

'That must have left some scars on you,' Hal remarked, expressing the compassion he was feeling that she'd endured such a horrendous experience. It explained a lot about why she was so guarded and self-contained, so determined to protect herself from similar predators.

Grimacing, Kit gave a brief shake of her head. Her blue eyes were like the most intense moonlit stars they were so bright.

'Scars heal…but unfortunately memories don't. But you were right…that Rigden chap really *is* a weasel. What decent, right-minded man would mock a friend because he had lost a bet and suffered serious injury? It's clear he doesn't have any principles. It's none of my business, and I don't mean to be presumptuous, but I'd steer clear of him in the future, if I were you.'

'Trust me. I *will*. I only wish I'd known the low-life was going to be dining here today—I would have suggested we went somewhere else. He keeps trying to rile me because he's still mad that I broke off our partnership.'

'So *he's* your ex-business partner? If you don't mind my asking, what on earth made you go into business with someone like him?'

'Ever heard the saying that a salesman can always be sold to?' Shrugging his shoulders, Hal was still pained to admit he'd been so gullible. 'I was in my early twenties when he approached me, having heard about the success I'd been having, and I was eager to prove to my father that I could do even better. So when Simon offered me what sounded like a good deal at the time I suppose I let down my usual guard and fell for his convincing spiel. He was an experienced businessman in the industry that interested me the most, and his record of success was impressive.'

He gave a wry grimace.

'Anyway, getting back to the skiing incident, when I saw him on the slopes at Aspen the only reason I agreed to his stupid bet was because I was certain I could beat him. I'd never lost a similar challenge before. But the truth is I was an egotistical idiot and I paid the price. I should have just walked away. But I want to sincerely apologise for Rigden's insulting you, Kit. If I were back on my feet *he* would have been the one who was immobilised.'

The comment clearly perturbed her.

'I can understand the impulse, but I abhor violence. It doesn't solve anything in my view. Doesn't the fact that there are so many wars in the world tell you that? It would be much better to talk things out or simply just ignore him. That would wound him more.'

An amused quirk lifted a corner of his lips. 'Well, the fact that you made it clear you weren't interested and then warned him what might happen if he continued to make a nuisance of himself was more than enough to see him off. You were quite formidable in your defence of me, Kit. I'm seriously impressed. The only other person who would have been quite so protective is my sister Sam.'

Giving him a captivating smile, Kit picked up the pristine silver cutlery she had laid at the side of her dinner plate 'I'll take that as a compliment. But now I think we should finish eating our meal before it gets cold, don't you?'

'I can always get the waiter to bring us fresh food if need be.'

'And waste all that money you're paying for what we've got already? No chance!'

Kit was deeply reflective on their return to the apartment. The appearance of Simon Rigden at the restaurant had given her a graphic insight into Hal's regret about going into partnership with such a man. *'A salesman can always be sold to,'* he'd said drolly. One thing was certain: she was sure he'd never be sold to by such a merciless shark again.

Walking beside him over to the couch, where he carefully lowered himself onto the firm leather seats and handed her his walking aids, Kit noticed that he looked particularly tired—as if the outing had been more of a strain than he wanted to let on. Not only had it been his first visit to a restaurant since his accident but, along with negotiating the challenge of appearing in public again when he wasn't as fit as he wanted to be, he had been confronted by the one person who was *guaranteed* to raise his stress levels... Kit hoped it wouldn't set his recovery back in any way.

Intermingled with those thoughts was the memory of telling Hal about her mother and her history of failed relationships due to her poor choice of men. Would she have revealed something so personal if Simon Rigden hadn't presented himself at their table to mock him?

'I'm going to relax for a while. Why don't you take the opportunity to do the same?'

Hal broke into her reverie with a beguiling smile. Was the man aware that if that smile were flashed up on a cinema screen it would have every woman and girl in the vicinity aching with longing for an opportunity to be intimately acquainted with him? Her body warmed helplessly. For Kit it was a new experience to be so acutely aware of a man...to the point where almost every other thought in her head evaporated when he directed that chameleon golden-eyed glance at her.

'Later on this evening I thought we could watch a

couple of movies together and afterwards have a talk about them?'

He settled back against the plumped-up cushions on the couch with his hands behind his head, which had the disconcerting result of drawing her gaze to the impressive muscular chest so lovingly hugged by his black cashmere sweater.

Her mouth nervously dried as he added, 'Are you up for that? And don't you dare tell me it's what I'm paying you for.'

'I'd love to do that…watch a couple of movies with you, I mean. But I think that I'll pass on your suggestion to relax. I know that Mrs Baker has been in today to clean the house, but I'd like to check if there's anything else that needs doing and if we need any supplies from the supermarket. If you're resting, it would be a good opportunity. I know you probably won't like me for saying it, but you're not paying me to be idle. Besides, I like to keep busy and do what I can to make things a little easier for my clients. Talking of which…' Kit couldn't resist smiling '…I'd like to ice that leg for you at some point and check that everything's okay.'

'Everything's fine.' Hal moved his hands from behind his head to drive his fingers a tad irritably through his dark hair. 'I'd tell you if it wasn't…*Nurse* Blessington.'

Kit feigned a disapproving look. 'I don't profess to be a nurse, but I know what has to be done and how to do it, so I don't mind if you think I'm a little bossy. Anyway, you should rest now. Just behave yourself while I'm gone,' she chided, 'and don't do anything you shouldn't.'

'Really?' he mocked. The devastating glint in his eye made her legs turn to mush. 'Like what, for instance?'

Flustered, she hurried across to the door and opened it. 'Oh, I don't know… Abseiling out of the window, perhaps? One thing's for sure: if there's any mischief to be found you're just the man to find it…intrepid thrill-seeker that you are!'

His delighted laughter followed her all the way down the hall and into the kitchen…

CHAPTER SEVEN

AT HAL'S INVITATION, Kit sat next to him on the couch as they watched the first film, making sure to leave a decent amount of space between them. But he had dimmed the lights, and even though the film's story was engrossing she couldn't relax because of her heightened awareness of everything about him.

Not that he had to rely on anything external to enhance his undoubted appeal, but did he *have* to wear such a provocatively arresting aftershave? The scent was seriously taunting her and after having experienced his kiss in the bathroom—albeit a too brief one—she could hardly think about much else other than sex! The thrill of his unexpected caress had seriously excited her, and it didn't help that she hadn't known a man's touch since the only other man she had gone to bed with had turned out to be a liar and a cheat.

The celibacy she'd imposed on herself since that episode had never backfired on her in such a disturbing and inconvenient way before. It surely wasn't the brightest idea she'd ever had to lust after her boss, even though Hal Treverne was pretty impossible to resist!

Clearing her throat, she absently curled a long strand of her burnished copper hair round her finger.

'Are you okay?'

Turning her head at the question, Kit curved her lips in an automatic smile. 'Yes, I'm fine.'

Her quick-fire reply was hasty and unsure, and the smile that accompanied it was by no means meant to be invitational or provocative, but her companion's arresting golden eyes darkened visibly in response. He also shifted in his seat, as though suddenly uncomfortable with his position. One thing was immediately clear. *He was in no hurry to get back to the film.*

'Is it me or has it got seriously hot in here?' he commented.

Over the slow and heavy thud of her heartbeat Kit tried her best to think straight. 'It *is* quite warm,' she agreed. 'Perhaps I should turn the heating down a little?'

'It won't make any difference.'

Her companion's lips shaped a compellingly wry grin that displayed his perfectly even white teeth and once again made Kit think he ought to be in the movies. But right then, in this dimly lit state-of-the-art modern living room, she was very glad that he wasn't. She had no desire to share him with anyone…let alone the whole world.

'Well, then, I suppose we'd better just watch the movie.'

Glancing away, she attempted to focus on the large screen facing her instead of on Hal, in a bid to not to be so distracted by him. But he was right. It *was* hot in here—and it wasn't just down to the very efficient heating system.

'Kit?'

'Yes?'

'Why don't you move a little nearer? It's a big couch and it feels like you're miles away.'

'Why do you need me to move nearer? Are you in pain? Shall I get your medication?'

In answer his golden eyes transmitted the kind of simmering heat reserved for burning embers, and the raw, impassioned hunger Kit saw reflected there was impossible to ignore. Her slender thighs, clad in black leggings beneath a matching roomy sweater, clenched defensively together. But in truth she knew she was on a hiding to nothing. A shiver convulsed her slender frame. If she hoped to be able to ride out the merciless electric storm confronting her, then it was already clear she was odds-on to lose.

'I'm not in pain, but if I was the only thing that would help ease it is *you*, Kit.'

Her eyes widening, she replied tremulously, 'Don't say that—at least not in that way. You hired me to work for you. Nothing else. I would never jeopardise my job by—by...' Embarrassingly, she ran out of the ability to finish her sentence.

Lifting a wry eyebrow, Hal sighed. It didn't help Kit's case that the gesture made him look irresistibly endearing...almost boyish.

'What you've said is true,' he said. 'But in the past couple of days I've developed feelings for you that go beyond just wanting you to work for me and they won't go away. I may have a broken leg, but that doesn't stop me from having the same needs as any other able-bodied red-blooded man.'

Curling her hair behind her ear, Kit knew it was a delaying tactic, but still she asked softly, 'Exactly what kind of needs are we talking about?'

'Scoot up next to me and I'll tell you. Better still, I'll demonstrate.'

'No.'

'Come on. I dare you. I want to try an experiment.'

She wanted to say something…*anything*. But forming words seemed impossible when her mouth had suddenly gone dry as sand and her tongue didn't respond in tandem with her brain. Hal Treverne had put her in a dizzying spin and it wasn't a state she was familiar with. She'd frequently anguished about her mother not having any common sense when it came to men, but where was hers now, when she needed it? Perhaps more than she'd ever needed it before?

Moistening her suddenly dry lips with her tongue, she made herself ask, 'What kind of experiment are you talking about?'

Hal's glance was unwaveringly direct.

'I want to kiss you, Katherine with a K. *Properly* this time. And I want you to kiss me back. If neither of us enjoy the experience then there's no harm done. We'll simply carry on as before. I want to reassure you that there's no danger of your job being jeopardised. I give you my word on that. You'll stay until our arrangement naturally comes to an end—when I'm completely mobile again. Agreed?'

The silence that followed this inflammatory statement was deafening.

Hal was gesturing for Kit to move closer, and when she gazed back into his eyes the sight was akin to gazing into a mirage of mesmerising crystal waters after she'd stumbled through a burning hot desert without hope of ever having a drink again.

How could she possibly ignore the chance that her

mirage might turn out to be a genuine vision and that it would save her life if she drank from it?

She reached out her hand to slide it over Hal's. His skin was silkily smooth and warm, as it always was. But this time she had permission to actively *enjoy* the experience—not just tend to his practical needs as she normally did.

With a heated, lazy smile he tugged her hand to bring her close into his side. Before Kit even had time to gasp he'd pushed aside the heavy fall of her hair and laid his palm against her nape. *Everything tingled.* Then he hungrily drew her head towards his. Any opportunity or desire for further conversation disappeared abruptly the instant he touched his lips to hers. The texture of them was like the most seductive velvet and they tasted like nectar.

When Hal's tongue dived into her mouth and duelled with hers pleasure such as she'd never known before suffused her—a delight so intensely hot and sensual that it was like a tropical storm descending out of a summer sky. Its sudden surprising appearance gave her no chance to find shelter. The only thing she could do was surrender, give herself up to its fierce elemental nature with no thought or concern of where the experience might lead her. *Was she brave enough to do that?* The more Hal kissed her, the more she wanted to fly into the face of her fear and challenge it.

Then he cupped her breast through her sweater, evoking a ravenous need in her blood that made her feel as if she was losing her mind with no hope of ever thinking straight again…like someone standing too close to a crumbling cliff-edge and dangerously being compelled to jump. Why did she suddenly feel that she would willingly sacrifice her dream of a safe place, a bolthole she could call her own, to travel into the unknown with him?

With a helpless whimper Kit anchored her hands round Hal's iron-hard biceps, her fingers gripping hard, wishing she had the courage to lift up his sweater so that she might touch him more intimately and press her body into his.

Hal's head and heart were reeling. He knew what it was like occasionally to drink more than one generous glass of intoxicating red wine at dinner, to have his head spin and his limbs turn to water, but never before had he experienced sensations as dizzyingly seductive and addictive as this! Kit's ravishing mouth and silken tongue were so sinfully delicious that he knew he could willingly be a slave to her kisses for a very long time indeed, whilst her *body...* Her body and her scent aroused him more than any other woman's had ever aroused him before.

The need to take this so-called experiment further was growing more and more demanding. He was so hot and hard that he had to tear his lips away from Kit's to take a steadying breath and try to calm his escalating need. As he moved his hands up to cup her face Hal's breath felt no less steady as he stared hungrily down into the incandescent blue eyes that gazed back at him. They looked as stunned and as intoxicated as he was.

'I want to take you to bed, Kit.' With a wry smile he added, 'Let me rephrase that. I *need* to take you to bed. Our little experiment was more...much more success-ful than I'd hoped it would be.'

To his surprise, Kit responded with a troubled sigh.

'We can't always have what we want or—or need,

Hal…and perhaps giving in to our base desires isn't the best thing to do for either of us. I won't deny that I find you attractive, but if you seriously think about this you'll know it isn't a good idea to take things any further. We've already crossed a boundary I vowed never to cross with a client. You've been hurt in an accident and forced to take a much slower pace than you're used to while you recuperate, and I've been hired to help you.'

Reaching up, she gently freed his hands from round her face and sat back against the couch's sumptuous leather upholstery, a shapely leg tucked beneath her.

'It's understandable that you're feeling frustrated and lonely, but I'm not the cure for either of those states— even though you might think I am.' Visibly blushing she added, 'Your kiss was lovely, and so are you. But I'd rather you remembered me as a reliable and competent help when you most needed it than some convenient woman you took to bed simply because you were feeling horny.'

As shocked surprise eddied through him Hal hardly knew what to say. Kit had told him he was 'lovely' and yet she clearly didn't trust his motives. A thought that might explain why she was so uneasy about taking things further suddenly struck him.

'You think I'm just the same as one of those low-lifes who used your mother then abandoned her. That's it, isn't it?' He cursed out loud because he knew it was true.

'No. Of course I don't think that!' Her mouth shaping a painful grimace, Kit folded her arms over her chest and dipped her head. The sudden movement caused her glorious hair to tumble forward onto her shoulders in a riot of silken burnished waves.

Hal sucked in a breath. The sight was so beautiful…

'I know you're not like them,' she declared. 'But I have to protect myself. There's no one else looking out for me but *me*. I've got a reputation for being competent and reliable at the agency and I need a good reference when I leave you if I'm to get another job as good as this. Don't you understand?'

Starting to feel a little calmer, Hal was thoughtful. 'I've given you my word that you won't lose this job, and if you see it through to the end of course I'll give you a good reference…the *best*. I want to reassure you about that. But I can't pretend it's going to make me want you any less, Kit, or that you'll stop thinking about that kiss we just shared.'

'Okay.' She smiled, but it was plain to see her expression was still guarded. 'I'm flattered that you want me—I really am. I know that you could probably just pick up the phone and have any woman that you want. And I'm sorry if I offended you with what I said about you being—'

'Horny?' he finished helpfully.

'Sometimes I'm a little too quick to speak my mind.'

'Do you think I don't know that by now?'

'Anyway…' Uncurling her leg from beneath her, Kit ran her hand over her hair, as if to tidy it, then positioned herself more comfortably against the cushions. 'Why don't we just finish watching the film? I was really starting to enjoy it.'

Hal's strongly defined jaw clenched ruefully. 'There's something else I'd much rather do, but seeing as I'm a gentleman this time I'll give you the prerogative of choosing the evening's entertainment. Next time it will be *my* turn.'

'If you're no longer so keen on watching the film perhaps you might like a game of chess instead?' The look she gave him was innocence personified. 'But if we play I warn you I'm no push-over. I don't take any prisoners. I play to win!'

His blood heated again, painfully reminding him of what he'd given up in deference to reassuring Kit that he was no ruthless playboy who believed it was his God-given right to take what he wanted. Lowering his voice, he remarked, 'So do I, sweetheart. I don't see the point of playing a game if I don't come out on top. After all, being on top is what I do best.'

Hal couldn't deny the sense of satisfaction that pulsed through him when her pretty cheeks turned re-vealingly pink…

Over the next few days Hal played the part of the gen-tleman he professed to be to the max. Gone was the teasing, provocative banter that Kit had come to love and expect, that suggested he was more bad boy than gentleman. A much more sedate, thoughtful man took his place. In fact he'd become so quiet that she fretted his leg wasn't healing as well as it should be and that it was seriously bothering him. When she checked with him he always immediately denied anything was amiss and returned to the book he was reading, or to his study to work, with an expression that told her friendly con-versation was off the agenda and he would prefer not to be disturbed.

There was no more talk of him choosing their nightly entertainment either. Kit couldn't deny she wasn't upset about that. *Her nightly dreams were all about Hal.* So much so that she sometimes woke up in a sweat, with her heart racing dizzyingly. Her visions of him and her together were so real that she was crushed when she woke up and realised they were just nocturnal fantasies. She might get to the end of this job with her self-enforced celibacy intact, but that didn't mean she would be remotely happy about it—not when her heart already ached at the mere idea of parting from Hal for good.

When the nurse paid her next visit to examine his injured leg and with a cheerful smile declared it to be 'healing nicely', adding that it was just a matter of time before he would return to full strength, to Kit's mind Hal didn't seem entirely convinced. When the nurse went on to say that he should take advantage of some regular physiotherapy before seeing his consultant again, and that Kit should make sure to keep up the RICE treatment, he gave a brief nod of agreement, thanked her for the advice and saw her to the door in his wheelchair.

He still wasn't in the mood for conversation, it seemed...

The night after the nurse's visit Kit lay in bed, staring up at the shadowed ceiling in her bedroom for what seemed like hours, because she'd been alternately teased and tormented by the memory of Hal's taste in her mouth and his hands on her body and as a result sleep evaded her. But eventually she fell into a fitful doze.

A loud shout woke her up. Immediately responding, she hurriedly pushed aside the sheets and counterpane and scrambled to her feet. Without even pausing to grab the striped cotton robe she'd draped over the back of a slipper chair, she ran outside into the corridor and pushed opened Hal's bedroom door.

The soft light in the hallway more than adequately

illuminated the room. Wearing navy silk boxers, Hal was positioned half in and half out of the voluminous bed, gripping onto the oyster-coloured silk sheets for grim death as his cast-covered leg precariously slid towards the floor.

Kit grabbed hold of him to prevent him from falling just in the nick of time. His broad, hard-muscled back was slippery with sweat and it was no easy feat to lift and push his heavy masculine frame safely back onto the bed, because he was clearly still half asleep and in no position to help her. Thankfully her reaction had been lightning-quick and had saved the day. A heavy fall onto that broken bone of his would have set him back several months at least, she was sure.

As he fell back against the pillows and stared dazedly up at her she gently ran her hand over his forehead, pushing back the rebellious dark curls that brushed against it.

'Are you okay? You gave me an almighty shock when I heard you cry out like that.'

'I'm fine.' Although Hal's smile was definitely on the drowsy side, his mercurial hazel eyes still managed a mischievous twinkle. 'Thanks to you. You really are my guardian angel, aren't you, Kit? Quite apt that you should rescue me when I was dreaming that you were in my arms.'

Still leaning over him, Kit turned as still as a statue. The remark had sent her own temperature skyrocketing and she was suddenly aware that the only thing separating them was the flimsy chemise she wore, which she'd impulsively bought from a vintage market stall in the Portobello Road. In truth, it was totally impractical, but she loved it. With its spaghetti shoulder straps, and a scooped neckline that just about covered her breasts, it was probably the most feminine item of clothing she possessed. And beneath the hyacinth-coloured material, apart from her panties, she was as bare as the day she was born.

'It must have been quite a dream if it nearly made you fall out of bed,' she replied huskily.

'It was. If it was graded by a panel of judges, the medal it would win would definitely be gold.'

'What were you doing…? *Wrestling* with me?'

Hal's chameleon golden-eyed gaze was no longer drowsy but wide and alert. In a flash his hands moved to fasten themselves round Kit's slender-boned wrists and her heart thudded so hard in surprise that the desire to be free again didn't even cross her mind.

'I was passionately making love to you, and I guess we both got a little carried away.' He smiled teasingly.

Riveted, Kit stared. 'Well…'

His indisputably aroused gaze was roaming over the curves of her creamy breasts in the body-skimming nightwear and she was only too aware that his own magnificent bare chest was mere tantalising inches away from hers,

'I'd advise you to try and have less, shall we say… *energetic* dreams in future. Especially when they could potentially endanger your health.'

'What if I think the dream was worth the potential danger? I'm not a man who plays safe. I like to take risks, remember?'

His well-shaped lips formed a slow, seductive smile and the heat from his body mingled with his arresting cologne and made Kit feel seriously weak. As she stared back into his chiselled handsome face any desire to do the sensible thing and free herself completely deserted her.

'I know,' she answered softly. 'It's what you're famous for, isn't it? Taking risks, I mean. But seriously, Hal, I've been so worried. You've hardly spoken a word to me over the past few days. Is there something wrong that you're not telling me about?'

'No, sweetheart. There's nothing bothering me other than frustration at so stupidly injuring myself and not being able to take control of things as I usually do.'

Kit breathed out a relieved sigh. 'Is that all? Don't you know those feelings aren't a permanent state? Bones heal and your frustration will fade just as soon as you're up and about again, like you were before. In no time at all this setback will be nothing but a distant memory. I promise.'

'Hmm, you're probably right. But, talking of another kind of frustration, did I tell you how sexy I think that little number you're *almost* wearing is?' he murmured, deftly pushing aside the inadequate spaghetti straps so that they slid down over her slim arms and caused the bodice of her chemise to reveal even more of her. 'Do you have *any* idea how beautiful you are?' he husked, his darkened gaze avidly roaming her now almost completely exposed bare breasts.

The cool night air that drifted in from the partially opened window skimmed her nipples and hardened them to prickling, tight steel buds. But Kit knew in truth it wasn't anything external that made her react physically like that. It was her desire and hunger for Hal, and its force was like a torrid drowning wave she couldn't do anything but surrender to.

'I want to make love to you, Kit. Will you let me?'

'What about—what about your injured leg? I don't want to risk hurting you.'

For answer he put his fingers across her lips to quieten her. 'I'm sure that between us we can find a position where there'll be no risk to my leg. Let's work it out, shall we? It will be an adventure.' His compelling eyes darkened even more. 'Are you in the mood for an adventure, Kit? I'm hoping that the answer is yes.'

Before she could utter a word Hal's hands were driving through her hair, pulling her down on top of him and searing her lips with urgent scalding kisses that made her gasp and moan for more. She was all but on fire for him. The temperature of her blood surely couldn't be far from reaching boiling point, and she didn't resist when he guided her carefully over him so that she was sitting astride his toned, fit body.

As she settled herself straight away Kit became intimately aware of the steely hardness beneath the sensuous silk of his shorts, but she didn't encourage or succumb to inviting his possession straight away, no matter how eager she felt. She didn't just want to *receive* pleasure; she wanted to *give* it too. Sitting back for a moment to observe him, she knew her appreciative smile couldn't help but be seductive. Henry Treverne was one of the most beautiful men she had ever seen, and she wanted to make the most of her time with him—however long or short that might turn out to be.

With a soft sigh Kit bent her head again. But instead of meeting his lips she slowly licked down his chest, from his flat male nipples to the column of dark silky hair that disappeared into his boxers.

CHAPTER EIGHT

'Do YOU KNOW what you're doing to me, woman?' Hal growled as Kit teased and taunted him by swirling her indescribably silky tongue round his nipples, then slowly and deliberately sweeping it down to his navel.

Her blue eyes twinkling, she lifted her head and gave him the most maddeningly innocent smile. 'I like to think I'm doing something nice. Don't you like it?'

'Of course I like it! But I want you to come back up here so that I can do the same to you.'

'All right, then. Your wish is my command.'

'Don't say that or you may find I have a veritable list of wishes that will keep you here for the rest of the night and most of tomorrow too. What do you think about that?'

'I'm beginning to see that you have a very creative mind, Mr Treverne. But if I don't agree with any of your requests I'll simply make myself scarce and go back to bed.'

She made this declaration as she rose to face him, and it took every ounce of will Hal possessed to suppress a heartfelt groan at the arresting sight she made. With her fiery copper hair tumbling onto her bared rosy-tipped breasts Kit reminded him of the eponymous

Moll Flanders from the classic Defoe novel. As well as being bewitchingly beautiful, everything about her was irresistibly sexy. He'd defy any red-blooded male not to want to possess her.

Reaching out his hands to cup her breasts, he luxuriated in the soft weight and satiny feel of them as he stroked and teased the rigid nipples. Then, unable to deny his growing need to know her more intimately, he captured one of them between his lips and suckled and laved until she cried out and her head fell forward onto his chest. It was apparent that his lover had experienced a spontaneous release, and Hal couldn't deny the sense of privilege that made him feel…that he could do that for her.

He was gratified that she was so exquisitely sensitive. *Had she been as sensitive as this with any other of the lovers she'd had in the past?* The thought struck a discordant jealous note that briefly unsettled him. But he refused to let it taint his pleasure for long.

With a smile, he tenderly smoothed his hand down over the tumbling red-gold curls that nestled just beneath his chin. When Kit tipped up her head to glance at him her cheeks had the bloom of a ripe red apple and her blue-eyed glance appeared surprisingly guilty.

'I—I don't know what to say…'

'Did you enjoy it?'

She blushed again. 'Yes, I did.'

'Well, there's no need to feel guilty if you enjoyed it, is there? I don't want either of us to have any regrets about being together like this. In truth, the attraction we feel for each other has been building up for a while—you know that. And I don't want you to feel guilty just because you experienced pleasure. Trust me, there's going to be plenty more of that coming your way. We haven't finished yet. Not by a long chalk. But first...' he jerked his head towards the satinwood cabinet next to the bed '...I think I'm going to need to use some protection—that's unless you're already covered?'

Sliding carefully to the side of the bed, Kit sat up, her hands immediately adjusting the thin straps of her chemise back over her shoulders and tugging the bodice up higher to cover her breasts.

'I'm not on the pill, if that's what you mean. There's been no need. Just in case you want to know, I haven't had sex in a very long time.'

Hal's heart missed a beat. 'How long?'

She frowned. 'The last time...and the *first* time, in fact—was when I was seduced by a man who turned out to be married. It only happened the once.' Her shoulders lifted in a pained shrug. 'It was a stupid mistake that I deeply regret. I'm just thankful that I had the common sense to make sure he used protection.'

For a moment Hal didn't know what to say. When he finally managed to make sense of his feelings, he asked, 'And when did this happen?'

'I'd just turned twenty-one and had gone to a club with some friends. That's where I met him. Anyway, like I said, it was a long time ago.'

'And since then you've really never been with anyone else?'

'No.'

'Why not?'

'Do you really need to ask? Don't you think I'd be wary of men after what happened? Being deceived like that made me feel dirty. I never want to experience such a feeling again, and it made me more aware than ever that relationships shouldn't be a priority—that I should just focus on trying to make a better life for myself. That was and still *is* my main priority. Shall I get the protection for you?'

With a slightly bemused nod of his dark head Hal indicated his agreement even as he resolved to delve a little deeper into her surprising confession at the earliest opportunity—to find out a bit more about the cheating rat who had stolen her virginity and deceived her.

'You'll find some in the second drawer down.'

As soon as Kit had handed the foil packet over to him he wasted no time in pulling her back against his chest and passionately claiming her lips in a languorous open-mouthed kiss. As he did so he tugged down the straps of her chemise until he was satisfied he could feel her lovely breasts again. Then, still kissing her, he shaped his hands over her pretty bottom and started to ease her panties down over her svelte hips as much as he could manage without jeopardising his injured leg.

Although he was more than ready to take her, and almost in pain because his desire was so acute, Hal didn't want to rush anything, so he made sure to take his time exploring his lover's supple and slender body. *It was hardly a sacrifice…* Not when her skin was as soft as down and as satiny-smooth as the finest silk. And, being that her only experience of lovemaking had been with a man who had lied to her about being free so that he could get what he wanted from her, Hal's greatest desire was to make this experience with him one Kit would *never* forget—but only for the best of reasons. He wasn't promising her something he couldn't deliver, but he honestly wanted to help her erase that painful episode from her mind and replace it with a much better one.

Earlier Hal had joked that he liked to be on top, but because of his injury it was only natural that Kit should straddle him, and with her surprisingly strong slender thighs clasping him, and her tumbled copper hair and bare tip-tilted breasts on seductive view for his personal pleasure and edification, he had no qualms in silently admitting that, in truth, he actually had the best position of all…

With his hands settling either side of her womanly hips, Hal suddenly couldn't wait any longer to fulfil his growing need for her—and told her so. 'If I don't take you now, angel, I might—just *might*—lose my mind. But you'll have to help me take these boxers off.' When she'd accomplished the task he told her, 'Now it's your turn.'

With the same graceful and athletic prowess she'd used to remove his boxers, and mindful again not to jar the cast on his leg, Kit reached down and carefully slid her flimsy underwear down to her ankles. Then she scrunched the delicate cotton into a ball and threw it onto the floor.

When she resumed her position, Hal murmured huskily, 'You were gone too long, baby.' Hungrily fastening his hands either side of her flushed face, beneath the bewitching cascade of her burnished copper hair, he finished, 'I missed you.'

'I missed you too.' She bent down teasingly to brush her fulsome moist lips against his mouth, making him groan.

Before he could completely surrender to his burning desire he ripped open the silver foil packet he still held in his closed fist and fitted the latex protection over his member. *He was rock-hard*. The soft gasp Kit couldn't prevent feathered over him. Reaching for her once again, Hal knew it wouldn't be easy for him to be as mindful of her inexperience as he would like to be, and as much as she deserved, and he honestly regretted that. But his hunger for this woman was off the scale…

Never before in his history of conquests had it been this wanton or voracious. When he placed the tip of his member at her moist entrance and pushed upwards without preamble her satin heat all but overwhelmed him. He had no choice but to take things slowly or his love-making would be over almost as soon as it had begun.

Any tension Kit might have felt at the thought of properly uniting her body with a man's after five long years of sexual abstinence quickly disappeared the moment Hal's hard silken manhood entered her body. *It was as though she'd been waiting all this time just for him*. Although her feminine muscles might be understandably tight due to her inexperience, Hal's initial thrust had not been as painful or shockingly invasive as she'd expected. In fact after a brief searing sting his possession hardly made her flinch at all it was so natural. And the fact didn't detract from the inconceivable pleasure that filled her.

It was like drowning in a sea of the most exquisite honey. She'd honestly never felt more alive or glad to be a woman as she did right then. And as he drove into her again and again, and she allowed herself to relax completely, she didn't have the slightest reticence about meeting his voracious hunger with her own, bending her head greedily to kiss the side of his chiselled jaw and forehead and nip the velvet lobe of his ear.

How was it possible that a man's body could taste this good or feel so wonderful? she mused. It made her wonder how she'd survived so long without such sublime intimacy and gratification. The heat that filled her made her feel as though her blood was being lit by a fire. A fire whose flames took a sudden fierce hold to lick higher and higher. In fact it grew so hot that when Hal clasped her head between his hands to kiss her more deeply it couldn't help but ignite sparks and reach a crescendo.

She already knew she was sensitive to his touch—that had been highlighted by her spontaneous climax when he'd kissed her breasts earlier. Now, as Kit gasped her pleasure into his mouth, the sensation that poured through her was akin to riding a wave whose natural destiny was to join the falls that plunged over a cliff edge into a crystal-clear sun-kissed ocean. It was the most exhilarating ride she had ever experienced, and it was everything she'd dreamed it would be. Her heart had never beaten so hard or so fast with excitement.

Even as she stilled breathlessly Hal held her tightly against him. Once more his narrow athletic hips rocked against her smooth inner thighs and his rhythmic thrusts grew deeper and more purposeful. The helpless shout he released as his desire reached its peak echoed round the room. Apart from their preoccupied presence the air was almost preternaturally still. Just as if it had been waiting for their breathless sighs of pleasure and satisfaction to fill it.

Seeing a muscle in the side of her lover's lean, carved face suddenly flinch, Kit eased herself up, her heartbeat accelerating for an entirely different reason.

'Are you all right? Have I leant too hard on your leg and hurt it? Tell me, Hal…I need to know.'

Even as she carefully disengaged her body from his and moved to lie next to him he straight away hauled her back against his chest and drove his hands through her hair.

'Stop worrying about me and let me tell you how amazing that was—how utterly delicious and gorgeous you are.'

'It's my job to be concerned about you, Hal.'

He raised a lightly mocking eyebrow. 'Does that mean you wouldn't worry about me unless you were being paid to?'

A mortifying wave of heat assailed her. In her mind Kit couldn't help privately cursing her inability to relax right then and say what she really wanted to say—that she cared for him more than she'd ever cared for anyone before and that it scared her, that she hated the idea of him being in pain and wished that it was somehow in her power to spare him the hurt.

'Of course it doesn't. When I saw you wince then I was just concerned that we might have put too much strain on your femur and maybe damaged it even more.'

With a soft chuckle Hal slid his hand beneath her delicate jaw and gazed deeply into her eyes. 'Don't you know that what we just did helped me feel the best that I've felt in a very long time? I mean it. Not just because it was great sex…and it *was*…but because you're a genuinely compassionate and caring woman and I'm so pleased that I've met you, Kit.'

She'd never been remotely easy with receiving compliments and now she found out that it was even harder receiving them from Hal. It was hard because it really mattered to have his good opinion.

'Thank you. It's very sweet of you to say so.'

His lips hitched in a rueful grimace. 'Sweet? I can honestly say that no-one's ever accused me of being *that* before.'

'Not even your mother when you were a little boy?'

In a flash his expression darkened. 'My mother left when Sam and I were kids. I have no memory of her ever calling me anything endearing or anything else, for that matter. Shall we change the subject?'

Kit was mortified that she'd inadvertently hurt him with her remark. 'I'm sorry I said that. I didn't know.'

Taking a deep breath in, Hal sighed, 'Of course you didn't—how could you? And how could I possibly be offended because you've stumbled on a subject that you weren't even aware might be awkward for me?' His gaze was distant and reflective for a moment, but it wasn't long before he returned his attention to Kit and smiled. 'One day I might tell you a bit more about my tale of woe, but not right now.' His strong arms encircled her waist. 'The only thing I want to do right now is hold you and breathe you in. I love that scent you're wearing…what's it called? It smells very natural.'

'It *is* natural. It's just me. I've never had any cause to wear scent to bed.'

'And you don't have one now, sweetheart. I love the fact that the alluring perfume I can detect on your skin is purely your own natural scent. You know what? I want to fall asleep with you beside me tonight, Kit. Will you stay with me until the morning? If it's any incentive, I promise you I don't snore.'

'Even if you did I'd probably just grin and bear it because you're so hunky,' she teased.

'You think so?'

Beneath his shadowed complexion she saw him colour.

'I confess it's not the first time I've been called that. The tabloids use the word with monotonous regularity to describe me when they're spouting some spurious story about some model or soap starlet they want to portray as being linked with me. It gets a little tiresome, to tell you the truth. The phrase "Hunky Hal Treverne" makes me feel more like a stereotype than a person. Although I have to say the description sounds much more complimentary coming from *you*, sweetheart.'

'Oh…' Kit couldn't help feeling a little defensive at his comment that the tabloid press used the word with 'monotonous regularity'. Did he think that was where she had got it from? If he did, then it didn't suggest she had much discernment.

It hit a particularly sensitive nerve to be inadvertently reminded that she wasn't as well-educated as a lot of women her age, who'd perhaps gone on to university when they'd left school. *In truth, it was one of the big regrets of her life.* As for reading the tabloids—she didn't give them the time of day. She'd probably seen the more salacious headlines about Hal on the internet…not because she'd deliberately sought them out but because along with other celebrity gossip they'd flashed up on the site she used to check her e-mail from time to time.

But his comment also reminded her that not only was he an educated man himself but also the son of landed gentry, and suddenly the jolting realisation made Kit's heart sink like a stone. If their lovemaking had lulled her even for a second into believing the improbable fantasy that they might go on to enjoy a *real* relationship then she'd best dissuade herself of such an idea as quickly as possible. Hadn't she promised herself she'd never go down the same soulless destructive path with men as her mother had? *She'd already made one unfortunate mistake in trusting a man.*

Hal Treverne was destined to marry a woman from his own privileged class—not someone like Kit, just an ordinary working class girl, whose father had been a Romany gypsy who had abandoned her mother when he'd found out she was pregnant. Sooner or later Hal would wake up to the fact she wasn't in his league and no doubt regret bedding her. The thought that he wouldn't think that their intimacy was anything special as time went by almost made her want to *weep*.

Because she'd suddenly fallen silent, Hal looked concerned. The softly diffused lighting streaming in through the partially opened door highlighted his compelling gaze, made his irises glint like gold.

'What's wrong? You've suddenly gone quiet on me.'

As she tried to tidy the now crumpled silk chemise so that it covered her a bit more, Kit's smile was tremulous. 'I don't think I *will* spend the night with you, if you don't mind? I need to be up early to see to a few things…'

'What things are those?'

'Well, I—I need to make a shopping list, and also figure out menus for the day.'

'If that means you can't spend the night with me then we'll simply order in some food instead. Didn't my sister tell you that your main priority should be meeting my needs?'

'You *are* the priority…of course you are…but—'

'I don't like the sound of that "but",' Hal commented, sounding a bit more than vaguely irritated. 'Go on.'

'It probably wasn't a very good idea…us getting together like, this I mean.'

'Are you saying that you regret it?' Now his expression was seriously perturbed.

She coloured a little. 'Not the experience—no. It's just that—well, it could make our day-to-day relationship rather awkward. It's still going to be quite a while before you can get around completely unaided and, like you said, your needs have to take priority. Anything that detracts from that wouldn't be good. Perhaps it might be best if you contacted the agency and asked for someone else to come in and help you? Someone more impartial than I'm able to be now.'

'Stop it. Stop this nonsense right this minute.'

The scowl on his handsome face was nothing less than formidable, and Kit's pulse skittered in alarm.

'I promised you that whatever happened between us it wouldn't jeopardise your job, and I meant it. If you think I've changed my mind then you're crazy. Just because I desire you it doesn't mean that I don't need your help any more. And I don't want someone else from the damn agency. All I want is you.'

'That's all well and good, Hal, but I'm just trying to think of what's best for you. Can't you see that?'

'And what about *you*, Kit? Do you really think it's best for you that you leave me high and dry with no new job lined up, after you've promised to stay with me at least until I'm mobile again?'

Hearing the sincerity in Hal's tone, along with the fear that she might just up and leave him, Kit couldn't deny her relief that he wanted her to stay. He was right—she'd made him a promise. And, no, she *didn't* have another job lined up, and it *would* hurt her just as much as it would hurt him to walk out now.

Knowing she should stay if she wanted to preserve her hard-won reputation with the agency and secure another job afterwards, she resigned herself to doing just that.

As far as her relationship with Hal was concerned she wouldn't expect anything more from him other than his thanks and respect when her job here was done, and as long as she had that, given time, she would get over this heartfelt attraction for him. If she was going to live the dependable and comfortable existence that she longed for and buy herself that little bolthole she'd been so diligently saving for, then the sooner she got over him the better she would be for it.

'Okay. No doubt you're right. I *would* be letting myself down if I didn't see the job through—although I am disappointed in myself because I broke a cast-iron rule not to get personally involved with a client. If I'm to continue to do my job well, Hal, I can't risk a repeat of what happened between us tonight. You know, I can't.'

CHAPTER NINE

HAL STARED AT Kit in disbelief. Did she really think to draw a line under what they had just shared as if it had never happened? It looked as if she *did*. She was already getting out of bed and turning her back on him, her hands tugging down her pretty silk chemise as if to hide herself—almost as if she was ashamed of succumbing to their passionate union. He couldn't bear the thought that the only reason she'd agreed to stay was to fulfil her contract with the agency, not because of any personal regard for him...

Manoeuvring himself upright, he ground out, 'Did I delude myself that what we just shared meant something to you, Kit? I mean, other than just fulfilling a very basic need?'

She turned her head at that, and her oval face was as pale as a winter moon even in the dimmed light that streamed in from the corridor.

'I'm not saying it didn't mean anything. I'm just saying that it can't happen again. You must know it can't. I'm a realist, if nothing else, and this impetuous turning in the road that we've suddenly taken can only lead to a dead-end. When you're back on your feet again you'll realise that and be glad that we didn't take it any further.'

'Will I? You know that for a fact, do you?'

Her eyes were downcast for a moment. Then, as if garnering more determination to stick to her decision, Kit lifted her head. 'Now, tell me—do you need anything before I go back to my room? I can help you into the bathroom, if you'd like?'

'So you intend to play the coolly professional nurse from now on rather than my lover?' Hal found it hard to prevent the anger and resentment that seeped into his tone. 'I know which one I prefer, and it isn't the nurse.'

Her lovely blue eyes reflected her anguish at his stinging remark.

'My intention is to fulfil my obligation to both you and the agency.' Her restless twisting hands confirmed that his words had hurt her. 'I won't say any more than that. I'd better let you rest. I'm very tired and I need to get some sleep. You must be tired too, so I'll say goodnight.'

She stooped to collect the scrunched-up underwear she'd disposed of earlier, when Hal had enticed her into bed, and as he watched her Hal's resentment curdled like bitter aloes in the pit of his stomach. *He was so sick of being abandoned.* It was becoming a soul-destroying pattern in his life. It had started with his mother, and then his father, who—no matter what Hal achieved or did—would never be proud of him. He hadn't even been able to put his cynical judgement of his son aside to visit him in the hospital when he'd been injured. *And now Kit—the woman he found himself more attracted to than any other—was turning her back on him...*

Gritting his teeth and shoving his hair back from his

forehead, he said scathingly, 'I'll be sure to call on you if I need anything. I'd keep your door open, if I were you…just in case you don't hear me should I call out your name. It wouldn't bode well for your exemplary record at the agency if I were to fall out of bed again and injure myself, would it?'

Her cheeks reddening, Kit said quietly, 'I would never let anything like that happen to you. You have my word on that. And it's not just about protecting my record with the agency. I—I care about what happens to you.'

'Do you really?'

'Yes, I do. Anyway, I'll make sure to keep my door ajar so I can hear you, should you need me.'

'I need you *now*, but you don't seem to care about that. If you did then you'd stay the night with me as I asked.'

Hal caught a glimpse of what looked like regret in her bewitching blue eyes and for a moment his heart leapt with hope that she might change her mind. But instead she gracefully moved across to the door and went out, making sure to leave it slightly ajar instead of shutting it completely.

'Damn and blast it all to hell!' Dropping back down against his pillows, he freely gave vent to his anger and frustration…

He'd had the most diabolical night's sleep—perhaps an hour or two at most. So when he wheeled himself into the kitchen the next morning in search of Kit and a cup of much-needed coffee Hal wasn't exactly predisposed to be either amenable or pleasant.

Nor was he easily going to forgive her for not accepting his invitation to spend the night with him—even though he'd reflected afterwards that it was probably a good thing that she hadn't. After all, his romantic interludes had always been on *his* terms, not his lover's, and that was the way he liked it. Certainly he had never invited any of his partners to spend the night with him before. It shouldn't be any different with Kit—no matter *how* much he desired her. Nor should he behave as if it remotely disturbed him that she'd refused his invitation to stay the night. If she intuited that he needed her more than he let on then that would make him vulnerable, and that was the one thing he wanted to avoid…

Usually when something was troubling him Hal's habit was to take some exercise—either to jog, run or take a bike-ride—so that he could think what to do. Because all of those outlets were denied him right now the sensation that the walls of his surroundings were pressing in on him added to the already considerable stress he was under. He longed to get out—to fill his lungs with some fresh air and breathe freely again.

Kit was standing by the worktop waiting for the kettle to boil when he entered. Her beautiful red hair had been curtailed into two neat plaits, and dressed in jeans and a tunic-style white shirt—wearing no make-up as far as he could tell—she looked just like a schoolgirl. Despite his irritability, Hal's heart missed a beat. He might be mad at her for running out on him last night, but it didn't make him want her any less. The blood in his veins was already simmering at the mere sight of her, and the thought that he might never again have her in his bed soured his already dark mood even more.

'Morning,' he muttered, deliberately averting his gaze and wheeling himself across to the table.

'I was just about to bring you in some coffee and toast and help you to get dressed.' She stopped speaking and sighed, and Hal couldn't resist lifting his head to check out her expression. 'But I see you've managed it without me,' she finished.

'I'm not entirely helpless,' he returned gruffly. To his astonishment, her lips curved in an amused smile—which wasn't the reaction he'd expected. 'What's so funny?' he demanded, privately furious that she might be mocking him.

The smile vanished. 'You've put your sweater on back to front.'

Glancing downwards, Hal saw that she was right. The grey cashmere V-neck was indeed back to front. Hardly welcoming the fact being pointed out to him, he muttered a curse and then impatiently pulled it up over his head. Bare-chested, it didn't help to maintain his dignity when he got into a tussle with one of the sleeves in an attempt to turn the sweater the right way round so he that could put it back on again.

Kit instantly reacted. 'Let me help you.'

Presenting herself in front of him, she carefully relieved Hal of the cashmere, sorted it out so he could put it back on, and gently pulled the jumper down over his head. By the time she'd completed the task, tugging it gently but firmly down to his hard lean waist as though he were a child, his heart was thudding fit to burst. It didn't help matters that he found it almost unbearable to be so close to her and not be able to spontaneously reach out, pull her down onto his lap and embrace her.

'For God's sake, stop fussing, woman! How old do you think I am? *Three?* If you want something useful to do you can go and see to my coffee and toast.'

'I intend to do just that,' she answered primly, her hands crossed over her chest. 'But a simple thank you for helping you out wouldn't go amiss. My mother may not have been an educated woman, or have been able to afford for me to stay on at school, but the one thing she absolutely insisted on when she raised me was my having good manners. I think manners can tell you a lot about a person.'

The revealing comment stopped Hal from coming back at her with a cutting or flippant rejoinder. He frowned. 'Does it bother you that you had to leave school early and didn't get a better education?'

At first she turned away from him. But she turned back again almost immediately, her hands on her hips and her cheeks flushed. 'It depends what you mean by "a better education". I may not have been to college or university, or studied for a profession, but I'm not stupid. I've learned a lot on my way to becoming a fully-fledged adult—including the wisdom to know what's best for me and the importance of making good decisions. I've learned that you suffer if you don't. There are a lot of important facts about life that even a privileged or expensive education can't buy, you know.'

'Are you perhaps suggesting that my own education was privileged and expensive?'

The rosy tint on Kit's alabaster cheeks grew even pinker. 'It's pretty well documented that it was. Are you saying that's not true?'

'It's true. I did indeed have a privileged and expensive education. I also grew up with the proverbial silver spoon in my mouth. But does that make me a bad person? A person you wouldn't think it worthwhile getting to know? I may have had most of the material advantages that a lot of people aspire to having, but that doesn't protect a person from experiencing the challenges we all have to face as humans and nor should it.'

To his surprise Hal's heart was racing as he came to the end of his little speech, and he realised just how much resentment and hurt he'd harboured over the years at being perceived as 'having it all'—meaning he couldn't possibly understand what it was like to go without anything and therefore his opinion shouldn't count. *That just wasn't true.* He *did* know what it was like to go without. The most fundamental thing a human being needed in life was to know that he was loved, Hal believed. But aside from the love of his sister Sam that was the commodity that he had been bereft of most of all.

'You said—you said that you'd tell me more about your mother leaving. Was that one of the challenges you meant?'

It was extraordinary how Kit seemed to have the unerring ability to get straight to the heart of something, he thought. Rubbing his hand round his jaw, Hal shook his head. 'I don't want to talk about that. Maybe if you'd consented to spending the night with me I might have told you. But all I want right now is my breakfast, and after that I just want to get out of here for a while.'

'I'm sorry that you no longer want to tell me about your past…about your mother I mean. But I understand why you don't. You think that I let you down by not agreeing to stay with you last night. Maybe you even think it was easy for me to make the decision. I assure you it wasn't. I was only trying to do what was best for both of us. Anyway, you said you wanted to get out. Any idea where you want to go?'

Not missing the fact that there was a telling break in

her voice—as if she was striving to put on a brave face
and show she didn't care that he'd refused to tell her
about his mother's desertion—Hal lifted his shoulders
in a shrug even as his heart ached to tell her *everything*.

'I don't care. Anywhere that's not here would be a
good start. If I was mobile I'd go for a run, or even a
walk. I can't do that so I'll leave it up to you to come
up with an idea of what to do. I just hate being cooped
up like this.'

Flipping one of her burnished copper plaits over her
shoulder, Kit surprised him with a smile. The sight was
like a welcome glimpse of the sun coming out on a day
that was cloudy and grey, and it didn't fail to warm
Hal's heart.

'Well, there's no need to stay here feeling like you're
a prisoner in your own home,' she announced. 'We
should get out and get some fresh air. Leave it to me.
I'll mull over where we can go while I get you your
breakfast.'

Kit's resolution to distance herself emotionally and
physically from Hal was severely tested that morning.
She'd been able to tell the instant he'd come into the
kitchen that he hadn't had much sleep. And it wasn't
just because he hadn't had a shave. His lean, carved
features looked almost haggard, and she couldn't help
feeling guilty that her decision not to spend the rest of
the night with him was the cause. *She hadn't had a lot
of sleep herself for the same reason.*

And when he'd struggled to put his sweater back on,
after inadvertently donning it back to front, the sight
of his broad tanned shoulders and heavenly chest had
made her insides flip at the memory of how incredible

it had felt to make love with him. Without a doubt she knew that the act of passion they'd shared had been not just irresistible but *necessary* too.

Not that Kit had needed reminding. Her body still ached and tingled from Hal's ardent attentions and she longed to be able to share with him how he'd made her feel. She'd never felt particularly attractive or sensual, but he had helped her feel both of those things last night. Now she was torn between following her heart and her finely honed instinct for self-preservation, and therein lay the dilemma.

Not wanting to dwell on her own inner turmoil above seeing to Hal's desire to get out of the apartment for a while, she had an idea. As he finished his breakfast at the table she said brightly, 'I've thought of where we can go.'

'Have you?'

Throwing down his napkin with a weary air, he didn't sound remotely interested or impressed, and she could tell that a bit of downheartedness and despair had crept in. It made her all the more determined to lift his spirits and proceed with the plan she'd come up with.

'Yes, I have. I just want to clear away the breakfast things and then we can go. I think we're going to need our jackets and scarves because it looks quite cold and blustery out there this morning.' She glanced out of the window at the overcast skies and at the windblown leaves that were occasionally flying past, plastering themselves to the panes of glass. 'Would you like to read the newspaper while I stack the dishwasher? I found it on the mat this morning.'

'I may as well.'

Clearly resigned, Hal didn't let his returning glance

linger for too long, Kit noticed—as if he'd resolved not to be quite so friendly. The mere thought cut her to the quick. The sooner they were out in the open the better. It would give them both a chance to clear their heads and it would be good to blow the cobwebs away—especially as neither of them had had much sleep last night.

The household tasks completed, Kit moved across the kitchen to where Hal still sat perusing the newspaper. Without asking his permission, she plucked it out of his hands.

'Hey! What do you think you're doing?' His expression was furious.

'You said you wanted to go out, remember? You can read the newspaper when we get back.'

Deftly folding the broadsheet, she dropped it down onto the table. Then, taking a firm hold of the wheelchair's handles, she turned it forthrightly towards the door.

Still seething, Hal remarked sardonically, 'I was in the middle of reading an interesting article about the number of people losing their jobs…particularly *women*. Apparently it's a real problem.'

'Is it really? I don't expect it will be a problem for very long. Not with women's ingenuity and resourcefulness at finding replacement situations. We're very good at rising to a challenge and getting ourselves out of a tough spot…it comes from centuries of having to take care of not so ingenious and resourceful men!'

'You should be a comedian. Anyone ever tell you that?'

Helplessly, Kit's lips twitched in amusement. 'No. They haven't. But I'll bear it in mind should I ever find myself without a job. I can turn my hand to most things if I have to.'

'Hmm...'

His shoulders had stiffened. It definitely irked him whenever she got the better of him, she noticed.

'Presumably we're travelling to our destination by car?' he asked, swiftly changing the subject.

'No, we're not. I'm going to push you in your chair.'

'I don't think so.' He twisted round with a belligerent glare that might have intimidated her if she hadn't known better. 'If we're not going in the car then I'll take my crutches and walk,' he declared.

'Not today you won't, sunshine.'

They were travelling down the spacious hallway with its gleaming parquet flooring, and when she reached the coatstand at the end Kit reached up for Hal's chocolate-coloured suede jacket and briskly handed it to him.

'I want you to get out into the fresh air, but we're going too far for you to use crutches. By the way, have you got a scarf? I don't want you getting cold.'

'I'm warning you, Katherine with a K, if you persist in treating me like some dull-witted imbecile then I'll call a cab to take me wherever I want to go and I won't let you know when I'll be back. Then you'll be forced to stay here on your own and soberly contemplate at what point you pushed me too far!'

Kit had never seen a man look so adorable when he was angry, but Hal Treverne cornered the market in sheer adorability in her opinion—*whatever* his mood. However, right then she didn't think he would appreciate her telling him so. The reason he was angry, she guessed, was because he couldn't get around with the effortless ease he was accustomed to and it made him feel vulnerable.

She knew how frightening that was for anyone who strove to be in sole command of his destiny—especially when events didn't always pan out as he wanted them to. Kit found it easy to empathise because she'd often felt that same sense of frightening vulnerability too. Especially when she'd lived at home with her mother and daily anticipated the rollercoaster existence they were living spinning even further out of control...

'I don't want to make you mad at me,' she said.

Before she thought about the wisdom of her action she brought her hand down on the top of his head and lightly ruffled his hair. Just as she was about to draw away, Hal caught her by the wrist. Almost immediately his hold tightened.

'Then don't imagine that you're the one in charge—because you're *not*.'

Even as he warned her Kit saw that his golden eyes were no longer glinting with fury but with something else far more disturbing. Meeting his gaze, she felt as if she'd been steeped in a vat of warm honey.

'One kiss,' he murmured, the timbre of his voice lowering huskily. 'One kiss and I'll let you take me wherever you want to—even in this dratted wheelchair.'

She made a half-hearted attempt at freeing her wrist, but her arm had slackened weakly the moment Hal had taken it prisoner.

'I told you—I can't do that any more.' Even to her own ears her answer sounded less than convincing.

His dark brows beetled in a mocking frown. 'In my dictionary there's no such word as "can't", sweetheart.'

'I think you'll find that there is. Maybe not in yours,

but in most dictionaries the term is described as a contraction. Perhaps you need to update your volume?'

Even as she came back with the witty rejoinder Kit's heart was hammering, because she knew that this was one situation where she wouldn't get the better of him. Not this time.

'You're too clever for your own good, Kit Blessington. Now, shut up and let me kiss you.'

Pulling her down to him, he crushed her lips beneath the slightly rough, melting warmth of his own. With a surrendering gasp she allowed her mouth to be thoroughly captured, offering not the slightest resistance as his tongue swept its satin interior and his hands cupped her face. The taste and feel of him was like being given the keys to Nirvana. The pleasure he gave her was almost indescribable.

How was she supposed to keep to her resolve not to be intimate with him again? Hal Treverne was in her blood, like a raging fever that wouldn't be cooled, and Kit knew she was fast becoming addicted to him. More than that, she realised, she was deeply in love with him. The thought wrenched a partly shocked, partly despairing groan from her. Despite her heartfelt vow not to, it seemed she was intent on repeating her mother's reckless folly all over again.

'We should—we should get going,' she murmured.

With her legs decidedly unsteady, she stepped abruptly away from Hal and reached up to the hook on the coatstand for her warm sheepskin-lined jacket. Draping a purple scarf around her neck and loosely knotting it, she saw that Hal was fastening his suede jacket with a somewhat bemused expression on his face.

'That kiss was like having a warming dram of

whisky before we set out on our expedition into the cold.' He grinned. 'I can't pretend I won't be tempted to have another one on our return. Lead the way, Captain.'

With a charming, mocking salute, he defied her not to give him an argument.

CHAPTER TEN

THE WIND WAS particularly raw and unforgiving that day. As Kit briskly pushed Hal's wheelchair along the smooth concreted paths in the park she knew that being forced to be static wasn't helping him maintain his body's warmth. He would have hated it, but she wished she'd brought a rug to tuck round him. She'd be willing to endure his angry glares if it made him feel more comfortable.

As if reading her mind, Hal piped up, 'It's warmer than this climbing a glacier! I can't say I'm exactly bowled over by this expedition, Kit.'

'It's not an expedition. It's meant to be a pleasurable stroll. I know it's cold, but at least we're out in the fresh air. There's a charming little café at the other side of the park and we'll head over there soon. But first I think we should take a little exercise, don't you?'

His broad shoulders tensed as he turned round to observe her. His chiselled profile was far from amused.

'That's not very funny and I don't appreciate the joke.'

'I'm not mocking you, Hal.' Swallowing hard, Kit frowned in apology. 'I just want you to know that even though you can't get around like you normally do right now you can still have fun.'

'This is your idea of *fun*?'

'Anything can be fun if you have the right attitude. How about this, for instance? Make sure you're holding on.'

Taking a deep breath, she firmed her gloved hands round the wheelchair's handles and started to run at full pelt down the path. Fortunately the park was sparsely populated that morning, the path was wide, and the only person they passed was an elderly man walking his terrier. As the trees, lake and the benches on the path flew by she couldn't help laughing out loud. Inside, she was suddenly filled with the kind of joy she very rarely *if ever* felt. The discovery that it was immensely liberating going against the conformity of what people expected made her want to do it more often.

At first it seemed as though her madcap idea had stunned Hal into silence, but as she continued to push him at speed down the path, he shouted up to her, 'You are one crazy woman, Kit Blessington. Do you know that?'

'Are you having fun now?' she shouted back.

'Hell, yes! Can't you go any faster?'

Kit kept her promise and after making their way across to the other side of the park, out of breath and with her cheeks healthily pink, she took Hal to the café she'd mentioned for coffee and cake. The table they selected had a wonderful view of the sparkling lake—at last the sun had started to shine, making the blue-green water shimmer like diamonds. Gratefully curling her hands round her hot mug of coffee, and observing the heightened colour in the sculpted planes of Hal's handsome face as well, she knew a delicious sense of well-being that she wished she could bottle.

'Feeling a bit warmer now?' She smiled.

'I feel strangely like I've run a marathon.' The corner of his lips quirked beguilingly. 'Well…maybe a *half* marathon. You were right—that *was* fun.'

'Good. I had fun too. What's the fruitcake like?'

Hal was already shaking his head and returning the slice of cake he'd just taken a bite out of to his plate. 'Nowhere near the standard of yours. Six out of ten, I'd say.'

'And mine is…?'

'You're a bad girl, fishing for compliments like that.'

His voice lowered to a smoky cadence that heated Kit's blood and made the tips of her breasts prickle hotly inside her bra.

'But I'll still tell you. You're definitely a ten. I can't fault you, it seems.'

'We're talking about my cake…*aren't we?*'

'Are we?' Leaning across the table, Hal reached for her hand, lifted it to his lips and kissed it. 'The truth is you make me giddy. The line between reality and fantasy always seems to be blurred when I look at you, Kit.'

He meant every word. Her presence in his life was growing more and more essential to his well-being—and not just because she had appeared in his life exactly when he needed her. As he gazed into her bewitching summer-blue eyes his heart gently pounded inside his chest. He'd climbed mountains and navigated raging rivers in his search for thrills and excitement. He had taken recording artists to the pinnacle of their careers because he'd believed in them when no one else had, where no one would take the risk of backing an unknown. But nothing he'd done or achieved in his life could beat what he felt when he was next to this woman…no wonder she made him giddy!

Kit's face flushed even pinker at his comment.

'It's probably the fresh air and the unexpected speed at which I pushed you in the chair that's made you giddy,' she quipped, as if determined not to believe his declaration had been generated by any other reason than that.

There was one other younger couple in the café with them, and when Hal reached for Kit's hand and kissed it he noticed over her shoulder that the girl was sending him a pleased smile of acknowledgement—as if he'd suddenly been granted entry into an elite and prestigious club. *It was a good feeling.* Suddenly he didn't mind if people looked at him and Kit and imagined they were a bona-fide couple. In fact he hoped that they *did.* His sister Sam would be over the moon that he was even open to the idea.

'Will you tell me more about the married man you had a liaison with?' he asked, suddenly needing to know.

'All right…'

Even though the question had clearly discomfited her, Hal was pleased that Kit wasn't going to shy away from answering it.

'I told you it was my twenty-first birthday and my friends had taken me to a club? Well, there was a restaurant upstairs, where we had a meal, and he was one of the waiters there. Anyway, he was very attentive to all of us, but for some reason he was extra-attentive to me. Towards the end of the evening, when he'd finished his shift, he came to find me. I'm afraid I'd had a little too much to drink in a bid to cheer myself up, because turning twenty-one and not having anyone who mattered in my life except my mum had made me feel rather low, and when he offered to take me home I let him.'

She glanced away for a moment, as if cautious about revealing too much and perhaps being judged for it.

'Anyway, he helped me into the house, where I had a room upstairs. He—he started kissing me. I should have made him stop, but I was drunk and hardly knew what I was doing. I stupidly told him that I needed to lie down and he led me over to the bed.' Ruefully shaking her head, Kit grimaced. 'To cut a long story short, he had sex with me, and afterwards…just before he left… he told me he was married. He took great pleasure in telling me, I remember. That's it…end of story. In truth, I had a lucky escape.'

'And you didn't report him to the police?'

'Why? He just took what he thought was on offer. The whole fiasco was *my* fault. I did everything I shouldn't have. I'd had too much to drink and I let a stranger take me home. The only sensible thing I managed to do that night was to insist he wore protection. Luckily he'd brought some with him. It obviously wasn't the first time he'd taken advantage of a woman who really ought to have known better.'

Kit's blue-eyed glance was unwaveringly direct.

'You're probably wondering why I acted so stupidly. The truth is I let my guard down that night because I was flattered by his attention. Sometimes we all want to be liked and admired, don't we? That's all that sorry episode was about—a very human need to be noticed by someone.'

'But you let him take your virginity, Kit. That's the

saddest part of the story. I wish you could have given it to someone who saw it as the most precious gift a woman can give to a man.' *It grieved Hal more than he could possibly say that she hadn't.*

'So do I.' She fell silent for a moment. 'Anyway, now I've shared my story, will you tell me about your mother, Hal?'

As painful as the topic was, if he wanted things to progress further with Kit then Hal knew he couldn't avoid speaking about it any longer. Suddenly it was imperative that she grew to trust him—especially after what she'd just told him—and in order for her to do that he had to have the courage to open up to her about his past. *Who knew?* If he took the risk it might open the door to the possibility of them enjoying a genuine relationship. Hal at least had to try.

Holding her gaze across the table, he gave her a tentative smile. Did he really have the courage to be vulnerable enough to confess the wreckage of his past to this woman?

'All right, then. I'll tell you about her,' he agreed.

Her eyes widening, Kit gently loosened her hand from his and sat back in her seat to give him her full attention.

'My mother was very beautiful,' he went on, his hand tunnelling restlessly through his hair for a moment. 'And her bewitching looks drew men to her like bees to honey. My dad is a wealthy landowner, and even though he was mad about her when they first met and asked her to marry him his property and his estate always came first. She didn't appear to mind that too much. She loved the fact that he was landed gentry as well as being rich, but she didn't understand why he chose to work at all when he didn't have to. If she'd troubled to find out, she would have soon learned that taking care of the estate and the people who worked for him to maintain it was a matter of fierce pride to him. The estate has been in the family since the sixteenth century, and my dad wasn't going to be the one that saw it fall to rack and ruin, as he'd say. The charities he supported were also hugely important to him, and he'd hoped that my mother would see how being associated with them might help her. Given her PR background, he thought she might be able to help fundraise and organise events and might even enjoy it.

'He encouraged her to try and forge a good relationship with the staff on the estate and get to know them a little. To sum it up, my father believed that she needed a purpose…at least until children came along. She'd been flitting in and out of PR work when they'd first met, but her heart wasn't really in it. Turned out that she had her own ideas about what the "lady of the house" should do, and when she moved onto the estate with my dad it became clear that it wasn't very much.

'She couldn't hack the isolation of the countryside. She was a city girl through and through and she hated being alone when my dad was taking care of his business on the estate—especially as she craved attention round the clock. In a very rare and honest moment my father once told me that he'd hoped when she had me and Sam she would settle down a bit, be more content with her lot. But instead of becoming devoted to her family she grew more and more restless and started to have affairs.'

Grimacing, Hal shook his head.

'At first my father turned a blind eye, hoping she

would grow tired of her soulless behaviour and realise what she had at home…two children who adored her, and a husband who loved her enough to forgive her destructive behaviour and also hoped that given time she would change for the better.'

Clearing his throat, Hal picked up his mug of coffee and took a swig. At the same time he found himself examining Kit's pensive expression to try and gauge what she must be thinking about his faithless mother and his perhaps *too* patient, some might say foolishly deluded father. Henry Treverne Senior was a man who had never given up hope that his wife would come to see the error of her ways and be content just to be his partner and mother to their children.

'Unfortunately she never *did*…change for the better, I mean.' He shrugged. 'When Sam and I were nine and seven respectively she ran off with an Italian count and relocated to Venice. She never kept in touch, even though my father regularly wrote to her and told her how much Sam and I were missing her.' Hal bit down on his lip as a familiar scissor of pain jack-knifed through his heart at the memory.

Again he cleared his throat and took another swig of coffee. 'About six years ago—just about the time I started to make a name for myself in the music industry—my father was notified by the Italian authorities that she'd been killed in a car accident. Apparently the Count's twenty-one-year-old son from a previous marriage had been driving the car at the time and also lost his life. It was common knowledge in Venice that he and my mother had been having an affair. Doesn't make for a very pretty story, does it?'

'That's so sad. For *all* of you.' Her face paling a little,

Kit breathed out a soft, heartfelt sigh. 'Do you mind if I ask who looked after you and your sister when she left?'

Hal grimaced. 'A series of not very reliable nannies, I'm afraid. One or two of them might have stayed, given the chance, but my father didn't think any of them were good enough to mind his children. He was always finding fault with them for some reason or other. The truth is—courtesy of my beautiful, faithless mother, I think—he started to believe that women on the whole were fickle and not to be depended on. As soon as Sam and myself were old enough, he packed us off to boarding school.'

Taking another sip of coffee, he realised it was now practically cold. 'Ugh.' Wiping the back of his hand across his mouth, he returned the mug to the table, his avid gaze alighting on Kit. 'We could be close…me and my father, I mean. But he couldn't see why I wanted to leave and branch out on my own in a career when I was going to one day inherit the estate and title from him. He still doesn't understand my reasons for wanting to be completely independent and neither does he see—in *his* words—why I "recklessly" risk my life in pursuing extreme sports.'

Kit's smooth brow puckered in a frown. 'Is that why he didn't come and visit you in the hospital after your accident? You said that he'd e-mailed you saying "pride comes before a fall".'

With any other woman he would have been surprised she should remember such a detail, but *not* with Kit. Hal heaved a sigh. To be honest, he wanted to shake off that painful illustration of the chasm that had grown between him and his father but he just couldn't.

'Trouble is he was right, you know? The only reason I agreed to that stupid bet with Rigden was because I *had* to prove I was better than him. Sometimes I *am* proud...too proud to see reason and let common sense rule.'

Ruefully he tapped his knuckles against his cast. 'This injury being a case in point. But my dad's proud as well—too proud to admit that sometimes he might be wrong. He *should* have come to see me in the hospital!'

With a tender smile, Kit nodded her agreement. 'Yes, he should have. But perhaps he was unsure how his visit would be received by you—whether it would be welcome or not if there had been previous disagreement and tension between you? When you spend too much time apart from someone it's very easy to believe that you know them so well you can predict how they're going to react when you see them again. You don't consider that they might have moved on from their old behaviour or changed for the better. When was the last time you actually spent any time with your dad, Hal?'

He sensed the heat rise in his face even before he started to speak. Kit's words had definitely given him pause. 'I don't know...a few months, I suppose. I know that sounds bad, but I've always been too busy to organise anything. Besides...' he shrugged a shoulder '...I got fed up with listening to his criticisms every time we happened to speak.'

Leaning towards him, Kit gently laid her hand over his. Her blue eyes were so captivating that Hal temporarily forgot that he was aggrieved with his dad. It was like gazing back into the most serene and calm lake.

'Would you like to go and see him? If he won't come to you, maybe you should go to him?'

Ever since he'd had his accident in Aspen it had been

eating away at him that his father hadn't shown any evidence that he cared. Resentment was a bitter companion, and it was only apt to grow worse if not dealt with, he knew. Kit's suggestion that he make a conciliatory move and go and visit his father was so obvious, so eminently sensible, that he knew he couldn't resist it. Reliving some of the tensions of his past with her just now had made him suddenly yearn to make amends. Losing one parent was bad enough—never mind allowing your relationship with the remaining one to deteriorate so much that you barely spoke to each other.

'Once again your astute insight has floored me, Kit,' he told her. 'You're right…I should go and see my dad. It's crazy that I've put it off for so long. Will you drive me?'

Immediately she withdrew her hand from his and frowned. 'Of course I will, but…where does he live?'

'Hertfordshire.'

'And when would you like to make the trip?'

'I want to go today. We should strike while the iron's hot—before I have the chance to think about it too much and talk myself out of it.'

'Shouldn't you ring your dad first and check that he'll be home?'

An irresistibly boyish grin split his lips wide. 'I probably should, but I won't. I'd rather just turn up and surprise him. Even if he's out, his housekeeper will let us in. He'll come back sooner or later. By the way—we ought to pack an overnight bag. It's too late to travel there and back today.'

Slowly, Kit nodded. 'Well, if you think that's all right, then of course we can go today. But first of all

I'd like to ice that knee for you, and then you should rest for a while. We can go after that.'

'I can rest in the car. After all, I don't have to worry about driving.'

Zipping up his jacket, Hal was surprised at how enthused he suddenly felt about the idea of making amends with his father. It would also be good to see his childhood home again, despite his fractured upbringing. Falteringham House, the Treverne estate, was breathlessly stunning, and he'd honestly missed it. Any man would be proud to have connections with such beauty, grandeur and history. But most of all Hal realised he was looking forward to introducing it to Kit.

'Come on, Nurse Blessington,' he urged with a smile. 'Let's get going, shall we?'

Kit had honed a helpful ability to get packing down to a fine art. She'd *had* to when she was so often moving from place to place for work. But when she stepped out of her bedroom to find Hal patiently leaning against the wall on his crutches, a classy leather tote down by his feet, she couldn't help smiling.

'That was quick. I see you're all packed and ready. I was just about to come and find you to help.'

'No need. I'm nothing if not prepared,' he quipped, an irresistible twinkle in his chameleon hazel eyes. 'I often have to jet off somewhere at the drop of a hat, so it pays to at least have one well-equipped bag ready. I see you've changed your hairstyle... I have to say I approve. The schoolgirl plaits were definitely cute, but I much prefer it when you look like one of Millais's models.'

After swapping her jeans and shirt for a smart pair of black trousers and a dove-grey Arran sweater Kit had quickly dismantled her plaits and shaken her hair loose. Once again the fiery copper waves tumbled freely over her shoulders, and they helped give her a sense of confidence she found herself suddenly in dire need of. If her one claim to beauty couldn't help her to that end, then what *could*?

The prospect of meeting Hal's upper-crust father, as well as visiting his ancestral family home, was seriously daunting. Although she was all but certain that it would—at last—dash any pointless hope she might be secretly nurturing that she could have a future with him. Best she just keep on reminding herself that if she continued to work hard then one day soon she would have the precious home of her own that she longed for. And she wouldn't have to depend on any man—even if she was head over heels in love with him—to provide it for her.

It was close to dusk by the time they reached the end of a long tree-lined drive and pulled up outside the esteemed manor house where Hal had grown up. Surrounded by lush parkland, the building was frighteningly imposing, Kit saw, even in the gloomy half-light of the day. Its Elizabethan windows and stone turrets made it look almost ethereal. And, apart from the late-afternoon birdsong, the silence that cloaked the area was eerily tangible. When she switched off the car's ignition and turned round to observe her passenger in the seat that she'd extended for him, so he could stretch out his injured leg, she saw immediately that his handsome face looked perturbed.

'What's up?' she asked. 'I'm sorry if it was a little

bumpy coming down the drive. You're not in pain, I hope?'

'Unless you have the power to go back to Elizabethan times and predict that we'll be driving round in engine-driven motor cars in five hundred years' time, so we had better level the road, there's not much you can do about the bumpy drive, I'm afraid. The surface has always been uneven and slightly bowed. And, in answer to your second question, I'm not in pain. But thanks for asking.'

Clamping down on her automatic response—*It's my job to ask how you're feeling*—Kit somehow shaped her lips into a smile. 'Anyway, it looks like an amazing house. It must have been wonderful, growing up with so much space around you. The places me and my mum lived in were always so cramped and small.'

Hal's gaze narrowed interestedly. 'I've been meaning to ask you…where does your mother live now? Is she on her own or does she have a partner?'

It had never been easy to talk about her mum at the best of times, and it wasn't any easier now. Inevitably, even though she had forged a life of her own and didn't regret it, Kit couldn't help sometimes feeling guilty that she didn't make herself as available to her as she'd used to. But the last time they'd spoken on the phone, Elizabeth Blessington had told her that she'd tentatively been dating the widower who lived next door to the building where her little flat was housed. It was early days yet, she'd stated, her tone sounding uncharacteristically cautious, but she had high hopes that it might blossom into something special.

Tucking some hair behind her ear, Kit stopped frowning and lifted her gaze back to Hal's.

'She lives in London and, yes, she lives alone. But she's recently started dating a widower who lives nearby, so I'm sure she has company from time to time. Anyway, shouldn't we go and find out if your dad is in? I can wheel you in your chair, or would you prefer to use your walking aids?'

'I'll use the crutches. I'd prefer to confront my dad when I'm standing upright.' His lips thinned ruefully.

'"Confront"?'

'Wrong word. Come on, let's go in.'

As they stood outside the imposing gabled front door Kit stole a glance at Hal to try and ascertain how he was feeling. His carved handsome face never failed to make her heart race, and it raced even more now because she'd intuited that he had mixed feelings about coming home to see his father again. She prayed the meeting would go well. The last thing he needed was to feel it hadn't been a success.

'If I didn't have to hold onto these damned crutches I'd hold your hand,' he said gruffly, a riveting dimple appearing at the side of his mouth.

Her insides cartwheeled pleasurably. 'I'm here for you, Hal. You don't have to worry.' Gently, Kit touched her hand to the back of his chocolate-brown jacket.

At that very same moment the door opened. A distinguished-looking man who looked to be in his sixties appeared. He had liberally greying dark hair that must once have been as strong and lustrous as the hair of the man standing beside her, and was dressed in casual country tweeds with a waxed jacket. Possessed of the same compelling hazel-eyed gaze as the younger man, he stared at Hal as though being confronted by a ghost.

Kit dropped her hand.

'Hello, Dad. Thought I'd surprise you.' His son greeted him diffidently.

'Why in God's name didn't you ring to let me know you were coming?' the other man responded.

He had the kind of resonant, booming voice usually attributed to distinguished actors who performed Shakespeare, and Kit didn't mind admitting that it startled her.

'I'll turn round and go back to London if it's inconvenient,' Hal countered immediately, unable to keep the hurt from his tone.

'Of course it's not inconvenient. If it's a surprise you hoped for then you've succeeded. I didn't mean that it was an unwelcome one. Come in, come in. It's clear you can't stand there for long on those crutches. It can hardly be good for you.'

'I'll help you,' Kit said quickly, her hand once again going to Hal's broad back to reassure him.

'And who might *you* be, young lady?' the older man asked pointedly, making no bones about looking her up and down.

Casting aside the uncomfortably warm sensation of self-consciousness that spread throughout her body, she determinedly lifted her head and silently defied him to find fault or look down his aristocratic nose at her for even a second.

'My name is Kit Blessington. Your son hired me to give him some practical help while he recuperates from his accident.'

'*Did* he, indeed?' There was a definite suggestion of a mocking smile around the mouth whose upper lip was decorated by a dark military-style moustache. 'Well, I'm Sir Henry Treverne—Hal's father—as I'm sure you've

gleaned by now. It's good to know that my son had the
foresight to get himself some help and support when
he needed it, for once. He usually insists on doing most
things alone, but I'm glad that on this occasion common sense prevailed.'

'Thanks for the vote of confidence,' Hal interjected
drolly. The strain of maintaining his upright pose with
the walking aids was suddenly reflected on his fur-
rowed brow. 'I hate to break up the party, but can we
go in now? And my companion and I wouldn't say no
to a cup of coffee and a sandwich. It's been a long, tir-
ing drive.'

'If you and Ms Blessington make your way into the
family drawing room, I'll go and find my housekeeper
and get her to organise it. Now, come in from the cold
and go and sit in front of the fire to warm up.'

Before he turned to follow his father inside the house
Hal deliberately caught Kit's eye and gave her a reassuring wink, as if he already knew that this visit wasn't
going to be an easy one for her either…

CHAPTER ELEVEN

A WARM FIRE was indeed blazing invitingly in the marble fireplace as they entered the family drawing room. It was a strange feeling, coming back to the room Hal had sat in so many times over the years with his father and sister…almost a surreal sensation—as if the past was nothing but a dream he'd conjured up. It was literally years since the three of them had spent any proper time together, and it was growing more and more unlikely that they ever *would*. The loving, caring family unit that he'd longed for them to become after his mother had left had never really become a reality.

Not liking the sombre direction his thoughts were taking him in—especially when he'd resolved to heal the rift with his father—Hal made his way across the expansive stone floor, liberally covered with hand-crafted Persian rugs, and carefully lowered himself onto one of the leather couches. Kit stayed close by him to help. As he sat she took his crutches away and laid them down on the floor, where he could easily reach them. Then, with a self-conscious smile she moved away.

It wasn't the reaction he'd anticipated. Whether she acknowledged it or not, there was a definite bond between them now, and in his mind their lovemaking last night had sealed that bond. He was no longer just a client she was working for, and she was no longer simply his hired help. With every fibre of Hal's being he ached for more intimate contact—or at least for them to be easy enough with each other that they would automatically sit together. With that in mind, he gestured for her to come back and join him. It was akin to receiving a blow when he saw that her pretty blue eyes were reticent.

'I'd better not. Your father might think it's not very professional of me to sit next to you. He might think that I—that we—' She was unable to finish the sentence and her cheeks coloured helplessly. As if desperately needing a distraction, she glanced round for a suitable place to sit. Selecting one of the armchairs positioned opposite Hal, she finally made herself comfortable.

'That we are up to no good?' he finished for her, his lips twisting wryly. 'I *hate* that expression. Even if he doesn't approve, do you think that's going to stop me from wanting you or showing *him* that I want you?'

Exasperation was close to getting the better of Hal, because the need to hold Kit close had been mercilessly taunting him all day. In contrast, she had been unbelievably composed and pragmatic. How on earth was he going to convince her that he was in earnest about how he felt? That he didn't just want a meaningless fling but something far more serious?

The depth and breadth of his intentions took him aback. Shaken, he shrugged off his jacket and dropped it onto the cushion beside him.

'I told you that I can't do this…that I—' She stopped.

'Need to be sensible?'

'I know that you don't want to hear that, but—'

'My housekeeper, Mary, is going to bring us in some refreshments, and after that she's going to go and get your rooms ready. I presume you and Miss Blessington *are* staying the night, Hal?'

His father's timing couldn't have been *worse,* Hal thought irritably. Yes, he wanted them to build bridges with him—that was why he was here—but equally he wanted to put things right between him and Kit—to get her to see that he wasn't the spoilt playboy used to getting his own way that she might secretly fear he was… not a man who wouldn't hesitate to use her and then cast her aside just as her mother's ex-boyfriends had done to *her.* But it looked as if that particular conversation would have to wait until later, when they could be alone.

'Yes, we are. I'd rather not ask Kit to drive us back to town tonight. And, by the way, I'm going to need a downstairs room—and so is Kit, in case I need her.'

'That won't be a problem. That's settled, then. So, how have things been since the accident?' his father asked, taking a seat in the high-backed armchair next to Kit.

The question was posed in the familiar non-committal and unemotional tone that Hal knew only too well. It was clearly too much to expect him to ask how he was *feeling.* Probably the only reason he'd referred to his son's injury was so that he could once again tell him how reckless he'd been, proving his opinion that pride came before a fall to be unerringly right.

Unable to help himself, Hal immediately made it his mission to disappoint him. 'Things are good—much better than I expected, given the debilitating nature of my injury.' Glancing over at Kit, he was surprised to see that her hands were folded almost demurely in her lap and her eyes were downcast, as if she didn't want to draw particular attention to herself…as if she believed she should be as unobtrusive as possible. Was it because coming face to face with the imposing grandeur of his home and meeting his father had overwhelmed her? Perhaps it had even made her nurse a feeling of inferiority? The mere thought that she might be entertaining such a self-deprecating idea made him see red. Apart from his sister, Hal didn't know one other woman who could match her for sheer class…

'In fact I went for a run in the park this morning. Didn't I, Kit?'

'This is a serious matter. I don't think it's something you should be joking about, Henry.'

The disapproving glance crossing his father's features, plus the more formal use of his name, made Hal bristle. 'Isn't it? If we can't laugh at the vicissitudes of life sometimes then we'll all be permanently addicted to tranquillisers merely to help us survive. Personally, I'd rather feel the pain than dull it or pretend it isn't there.'

'Your son wasn't entirely joking, Sir Henry,' Kit interjected calmly, leaping to Hal's defence. 'We *did* go for a run in the park. At least, *I* ran as I pushed him in his wheelchair.'

'Did you, indeed?' Staring at her, his father blustered, 'Did you *really* think that was a good idea when my son already has a broken leg, young woman? What if he had fallen out of the chair and hurt himself even more?'

'There was no chance of that. For goodness' sake, I'm an adult, not a child, and Kit was only trying to cheer me up.' Hal was rigid with anger. 'In any case, why is the thought of having some fun so alien to you,

Father? Not everything in life has to be so damn serious. Do you even *know* the concept of relaxation?'

To his surprise, the other man looked almost crestfallen.

'The truth is I probably don't,' he answered quietly. 'I've always felt that my responsibility for raising a family and leaving a healthy legacy for my children after I'm gone was paramount…just as my forebears did. *Too* serious a matter to take lightly and relax.'

'You drive yourself too hard. Sam and I have been independent for a long time now, Dad. I'd rather you stopped working so hard and just thought about what you wanted for yourself. Take some time out. Go on an extended holiday. You've got plenty of people working for you who could take care of things in your absence. Falteringham isn't going to go to rack and ruin if you're not here, as you fear it might. You should make a new priority to have some fun. Maybe even find yourself a nice woman?'

As Henry Treverne Senior's downturned mouth nudged into a surprising smile the drawing room door opened. Transporting a tray laden with cups, saucers, a plate of sandwiches and a full cafetière, the housekeeper—Mary—came into the room. She was a statuesque middle-aged woman with broad hips, bobbed brown hair and a clear open face that in her youth might have been called pretty.

Aware that they hadn't been introduced—his father's last housekeeper had retired a few months ago—Hal automatically gave the woman a welcoming smile. 'You must be Mary?' he said as she laid the tray down on the walnut coffee table in front of him. 'I'm Henry.' He held out his hand to shake hers.

Clearly surprised at a welcome she hadn't expected, the woman slid her palm into his and smiled back.

'It's nice to meet you, Mr Treverne. Your father is always singing your praises. I'm so sorry about your accident, by the way. But I'm sure it won't be too long before you're back on your feet again. Anyway, help yourself to coffee and sandwiches. If you want any more do let me know. In the meantime I'll be getting your rooms ready.'

When she'd departed, his father sat back in his chair and sighed.

'She's a breath of fresh air, that woman. I honestly don't know what I'd do without her.'

This frank confession, coming straight after Mary had told him that his father was always singing his praises, doubly stunned Hal. It opened the door to a distinct possibility that he had unfairly misjudged the man. Shaking his head in wonder, he said, 'If you feel like that then all I can say is welcome back to the land of the living. Good for you, Dad.' Glancing across the room at Kit, he felt his heart warm when he saw that her pretty mouth was curving in what looked to be an approving smile. 'Why don't you come over here and tuck into some of these sandwiches?' he invited her. 'They look seriously good.'

'My son is right, Miss Blessington. Or perhaps you wouldn't mind if I called you Kit? You must be hungry after making that long drive from London. You should definitely eat something.'

'Thank you. I will.'

When she'd reached the table Hal couldn't resist reaching for her hand and squeezing it. She didn't im- mediately pull away, as he'd thought she might, even though her smile was somewhat tentative and shy. Catching the unspoken question in his father's eyes, he realised he was watching them. But Hal honestly didn't care that he'd witnessed the fact that the relationship between him and Kit wasn't *entirely* a professional one. There was suddenly a great desire in him to be transparent for once—to be honest and open about his feelings and take the consequences, no matter how difficult or challenging they might be...

A short while later Kit was returning from the bathroom, just about to open the drawing room door to enter, when she heard Sir Henry's deeply resonant voice saying to his son, 'I must say your suggestion that I take an extended break sounds like a good one, Hal. I know I can rely on the staff here to take care of things in my absence. And while we're on the subject, have you had any more thoughts about one day coming home to take over the estate? I know you probably don't want to hear it, but I'm not getting any younger, and Falteringham needs some young blood in it again. Perhaps you need to think about marrying and having a family? Are you seeing any nice girls who might be suitable at the moment? The estate is your heritage, as well as your home, and I'd like you to help take it forward into the twenty-first century with a family of your own beside you.'

Outside the door, Kit froze and held her breath.

'Given that I've had a lot of time on my hands lately to reflect on things,' she heard Hal reply, 'you and the estate haven't been far from my mind. Yes, I would like to come back one day and take over the reins, with a wife and children of my own by my side...but just not right now. I'll know when the time is right.'

'Any idea when that might be?'

There was a pause, and then Hal sighed. 'No, Dad. I'm afraid you're just going to have to be patient.'

With her heart clamouring distressingly, Kit took a deep breath in and shakily curved her hand round the doorknob....

Dropping her holdall onto the end of the elegantly dressed half-tester bed in the room Mary had shown her into, Kit drew her hands down over her face and sighed heavily. She felt emotionally wrung out and weary to the bone. Even though she'd got through the rest of the evening without regretting that she'd agreed to Hal's request to take him back to his ancestral home, because it looked as if his father and he were honestly resolved on healing the rift between them, she was in utter turmoil about the discussion she'd heard between Hal and his father about him returning home one day to Falteringham House and assuming the ancestral role he'd be inheriting with a wife and children by his side.

Her memory of the conversation was upsettingly fixated on Sir Henry's enquiry as to whether Hal was seeing any 'nice' or 'suitable' girls at the moment. Nothing could have made her feel more out of place. Not just out of place, but heartsick, because she was in love with a man who was so clearly out of her league that it was pure fantasy to imagine even for an instant that she might have a future with him. Unfortunately Kit *wasn't* one of those 'nice' and 'suitable' girls that Hal's father wanted for his son. And, that being so, she would probably nurse her hurt and regret at not being able to be with Hal for ever.

You're such a fool, Kit... How could you have been so stupid? You're your mother all over again!

Furiously berating herself, she buried her face in her hands and cried and cried until she felt she couldn't cry any more. There wasn't a single place in her body where she didn't ache for Hal. Everything about him—the way he looked and smiled, the warm, sensual scent of his body, even the way he teased and provoked her to distraction—had ensured Kit would be an addict for him for life. It was as though he'd put her under a spell that she'd never be free of, no matter how hard she might try.

But, since she couldn't have him, the only thing she could look forward to was the prospect of the little bolt-hole she'd been working towards for most of her life. Making it into a reality. Perhaps when she had that she might at least have the satisfaction of achieving the one thing that she'd set out to do to make her life better. As for having a meaningful relationship... It was something that wasn't even remotely likely. Not now. *Not when Hal Treverne had ruined any chance that she'd ever be whole enough for anyone else again.*

Slipping off her shoes, she wearily tugged her sweater over her head and threw it onto the bed. Then she turned and headed for the bathroom. Usually a long hot soak in the tub was her therapy of choice to help soothe her and put things into perspective when she'd had a bad day. But, knowing that wasn't going to be the case tonight, she opted for a shower instead. After that she intended to go straight to bed.

At Sir Henry's suggestion she would take the opportunity to have an early night because he and his son had 'a lot to talk about'. She wasn't to worry, he'd said, because he would help Hal to his bedroom and see that he got his medication if he needed it. There was no need for them to disturb her. Every word of that little speech had sliced through Kit's heart like a sharpened scythe, because it had only served to remind her that she was already becoming superfluous to Hal's needs. The fact was he had access to a raft of people he could call upon for help if he wanted to. His wealth pretty much saw to that. *Would he even miss her when the time came for her to leave?* Kit speculated forlornly.

Underneath the hot spray of the shower, she disproved the belief that she had no more tears left to cry and helplessly, despairingly, cried again.

When she finally emerged from the glass cubicle she felt shaken and drained to the core. She didn't even feel as if she had the energy to dry herself. Scared at how powerfully she seemed to be unravelling, she determinedly switched her focus to the practicalities of getting ready for bed. To that end, she brushed her teeth, properly dried her hair, then unpacked her holdall to retrieve the cosily warm pyjamas she'd brought with her. They were a lot more practical than the silk chemise she'd worn the night Hal had seduced her, but the sight of them did little to help alleviate her sorrow. They were just another reminder that she'd never know another night of passion with the man she loved again.

Turning out the elegant lamp next to the bed, wanting to shut out not just the day's events but everything that troubled her, she closed her eyes. All she could do now was pray for an unbroken night's sleep in which to recover her strength and to somehow find the will and the means to overcome her sorrow so she could carry on with life regardless. God knew her mother

had had to do just that *more* than once. If she could
do it, then so could her daughter…

In Kit's dream, someone was tapping on the door. The
repetitive sound didn't seem to abate, and finally it
pierced her already fitful sleep and made her realise it
was no dream but solid, disturbing fact. Dazedly scrambling to sit up, she pushed back the silky curtain of hair
that brushed her face and stared over at the door. All
she could see beneath the edges was an unbroken sliver
of dimmed light that came from the corridor outside.
There was no evidence of anyone's feet moving. Her
head felt fuzzy and she couldn't think straight. Icy fear
had robbed her of the ability. Was she still dreaming?
It was hard to tell.

When the tapping sound abruptly ceased, she sucked
in a relieved breath and nervously glanced round the
room. Perhaps it *had* been a dream after all?

The moonlight outside her window dappled the
emerald-green counterpane that covered the bed with
haunting shadows, and did the same to the various
pieces of dark antique furniture that were arranged
round the room. Kit's heart galloped in fear in case a
ghost suddenly appeared. She was already frightened
out of her wits enough, without having to contend with
some ghostly apparition!

When another bout of tapping broke the uneasy silence that had descended, this time with a bit more
force, Kit remembered that Hal's room was next door.
What if he was in urgent need of her help? She was mortified that it hadn't registered before that the knocking
on the door was probably coming from *him*.

Shoving aside the counterpane, she swung her legs

over the side of the bed and hurried across the rug-covered stone flags to open the door. Her heart was already bumping anxiously against her ribs even before she set eyes on the man who waited outside. When she did, her heart bumped even harder. He was sleepy-eyed and tousle-haired, with a fresh growth of dark beard studding his chiselled jaw, and gazing into Hal's golden eyes was like stumbling onto a never-to-be forgotten glimpse of heaven.

'What's wrong?' she asked.

His answer was a provocative lopsided grin. 'Nothing now that I'm looking at you, angel.'

The smoky cadence of his voice somehow transmitted itself to Kit's muscles and made them feel dangerously weak. 'How long have you been knocking on the door?' she asked huskily. 'I thought I was dreaming.'

'I wasn't keeping track of the time. I just thought I'd stay here until I wore you down with my dogged persistence, got you to come and see who it was and hopefully let me in.'

Unconsciously clutching her pyjama top, agitatedly twisting the material into a knot in the process, Kit stared at him in disbelief, suddenly realising the only reason he was standing was because he was using his crutches to help him. Hadn't his father had the sense to get his wheelchair for him? She'd left him the car keys and had strongly emphasised that he shouldn't let his son rely solely on his walking aids to get to his room. He'd already told her that the guest rooms on the ground floor were right at the back of the house.

'Are you crazy? You should *never* have stood out there for so long. You'll have to come in and sit down on the bed for a while.'

'That invitation is music to my ears, sweetheart. I'm certainly not going to argue.' He winced a little, as though the strain of standing upright had unquestionably taxed him.

Again Kit berated herself for not doing her job properly—for leaving him. It didn't matter that he'd been with his father...no one knew better than *she* did what he needed. The impassioned thought sent a scalding, searing heat surging through her bloodstream that was like a swell of molten honey.

Biting down on her lip, she waited until Hal had passed her before shutting the door behind them. She noted he was still dressed in the clothes he'd been wearing to travel in. She had no idea of the time but it was obvious he hadn't been to bed yet. What did he think he was doing, staying up so late, when his surgeon had told him it was extremely important he got as much rest as possible while his leg healed?

'That's better.' Expelling a grateful sigh, he dropped down onto the rumpled green counterpane and handed her his crutches. 'Can you put these somewhere?'

'Sure.' Kit laid them against the striped green couch at the end of the bed, where they would be easily accessible. Then, folding her arms over her chest, she asked, 'Why on earth have you stayed up so late? Is there something you want to discuss that can't wait until the morning?'

His avid gaze intensifying a little, for a long moment Hal looked to be deep in thought. 'As a matter of fact, there is. But first I wanted to tell you something. My dad and I have been having a father and son talk—probably the first genuine discussion we've had for years. God knows it's long overdue. Turns out he doesn't think

I'm such a disaster after all. In fact he tells me he's more than a little awed by my success *and* my courage at pursuing my "hair-raising stunts" as he calls them—even though he can't always understand it. He's always thought that the reason I'm so reckless is because I don't value my life enough—that I must be suffering from some sort of depression brought about by my mother leaving when I was little. That seriously grieves him.

'He blames himself for not being there for me as often as he would have liked after she left, and he said that he wished it could have been different. But as well as making sure he's protecting mine and Sam's legacy he's so focused on taking care of the estate and the people who work for him because it's their livelihood too. He has to make those things his priority. Who could have predicted that he'd be so honest with me? You were right when you said I should come to see him, Kit. I'm glad that I did. Hearing the truth about how he really feels about me has helped lay a lot of the ghosts from my past that have haunted me to rest. Like any good parent, he just wanted the best for his children—even if I couldn't always see that that was his intention. Anyway, it feels good to clear the air and have the chance to repair things.'

'Then I suppose I shouldn't moan at you for staying up so late, since something good has come out it. But I don't think you should stay up for much longer. Not unless you intend to spend the whole of tomorrow resting and taking it easy. I think it's time you turned in and went to bed.'

One corner of Hal's engaging mouth lifted intriguingly. 'That brings me nicely to the main reason I knocked on your door sweetheart. I do indeed need to go to bed—but not on my own. I'd much rather have some company tonight and the company I want and need most in the world—not just for tonight—is *you,* Kit.'

Nothing could have prepared Kit for the dizzying joy that swept through her at his unexpected confession. In fact her feelings so overwhelmed her that she couldn't find the words or the actions to express how much they meant to her. But tainting her unexpected happiness was the distressing memory of the conversation she'd overheard between Hal and his father about him taking up his inheritance.

'I *can't* be the company you need most in the world, Hal,' she said soberly. 'Not when one day soon you'll be married to someone else…someone much more suitable than I am.'

'What on earth are you talking about? Who told you I'm soon going to be married to someone else?'

'It's obvious, isn't it? I didn't realise the extent and importance of your family legacy until I came here. It's understandable that you'll need to marry someone from your own class when one day you're going to inherit this estate.'

Frowning, Hal stared at her as though she were speaking a foreign language he didn't understand. Then comprehension dawned on him.

'Did you by any chance overhear a conversation between me and my dad? Specifically the part where he asked me if I would one day come back to take up my inheritance?'

Feeling uncomfortably guilty, Kit nodded. 'I did. I didn't mean to eavesdrop. It's just that I was on my way back from the bathroom and your father—well, he doesn't speak quietly.'

To her astonishment, Hal threw back his head and laughed.

'He certainly doesn't speak quietly,' he agreed. His expression quickly became serious again. 'What else did you hear?'

'I heard you tell him that you *would* marry one day and return, but only when the time was right. Then, when he asked you when that would be, I heard you tell him he had to be patient.'

'That's all? You didn't hear anything else?'

'No. That was enough.'

'Enough? For what, exactly?'

'It was enough to make me realise that I shouldn't delude myself that you'll ever want to have a serious relationship with *me*.'

'Is that really what you believe, Kit?' His brow furrowing in concern, Hal reached out a hand and curled it round her wrist. Then he pulled her towards him.

For a few moments she teetered, anxiously trying to regain her balance and not fall against him. But he was already winding his arms round her waist to steady her, and gazing up into her eyes as though he would never willingly tear his gaze away to look at anything else. At once the scent of his warm, virile body enveloped her and she knew that even if she could muster the most powerful will in the world she wouldn't be able to deny him anything that he desired if it gave him pleasure and made him happy.

'What am I to believe, if not that?'

'How about that I honestly want to have a serious relationship with you? That I'll go crazy if I can't have the one woman in the world who means more to me than anybody else?'

Every other thought in her head was obliterated at that heartfelt assertion. Sorrow seemed a million light years away when Hal looked at her the way he was looking at her now. As if she was something infinitely precious and he would willingly sacrifice everything he owned to keep her safe.

CHAPTER TWELVE

'I CAN HARDLY believe it,' Kit admitted softly.

'Well, you must—because it's the truth.'

Her handsome companion's voice was gravelly with emotion.

'You might travel to the ends of the earth, Kit Blessington, but wherever you go I swear I'll come and find you and bring you home.'

A warm surge of tears swam into her eyes. 'You mean it? You're not just saying that?'

Hal's handsome face was immediately perturbed. 'I might not always agree with everything you say or do when we're together, and I'm sure sometimes sparks will fly when I feel the need to hold my ground and you protest, but one thing I promise you: I will never lie to you about my feelings. You have my word on that.'

'What feelings are we talking about, Hal?' Right then it wouldn't have been difficult to convince Kit that she was dreaming. Having her wishes fulfilled had never happened very often, and more often than not she expected to be disappointed.

'Don't you know? Can't you guess? I thought I'd made it perfectly clear.'

It was hard to hear him over the sonorous thumping of her heart, let alone give herself permission to speculate. 'If it was so clear then I wouldn't need to ask, would I?'

Shaking his head, Hal bemusedly acceded to her tremulous suggestion. 'All right, then. I'll tell you.' His tawny, long-lashed eyes visibly darkened. 'I'm mad about you, Kit. To make it even clearer, so there's no possibility of confusion, I'm head-over-heels in love with you, and I'll happily spend the rest of my days showing you how much I mean that—mean it with all my heart.'

Kit stared at him in shock even as her heart leapt joyfully. 'You *really* love me? I mean—I know I'm not the type of girl you normally go for. I'm very ordinary. And I'm not just saying that because I'm fishing for compliments. I'm...I'm being realistic.'

'Well, maybe it's time you woke up to a new reality, Kit. One in which you start to realise how beautiful, sexy and desirable you truly are.'

She could still hardly believe what she was hearing. 'You know what? Not only do you have a worrying predilection for dangerous sports, Henry Treverne, but I've come to realise that you're a very dangerous man too.'

'Hmm...why do you say that, I wonder?' His lips quirking in a gentle grin, he tenderly pushed away some coiled Titian strands from the side of her face and let his palm linger there, intermittently stroking the pad of his thumb down over her cheek.

Inside the sprigged cotton of her pretty pyjamas, the tips of Kit's breasts—already so acutely sensitive whenever he was near—tingled and hardened. They surged against the lightweight material, desperately seeking his touch.

'I say it because it's true—and the reason I find you dangerous is because I love you too. And when you love someone it inevitably makes you vulnerable. That's something I vowed I'd never allow myself to be when I left home, because life with my mother—the one person I loved more than anybody else—was such an emotional rollercoaster ride it was frightening. I longed for some stability for us both when I was young—a place that we could call our own. But it didn't happen. Because whenever my mum met someone and started to trust them they usually ended up breaking her heart and fleecing her of every penny. Then we'd have to move on again. I constantly lived in fear that something would happen to her when she was down and upset about a man because I saw how vulnerable it made her. So I decided not to risk the same thing happening to me. The last thing I expected to happen when I came to work for you was that I'd come to love you, Hal.'

The sense of wonder at his revelation that he reciprocated her feelings couldn't prevent her still being anxious about the pain she'd suffer if anything ever happened to him—or, worse still, if he should ever leave her. But realising that was just old programming kicking in, because she'd grown up fearing that if she got involved with a man he would behave in the same destructive way as her mother's various unreliable boyfriends, Kit knew she had to trust that her own path was more hopeful. But she still wanted to come clean about her fears to Hal.

'I've guarded my heart against falling in love for so long because I've had no good example of a man being sincere or keeping his word, and I witnessed the devastation that caused my mum. I was determined not to repeat it. But nothing could have prepared me for a man like you, Hal.' She smiled. 'Or the effect that you would have on me. I found myself dangerously fascinated by you almost straight away, and that feeling has grown stronger. So much so that I can't be remotely sensible about what's the best course of action for me any more.'

'What kind of action does your *heart* want you to take?' Hal prompted, his tawny eyes turning to a deeply hypnotic liquid gold that silently and irrefutably conveyed how aroused he was.

Unable to deny her need to touch him intimately any longer, Kit slid her hand round the back of his neck and slowly brought his face towards hers.

'My heart tells me to kiss you until I'm drunk with the taste and flavour of you. Until it beats in tandem with yours. God knows I've tried, but I just can't seem to resist you. But I'm sure you know that already, don't you?'

'I don't take anything for granted where you're concerned, baby, but I was hoping you'd say that. And I want you to know that I'm so sorry you had such a rough time of it growing up. But that time is past. And if it's a place of your own that you want, then I'll get it for you. I'm no psychic, sweetheart, but I can tell you right now that your future is looking much brighter.'

Even though his loving words thrilled her, and reassured her that he understood her need for a place that she could call her own, Kit couldn't totally dispense with her anxiety about it. 'I—I don't just want a place of my own any more, Hal,' she said softly. 'I don't care where I live so long as I can be with you. Is that—is that possible, do you think?'

'Is it *possible*? Surely you know by now that's what I want too?'

Even before he crushed her lips beneath his Hal was expertly undoing Kit's buttons and sliding his hands inside the material of her pyjamas to cup her breasts. Then as their kiss deepened, with both their mouths opening hungrily to accommodate the other's searching tongue, his fingers tugged on the aching steel buds of her nipples to inflame them even more. If Kit thought anything at all in those incendiary few seconds, it was about for how long and how passionately he would pleasure her. In turn, would she be able to repay *him* with equal pleasure?

She needn't have worried. Proving he was as instinctive a lover as she could wish for, Hal's fingers and thumbs started to ease her pyjama bottoms down over her svelte hips. As soon as he'd done so his hand returned to slide between her silken thighs and stroke over the sensitive bud at her moist centre.

Trembling with anticipation, Kit tore her lips away from his and dropped her head down onto his iron-hard shoulder. She'd had no idea that such staggering gratification was even possible until she'd fallen in love with this man. 'Hal, please…' she couldn't help her voice breaking with need.

'There's no need to beg me for anything, baby,' he responded huskily. 'I know what you want and I know what you need. I know it because I feel the same. I want you so much that I think I'll die if I can't have you.'

He was kissing the smooth skin on her neck and nibbling it at the same time. Then in one smooth movement he lay back on the bed and, with his hands firmly on her hips, eased her body over his.

'I don't want you to die,' Kit breathed, her hands fumbling at the fly of his jeans and tugging them down as carefully as she could over his strong, muscular thighs. Her blood palpably thrummed, because the need to feel his possession suddenly grew urgent.

Hal didn't hesitate to oblige her. Shoving aside his black silk boxer shorts, he plunged his hardened silken shaft deep inside her and, lifting his hips, pressed upwards. Before, his persistent taps at her door had rendered her terrified, in case it was the precursor to a ghostly visitation, but now Kit's full-throated cries of pleasure echoed uninhibitedly round the room instead, banishing any sense of sadness and regret that it might previously have held.

If their loving had anything to do with it, from now on she knew that it would be passion and joy that the bricks and mortar here were imbued with. And as heady desire enslaved them, guaranteeing they would be seductively preoccupied long into the night, the forceful storm of their loving shut out every memory of past hurt and disappointment that might have haunted them, ensuring the future was suddenly not half so fearful as they might once have imagined.

Just before the dawn broke Kit fell asleep in Hal's arms. There was no question that she would do anything else. All self-doubt had fled. It had been replaced by calm, assured surrender to whatever came next. As long as they were together she knew she could face any adversity or sorrow and overcome it. That was what love did, she realised. It made you strong, *not* weak. All these years she'd been labouring under a cruel misconception. What was the point of living if you never experienced loving someone? If you were so afraid of being hurt that you never trusted the wisdom of your own heart? Searching for guarantees and trying to work it all out in your head, clearly wasn't the answer. Decisions should be made out of love, not fear. From now on, Kit vowed, that would be her mantra.

When she woke a few hours later her eyes opened to find Hal examining her thoughtfully, casually resting back on his elbow as he gazed down at her. His arresting golden eyes, hard chiselled jaw and curling tousled hair was definitely a sight she would never tire of waking up to.

'Are you all right?' she asked, suddenly afraid that he might have needed her but had decided against disturbing her to let her know.

'I'm fine. In fact I'm *more* than fine. I feel on top of the world. I've just been lying here wondering how on earth I've had the good fortune to attract someone as good and beautiful as you into my life.'

It wasn't easy for Kit to keep her humour at bay. 'Good fortune? Some people might think that the circumstances were a disaster. You broke your leg, remember? I suspect that had something to do with it.'

He scowled, gathered a coil of her russet hair between his fingers and for a few seconds examined it intently. 'I confess I was expecting a much more romantic reply than that, sweetheart. It's all well and good that one of your qualities is that you're eminently sensible and pragmatic, but I'd like to know that you can be dreamy and romantic too.'

She hastened to reassure him. 'I promise you I can. It's just that it's become rather a habit of mine to be sensible. In future one of the things I want to achieve is an ability to give myself permission to enjoy life more—to have fun and be silly if I want to and not worry about looking a fool.'

'I'm glad to hear it. But you could never look like a fool, Kit. Talking of achieving things—do you remember when you came into my study and asked if there was anything else I'd like to achieve, other than all the business awards and sporting accolades displayed round the room?'

She nodded. 'I do. As I recall, you said there *were* other things you'd like to achieve, and it did make me think.'

'There's not much you don't remember, is there? I'll have to watch out in the future if I dare forget your birthday or what kind of flowers you like. I'll definitely be in the doghouse if I do.' Grinning, Hal reached for her hand, then raised it to his lips and planted a kiss. 'Well, to expand on that comment, the one thing I want to achieve above everything else is to find the woman of my dreams, marry her, then settle down to have a family.'

As Kit all but held her breath his golden-eyed gaze deepened meaningfully.

'To that end, I'm asking you to marry me, Kit.'

She immediately sat up and stared at him. 'You're being serious?'

'I most certainly am. And, trust me, this moment will be imprinted on my memory for many years to come.' Disconcertingly, he chuckled. 'Not just because it's one of the most momentous occasions of my life, but because I won't be able to forget what you were wearing when I proposed.'

'What I'm wearing? But I'm—' Stricken with embarrassment, Kit realised she was naked. Her sensible pyjamas had long been dispensed with during the night. She made a grab for the counterpane and held it firmly over her breasts.

'Naked!' Hal finished for her, unrepentantly wrenching the counterpane back and giving her a lascivious smile. 'And that's just the way I want you. Because when you've given me your answer—and I'm hoping it's the one I want to hear...' He paused to deliver a tantalising little kiss on her mouth and then teasingly caught her lip between his teeth for a moment. 'I intend to shut out the world for the rest of the day...' another sizzling kiss was dropped at the satin juncture of her neck and shoulder '...and make wild, passionate love to you.'

It was difficult for Kit to comment because she was so stunned. Shyly, she determinedly freed the silk counterpane from his grip and tugged it back up over her breasts. 'I'm far from against the idea, but you're not supposed to overdo things, remember? We've already been up most of the night and... Exactly *how* wildly passionate are you intending to be?'

'That's for me to know and you to find out, angel. Now, stop wasting time worrying about me overdoing things, shut up, and let me propose again...but properly this time.'

Kit lost any inclination to argue. Keeping quiet was suddenly not such a challenge after all.

Pushing back his tousled dark hair, Hal made his handsome face assume a serious expression.

'Katherine Blessington, will you do me the honour of becoming my wife and making me happy...*far* happier than any man has a right to hope to be on this earth?'

'Yes, Henry Treverne, I will. I'll marry you. Because

I can't imagine ever living without you and I love you much more than words could ever say. But I still won't stop trying to find the right ones to tell you.'

His strong arms enveloped her then, and there was a magical sense of time standing still. It wasn't just Hal who would remember these precious moments forever. *Kit would hold them in her heart until the day she died.*

A sudden sharp knock at the door made her gasp. Her pulse raced in shock. It raced even more when Hal's father's resonant voice enquired loudly, 'Hal? Are you and Ms Blessington ready for a cooked breakfast? I thought we could all have it in the dining room this morning, and Mary tells me it's going to be ready in about twenty minutes. Does that give you both enough time to shower and dress?'

Shaking his head in amusement, and hardly looking at all surprised, Hal answered, 'Make it half an hour and we'll be there on the dot. Thanks, Dad!'

'Don't mention it. It's nice to have you home, son.'

Sir Henry's receding footsteps echoed clearly round the room as he made his way back down the stone flags of the corridor.

'Your father sounded like he knew you were in here with me.' Kit's blue eyes widened in disbelief. 'How could he *possibly* know that?'

'I told him last night that I was going to pay you a visit and propose to you. Turns out he didn't have to be so patient in waiting for an answer as to when I'd marry and return home after all.'

'You mean—you mean you *discussed* the fact that you love me and want to marry me? What did he say? Was he surprised? I don't expect he was very happy.

I'm sure he must believe you could do a whole lot better for yourself than me. Tell me, Hal—was he angry?'

'Stop doubting and torturing yourself, will you? Of *course* he wasn't angry. My father knows how lucky I am to have found you, and he certainly doesn't think I could do any better. Class isn't such an issue nowadays—and nor should it be when two people fall in love. And I'm no Prince Charming, devoid of any faults, so don't kid yourself that I am, Kit. It's *me* who's the lucky one in this relationship. And the only thing my dad wants to be assured of is that I'm with someone I love, who loves me. He was as pleased as punch when I told him how I felt about you. He said he knew you were something special the moment he set eyes on you. Apparently my sister confirmed it for him. She talks to him on the phone at least once a day and she spoke very highly of you.'

'All right, then. You've convinced me.'

'Where are you going?'

Having thrown back the covers, Kit was hurriedly stepping into her pyjama bottoms and reaching for the top half that lay discarded on the counterpane. Her hair tumbled in a riot of burnished copper waves down over her slim pale shoulders and alluring naked breasts and Hal thought she resembled an enchanting elfin sprite from one of his and Sam's childhood fairy stories— but a very *sexy* red-haired sprite. He almost wanted to pinch himself, to check he wasn't dreaming that she'd agreed to marry him.

'I'm going to go and take a shower and then get dressed. I don't know about you, but I'm not going to turn down the offer of a cooked breakfast any time soon. When I'm done I'll come and help you.'

Hal couldn't help releasing a very audible curse and, echoing his frustration, his injured leg began to throb. 'It's bad enough that I have to endure the thought of you showering naked on your own when I want to join you. There's not much I can do about that…but then to suffer the indignity of you looking at me with those big baby-blue eyes like I'm some poor helpless invalid…' He cursed again and impatiently scraped his hair back off his forehead. 'You have no idea what I'd give to be able to get up and carry you into that blasted shower myself!'

'You're wrong, Hal.'

Her voice was more tenderly compassionate than he'd ever heard it before, and Kit returned to his side of the bed and carefully sat down.

Taking his hand in between hers, she said, 'I know how much it tears at your self-esteem and your pride that you can't do all the things you did with ease before the accident. But, honestly, with all the progress you're making it will be no time at all before you're walking around again, fully fit, *and* chasing me round the kitchen for a kiss to boot!'

'And joining you in the shower?' Despite the flash of irritability and frustration that had seized him, Kit's calm-voiced reassurance had done a lot to alleviate Hal's concerns. With pleasure, he saw that she was blushing too.

'I'll look forward to it,' she said, and smiled.

'Well, I suppose you'd better go and get ready. We shouldn't let that cooked breakfast go to waste, should we?'

'Are you kidding? Something tells me I'm going to need to eat all the cooked breakfasts I can get to build up my strength if I'm to meet your insatiable demands, Hal Treverne.'

Dropping a kiss on the side of his cheek, she got to her feet and disappeared into the bathroom…

EPILOGUE

One year later

KNOWING THAT HER adventurous husband was champing at the bit to be off on the most taxing mountaineering hike he'd undertaken since his leg had fully healed—this time on Ben Nevis, the highest mountain in Britain—Kit hesitated outside the stately bedroom in the private wing they'd made their home in at Falteringham House.

They'd moved in shortly after they'd married because Hal had decided it was time he came back to his ancestral home and learned the ropes of running the estate with his father. Kit had agreed. Although it wasn't easy, getting used to living in such a grand place, she was definitely adapting to it and had been delighted when her father-in-law, Sir Henry, had asked if she'd like to take over the PR aspects of running the estate. She'd taken to the job like a fish to water.

But now Hal was busy packing his gear to head off to Ben Nevis, and she couldn't help anxiously biting down on her lip at the thought of the adventure he had ahead of him. He would only be gone for the weekend, but any separation from him had to be endured always seemed like purgatory to Kit. Sometimes she would swear that they were literally two halves of the same soul, and even after nearly a year's marriage their need for each other seemed to grow even greater, *not* lessen. However, she had promised him on their wedding day that she would never seek to curtail the sports and adventures that gave him pleasure just because she was fearful of the danger he might put himself in. Hal was a loving and devoted husband, and challenging himself was part of who he was. Kit wouldn't want him to be any different.

But maybe today she had good reason to revise that view...

Lifting her hand and briefly sucking in a steadying breath, she rapped on the walnut door. 'Hal? I know you're busy, but can I come in for a minute?'

No sooner had she finished speaking than he opened the door, and just as though she'd been brought face to face with his six-foot-two, straight-legged frame for the very first time her heart skipped a beat. He was wearing faded jeans and a dark blue chambray shirt, and his tawny chameleon eyes glinted with pleasure as soon as they alighted on his wife's face.

Straight away his arms encircled her waist to bring her close against him. 'Since when do you need to knock on the door to ask if you can come in? This is your bedroom too, sweetheart.'

'I know.' She smiled, but her voice was perhaps not as steady as she would have liked it to be. 'I just thought I'd see how you were getting on with your packing and if you needed any help.'

'You can't resist offering to help me, can you?' Hal lowered his head to brush his warm lips tenderly across his wife's. 'I know you mean well, angel, but I've been climbing and hiking long enough over the years to know the drill for how to pack and what to take.' His smooth brow puckered for a moment. 'But that's not it, is it? I mean that's not the reason you wanted to come in and talk to me? Is everything okay? I know you've been feeling a little under par since we came back from our trip to Morocco a few weeks ago. Do you think it's something you ate that's caused it?'

'No, Hal, I don't think I've been under par because of something I ate.' Apprehensively Kit lifted her gaze to his. 'I've just found out that I'm pregnant.'

'What?' His expression was so shocked it was almost comical.

'I'm pregnant.'

'How do you know? Have you been to see a doctor?'

Her stomach plunged at the uncertainty in her husband's tone. 'Don't you believe me?'

'If you tell me it's true then of course I believe you— but how do you know you haven't made a mistake? That it's not just some kind of tummy bug? I've heard there's one going round...'

'I bought a pregnancy test and it was positive. I'm going to have a baby, Hal. Do you mind? I know the news probably could have come at a more conducive time, seeing as you're about to make your first mountaineering trip since the accident, but I hoped it might make you determined to be extra careful when you're up on that mountain and to come home to me just as soon as you can so that we can celebrate.'

'I'm going to be a father... We're going to be *parents*!'

Lifting her high into his arms, Hal hugged her hard

and swung her round in a circle with delight. Then he kissed her hungrily and passionately until she had to push against him to let her up for air. Dizzy with relief that he shared her joy that they were going to have a child, Kit cupped Hal's chiselled jaw and smiled tenderly up into his eyes—eyes she now knew she'd lost her heart to from the very first glance.

'I'm so glad that you're pleased about it, Hal. For a moment there I was afraid you might not be.'

He gave her a bemused look. 'Why on earth would you think that? I told you on the day I asked you to marry me that it was what I wanted most in the world—to marry the woman of my dreams and settle down and have a family. Don't you remember?'

Kit sighed as Hal delivered her safely to the ground again. 'I remember. But I don't want you to settle down, my love. It's never going to be in your nature to just be content with raising a family—and that's not a criticism. I know you have to run the estate, but that's no reason not to do the things you love as well…the sports and the challenges that give you pleasure. As long as you promise not to take too many unnecessary risks—because I want you to come home in one piece to me and our children—then that's fine by me. You wouldn't be the adventurous and brave man I married if I tried to change you in any way. I love you just as you are, Hal Treverne.'

'And I adore you, Katherine Treverne. And I promise that from now on I will never take any dangerous risks that I don't have to. You and our children will always be the most important things to me in the world. And talking of celebrating our good news…I don't have to leave for Ben Nevis for a while yet, so why don't we start our celebrations early?'

He was already lightly pushing her towards the vast king-sized bed that they shared and Kit didn't have a single thought in her head to protest, no matter how 'under par' she felt.

Hal and their marriage meant everything in the world to her, and for as long as they lived she would happily take every opportunity she could to let him know it.

* * * * *

A sneaky peek at next month…

MODERN™

INTERNATIONAL AFFAIRS, SEDUCTION & PASSION GUARANTEED

My wish list for next month's titles…

In stores from 17th January 2014:

❏ A Bargain with the Enemy — Carole Mortimer
❏ Shamed in the Sands — Sharon Kendrick
❏ When Falcone's World Stops Turning — Abby Green
❏ An Exquisite Challenge — Jennifer Hayward

In stores from 7th February 2014:

❏ A Secret Until Now — Kim Lawrence
❏ Seduction Never Lies — Sara Craven
❏ Securing the Greek's Legacy — Julia James
❏ A Debt Paid in Passion — Dani Collins

Available at WHSmith, Tesco, Asda, Eason, Amazon and Apple

Just can't wait?

Visit us Online

You can buy our books online a month before they hit the shops! **www.millsandboon.co.uk**

0114/0

Special Offers

Every month we put together collections and longer reads written by your favourite authors.

Here are some of next month's highlights— and don't miss our fabulous discount online!

On sale 7th February   On sale 17th January   On sale 7th February

The *Royal* HOUSE OF KAREDES

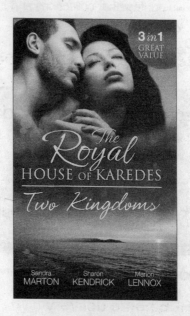

TWO CROWNS, TWO ISLANDS, ONE LEGACY

One royal family, torn apart by pride and its lust for power, reunited by purity and passion

Meet the Karedes now, at:
www.millsandboon.co.uk

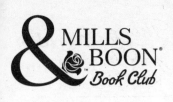 

Join the Mills & Boon Book Club

Subscribe to **Modern**™ today for 3, 6 or 12 months and you could **save over £40!**

We'll also treat you to these fabulous extras:

- ❧ **FREE L'Occitane gift set worth £10**
- ❧ **FREE home delivery**
- ❧ **Rewards scheme, exclusive offers…and much more!**

Subscribe now and save over £40
www.millsandboon.co.uk/subscribeme

The World of Mills & Boon®

There's a Mills & Boon® series that's perfect for you. We publish ten series and, with new titles every month, you never have to wait long for your favourite to come along.

Blaze.
Scorching hot, sexy reads
4 new stories every month

By Request
Relive the romance with the best of the best
9 new stories every month

Cherish™
Romance to melt the heart every time
12 new stories every month

Desire™
Passionate and dramatic love stories
8 new stories every month

M&B/WORLD3

Discover more romance at

www.millsandboon.co.uk

- ❤ WIN great prizes in our exclusive competitions
- ❤ BUY new titles before they hit the shops
- ❤ BROWSE new books and REVIEW your favourites
- ❤ SAVE on new books with the Mills & Boon® Bookclub™
- ❤ DISCOVER new authors

PLUS, to chat about your favourite reads, get the latest news and find special offers:

- 📘 Find us on facebook.com/millsandboon
- 🐦 Follow us on twitter.com/millsandboonuk
- ❤ Sign up to our newsletter at millsandboon.co.uk